THE GOLDEN HARVEST

THE GOLDEN HARVEST

JORGE AMADO

TRANSLATED BY CLIFFORD E. LANDERS

AVON BOOKS ▲ NEW YORK

THE GOLDEN HARVEST is an original publication of Avon Books. This work is a novel. Any similarity to actual persons or events is purely coincidental.

Originally published as *São Jorge dos Ilhéus* by Livraria Martines Editora, Sao Paulo, Brazil

AVON BOOKS
A division of
The Hearst Corporation
1350 Avenue of the Americas
New York, New York 10019

Copyright © 1944 by Jorge Amado
English translation copyright © 1992 by Clifford E. Landers
Cover illustration by Terry Widener
Published by arrangement with Thomas Colchie
Library of Congress Catalog Card Number: 91-92458
ISBN: 0-380-76100-9

First Avon Books Trade Printing: August 1992

AVON TRADEMARK REG. U.S. PAT. OFF. AND IN OTHER COUNTRIES, MARCA REGISTRADA, HECHO EN U.S.A.

Printed in the U.S.A.

OPM   10   9   8   7   6   5   4   3   2   1

Contents

The Land Brings Forth Fruits of Gold

The Land Changes Hands

The Land Brings Forth
Fruits of Gold

The "Queen of the South"

$\boxed{1}$

And, suddenly, as the plane veered from its southbound course, the city appeared before the travelers' eyes. They were no longer flying over the green sea. First came the coconut trees, and immediately afterwards Conquest Hill. The pilot turned the plane, and the passengers on the left side could see the city of Ilhéus moving as in a post card. Descending in poor, zigzagging streets down the proletarian hillside, it stretched opulently along the recently built avenues between river and sea that ended at the beach, then resuming in the houses on Pontal Island with their cheerful gardens, once again proletarian it climbed the tin and wooden houses of Unhão Hill. A passenger counted eight ships in the harbor, besides the large sailboats and innumerable small vessels. The port appeared larger than the city itself. The passenger shouted this observation to Carlos Zude, but he was looking at the bathers on the beach, minuscule black dots running on the whiteness of the sand toward the foamy opening of the waves. Julieta must be there, taking her sunbath, batting a *peteca* back and forth with her friends. Carlos Zude noticed that someone on the beach was waving at the plane. It might even be Julieta. Carlos Zude could not tell if the person waving, a mere black dot lost in the whiteness of the sand, was a man or a woman. But it could well be Julieta; she knew he was coming on that plane. Carlos Zude answered the greeting, waving his hand behind the glass. But the pilot maneuvered again and the beach disappeared. Carlos's gesture was lost among the trees of the hillside, against which the plane seemed determined to dash itself in a collective suicide. It dropped rapidly. Above, the blue sky was dotted with fleeting white clouds. Leaving the hill behind, the plane descended smoothly over the river, slowing its propellers, and came to a stop beside the airport of the American company, next to the railroad tracks. The

5

German company's airport was farther off, and passengers had to
be transported to the dock in launches. The flight attendant opened
the door, and the airport workers attached the steps. Carlos Zude was
the first passenger to leave the plane. The young man, who worked in the
office and had come to meet him, rushed forward in greeting, a smile
on his lips.

"Did you have a good trip, Mr. Carlos?"

He shook his employer's hand.

"Wonderful"—he glanced at his wristwatch—"an hour from Bahia
to here. Fifty-five minutes . . ."

"That makes it worth the trouble . . ." the young man commented.

He took the briefcase Carlos was carrying, heavy with papers. The
suitcases were being brought by a black porter. Taxis honked, looking
for customers. Carlos walked over the railroad bridge, the employee
a few paces behind, admiring the elegance of his boss, the type of
man he would like to be. The gray strands of hair gave him a look of
nobility rather than age. He wore the finest in clothes and shoes, and the
employee admired above all the easy, natural gestures of a gentleman,
from his walk to his way of laughing, so natural that they seemed the
result of lengthy study and lengthy training. The plane roared again,
the passengers had boarded, the attendant closed the door, and the
machine glided along the waters of the river, quickly gaining altitude
and disappearing toward the south, bound for Rio de Janeiro.

The chauffeur opened the door of the Buick. Once again the employee
admired the seigneurial casualness with which Carlos Zude shook
hands with the driver and thanked him for his welcome. A real
aristocrat . . .

Carlos Zude got into the car. The employee, seated beside the chauffeur, turned around and said, "We were expecting you Thursday . . ."

"I couldn't get a place on the plane. They're packed these days,
every seat taken. To get here today I had to book the flight three days
in advance."

His gesture gave the impression that he would take care of the entire
matter.

"The Americans are putting a plane into service exclusively between
Ilhéus and Bahia. Two flights a day . . ."

"Fantastic!" exclaimed the employee.

Carlos Zude continued: "I spoke with the manager. It's quite a deal for
them . . . He's an intelligent American. He understood and guaranteed
the problem would be solved within a month. Two flights a day."

He gave details as if the business were his own:

"They can bring down the price a little, and if the colonels get over
their fear of air travel . . ."

The employee laughed. "Huh, they will ... I remember Colonel Maneca Dantas ... When the first air service began, the one the Germans ran, with a stop here, the colonel told me that the only way he'd die in a plane crash was if one fell on him. But ever since he was forced to travel to see his son who was sick—the one who just graduated," he explained, "it's the only way he travels ..."

The employee had never talked so much in the presence of Carlos Zude and felt a certain misgiving. But the boss smiled approvingly and commented: "They're like frightened children ..."

The employee found this a perfect image and, as he harbored literary ambitions, thought about repeating it that night, as his own, at the meeting of the Commercial Employees Association. The car was passing through the streets of the railroad company, entering the city's business district, en route to the port. The employee remembered the message:

"Oh! Mr. Carlos ... Dona Julieta phoned and asked me to let you know she's at the beach ..."

"Thank you very much ..." The indifferent voice of the aristocrat.

Carlos Zude thought once again about Julieta. She would be in her tiny swimsuit, playing *peteca* or diving into the waves of that dangerous sea with her intrepid courage. He patted the pocket that held the necklace he had bought in Bahia. He pictured it around his wife's tawny neck and smiled. *She was the most beautiful woman in the world ...*

The car stopped. The chauffeur opened the door and Carlos got out.

"Wait for me, José, I'll be right back."

The chauffeur nodded, closed the car door, and went through the wide main door of the Zude Brothers & Co. export firm, but did not go to the elevator like Carlos and the employee. He went instead into one of the enormous rooms on the ground floor. Nowadays the firm was a four-story building, near the harbor in the same location as the former two-story structure. The ground floor was a warehouse and cacao-bagging area, two immense rooms filled to the ceiling with dark beans from which emanated the smell of chocolate. Climbing over the mountain of cacao, men naked to the waist filled sacks with the beans. Others weighed sacks, adjusting them to the exact weight of sixty kilos, and afterwards the women stitched the mouths of the sacks with surprising speed. On each sack a twelve-year-old boy stenciled in red letters:

ZUDE BROTHERS & CO.
Exporters

Trucks backed into the rear of the warehouse. Porters, doubled over under the weight, hauled sacks on their backs. The sacks fell with a muffled thud onto the trucks, the drivers put their motors in gear and pulled away down the street, coming to a stop at the pier. Porters reappeared, and once again their backs bent under the weight of their load. Running along the bridge they seemed like some kind of strange being, black men with enormous hunchbacks. The Swedish ship, huge and gray, swallowed up the cacao. Sailors, drunk and speaking a strange language, descended the gangplank.

José leaned against a wall and watched the work, looking at Rosa as she stitched sacks, her lips taut and her eyes alert. The chauffeur's almost-smiling lips wore the smile of a ladies' man, but Rosa didn't see him, preoccupied with the rhythm of her work. Hoping to exchange a smile with the mulatto woman, José spent another minute watching her, then shrugged his shoulders in a gesture of resignation and returned to the car. *That tame cuckold is dying to see his wife, he might be back any minute . . .*

Number 72, who was passing by, laughed from beneath his sack of cacao, and José laughed also at the insult murmured between his teeth.

Carlos Zude really *was* dying to see his wife. He had gone up in the elevator, crossed quickly through the offices, where the employees rose as he passed, and opened a door over which a metal plaque read:

DIRECTOR
Private

He sat at the chair behind the desk. The employee who had gone to meet him put the briefcase on the table and waited till Carlos Zude spoke.

"Very good, Reinaldo. Send Mr. Martins in."

The employee acknowledged the order and left, nearly at a run. Carlos Zude turned in his swivel chair and looked out the broad window at the movement of passing trucks on the street. A bus was leaving for Itabuna. The manager entered the office, having come on the run, and panted: "I was supervising a shipment . . ."

After the handshake and routine questions about the trip, he also stood waiting. Carlos opened the briefcase, spread some papers on the table, and indicated a chair to the manager.

"The business is taken care of . . . A million and a half kilos sold at twenty mil-réis per fifteen kilos . . . I closed the deal by cable yesterday."

The manager was surprised. "You got twenty mil-réis? And you only sold a million and a half?" There was a certain timid tone of reproach in his voice. "We still have two point seven million on hand . . ."

Carlos Zude smiled. On the opposite wall the enlargement of a picture of old Maximiliano Campos returned his smile. He had, in a manner of speaking, built the firm of Zude Brothers & Co., cacao exporters. He had passed away ten years ago, and with his dying words had advised Rômulo, the older of the two Zude brothers, to dedicate the firm's activities exclusively to cacao. Carlos had followed that advice, and today the Zude fortune had tripled. In the photo Maximiliano's wise smile responded to Carlos's good-humored smile. The old man understood, he really understood cacao. He had come to Ilhéus when cacao first arrived on the scene. Carlos turned back to the manager and explained in a voice that betrayed a tiny trace of vanity:

"Only a million and a half, Mr. Martins, and I'm not sure I didn't sell too much . . . There was a time, Martins, when buyers could name their price. They paid whatever they felt like paying. Ilhéus cacao was nothing, it had no impact on the market. It lagged behind the rest. In those days—I don't know if you've heard about it—our firm was small. Instead of this building it was a crummy two-story building that didn't even belong to us, it was rented. That was twenty-five years ago, Mr. Martins . . ."

The manager nodded his agreement, uncertain of his boss's point. Carlos Zude stretched his legs and continued:

"Only a million and a half, Mr. Martins, and maybe I should sell only half that amount. I'll tell you something: cacao is going to go up like never before. Don't be surprised if it hits thirty mil-réis this year . . ."

"Thirty? Could be . . ."

Carlos Zude noted doubt in the manager's face and voice. He smiled more broadly; it was for Maximiliano Campos that he smiled.

"I sold a million and a half kilos but that wasn't why my trip was advantageous, Mr. Martins. It was because I had a long talk in Bahia with Karbanks, and he agrees with me. I got the word from him about a series of matters. The price of cacao is going to rise like never before, unlike anything ever imagined. Ilhéus will be swimming in gold . . . Do you know what percentage of the world's cacao comes from Ilhéus?"

The manager did know, and gave some numbers, looking at his superior in admiration. Martins considered himself a good manager, beyond a doubt, careful in his dealings, meticulous and hardworking, but he lacked the business genius of his superior. Carlos stood up, stuck his fingers in his vest in a characteristic gesture.

"The time has come, Mr. Martins, for the Americans to pay the price we ask. From now on the price is going to be set here in

Ilhéus, not in New York . . ." In the photograph, Maximiliano was smiling.

The manager waited. Carlos Zude looked out the window at the passersby. The smell of cacao drifting into the office was a good smell.

"What are the current rates?"

"Superior, eighteen thousand three hundred. Good, seventeen thousand nine hundred. Standard, seventeen thousand four hundred."

"Exclusive of delivery costs?"

"Yes. The delivery price is eighteen thousand nine hundred for Superior. A good price . . ."

"A bad price, Mr. Martins. New York's price. I want you to hit the street and make the colonels an offer: anyone who wants to sell their crop, exclusive of delivery costs, we'll pay—"

He paused briefly, his mouth twisted, thinking.

"Nineteen mil-réis."

"Nineteen per fifteen kilos?" Fear was back in Martins's voice.

Carlos Zude smoothed the crease of his trousers.

"Yes, nineteen, Mr. Martins. And you can go as high as nineteen five . . . And soon, don't be surprised if we're paying twenty or twenty-five."

The manager was engulfed in doubts. Carlos lowered his voice. "And, by the end of the year, chocolate manufacturers will be paying us thirty or more for every fifteen kilos."

In a firm voice: "They'll pay the price we ask . . ."

"It's amazing," the manager said.

Carlos Zude gave his final orders: "Phone the other exporters—use my name and Karbanks's—and invite them to a meeting tonight at the Commercial Association. Set it for nine o'clock and make sure everyone's there. Say it's important; use my name and Karbanks's."

"Certainly."

Carlos collected the papers, handed some to the manager, shook his hand, went back through rooms where sweating employees rose at his approach, and took the elevator. At the door he looked at the movement in the streets, at the men hurrying past. At a nearby bar many people chatted. The theater displayed photos of a coming film. José held the car door open. Porters passed bearing sacks of cacao on their backs. At the Grand Travelers Hotel people were entering and leaving. A ship's whistle sounded at the dock. Carlos Zude smiled once again: he was pleased with himself, with the admiration that surrounded him, the employee who had met him at the pier, the openmouthed manager, the men who removed their hats as he passed. He would like Julieta to be at his side there at the company's main entrance, on that business day in the city. He would point out to her the intense movement centering on the port and perhaps then she'd understand the necessity for living here a few more years instead of on the beaches of Rio de Janeiro. He recalled the stories that Maximiliano used to enjoy telling on his trips to Bahia about this land's past, about the Ilhéus of thirty years ago. There was one Carlos especially liked. It dealt with a bearded colonel, revolver at his side, riding crop in hand, with a stern countenance and a calm voice, to whom merchants would point as he crossed the streets: "He's the owner of the land!"

The owner of the land, that's what they'd say about him one day. About him and Julieta . . , The owners of the land.

He got into the car: "Home, José."

José blew the horn and a porter moved aside as the car pulled out. Carlos Zude took the pearl necklace from his pocket. *I want to see her nude, completely nude, with nothing but the necklace falling from her neck to her breasts.* He closed his eyes to imagine it more clearly.

2

Carlos put on his bathing suit, had a glass of vermouth in the dining room, and went out onto the hot asphalt of the avenue, whistling a currently popular samba. He took large steps, advancing in small hops over the asphalt made scorching hot by the sun. A boy on a bench, practicing his sport of spitting on the beach, looked up from his immensely pleasurable task as Carlos passed. He couldn't resist a sarcastic guffaw at the sight of the potbellied man, his paunch spilling over his trunks and contrasting with his skinny legs, springing over the asphalt in little hops. The laughter pierced Carlos Zude's happiness, injecting an unpleasant note into such a joyous morning. He pretended not to hear but stopped hopping, his feet burning from the contact with the blazing ground. Unintentionally he looked at his belly: he could see he wasn't the same good-looking young man who had swept women off their feet twenty-odd years ago. He was forty-four, and he liked highly seasoned meals, those tasty Bahian foods; fat had begun to take its toll and was deforming his body. "A dilated stomach," the doctor said. Dressed, it was a different story. His clothes of finest cashmere, cut by the most famous tailor in Bahia, the beautiful ties, the specially-made shoes, and the belt—especially the belt—hid his paunch and made him look at least ten years younger. The only other thing was the gray hair, but that even gave him a romantic air, according to Julieta. He was a little the worse for wear, no denying that. A little or a lot? The result of all those years of partying while Rômulo busied himself with the company's future. His older brother had let him live like a playboy till almost the age of thirty, when Carlos had finally decided to abandon his medical studies. He had attempted to introduce a new approach in the college: replacing classes with nights in cabarets, mornings spent between the sheets and in women's arms, afternoons in movie theaters, taking strolls, seeking to arouse women. He was twenty-nine when he came to work in the firm, and although he retained the night-owl habits of a drinker and womanizer, he demonstrated a remarkable head for business. He was the first to understand and staunchly support Maximiliano Campos's ideas, in the sense of completely abandoning tobacco and cotton to dedicate themselves exclusively to cacao. When Maximiliano died, Carlos took over the branch office in Ilhéus, spending long months in the south of the state buying cacao and building up the firm, transforming it into one of the largest exporters of the product. And he came to be a great admirer of the region; his friends already called him "Ilheense," a man from Ilhéus. When Rômulo died, leaving him his house and the care of his widow and children, he made the definitive decision to abandon other products and concentrate on cacao. It was then that he moved the firm's headquarters to Ilhéus, constructed the new building, and began to think about getting married. This was really his sister-in-law's idea more than his. He merely missed the women of Bahia, the French and Polish women who had taught him sexual refinements that made it difficult for him to accept the rudimentary lovemaking of the lovers he found in Ilhéus. His sister-in-law complained that he was "becoming an incorrigible, melancholy bachelor." In the absence of worthwhile women in Ilhéus, Carlos abandoned himself to drink, influenced by the example of the colonels, who could drink all afternoon and night without the alcohol having any effect. Although she never said so, his sister-in-law was afraid that drink would ruin Carlos, making him unfit to carry out business, thus hurting the firm and in consequence her children, of whom he was guardian. She began a marriage campaign by looking for girlfriends for Carlos. But possibly he never would have married if, at a party in Bahia, he had not met Julieta Sanchez Rocha, the daughter of old man Rocha, a wine merchant in the lower city. Julieta's mother, when she was young, had already been famous in the streets of Bahia for her beauty. And for hot-bloodedness as much as beauty, to the point that none could vouch for her faithfulness. It was said she had turned the head of even a governor of the state . . . Her daughter had inherited her beauty, and had the young men of the capital at her feet. Dark Spanish skin, black hair, deep and languid eyes—all this in the agile, supple body of an athletic girl whose romantic and mysterious eyes, sweet as a rapture, highlighted a tangible sensuality. From suppliant eyes a languor cascaded over the girl's trim body.

Carlos Zude fell in love. The night he met her she was with a young and jaunty naval officer. At the table, Carlos's friends commented on how gracefully she did the latest dance imported from the United States, pressed against the young man.

"Close together, aren't they?"

"She's really something . . ." the other man said.

The third man imagined the erotic subtleties he could teach Julieta in bed. He clicked his tongue in an immoral sound full of desire and suggestiveness. Carlos Zude said nothing; he merely looked at her, continuing to follow her with his eyes when she sat down. She laughed frequently, her teeth small and white like those of a pedigreed dog (the image came from one of Carlos's friends), her voice warm and throaty. A mutual acquaintance introduced them and they danced. The naval officer was soon forgotten, and seven months later they were married and traveled to Europe, Carlos Zude deeply in love with his wife. That passion still endured three years later. Three happy years, Carlos thought. He remembered that Vasco, his longtime cabaret companion, had doubted the possibility of his finding happiness in marriage. Especially with Julieta, with her restless and powerful flesh of a woman of twenty, a body that longed for a man, but a strong man who could satisfy the sexual hunger that shone in her coquettish eyes. Vasco said this with characteristically brutal frankness, hammering away at the age difference between the couple: Julieta at twenty and thirsting for a man, Carlos at forty and weary of women. Carlos took umbrage at the adjective; he was not weary of women, and besides he had mastered the science of love, complete with details which allowed him to supplant the drive of youth with certain advantages. Today, content, he could laugh. Vasco's gloomy predictions had not come to pass, and Julieta had grown accustomed to him. Carlos had enfolded her in his net of sexual refinements and unhurried lovemaking, the delight of elegant variations, with something new every day. At the beginning of their married life she was raw sexual drive, a moment of strangulated agony in the immediate and rapid sex act. And she wanted more, like a hungry child. In the first few days Carlos gave of himself as if he were a millionaire. But he had a plan, and he carried it out. Bit by bit he gave less, but with more technique, thus accustoming her body to the subtle caresses he had learned at the hands of experienced prostitutes. And he lost any fear of the future when he noticed that Julieta had stopped gazing with a melancholy expression at twenty-year-old men, convinced as she was that nothing could be better than a man experienced in life and love. She even stopped talking constantly—unlike before—about moving to Rio and the house he had promised her on Copacabana Beach. Carlos had convinced her of the absolute necessity of living for a time in Ilhéus, where he was indispensable and irreplaceable. Not only was there not a single individual capable of running the export firm; Carlos was also aware that the time to rest had not yet come. There was still much to do before his plans were complete. He was not yet the "owner of the land." Within his overall commercial outlook for cacao Carlos Zude had grand projects brewing. In just a few more years, he told Julieta, the firm would be running itself and they could go live in Rio or Europe. But he was needed during those few years, badly needed, and he was stuck here. Julieta had asked him to set a time limit. Carlos was rather vague: four or five years, who could say?

Three years had already gone by. And only this morning had he become certain that his projects were under way. Now he could tell Julieta they wouldn't have to live in Ilhéus more than another four or five years. If it were up to him he wouldn't leave at all. He liked the city and its people, and he liked cacao. It was Julieta who was not satisfied by her frequent trips to Bahia, her two trips to Rio—one by plane when the Americans inaugurated their airline. She still dreamed of the big cities, Rio and São Paulo, the casinos, the beaches, the theaters and movie houses. Carlos understood her: Ilhéus was a commercial city with few amusements, swept up in the cacao trade, hardly the ideal place for a woman brought up in high society and used to the capital cities. By way of compensation, what commercial might it possessed! They called Ilhéus "Queen of the South" in honor of its riches. It was the fifth largest port of export in the country, and through it passed all the cacao in Bahia, 98 percent of all the cacao in Brazil, a large share of the total world production of cacao. Few cities in Brazil had seen such rapid growth. More new streets were being opened, and construction was booming; in addition it was one of the richest cities, with money flowing freely in its prosperous business sector. Moreover, it was a pretty city, crisscrossed by squares and gardens, with well-paved streets, good lighting, and fine water and sewage facilities. Even so, Carlos had to admit, it was a far cry from the great capitals with their amusements, their happy and ingratiating way of life. Ilhéus was a business city of rough planters that still retained many patriarchal customs. Married women lived out their lives inside their houses taking care of the cooking and the children. The colonels' wives were women devoid of culture and refinement; no wonder Julieta felt like a displaced person. If not for the Englishmen and Swedes from the consulates, the railroad and the shipping company, she'd have no one to join her for cocktails when Carlos left on one of his frequent business trips to Bahia. Julieta had little to do with the local society wives. Her manners shocked them, and to the colonels' wives her zest for sports seemed suspicious and frivolous. Carlos Zude laughs, remembering the face of Dona Auricídia, Colonel Maneca Dantas's wife, when at a dinner she had given for them, she saw Julieta light a cigarette . . .

Carlos Zude runs along the beach, his thin legs supporting his large belly. In the distance boys are playing soccer in the sand. Carlos pants from running. He's getting old . . . Forty-four . . . Any little sprint tires him, and his paunch feels heavy. He makes out Julieta's form under the large red beach umbrella. Her dark hair stands out between the blond heads of the Gersons, the Swedish couple from the consulate. The one standing, eating ice cream, is Mr. Brown, the chief engineer from the railroad. He has the body of an athlete, although he must be the same age as Carlos, perhaps a bit older. Carlos thinks about the differences in upbringing. He'd never played sports; to learn to read he had spent his childhood with books, difficult and unappealing books. Now at forty-four he's potbellied with skinny legs and a puffy face. Dressed, he looks fine, but like this, in a bathing suit, he looks . . . worn-out. The Englishman is an athlete. Carlos thinks that, if they have a son, he'll be educated in an English school. They'll send him to either England or the United States.

Mr. Brown sees him, and Julieta rises and waves to him. Carlos stops when he sees her on her feet, standing on tiptoe, her hand in the air waving a greeting. She stands like a statue erected in the tropical sun. Carlos Zude is moved by the sight of his wife. And he imagines that, athletic as she is, she will not age, that body he adores will never turn into the flaccid body of an old woman . . . Carlos runs faster (oh, these skinny legs . . .), runs to meet Julieta. The Swedes and the Englishman may think it ridiculous, but he takes her in his arms and kisses her on the mouth, a prolonged kiss in which Julieta's lips disappear under her husband's mustache. One of the boys playing soccer comes after the errant ball and stops, watching the exciting scene. Carlos's eyes are closed. So are Julieta's, but she has seen the Englishman and the Swedes, athletes all, seen the exciting figure of Guni, a match for that of any adolescent.

The boy, before kicking the cloth ball to resume the game, yells to Carlos Zude: "Go for it, old man . . ."

3

The man took the flyer from the hand of the boy distributing it on the street and read indifferently:

PUBLIC NOTICE

Marinho Santos advises the public that, having acquired the Pirangi bus formerly belonging to Mr. Zum-Zum, licensed for Mondays, Wednesdays, and Fridays, the following prices have been established:

ITABUNA	...........4$000
PIRANGI	.............5$000
GUARACI	..........8$000
round trip	...........15$000

I do this in order to better serve a public which hitherto has been driven away by absurd prices, for in the ten years that I have been the owner of Buses, on other lines, charging more or less the above prices, I have not had to relinquish possession of any of them and have always paid my debts promptly. And Always Getting Ahead. Further, with this Bus I now have a Fleet of fifteen Buses, which enables me to handle service of all kinds without any misgivings on the part of my riders.

THE NEW BUS
will soon be here.
Mondays, Wednesdays, Fridays—price 15$000
round trip to GUARACI

17

The man continued reading, then threw the advertisement in the
street. He commented to whoever might care to listen, "The way this
competition thing is going, they're going to end up paying passengers
to ride. They really are . . ."

4

The bus was leaving for Guaraci, newest of the towns that had sprung up in the cacao zone. It was near the division line between the Ilhéus county limits and the backlands at the edge of the Baforé mountain range, where cacao cultivation blended into cattle raising.

A woman in the bus was screaming at her husband, who was talking at the door of a tavern: "It's time to go, Filomeno . . . Hurry up, you loafer!"

The passengers laughed. The bus was full. Marinho Santos was checking the work of the collector, who went from seat to seat selling tickets. The driver put the engine in gear; the tardy passenger got in and started arguing with his wife. The collector complained about a man who had given him a 500 mil-réis bill to pay the fare to Itabuna—four mil-réis. Marinho Santos nipped the incident in the bud by pulling out a wad of bills and making change.

A passenger complained: "Is this piece of junk going to leave or not?"

Another came to his support: "You'd think they'd never heard of a schedule . . . It doesn't mean a thing . . ."

"You'd never know this was a civilized country," said a third.

A man came running down the street, suitcase in hand. Marinho Santos informed him, "It's full. Not a seat left . . ."

The passengers smiled at the disappointed look on the latecomer's face. Marinho said consolingly, "There's another one leaving in an hour. You can wait in the station if you want to."

The man walked toward the station. Marinho Santos banged his fist on the side of the bus; the driver blew his horn to clear away the baggage carriers and headed toward the highway. In the bus, men in worsted suits, on their way to Itabuna or Pirangi, mixed with people

19

heading for plantations, dressed in riding breeches and boots. Despite the jolting of the bus, a Syrian was attempting to sell some necklaces and rings to a farm worker who fingered them suspiciously.

"Is highest quality, customer . . ." the Syrian said in his clumsy speech, pointing to the glass of the rings and displaying cheap, cheery necklaces.

The farm worker studied them. He had never seen such an obviously fake ring—fake gold, fake diamond, but pretty nevertheless.

"That thing won't last two days . . ."

"Guaranteed for two years . . ."

The Syrian raised his hands in strange and impressive oaths: "I swear from God, customer. Customer never see a more pretty present . . ." He pronounced it "bresent," his tongue suffering from forming what for him were difficult words. The worker argued prices a bit longer, then took from his pocket a large red kerchief tied with a knot. Untying the knot, he removed some small bills and a few coins. He slowly counted out the agreed-upon price, still complaining and asking for a reduction. The Syrian swore it was impossible.

"Swear I no can, friend." He pronounced it "briend," and displaying his sincere and humble eyes, reached out his hand and took the money. At the last moment the customer decided to switch the ring for a necklace of blue beads, whose fleeting beauty might perhaps outlast that of the patently fake ring. The Syrian made the trade, swearing that he was losing in the exchange. He assumed a victimized air, the voice of a victim, his eyes near tears in the daily theatrical routine that was his stock in trade. On his back was the trinket-filled peddler's case he carried from one plantation to the next, bearing the only luxuries peasant women could afford: his fake necklaces, false rings, flashy but cheap cloth, colored kerchiefs, images of miracle-working saints.

Conversation spread through the bus, involving men and women, planters and farm workers, as well as contracted immigrant workers.

"Cacao's bringing a good price this year . . ."

"And it's going even higher, God willing . . ." said a woman, crossing herself. She wore a kerchief on her head and a fatigued expression in her lifeless eyes.

"Don't look to me like it'll go beyond nineteen . . ." said her husband beside her, a thin, hunched-over old man.

"Ha . . ." another worker said. "Just today Mr. Martins, from the Zude company, was payin' nineteen against future delivery."

"Against future delivery?"

"That's what I said . . ."

"Then it's gonna go up . . ."

"I don't believe it. Cacao at twenty is better'n gold on the ground that you scoop up with your bare hands. It'll never reach twenty . . ."

The driver joined in, almost letting go of the wheel. "Don't you doubt it, Mr. Clementino, it'll get there. We're in for a boom, bigger'n the one in 'fourteen, the one caused by the war . . ."

Clementino decided to ask the informed opinion of Captain João Magalhães. What remained of the João Magalhães who thirty years earlier had arrived in the port of Ilhéus, in search of easy poker winnings at the expense of colonels with little experience at gambling? He had aged greatly in those years, and not even a certain young woman in Rio de Janeiro who had come to disdain him (when she discovered he was nothing but a professional gambler and not the businessman he pretended to be) and who was never to marry after spurning his proposal, perhaps not even she, who still kept him in her heart, would have recognized him. Countless wrinkles furrow the captain's face. His hands bear large calluses, a far cry from the well-kept hands of the dandy of so many years before. His hair, scorched by the sun, is a stranger to combs. He is unshaven, and a straw cigarette dangles from the corner of his mouth. He is wearing a worsted jacket and a khaki vest and carries a riding crop in his hand. All that remains of those distant times is the title of captain by which he's known, and an engineer's ring with which he refused to part. Clementino asks his opinion.

"What do you think, Captain? Is cacao gonna hit twenty this year?"

João Magalhães takes a puff of his cigarette. "Higher than that, Clementino. A boom is coming, all right . . ."

The others perk up their ears, even the driver.

"Do you have some inside information?"

"Only what I read in the newspapers . . ."

"And what's that?"

Captain João Magalhães relates what he read in the papers about the blight in the cacao fields in Ecuador, where the entire crop had been wiped out. He speaks with animation, gesturing and explaining in detail, inventing newspaper stories to supplement those he had actually read. The others listen with eyes and ears open, eager for those optimistic words. Captain João Magalhães also listens with satisfaction to his own words, remembering for the moment the young man of thirty years ago who recounted poker stories about astounding plays and impressive bluffs. But now he is a man past fifty, of which close to thirty years have been spent in these lands of Ilhéus, planting and harvesting cacao. He had given up poker long ago, only playing now and then in family games, occasionally teaching tricks of the trade to astonished friends. Now only cacao interests him, a much more dangerous game. Sinhô Badaró, his father-in-law, was right when he said that the land grabbed

hold of people and never let go. It was the sticky substance exuded by
soft cacao . . . He had gotten it on his feet, just as Dona Ana Badaró
had gotten it in her eyes. They had married in the awful year at the
end of the fighting over Sequeiro Grande, the year Juca died, the
government intervened, and the Badaró plantation house was attacked.
The plantation was left in ruins. Less than from the wound from which
he never completely recovered, Sinhô Badaró died some years later of
grief, of shame at no longer being the landowner he once was. When he
went to the city he was not pointed out. He walked by like anyone else,
limping from the wound in his leg; he was a plantation owner in debt.
He had emerged from the fighting deeply in debt and with his fields in
disarray. When he died, Sinhô was still paying off his debts, rebuilding
what he could of his property, replanting the burned-out fields, cutting
down the few trees that remained, with his son-in-law living on the
plantation, working day and night. The doctor said it was his heart.
João Magalhães never believed it. To him, Sinhô Badaró had died of
shame, the shame of seeing one of his promissory notes challenged in
a notary's office in the city. In any case, while he was alive things had
gone well. But as soon as he died, Olga, Sinhô's sister-in-law, and his
brother-in-law, the widower of Sinhô's sister who had died in Bahia,
asked for a survey and division of the lands. Old doctor's bills also
showed up, along with bills from the lawyer Genaro, who asked to be
paid for years of legal representation, forgetting that he owed his own
land to the Badaró family when they were the political kingpins of the
zone. The plantation was broken up. Olga sold her part immediately,
at a good price, and left for Bahia, where she was living with a young
man who worked at the branch of the Bank of Brazil in Ilhéus and had
long been interested in her. While Sinhô was still alive, Olga ignored
him; she was truly afraid of her brother-in-law. But he was hardly in
the ground before she demanded her share of the landholding and sold
it for cash. Luckily for her, there were lots of buyers, and she got a good
price. She went looking for the bank employee, who was now working
in the Bahia office. Rumor had it that she was living with him as if they
were married, in scandalous luxury. The husband of the other sister also
sold his share. João Magalhães tried to reach an agreement with him to
buy it, but he wanted cash on the spot to sink into his business in Bahia.
João was unable to get a loan, and the land was sold to someone else.
João Magalhães and Dona Ana retained ownership of the cacao fields
which produced nearly twenty-three thousand kilos, with enough land
for forty-five thousand if they had the money for planting. Their lands
now were scarcely larger than those the Badarós had given as a gift to
Antônio Vítor, the hired gun who had gotten married the same day as
João Magalhães. Of the wealth of the Badarós, those "owners of

the land," there remained only these fields—and João Magalhães and Dona Ana. The land must have been worth around two hundred thousand réis in those days. They had enough to get by on, as they said in those parts, falling between the small growers, who produced fewer than fifteen thousand kilos, and the large plantation owners, who harvested sixty thousand or seventy-five thousand. One day they might make it to forty-five thousand, buy more land, and little by little rebuild the lost wealth. João Magalhães had made the attempt many times in the last thirty years. He tried unsuccessfully to apply his poker tricks to that new game. It was only with difficulty that he managed to pay off the remaining debts. The plantation ate up the profits of each harvest through necessary improvements, the electric kiln for drying cacao in the winter, the pruning of older fields, and the planting of new fields using modern methods as the older fields, planted almost at random by Dona Ana's grandfather, began to decline in production. Little by little, João Magalhães learned the secrets of cacao and how to come to terms with the demands of life on the plantation. In the early times—the most difficult—he had thought of running away, abandoning everything and returning to his previous free and easy life. The day he watched the departure of Margot (as she waved her handkerchief from the ship's rail), returning to other lands, leaving all that the cacao zone represented, João Magalhães felt like going to the Bahiana Shipping Company and buying a ticket. He still had his gambler's hands and his facility with a deck of cards. But he was beyond saving, the prisoner of cacao. There lay within him a certain strange kind of loyalty that kept him faithful to the Badarós, to Dona Ana's eyes, to the soil of the plantation. And Dona Ana would never agree to leave this area and live by their wits somewhere else.

The captain dedicated himself totally to cacao, which had come to be his sole concern. Four children were born, a boy and three girls. The boy died a few days after birth; the girls grew up and got married, one by one, poor marriages, the best being that of the youngest daughter, who married a doctor with a practice in Pirangi. The other two married small growers with little land and less money. Dona Ana had grown old in the kitchen of the plantation house, alongside the pots and pans. So had the captain. His hair was mostly white and his face was covered with wrinkles. He had forgotten the fighting at Sequeiro Grande and even had personal dealings with Colonel Horácio, who at eighty-odd was on his last legs, but rich and still feared. Now and then they talked about old times. The colonel spoke without rancor of bygone days, and once when João Magalhães was in a bind for money when the early stages of a drought ruined a year's crop, the only reason he didn't ask Colonel Horácio for a loan was in order not to displease Dona Ana, who wept in humiliation when he broached the subject to her. He took a loan from a small bank at high interest; he was a long time paying it off. Cursing Dona Ana's pride, he said, "Pride is a luxury the poor can't afford . . ."

Such had been his life for thirty years. His life had been cacao and nothing else: the rise and fall of prices, waiting for rain for the crops, waiting for sun to dry the beans. All the rest—the birth of the children, the death of the boy (who was named Juca), the death of Sinhô, the daughters' weddings—were more or less important incidents, but only incidents. What really mattered was cacao, only cacao.

Today João Magalhães is returning to the plantation happy: all indications are that cacao is about to go up like crazy. He came to Ilhéus to sell this year's crop but saw the drift of things, the offer made by Martins, Zude's manager, and decided not to sell. They were too eager, a sign that cacao was going to go up . . . It was better to wait. Besides, he had seen that piece in the newspaper about the cacao in Ecuador . . .

He explained to the listeners on the bus his thoughts on the situation: "There's going to be an increase, a big one . . . Stick with me and you won't go wrong. Only a fool would sell cacao now . . . You might as well throw it away . . ."

"Even at nineteen, Captain?"

"Nineteen . . . This year I'm going to sell my cacao for twenty-two . . . Didn't I tell you that the newspaper . . ."

He poured out details, further explanations. He had changed a great deal on the outside, gotten older, his gambler's elegance something long past, but he had retained the enthusiasm, the love of adventure and the unforeseen, that had brought him to this land thirty years before. And it was love of adventure that kept him there, in the battles for Sequeiro Grande, in Dona Ana Badaró's eyes. Now he's risking everything on the chances of a price increase, optimistic and wearing the same smile as always, the smile that had brought him through the worst days of debts and hardships. But, if the increase comes . . .

Everyone agreed with him. The woman who had spoken first made the sign of the cross again and said, "I pray an angel is speaking through your lips, Captain."

The bus rolls down the highway carved from the mountain, which it climbs in dangerous curves. A group of workers steps aside to make way for it. But the bus stops, and the driver gets out to look for water for the overheated engine. The Syrian makes use of the stop to open his peddler's case and show the cuts of cheap silk. He high-pressures João Magalhães to buy one as a gift for his wife. João Magalhães examines the fabric, tempted by the flashy pattern. The driver, as the bus pulls out, turns around and asks the question in everyone's heart, a question that makes Captain João Magalhães forget the Syrian and his silks.

"But what if it doesn't rain, what good are high prices then? Where's the cacao to sell? No rain, no crop . . ."

The discussion resumes, of interest to everyone on the bus. Captain João Magalhães thinks it will rain heavily. He recalls previous years when in this month, without any warning, rain suddenly began to fall. After all, Ilhéus wasn't Ceará, a land of droughts. But someone pointed out that clearing the large forests had reduced the rainfall. The captain disagreed:

"Even so, drought is a rare thing around here . . ."

The Syrian took advantage of the ensuing silence to insinuate himself once more, the piece of silk in his hand, his voice almost pleading: "Buy, Captain . . . I give it for four mil-réis the meter. I swear I lose money . . . Swear from God . . ."

But João Magalhães did not hear him because someone was pointing to the hillside, where the sun-scorched weeds were turning yellow: "It may not rain . . ."

"God forbid," prayed the woman.

And every heart, even the Syrian's, shared the woman's wish, lifting their eyes from the weeds to the clear sky, looking for clouds and rain that did not exist. Only a blue sky where a coppery red sun marked high noon.

5

The clock in the bar struck twelve. The lawyer Rui Dantas, spotting
Pepe Espinola's game and the dice spread on the table, repeated the
classic and infamous witticism, "Anybody can do it once."

He gathered the dice in the leather cup, or "bog," covered it with his
palm, shook it, pretended to spit over the back of his hand for luck,
then rolled the dice.

"I'm going to try for another."

He scattered the dice on the table and watched, ready to chant out
the results. Espinola watched also, his pale face made even paler by
the powder he used, a solid color from chin to shiny bald head, where
the sparse strands of hair were carefully combed. The die that was still
rolling came to a stop, momentarily undecided between the ace and the
eight. It landed with the ace showing, making three of a kind.

"Three aces, in one roll," Espinola intoned.

But Rui Dantas, who had graduated only a few years before and
sported a large ruby on his finger, symbol of the legal profession, was
not satisfied and wanted more. "I'm going to make it five of a kind,
and in two rolls."

Espinola smiled, half generous, half ironic: *"No hace nada."*

Rui Dantas shook the "bog" once more, then threw the two remaining
dice onto the table: a queen and an eight. Espinola broadened his ironic
smile. The lawyer picked up the two dice again and had better luck: an
ace came up.

"Four aces in a thousand rolls."

"That's not permeeted." Espinola corrected his pronunciation at once:
"Permitted, I min."

"Mean." It was Rui who made the correction this time.

"Sí. Mean . . ."

26

"And it's *sim,* not *sí,*" Rui corrected, smiling.

Espinola gathered the dice. He rolled. Two pairs. He kept the larger, jacks. On the second roll he got his three of a kind, albeit a small three of a kind. He put all five dice back in the "bog" for his last roll. He was out of luck: no pairs.

It was Rui Dantas's turn to gloat: "Didn't I say anybody can do it once? I won the second round, let's play the rubber match . . ."

Espinola won the third and decisive round. Rui Dantas called the waiter and paid. Espinola ordered cigars. They watched the movement at the Ponto Chic Café, which was bursting with people. It was time for the prelunch drink, a habit of many years' standing that was introduced to the people of Ilhéus by the Englishmen who had come to begin construction of the railroad. The Englishmen who came later preserved the custom. There they were, engineers from the railroad and employees of the consulate, at a corner table, drinking their cocktails and playing poker dice. Businessmen and colonels occupied the remaining tables. From the other side of the street came the noise made by commercial employees in the Café Ilhéus. They did not frequent the Ponto Chic, the most important of the cafés in the business district and a meeting place for exporters, lawyers, Englishmen from the railroad, landowners, big businessmen, and some of the agronomists from the Experimental Cacao Station established by the governor of the state in Água Preta. Espinola lights his São Félix cigar. Colonel Frederico Pinto comes into the café, small and nervous, animation in his tiny eyes, and pounds Espinola on the back.

"Smoking a cigar before lunch . . . Something only a foreigner would do."

Espinola turns around to see Colonel Frederico shaking hands with Rui Dantas. "How are you, counselor? And how're Colonel Maneca and Dona Auricídia?"

Rui Dantas replies that both are well. The "old man," as he calls his father, was in Ilhéus last week. He inspected the plantation, waiting for rain . . . Colonel Frederico commented on the delay in the coming of the rains that year.

"It could ruin the early crop . . . If it doesn't rain in the next couple of weeks, I don't know . . . It'll be the end of the early crop." He had suddenly become serious.

Later, smiling broadly, he wanted to know "how those verses are coming along." He was referring to the sonnets that Rui Dantas published now and again in the *Ilhéus Daily* or the *Afternoon Journal,* two daily newspapers circulating in the city. There were also *The Century* and *The Day* in Itabuna, the neighboring city, but Rui Dantas seldom contributed to these because of the intense rivalry between intellectuals of the two

cities. Frederico Pinto did not even hear the young lawyer's reply. He had
already turned back to Espinola, clapping him on the shoulder, laughing
again at the Argentine's habit of smoking cigars before lunch. A cigar
was just the thing after a real lunch washed down with good wine—
a fish stew, for example. Like those they used to have at the Fazenda
dos Macacos—he directed himself to Rui again—fish fresh from the
river, a nicely done sauce of coconut milk, now there's a lunch. Then
you light your cigar and think about nothing . . .

"Except women," Espinola interjected.

Frederico Pinto felt a mild start. Could the foreigner suspect
something? There was so much gossip in Ilhéus. It didn't even seem
like a civilized place . . . When anyone hinted about the matter, Colonel
Frederico Pinto offered no denials; he merely smiled with a certain
vanity. Who in the city was unaware that the colonel was the lover of
the *gringa,* that splendid figure of a woman who was Lola Espinola,
Pepe's wife? The Espinolas' arrival in Ilhéus, some ten months earlier,
had introduced a new word into the heterogeneous Portuguese spoken
in the south of Bahia, already transformed by contact with black people,
who sweetened it, then later acquiring an admixture of English terms
brought by the railroad engineers and by the Americans in the Exporter.
To all this the word *rubia,* or blonde, was added. It came ashore written
in huge letters in the ads distributed from house to house, and on wall
posters, when Pepe and Lola arrived in town:

THE RUBIA LOLA,
IDOL OF AUDIENCES IN THE SOUTH

They danced tangos, and danced them well. Tall, supple, and blonde,
Lola pivoted her body, swaying to the rhythms of the effete dance.
Espinola was a good dancer, and onstage, dressed in tails, even his
baldness disappeared in the eyes of the women who watched the slow
movement of his body, only now beginning to thicken, as he executed
the deliberate steps of the dance, in which sensual instinct blended with
all the dramas of prostitution. They had the feeling that Pepe was luring
the woman, as snakes in the fields lure birds from the trees with their
hypnotic gaze. The swaying of the slow dance was like snakes' eyes,
eye meeting eye, as a man with neither money nor love took love and
money from the same woman.

The women followed Pepe Espinola's movements closely, his tailcoat
making him even darker, his agile body bending over his partner. But the
men had eyes only for the *rubia* Lola. In the packed theater there was
not a man, from the timid adolescents who worked in the stores to the
fat and moneyed colonels, who did not desire her that night. A worker

from Colonel Silvino's plantation, in Ilhéus for medical treatment and at the theater because someone had given him the ticket, would never forget her, and the Argentine *rubia* was, till the end of his wretched life as a worker in the cacao fields, the most beautiful thing he had ever seen, the most unforgettable moment.

Nor did Colonel Frederico Pinto, an undersized bundle of nerves, take his eyes for a moment from the shapely legs, the elegant bust, and plump buttocks of the Argentine woman. For him too, Lola was a vision from a dream, a novel and unexpected happening. He desired her with the force of a man who had spent thirty years in the wilderness, cutting down forests and planting cacao. With all the repressed longings that had lain dormant throughout his entire existence or had found release with his wife, Dona Augusta—who had aged rapidly under the stresses of country life and whose body had ballooned out of control from rich foods—or with mulatto prostitutes in dirty back streets in the red-light districts of small towns. Lola was unique, a refined flower in the middle of that coarse land. Colonel Frederico Pinto sweated in his front row seat. What he would have given to have that woman beside him in bed that night, her blonde hair, her legs, her breasts, her buttocks ah, those buttocks like the haunches of a full-bodied mare!

It was both a dream and a reality. Pepe Espinola only went onstage as a last resort, when overtaken by dark days that left no alternative. And all of it, the tangos they danced, the tangos she sang, those lyrics redolent of petty tragedies, love stories with a different kind of triangle—woman, pimp, and gigolo—Lola's beauty, more evident than ever under the footlights, all that was merely the hook (a hook with the best bait in the world, someone had once said, referring to Lola) to catch a fat fish. And Pepe Espinola often commented that the technique never failed.

One day in Pepe Espinola's youth, a day more remote than anyone looking at him and trying to guess his age would estimate, someone with long experience in life affirmed in a cabaret on the outskirts of Buenos Aires, on a night filled with tangos and women, "To be a gigolo is the highest calling to which a man can aspire . . ."

He was not bald in those days but had a fine black shock of hair that he kept slicked down and well combed on his pale head, eyes that strained to appear evil, nervous and delicate hands, and lips that were always whistling. He had already had some adventures, but those were not the decisive days for "Kid Pepe," as his friends in the neighborhood called him. Others called him "the poet," because he treated the cabaret women with such delicacy that he reminded them of a certain romantic poet who one memorable evening had amused the regulars with his strange and ridiculous gestures. Pepe's father, an underpaid civil servant, felt strongly that his son should make some decision about his future, expressing his thoughts in harsh words about the character of the youth, who was "no good, a rotten student and a rotten son." Only sixteen, Pepe was already coming home in the wee hours of the morning as if he were a man, and spending time with the worst sort of companions. Dinnertime was strained, as he sat silently through his father's complaints, then lit out for the street at the first opportunity. The storm at home continued, the civil servant hurling insults while his long-suffering wife offered unconvincing maternal rationalizations. One day things took a more dangerous turn; Pepe's father stated his intention to find his son a job—"any job, it didn't matter what"—being unwilling, he stated categorically, to go on supporting a freeloader.

It was just as he was facing the agonizing possibility of having to take a job in a store or shop that, at the cabaret, Pepe Espinola heard, from Dandy (no one ever knew for certain what his real name was), the phrase that struck him as more profound than anything to be found in the thickest and most abstruse philosophical treatise: "To be a gigolo is the highest calling to which a man can aspire . . ."

Dandy gave him other hints as well. With his connoisseur's eye he judged Pepe to be a natural for the profession. His delicate manner interspersed with sudden acts of brutality, his unruly mien, and his youth made him the ideal dreamed of by forty-year-old women with full purses and empty hearts. There was a blonde woman in the cabaret who fit the description, an Argentine who called herself French, and who pronounced with exceeding correctness the only eight words she knew in French. Let's tell the whole truth: Pepe first made his move with Fat Antônia, a huge prostitute greatly favored by the sailors. But Fat Antônia lacked the necessary emptiness of heart, and her attitude, on the night she single-handedly beat up two German sailors, gave Pepe pause. It was then he turned to the Frenchwoman and began to concentrate on her. To tell the truth, Pepe fell in love with the woman, and Dandy's praises about how he, just a beginner, carried off his role of gigolo were undeserved. Pepe at seventeen burned with ardor for the forty-year-old Jacqueline (whose birth certificate read Luisa). She showered him with money, and Pepe led the easy life for six months, having told his family he worked nights in a bar. But Jacqueline spent so much time with her lover that she forgot the paying customers, and money became tight. Dandy advised Pepe that the time had come to look for someone else, a woman who was more conscientious about her duties to her gigolo. Pepe resisted the thought of separation. The woman's body, in the radiant beauty of its last moments of lushness, gripped the adolescent with the force of first love. But Pepe had chosen his profession and knew that it demanded sacrifices such as this. "One must have character," Dandy told him, when he realized what was going on, and in the end Pepe "had character."

He acted like a seasoned gigolo: one night he picked a fight over jealousy, took what little money she had from Jacqueline's purse, put on a gold wristwatch of hers, taunted her about her farce of French nationality, and walked away smiling. Jacqueline took poison that same night, and that memory, surfacing from time to time, casts a cloud of sadness over Pepe Espinola's happiness and peace of mind.

Thus he began his fine and meteoric career, which at one point elevated him to a prominent position in the cabarets and racetracks of Buenos Aires. They called him "the great Pepe," seen daily in the company of beautiful women, the gigolo of the city's most sought after demimondaines. He lived off a slim and internally sensual White Russian woman, who charged a fortune for a night of love granted to any degenerate millionaire. His women, of various races and colors, were the most beautiful ever to grace the cabarets of Buenos Aires, from the mulatto Brazilian chanteuse who made such a hit, to a dark, square-faced Dutch woman who lived off a beef exporter. No gigolo was more renowned or lived better. These were years of much money and high living. The knife scars on his hands, souvenirs of a scuffle in a nightclub; a few nights spent in a police precinct; and the beginnings of a lung ailment (an incipient accumulation of pus in his left lung), treated at the best sanatorium in Córdoba at the expense of Miss Kate, an American who was touring picturesque cabarets and had fallen in love with Pepe in the most shameful and romantic way—none of these incidents marred his happiness. Only after a binge would he recall the green-tinted face of Jacqueline lying in the coffin. Jacqueline, who had drunk poison one night long ago. Then he would suddenly turn cruel and beat the woman who was keeping him at the moment. He would curse life and swear that tomorrow he would visit his parents. But when tomorrow came, the crisis had passed. Pepe would not go to see his parents, which in reality was a good thing, for his father, a retired civil servant, had expressly forbidden him to set foot in the house, saying that Pepe had disgraced the family with his unworthy profession. Unworthy profession—! Pepe remembered Dandy's words: "The highest calling to which a man can aspire . . ."

Dandy had been outstripped by his pupil. In reality there was no comparison between a decadent cabaret gigolo on the outskirts of Buenos Aires and "the great Pepe," fought over by women, their purses and hearts opened wide. Pepe was not ungrateful to Dandy. When Dandy gave up the profession, visibly aged, more decadent than ever, and realizing that with false teeth he could no longer work "with the necessary dignity," Pepe found him a job as doorman at a downtown cabaret whose owner owed him a favor. That way Dandy need not exchange his tuxedo for something less elegant. On many a night he held the door for Pepe and the woman who loved and kept him at the moment, accepting the lavish tip with a comment the entire street could hear:

"I made him what he is today . . ."

But even for Pepe the years of glory began to fade. The "worthy" profession of gigolo has its age limits. Who can imagine a gigolo who isn't young and romantic looking? When he was around thirty, Pepe's hair began to conspire against him, falling out with surprising rapidity. When he became bald Pepe could no longer live off his "beautiful body," as he liked to put it. But he could still live off women. There was another profession, less romantic to be sure, which did not demand such physical attributes: that of pimp. This repelled Dandy, who found it unworthy of a man with any self-respect. He'd rather be a doorman than a pimp . . . Pepe thought differently. He recalled another statement of Dandy's: "One must have character." He became a pimp. Some years later the police interfered in his life to the point that he had to leave Argentina, taking Lola with him, whom he always introduced as his wife. They went to Rio de Janeiro.

It seems beyond dispute that Pepe Espinola was the first to introduce the badger game to Brazil. The badger game generated substantial revenues for Pepe and a great many emotions for Lola. They would rent an apartment in a residential high rise where they had already spotted a rich "client." Lola would bump into him by chance in the elevator, they would say hello, and the repeated meetings would lead to an acquaintanceship. One day, when Lola had sensed an awakening of the victim's interest, she would appear with tears in her eyes, the very soul of unhappiness. The rich man would ask what was wrong. Lola, wearing a dramatic expression, would lose no time telling him: she was unhappy in her marriage. Her husband, a monster, mistreated her; he was a materialistic and jealous lout, devoid of feeling, and didn't understand her. What man would have refused to console the *rubia* Lola, so pretty and so unlucky in marriage? In any case, the rich man was already interested in her to begin with. Events would then move swiftly, and after a few more talks Lola would open her apartment to her neighbor, who would either come down one flight or up one flight from the apartment he shared with his wife and children. He would arrive cautiously, for such an adventure in the same building where his family lived was not without danger, although that fact also lent it a special appeal. Lola would pretend to be even more frightened than he. She would speak of her fear of her husband, her terrible jealous husband who might cause a scandal, raise hell, or even kill someone. Then she would take the rich man into her arms, and the afternoons of love would last about a week, until one day—unexpectedly, since the "client" had already come to feel a sense of security—Pepe would burst into the room at the height of the lovers' ecstasy, a revolver in his hand, eyes blazing, and shout, "You bitch!"

Lola could not help admiring Pepe's acting, the way he screamed insults with fire in his eyes. He was a true artist. She loved him more each day. The rich man would lie in the bed, trembling. Generally the victim was a quiet businessman for whom scandal would have been a major embarrassment, especially a scandal in the same building where his family lived. He felt certain he was a dead man. Pepe would shout insults and threats. When he saw the "lover" was frightened out of his wits, he would soften his tone a bit, and when the rich man suggested there might be a way to make amends for everything, Pepe would undergo a short-lived crisis of dignity, then quickly prove willing to consider the possibility of cleansing his honor with something other than blood. He would speak at length about besmirched honor and set a high price, a very high price. After writing a check, the rich man would grab his clothes and escape, swearing he'd never again get involved with a married woman . . . During the run of the comedy, Lola would also receive some valuable gifts from the smitten man, so she and Pepe always showed a tidy profit for their efforts.

What ruined the badger game in Rio de Janeiro was overexposure. Pepe Espinola was not the only one using it. Others began to imitate the Argentine's methods, and one Brazilian even expanded it by raising the number of women to two, one of whom played the role of the husband's virgin sister, a dewy-eyed maiden who one day let herself be deflowered by a millionaire. Pepe did not have time to adopt this innovation, because one morning he woke up in jail, where he and Lola spent three months. He went to Bahia and lived there quietly for some time, for the Rio police had advised their Bahia counterparts about the couple, thus making it inadvisable to introduce the graceful badger game to the state capital. They bided their time, dancing in the most elegant local nightclub, then moved on to Ilhéus, under contract to perform at the São Jorge Theater. As soon as he disembarked, Pepe Espinola saw the enormous possibilities the rich city had to offer, with colonels who were pushovers for pretty women, in such short supply there. He stayed, earning money by gambling. His first business venture, still in operation, was to rent a house where he sold expensive drinks and where the colonels could play poker. Pepe himself did not play but took a cut for "expenses." He also charged for drinks and sandwiches. It was "in" to play at Pepe Espinola's house. In the game room, which was small and chic and where only a few were admitted, Lola paraded her supple body back and forth. Pepe toyed with the idea of putting in a roulette wheel.

One of the first regulars at the house was Colonel Frederico Pinto. When Pepe saw that the colonel was hopelessly taken with Lola, he decided to set up the badger game once again. He told Lola, who began playing her role. But the colonel was quite timid and took months to realize that it might be possible to get the woman into bed. Lola was earning a reputation as a "model wife," since for the game to work more effectively she exhibited complete indifference to the flattering comments from the colonels, the lawyers, and even Karbanks, the exporter. The comedy starring Frederico lasted longer than Pepe expected. And it was still running, for although the colonel was now Lola's lover, he showered her with so many gifts that Pepe had decided to delay the ending until Lola's small jewelry box was full. Then the colonel would pay dearly for the stains on Pepe Espinola's honor . . .

At the Ponto Chic, as Pepe and the colonel discussed brands of cigars, Rui Dantas, the lawyer, studied the colonel and Pepe, reflecting on the bad taste of women. While he, young and strong, wrote corny sonnets for her, she gave herself to a potbellied old colonel. It had to be for the money . . .

Rui Dantas, a lawyer without clients, son of a rich father, a bad poet and an unlucky gambler, can't understand Lola's taste. He too would give anything to have the *rubia* in his arms. Would he ever . . . He has no way of knowing that while he chats with the colonel, Pepe is thinking the time has come to ring down the curtain on Frederico's comedy and start another. And that for the new version he has cast as male lead Rui Dantas, son of Colonel Maneca Dantas, owner of the Fazenda dos Macacos plantation and a very rich man. Rui is sad. Lola is so far away, he'll never have her. What he would pay to take her and caress her body . . . As if guessing these thoughts, as soon as the colonel leaves, Pepe invites him to have lunch at their house:

"The *invitación* is from Lola. She is liking you very much . . ." He was trying to speak Portuguese.

Rui Dantas's eyes take on a new light. He would write a sonnet for her. That very day. A quite romantic one, with difficult rhymes. He paid for Pepe's cigars.

6

Including its warehouses, the Ilhéus Cacao Export Company occupied almost a square block. Nevertheless, the plaque bearing the name of the firm was small. The plaques of some of the companies that the Exporter (as everyone called it) represented were larger: the American aviation company, the Swedish shipping company, an American marine insurance company, and a typewriter company. The Exporter represented numerous other companies, but the totality of its activity as agent took up a minuscule part of the enormous offices and constituted a very small portion of its balance sheets. It is true that there one could buy a plane ticket, sign a contract to ship cacao on Swedish freighters, insure a house against fire, or buy a typewriter. But only a handful of employees were needed to handle these services. The rest, a large number, worked in the cacao trade. Cacao beans filled the warehouses that extended almost the entire length of the block. Along that stretch of the street the smell of chocolate was so strong it made people dizzy. The Ilhéus Cacao Export Company was the largest cacao exporter in the country.

The door of the office used by Karbanks when he was in Ilhéus bore a plaque reading GENERAL MANAGER. Karbanks liked night-clubs and drinking. He would walk down the street with his arm around the colonels' shoulders, talking with everyone. He was cheerful and courteous, but even so that large and corpulent American, red faced and sweating, with his loud voice and arms so long they had earned him the nickname "gorilla," remained a mystery to Ilhéus. There were various stories: that he represented large American interests in the area, that the Exporter wasn't really his and he was merely a high-level employee. For a time Ilhéus racked its brains trying to discover the secrets of the gigantic American but finally gave up and accepted him on his own terms.

35

To tell the truth, Karbanks was probably the best liked foreigner
in the cacao zone, with the exception of the Syrian Asfora, who became
a grower and whose daughters were married to Brazilians. Asfora was
not even considered a foreigner any longer. He had gone to Syria with
his wife and youngest daughter, the only one still single, to live out a
comfortable old age in his native land. But he returned before the year
was over, brought back by homesickness. He donned his riding boots
once again and set out for the plantation to grow and harvest cacao.

Since air travel had begun, Karbanks went to the United States
every year. Before that he had gone every other year, by ship. He
always came back with mechanical gifts—electric razors, small radios,
pencil sharpeners—for his closest friends among the colonels. But his
popularity came not from these trips but from the lack of importance
he gave to his position. He lived in the bars, talking, drinking, telling
jokes in his ungrammatical Portuguese. From time to time he would put
on a show in the cabaret, dancing drunkenly with some wench or other,
his enormous gorilla's body curved over the woman, his immense arms
flapping, his legs out of sync with the samba rhythms. His binges were
classics. On such nights he would start singing fox-trots in English.
It was Karbanks who, shortly thereafter, would support the Ipicilone
Group when it was formed in Ilhéus when cacao prices rose.

He liked to use slang terms having to do with cacao, the words
coming out a bit at a time, his pronunciation heavy. It is a matter
of record that it was he who succeeded in getting a contract with
the Swedish shipping company to bring in the large freighters, thus
making possible export of cacao directly from Ilhéus to the United
States, Germany, and northern Europe. And it had been he, with the
help of Carlos Zude and the other exporters, who had forced the
federal government to make the necessary improvements to the sandbar,
opening the way to deep-draft vessels. Perhaps it is unjust to use the
term "forced" in relation to Karbanks, for he gave the impression of
being the last person on earth capable of forcing anyone to do anything.
There was even a coarse joke in Ilhéus on that subject: the cheekiest
men in town claimed that Karbanks had not married a girl from Ilhéus
because, since in Brazil girls were virgins when they got married, he
would have had to force his bride's hymen. The joke was told to
Karbanks and the exporter laughed loudly, shouting his favorite term:
"Astounding! Astounding!"

But the business about the sandbar was a fact. Insiders said that
the Exporter held a majority stock interest in the docks, acquired
from the heirs of Colonel Misael. And the income from the port
was enormous . . . They also said that behind the managers of the
Farmers' Aid Bank was the Exporter, that is, Karbanks. He and

Carlos Zude were everywhere; the only area they had not gone into, so far, was the plantations. No one yet fully realized that a struggle was nearing between the colonels, conquerors and planters of the land, and the exporters. For now they only realized that a rise in the price of cacao was coming, an unprecedented rise . . . But there was already much talk of Karbanks, of Zude, of Ribeiro & Co., of the Rauschnings, the Germans who ran another export house, of Reicher, a tight-fisted Jew, of the Nazi Schwartz. There was also talk of Correia, who had founded a small chocolate factory and paid for articles in the newspapers proving that he was performing a patriotic act by producing the chocolate in Brazil itself. But the most talked about matter of all was Karbanks's binges. Married ladies with their narrow point of view thought the American was a rich man who cared little about his reputation. Despite that opinion Karbanks was well liked. Neither the English, who lived in their own little circle, nor the Germans, who patronized the natives with a mixture of disdain and uneasiness, were looked upon with favor. They were in the city but not of it. Karbanks had lived in Ilhéus for many years. Arriving just as cacao was emerging as an economic force, he had founded the export house. It was an insignificant thing at first, possibly the smallest of the export companies. But Karbanks went to the United States, and when he returned the name of the company was changed from Frank Karbanks to Ilhéus Cacao Export Company. With the name change came an incredible increase in capital. In that same year Karbanks bought more cacao than any other exporter, and in the next year continued to expand his business, until today only Zude Brothers and Schwartz came close to him in volume. The Rauschnings only exported to Europe, and Reicher and Ribeiro, who exported to the United States and Argentina, were much smaller buyers. Karbanks bought almost 30 percent of all the cacao in the south of the state of Bahia.

Once during those years a rumor circulated insistently through Ilhéus, during one of Karbanks's stays in the United States: the Yankee was not coming back, he had been given a desk job in New York. The city deplored the event, for Karbanks would be sorely missed by the colonels and nightclub habitués. In fact another American did show up to take over Karbanks's office at the Exporter. He was thin, taciturn, and brusque, and business took a precipitous nosedive, which Maximiliano Campos took advantage of to lure away some of the Exporter's biggest planters, who from that time on began selling their cacao to him. The colonels did not know how to deal with that close-lipped American who never bought drinks, never accepted an invitation to have some coffee in the nearby bar, and never talked about women. The upshot was that

Karbanks returned and the thin, brusque American disappeared from
Ilhéus. Karbanks's return was accompanied by the return of prosperity
for the Exporter's business. There followed the matter of the docks
(which some thought was a very shady deal and involved politicians
from the capital), the founding of the bank, the contract for Swedish
ships, and exportation direct from the port of Ilhéus. Today the Ilhéus
Cacao Export Company occupied almost a block on the main business
street in the city, represented a series of companies, and had interests in
countless businesses. It controlled an absolute majority, for example, in
the highways that were giving the railroads a real run for their money.
And it enjoyed preference on the trucks that carried cacao from the
cities and towns connected to Ilhéus by the railroad: Itabuna, Ferradas,
Pirangi, Palestina, Banco da Vitória, and Guaraci.

The few Americans who worked for the Exporter were Protestants to
a man and all went to the English church that had been improvised in
a former cacao warehouse. Karbanks, despite also being a Protestant,
did not go to any church. Nonetheless he never failed to sponsor the
Catholic feast days of St. George and St. Sebastian, or Our Lady of
Vitória, and St. John. On the lists circulated by the bishop and priests
in order to raise money for these and other church feasts days, lists
carried by girls from the parochial school hand-picked for their good
looks, Karbanks's name was always one of the first, and next to it was
one of the largest contributions.

Also, on the large marble plaque on which were carved the names of
the largest contributors to the erecting of the new church of Our Lady
of Vitória, a lovely white chapel that the nuns had ordered built in front
of their school and which dominated the city from the hillside, on that
plaque placed in the atrium one could also read Karbanks's name, just
below the mayor's. The American had given twenty thousand réis for
the work. The plaque was one of the few places one could see his full
name: Mr. Frank Morgan X. Karbanks.

7

Rising from the chair where he was listening to the singing of the thrush, the poet Sérgio Moura reluctantly answered the telephone. He heard the faraway, friendly voice of Martins, the manager for Zude Brothers & Co.

"Mr. Moura?"

"Speaking."

The scene was the new building of the Ilhéus Commercial Association, next to the nicest garden in town and almost directly across from City Hall. The building was a testimony to the strength of the city's progress, the strength of the so-called "conservative classes": huge, imposing, with a large marble lobby, sumptuous stairs, and expensive carpets. It had a library, whose books were not virgin of readers solely because the poet Sérgio Moura could take advantage of his position as executive secretary of the association to read them. It was also because of him that orchids (which grew profusely on the land near the beach without anyone noticing them) graced the gardens in the rear, where close to two dozen melodious songbirds took the poet's attention from the numbers before him marking the level of cacao exports and the commercial activity of the zone—cold numbers like gentlemen in stiff collars. The thrush trilled in the first hour of afternoon. The poet Sérgio Moura lived in the association building itself, and as he had food sent in, would go days without stepping outside. Still, someone who fancied himself a psychologist had said that the only person who saw everything that went on in Ilhéus, and above all drew correct conclusions about it, was the poet Sérgio Moura. It may have been an exaggeration, but there was reason to exaggerate.

Martins's voice on the telephone. "It's Martins."

"Yes?"

"A meeting of exporters has been called for tonight to be held there."

"What time?"

"Nine o'clock . . ."

"All right."

"You can see about—"

"Whiskey? No problem . . . How could exporters hold a meeting without whiskey?"

Martins was unsure whether he liked Sérgio Moura, or feared him. In any case he decided to disclose the news: "Did you hear, Mr. Moura? It looks like we're in for a price increase, and a big one . . ."

The poet wrinkled his forehead. "An increase?"

"That's what the meeting is about . . . I don't know all the details . . ."

"Does anyone?" asked the poet.

"Right . . ."

"Well, see you tonight . . ."

"See you later, Mr. Moura. Remember, you didn't hear it from me . . ."

"Don't worry."

The thrush continued to sing its sweet melodies of a lost forest. The poet Sérgio Moura went to the cage, where a bright yellow bird warbled its painful song with all its heart. The poet was tall and thin, wore blue worsted, and looked a bit like an ironic bird with his fleeting smile that spread from mouth to eyes. At one time he had been quite thin and weak. But one day there was a street incident, the only street incident in his entire life, and he decided to exercise and strengthen his body. Some people laughed at him. Sérgio hired a trainer and bought equipment. It took a year, but he was a different man. He never got his revenge on the guy who had insulted him—the man had left town—but he still harbored the hope that one day their paths would cross. In reality no one bothered the poet anymore, and if he was already respected for other reasons ("that one is more poisonous than a viper," the attorney Rui Dantas had said when, still a law student, Rui published his first sonnets, which gave the poet a good laugh), now they respected him even more.

The thrush sang and the poet Sérgio Moura thought. A price increase . . . Why in the world would exporters be in favor of a price increase? At first glance prices were ideal for exporters the way they were. Prices dictated by New York buyers . . . For some time now, had they desired, Ilhéus exporters could have set the price . . . Where else could the United States turn to for the cacao it needed for internal consumption? The poet remembers the cable he had clipped from the newspaper, about the wipeout of the Ecuadorian crop. The blight had consumed the flowers and small buds. In Ecuador, unlike Ilhéus, the growers did not raise a certain type of ant on the leaves of the cacao trees. The ant, without harming the trees, eliminates the blight. All the wealth of Ilhéus depended on an ant . . . The poet thought the ant merited a poem from him, one of those modern poems that so scandalized the city (which no longer laughed at him as before, for two or three important critics in Rio and São Paulo had written articles praising the poet Sérgio Moura to the skies, critics with whom it was impossible to disagree without appearing ignorant). The pixixica ant . . . The truth of the matter, my dear sweet-singing thrush, is that the exporters could have forced a price increase for some time . . . The poet had always thought that wasn't in the exporters' interests. Why the increase? In his conversations with the thrushes, canaries, and other birds, the poet had already told them something about the struggle he foresaw between the large exporters and the owners of the land, the large planters, those conquerors of the forest who thirty years earlier had stepped over so many corpses to plant cacao trees, a struggle that would also drag in the small farmers who tilled their fields with their families, men, women, and children all working together. The exporters were only middlemen but were becoming the true owners of cacao, those who profited most from its cultivation. The small farmers, poor devils, faced a constant struggle to avoid being swallowed up by the large growers. Behind the scenes the exporters encouraged the struggle, helping the small producer with loans, subdividing the plantations in order to avoid having the crops fall into a small number of hands that could dictate prices. Now this business about the price increase . . . Why? The increase would strengthen the colonels, the large growers. The poet couldn't see what was in it for the exporters.

One canary was named Karl Marx, which was no doubt a scandal in the Ilhéus Commercial Association. The poet was well read in Marx and revolutionary economists. But then in what subject was Sérgio Moura not well read?

He had come to Ilhéus from a much smaller city where he had worked in a wretched civil service job. He had come to work on the *Ilhéus Daily*, the first newspaper founded in the city. He hadn't remained for long, finding the atmosphere uncongenial. The position as executive secretary of the Commercial Association not only gave him a salary sufficient for the elegant life-style to which he aspired, but also made it possible for him to read and write undisturbed. Which is how the poet Sérgio Moura came to understand Marx better than almost anyone in the state. In one sense it was a futile understanding, since the poet kept it to himself and made no use of it. He never went, for example, to the meetings at the home of Edison, a shoemaker who lived in Snake Island. Still, his readings had left their mark on Sérgio's poetry, which had forsworn sonnets with obscure rhymes and carefully scanned alexandrines for poems with liberal and sonorous rhythms and meaningful content. It was curious that his revolutionary work had no impact to speak of in Ilhéus but did have a certain impact among young intellectuals in the large cities. One of his poems, "Two Celebrations in the Sea," had been a success in Rio, São Paulo, and Recife. It told the story that once, a book by Freud fell into the sea, which brought about a "celebration in the sea." The mermaids removed their fish tails and began to make love without guilt. Later, on another occasion, it was a book by Marx that fell in, and a second celebration took place in the sea. All the fishes held a meeting and went to the palace of the sea king, who was the shark, and killed him and were thereafter forever free under the waves. Such was Sérgio Moura's poetry these days.

He was much the topic of discussion when he first came to Ilhéus. He never went to cafés, never set foot in a nightclub, and lived isolated from others.

But little by little Ilhéus got used to the poet Sérgio Moura. The favorable reviews of his work (still unpublished in book form) offered by critics in Rio and São Paulo were crucial to his acceptance. The townspeople made allowance for his biting comments on local scandals, his refusal to participate in the commercial employees' literary society, and his "air of absurd superiority," as the attorney Rui Dantas put it. The poet repaid that acceptance with a poem about Ilhéus which was now declaimed at festivals.

Now and again Joaquim, the driver, came to the Commercial Association to chat with the poet. He would speak to him about economic problems and they would argue amidst trilling of birds and statistics of cacao exports.

An editor of the *Ilhéus Daily* often said that the following phrase, spoken by Sérgio Moura, explained his complex personality in its entirety: "I wanted to be a bishop . . ."

He was merely executive secretary of the Ilhéus Commercial Association, earning his salary by sitting through the discussions of the planters, businessmen, and exporters at their weekly meetings. But he passed the time by writing his poems (lately he had turned to folklore, creating lengthy poems about the cacao zone), listening to the birds, picking orchids, and reading Marx and his fellow revolutionaries. In that city of so many conflicts about money, of so many struggles over land and plantations, of shady land deals known locally as "dodges," a city with a tradition of violent death, he would walk down the street as the sun set behind the coconut trees, an ironic smile on his face, admiring the lights as they came on at the top of Conquest Hill, across from Vitória Cemetery. The only thing lessening his tranquillity was threats from leaders of the local fascist party, who, for reasons the poet had yet to discover, considered him an extremely dangerous element. It was well known in fascist circles that the list of those to be shot when victory came, a list drawn up by the local Supreme Leader, was headed by the name of the poet.

The poet stands before the sweet-throated thrush, thinking. Why a price increase? It was strange; he could see no advantage in it for the exporters . . . What the devil was it that they wanted? Anyway . . . The poet shrugged, stuck a finger into the cage, where the tame bird allowed him to scratch its head. Then he went back to the children's poem he was working on, the story of a thrush who one day rounded up all the caged thrushes and organized a songbirds' strike. Immediately they all stopped singing. The poem, a new fable, was coming along nicely. But now the poet was stuck for the precise word, the exact term he needed. The increase . . . He should have a talk with Joaquim. Thinking of Joaquim, his thoughts shifted to the plantation workers. The price increase didn't mean a thing to them. They would continue in their same miserable existence; nothing would change that, be it the progress of the zone or the growing wealth of the colonels. A friend of Joaquim's had worked on a cacao plantation for six months just to see firsthand what it was like . . . The courage of the man . . . The increase wouldn't help the workers. What it would do was enhance the size of the large plantations, but what the devil did the exporters have to gain from that? Why were they forcing the issue?

The thrush ends his song. The orchids open their fleshy blossoms in voluptuous color. The poet goes to the open window looking out onto the quiet street. In the garden, he sees Julieta, elegant and beautiful, approaching. She nods a slight greeting. Sérgio Moura responds, his eyes fixed on the woman's buttocks, her long-desired buttocks. Long desired and unattainable . . . An exporter's wife . . . Not even with the increase . . . But Julieta is coming toward the Association; what can she want? The poet goes to receive her at the door. She's looking for books from the library; her Swedish friend wants to read something in Brazilian literature, and Julieta has come to ask the poet's opinion.

"What should I recommend?"

She smells of expensive perfume and is wearing a pearl necklace around her creamy neck. If someone had told the poet Sérgio Moura that the desire he felt was exactly like that of the exporter Carlos Zude, he might have taken offense and responded with trenchant irony. But at that instant the poet is imagining Julieta naked, the necklace tumbling over the firm breasts under her dress. She was emitting tiny shouts, clapping her hands.

"The birds are so pretty . . . And the orchids are wonderful!"

The loveliest of the orchids is now over her breast. She listened to the titles and asked him to make a list.

"Why don't you bring it when you come to our house? You never go anywhere for conversation, you're like a monk . . . We're having a small party tomorrow, it's my birthday . . . Why don't you come? I haven't invited you before because they told me you never accept invitations because you're so proud . . . Won't you come?"

Her perfume lingered in the room after she left. Was the increase of any importance to her? Did the workers, the base of that entire pyramid made up of cacao beans, even suspect the existence of a woman as beautiful, as elegant and well-groomed as she?

Definitely, the best thing would be to send a message to Joaquim. The poet summons the custodian, tells him to buy the whiskey, ice, and sandwiches for the meeting that evening: "On your way tell Joaquim to stop by . . ."

Now he wishes only to think about a love poem, a poem for Julieta:

> *Beyond a doubt you come from distant shores,*
> *In flight from Ship Catarineta . . .*

Was there some mystery behind this business of the increase? What the devil could it be? The poet Sérgio Moura is unable to write his poem that day. Even he feels the weight of cacao, in this city of Ilhéus in these times of ours.

8

To better explain his still confused thoughts, the poet Sérgio Moura translated for Joaquim the following passage from an article the Commercial Association had received from the United States. He did so with some difficulty, since he didn't speak English well; Joaquim listened, serious and attentive.

The cacao tree is native to the Amazon region. It is grown in the states of Bahia, Pará, Amazonas, and Espírito Santo. Pará was the first state to begin cacao cultivation. It planted the first tree in 1677 and in 1836 the first sprout was taken to the state of Bahia, where it gave rise to vast plantations.

After the Gold Coast, Brazil is the largest producer of cacao in the world, and in that country, Bahia is the state which grows the largest quantity, i.e., 98 percent. The Bahian cacao zone comprises a 500-kilometer strip along the coast, the width varying up to a maximum of 150 kilometers. Almost all of the cacao crop comes from a continuous area of 20,000 square kilometers beginning at Belmonte, in the south, and terminating at Santarém, in the north of the state. The highly fertile soil there created for the cacao tree conditions more appropriate to its growth than it had found in its native Amazon region.

Cacao is shipped from Brazil through the ports of Ilhéus and Bahia in the state of Bahia; Belém in the state of Pará, Vitória in the state of Espírito Santo; and Itacoatiara and Manaus in the state of Amazonas. The product is exported mainly to the United States, Brazil's largest market for cacao. Last year the United States purchased 88,202 metric tons from Brazil, Germany 19,228 metric tons, and Italy 6,541 metric tons; smaller amounts were exported to Argentina, Sweden, Holland, Columbia, Denmark, Norway, Uruguay, Belgium, France, and other countries. Brazil's domestic use of cacao is small, as it is a product used primarily in cold countries. For this reason, Brazil's production is mostly for export.

Cacao is high on Brazil's list of exports, second only to coffee and cotton. The U.S. market, which consumes more than 40 percent of the world's cacao supply for making chocolates, candy, cocoa powder, cocoa butter, and pharmaceutical products, has in recent years given preference to Brazilian cacao.

Figures followed, large figures showing the crop totals for the last ten years and the unstinting growth in production. The driver spread his arms in a gesture that encompassed not only the room in the Commercial Association but also the city of Ilhéus, the county, and the whole of the cacao zone with its plantations awaiting the rain that would fill their trees with gold-colored fruit.

"It's imperialism, Sérgio, my friend, it's imperialism. It's looking to gobble up all of this . . ."

In the poet's crazed fantasy, conjured up by the driver's tragic gesture, it appeared as a timeless monster with a hundred ravenous mouths that devoured everything: the port of Ilhéus, the chocolate factory, the workers, the plantations with their colonels and their field hands, the small farmers' plots, the stevedores at the docks, the buses and their passengers, Julieta and the birds, the genitalia-like orchids.

The driver's voice, accompanying his expansive gesture, had the sound of prophecy: "Imperialism is going to gobble up everything!"

Amidst the well-tended beds of roses, carnations, and violets, day was fading into a sweet twilight over the Ilhéus Commercial Association. At the door of City Hall the mayor, fat and smiling, was getting into the official car. On the pole above the tall City Hall building the green and yellow Brazilian national banner flapped lightly in the smooth, soft breeze of day's end. The poet Sérgio Moura could still see the monster emerging from Joaquim's dramatic gesture as it fled through the window, an immense and insatiable dragon that turned into a black cloud in the deep blue sky over the city of cacao. Slowly it grew, covering everything—the solemn City Hall, the blood-red roses in the garden, the colonels' mansions, the poor hillside populated by workers, the birds in the trees. Heading toward the plantations, it blocked out the flag as well. The poet saw it all with his hallucinating eyes, his clairvoyant eyes. A fearsome dragon, a dark cloud in the peaceful blue sky.

A man cut across the street almost at a run, shouting at another man at the other end of the square, his voice echoing joyfully in the twilight: "Hey buddy! It's gonna rain tonight! Everything's saved, thank God!"

A bird sang its farewell to the day.

9

As twilight fell on Ilhéus, business was hastily concluded, iron doors drew shut over the cacao warehouses, church bells pealed their blessing, and the sad voice of Lola Espinola sang a tango about drunken sprees, betrayal, and the suffering of love. His eyes half closed, Pepe listened, and in his heart rose once again images of cabarets on the outskirts of Buenos Aires, of women in the chill morning hours, of men with cynical smiles. The words of the tango brought back nights from the past, of ever-recurring betrayal, binges to forget, wretched dramas of social outcasts, dramas melancholy and pungent in their squalor. The sordid love of pimps and gigolos, a love intermingled with money made in bed, tragedies played out in the often lugubrious space of cabarets that claimed to sell happiness at prices accessible to all. Lola's voice, drawn out as if steeped in cheap liquor, seemed steeped in pain as well:

> "Tonight I'll drink my fill,
> I'll drain the cup till it's dry,
> And once again forget . . ."

Colonel Frederico Pinto, moving in his chair, smiled at the woman. He had chosen that chair deliberately. From it he could smile as much as he liked, wink, blow little kisses with his lips, without the others seeing, since he had his back to both Pepe and Rui Dantas, who was seated on the sofa behind him. The lyrics of the tango meant nothing to the colonel, ignorant of the twisted Spanish with its truncated words, the language of the bordellos of Buenos Aires. But the music, slow and corrupt, reminds him of nights in bed, nights that Colonel Frederico had never imagined existed. In his relations with his wife, a certain modesty-laden graveness had always prevailed. They slept together,

47

they made children. That's what it was: they made children. But in
reality Frederico was not even familiar with the details of his wife's
body, a body which had grown year by year until it transformed
itself into that amorphous, shocking mass of flesh. From his sexual
contact with his wife, Frederico kept only the pitiful memory of the
small cries she made at the conclusion of the act. He, in fact, would
usually finish before her, and those cries, coming from such a huge
body, disgusted him. Such contacts were becoming rarer by the day,
as the colonel, whenever he visited the city or towns, sought out
prostitutes with bodies more well proportioned than his wife's. It
was from them that the colonel learned some of those caresses
that prolong lovemaking. But even so, they were performed in that
professional manner that shocked even a man like Colonel Frederico
Pinto. Lola was the revelation of everything—of love, of caresses,
of life itself. To that nervous, rich little man, a planter who had spent
most of his life among the trees and animals of the forest, Lola was the
highest good the world had to offer, a beauty never before seen, an
unexpected and final delirium. Frederico Pinto had a wife, children,
and a cacao plantation. He was respected throughout the zone, he was
one of the powerful men of the land. But he would have willingly left
all that, the land, the plantations, his wife and children, to follow Lola
wherever the path might lead. His possessing the blonde Argentine
woman had brought him a wealth of new feelings. He felt like a young
man starting out in life. To be sure, many thought him ridiculous, but
the colonel was unaware of that. He lived like someone from another
planet, in a dreamworld. Those incredibly subtle caresses which Lola
made part of the sex act didn't cause the colonel to deem her merely
a more refined prostitute than the rest. Just the opposite: they made
him consider her more worthy and more pure. To him those caresses,
those lips that traversed his body in lingering kisses, those hands as
wise as sex organs, that corrupted mouth—to him it all seemed like
love, extraordinary love, with no hint of vice. To him there is nothing
of vice in the tango she sings, merely sadness, verses of love directed
at him in her melodious voice. The colonel opens and shuts his lips,
directing ridiculous little kisses at the woman as she sings.

   Rui Dantas affects a maturity that he does not possess. He assumed
a very romantic pose, standing beside the sofa, his eyes on the woman,
his impassioned and grave eyes. Lola is older than he and Rui feels the
need to appear, rather than a recent college graduate, a man capable of
possessing and dominating her. He stares at her, at once arrogant and
tender, but his heart beats rapidly in his chest. Gradually he thought
of a sonnet in which he compared himself to a butterfly fluttering
around a rose of incomparable beauty. But alas! the rose had thorns,

the thorns of indifference, which ripped the butterfly's wings. The final image was really quite banal: the butterfly's wings were Rui Dantas's heart. But the young man was pleased with himself, certain that the verses would capture once and for all the elusive love of Lola Espinola. So he watches her, half grave, half romantic. Anyone coming in from the street would get the impression that he was trying to hypnotize the singer. Lola's voice fills the room, her eyes travel over the three men, one by one. Her voice, falling on each man, arouses a different sentiment in each heart. Pepe knows it is for him that she sings those unhappy Argentine tunes. Rui Dantas thinks she sings those sad love songs for him. The colonel knows that she is inviting him to lovemaking, an invitation in a foreign tongue.

But Lola is singing only for herself, such is her desire that afternoon, her desire for that night:

> "Tonight I'll drink my fill,
> I'll drain the cup till it's dry,
> And once again forget . . ."

This is a sad and dirty life. The only thing is to drink till you collapse, suck bottles and more bottles till you can't think anymore, till you forget everything, everything, everything. Pepe would beat her if he knew what she was thinking; Frederico would give her a ring, a necklace, a bracelet, or some other expensive piece of jewelry. Rui would ask her to marry him. All three things were senseless, vain, depressing. Lola wants none of that. She wants only to drink, drink in order not to think. Drink till she can fall asleep, and thus forget. Her voice goes from man to man, her eyes from one to the next. It is like a sob, but no one hears:

> "And once again forget . . ."

Lola is infinitely weary.

10

Julieta Zude is also infinitely weary. Sunset, falling on the sea like trickles of blood, increases her despair. It's like a sickness . . . As if every muscle, every bit of her flesh were rotting. Weariness. Weariness of everything and everyone. She adjusts herself in the window, where she is sitting on the sill. On the avenue in front of the building a passerby stops to get a better look at the bit of thigh she exposes. Julieta does not smile in amusement as she would on any other occasion. She withdraws her leg, straightens her dress; the onlooker moves on. Bloodstains cleave the dark green sea. The deserted street is silent. In the distance, urchins are playing soccer. They are abandoned children, and Julieta concerns herself with them for a short minute, thinking about how they never tire of playing soccer. They were already on the beach by morning, with their cloth ball, their happy shouts, their mischievous expressions. Now it is dusk and they have returned once more to their favorite game. And they shout and laugh and run. *They're happy*, Julieta thinks.

Why the devil can't she take her eyes off that bloodstained sea today? It looks like a painting . . . It reminds her of the paintings she saw in the exhibition in Rio de Janeiro. But those were static things, and didn't cause her the anxiety she feels now in the presence of the real sunset. While the others—the wives of friends, well-read ladies of Rio—stood before the paintings eagerly voicing their admiration ("Look at that sunset! It's superb!"), she had remained silent, unreached by any emotion. She was thinking about the casino, where that night she would see Otávio. But now, the dying sun spilling its blood over the sea and the silent street at twilight only served to increase Julieta's fatigue. She stretched her arms, yawning.

"I've got the neura . . ."

50

It was Otávio who had told her that, during their last days of love in Rio. When she complained of fatigue, that mysterious illness, he laughed, took her in his arms, and explained. "It's neura, baby. Neurasthenia . . . A disease you rich people get . . . It comes from not having enough to do . . ."

Whatever it was, it was terrible. It came on gradually, took over her body slowly, an all-encompassing sadness, apathy, a desire to die. "It comes from not having enough to do . . ." Julieta would like to blame the city of Ilhéus, where she is forced to live, for her neurasthenia. There was a time when she would do so, torturing Carlos, complaining, saying she wanted to travel, asking for trips to Rio. But here or there, whether in a small town or the great capital, the "neura" would return to possess her, settling in her breast and weighing on her heart. Sometimes it would happen at the height of a party. Everyone else would be happy, but she would become serious, distant and weary of it all, apathetic about everything. She had tried drinking; it made things worse. She would be taken by a desire to cry, an endless agony and despair. Madame Lisboa— so beautiful and gentle!—to whom she had opened her heart on her first trip to Rio, took her head between her hands, kissed her maternally on the brow (she was scarcely older than Julieta but knew how to be motherly and give advice), and said:

"It's lack of love, my dear. I was that way once. Tired of everything, restless, unhappy. Then I found out it was only my husband I was tired of. That's when I began to take lovers . . . It worked wonders for me . . ."

It was Madame Lisboa who introduced her to Otávio, on the pretext of a medical checkup. The doctor's office looked more like a boudoir. And it was there in the office, on her second visit, when she went by herself, that he possessed her. He was Julieta's first lover, and the truth is that—though Otávio was only thirty—her lover was frighteningly like her husband. The same topics of conversation, the same words, the same ambitions, the same unbounded selfishness. They were even alike in the way they made love. So Julieta sank once again into the sadness of her life, apathetic toward everything.

Her mother, who was both beautiful and well read, had passed on to her the habit of reading. Julieta shut herself up with her books. Light and miscellaneous reading, French adultery novels, weightier novels, detective stories. Then Jack, the engineer with the railroad, came along. He had arrived from England when Carlos was beginning to gather the foreign colony in the mansion in Ilhéus, especially the English and Swedes. Julieta was yawning in the indifferent company of Guni and Mr. Brown when, one day, they introduced her to Jack, who had just arrived. She was almost a child, happy and crazy, completely empty, smiling and full of animal energy. Julieta spent a delicious week

in her anxiety to make love to him. In those first days of love, when
every precaution was taken so he could come to her house or she could
meet him in his cramped quarters beyond the railroad tracks, Julieta was
happy. Jack, unlike Otávio, did not remind her of her husband. He was
a little boy eager for love, a small animal full of desire, and Julieta took
delight in teaching him the perversions in which she was so skilled. But it
didn't last long. She grew tired of him with surprising rapidity. Jack had
nothing to offer her. Once the furious sex act was over, he had nothing
to say. He would do cartwheels for her, little childish acts of insanity,
but he made Julieta feel old. It was not enough for her, so she broke it
off. Jack nearly went mad; he threatened her, tried to strike her the last
time they spoke. Finally he left town, somber and disillusioned. Julieta
felt no pity for him. She felt pity only for herself. Weariness . . .

Now there was Sérgio Moura . . . Why had she sought him out? Why
had she offered herself like some cheap tramp? She had already seen him
several times, said hello, but had never paid any attention to that man
with his ironic look and birdlike smile. But she had heard him talked
about so often, and always with suspicion and reservations, that when
the neura crisis hit her that morning, after the protracted sex act with
which she had paid Carlos for that wonderful necklace, she had rushed
to the Commercial Association. She felt better when she returned, for
the poet had struck her as both timid and vaguely sarcastic, as if he
both feared and found amusement in her.

Stretched out in bed, Julieta Zude made plans. It had happened
that way before with Otávio, and with Jack. But the weariness was
returning, taking control of her body, stifling her heart. She felt the
urge to cry caught in her throat. She went to the window. Agony without
explanation: *One day I'll kill myself . . .*

Sunset ached in her body. Now even the urchins had left the beach,
tired of their play. They would sleep under bridges, on park benches,
in the space under abandoned houses. "Oh if I could only go with
them . . ." A rich people's disease, Otávio had said. It was complicated.
Try as she might, Julieta is unable to analyze her feelings. She takes
ferocious pleasure in making love. Her blood needs men, and at the
moment of love, the moment of giving herself, she loses herself, loses
all circumspection and descends to the depths of degradation. She even
lusts after many of the men who pass before her, and if she doesn't take
them, it's only because it is impossible. But as soon as she emerges from
the delirium of the sex act, the man—Carlos, Otávio, or Jack—no longer
interests her. Or is it that she no longer interests the man? Possessing her
was not enough to capture her heart, but it was all they had. Carlos still
concerns himself with her, but only with her comfort. He never guessed
she could become depressed, contemplate suicide, want to die . . .

She is weary of it all: of Carlos, cocktails, parties, trips, necklaces—and life. She is like a drowning man thrashing his hands in a final cry for help after his eyes have already closed, never to reopen. The sunset adds to Julieta Zude's unhappiness:

What an awful neura . . .

Will Sérgio be worth the trouble? Nothing in this world is worth the trouble . . . Are they all the same? If she could just die painlessly, gently . . . How good it must be to die . . . Julieta Zude is tired.

On the avenue the streetlights come on. Carlos's car comes up the street, honking its horn. *It's showtime*, Julieta thinks.

She is tired of acting.

11

Even in Rio de Janeiro the rapid progress of the city of Ilhéus was the subject of comment. Newspapers in the state capital had invented another name for her: "Queen of the South." Among the perpetually impoverished cities of the nation's interior, where only the state capitals mattered, Ilhéus stood out as a progressive and wealthy city. The county's one hundred and fifty thousand inhabitants included a high proportion of affluent men, compared with other counties in the interior. The city was pretty, abounding with blossoming flower gardens and the fine homes of the colonels' families. The entire portion along the ocean was residential, crossed by wide thoroughfares, one of which followed the curve of the sea in imitation of Copacabana Beach, in Rio de Janeiro. This was the site of the mansions of the richest colonels, luxuriously furnished, ostentatious two-story houses. They were as a rule quite ugly, solid and massive as if symbolizing the solidity of those men who had conquered the land. From these mansions emerged expensive automobiles, almost all American, a few European.

Along the river lay the city's business district, just beginning to look impressive with the tall buildings of the export houses, banks, and large hotels, and the immense warehouses at dockside. There were now four piers leading in from the bay, and beside them rested the ships— the modest ones of the Bahiana Shipping Company, the larger ones belonging to Lloyd Brasileiro and Costeira, the Swedish company's enormous black freighters, and the fragile boats of Ribeiro & Co. The port's movement was intense, and any inhabitant of the city could reel off the statistic found in the commercial annual reports: Ilhéus was the fifth largest port of export in the country. Through it passed all the cacao harvested in the outlying parts of the county and in the neighboring counties of Itabuna and Itapira, brought in by railroad and highway. The

Bahiana company's ships brought the cacao from countries farther to the south: Belmonte, Canavieiras, and Rio de Contas, as well as from Una and Porto Seguro in the north. All that cacao was amassed in the port of Ilhéus, in the warehouses beside the docks, and from there was shipped to the United States or Europe in the great Swedish ships, where blond sailors sang strange tunes that left the hearts of the mulatto women of Ilhéus aching with longing. Sometimes they also left in the shapely belly of one of these women a mixed-blood child with dark skin and blond hair.

On the coattails of Ilhéus's progress the cities of Itabuna and Itapira grew also, the former transforming itself into an important commercial city, the hub of an enormous network of highways, heart of the cacao zone; Itapira, though somewhat smaller, was growing daily. And not only these, but many other towns that had sprung up along the path of cacao: Pirangi and Água Preta, Palestina and Guaraci, Água Branca and Rio do Braço. The most important were Pirangi and Água Preta, which were true cities and zealously asserted their well-deserved independence, for few cities of the interior of the state boasted the degree of business and progress of these secondary centers.

But Ilhéus was the heart of it all. Into its port poured all the riches of the zone, riches which in reality were but one: cacao. A rich and proud city, "Queen of the South." That pride was reflected in every gesture of every inhabitant of the city. They referred to themselves not as Bahians but as Ilheenses. They said that one day southern Bahia would be a state and that Ilhéus would be its capital. It was often said that the city of Bahia had no theater to compare with the recently constructed Ilhéus Cine Theater, that buses in Ilhéus were superior to those in the capital, that the city had much more life than Bahia. They would cite Ilhéus's five movie houses, two of them—the Ilhéus and the São Jorge—quite good, the other three less important, one on Vitória Hill, another on Pontal Island. They also pointed to the nightclubs, which at that time numbered three but would very soon be five. They would cite the library of the Commercial Employees Association, saying that only the public library in the capital was better. If the discussions really got heated, they would even cite the poet Sérgio Moura: there was no better poet in the city of Bahia!

The two weekly newspapers of thirty years earlier—one opposition, the other supporting the government—no longer existed. Now there were two dailies. One, the *Afternoon Journal,* followed the official line; the other, the *Ilhéus Daily,* which claimed to be independent but in reality followed the opposition line. From time to time both published full-page ads for the Exporter and other firms and were unanimous in publicizing, on page one, the birthdays of Karbanks and the large plantation owners and exporters. They lacked the violence of language that characterized the weeklies of thirty years before. When they had occasion to refer to each another they used phrases such as "sister publication" and "fellow newspaper." Any disputes were with newspapers in Itabuna, disputes arising from the rivalry between the two cities. Even so, harsh words were rare.

Where the small Church of St. Sebastian had stood, work was under way on the new cathedral, ugly and majestic, worthy of a great capital, despite the fact that the people of Ilhéus continued as irreligious as ever. In front of the girls' parochial school a lovely church was going up, jutting out over the city. Nearby was the bishop's palace, more opulent—the Ilheenses affirmed—than the archbishop's residence in Bahia. It was a palace painted the color of clay, square and devoid of architectural grace. The parochial school's day students would pass it in the happy moment when classes ended for the day. And there, near the bishop's palace, their boyfriends came for them, and the couples descended the hill hand in hand.

If the parochial school, accredited as a girls' normal school by the state Secretary of Public Education, brought rich landowners' daughters to Ilhéus from the other cities of the south, the County High School of Ilhéus—the mayor's bold accomplishment, the finest in northern Brazil, as the press was wont to say—had the effect of an entire generation of boys from the south of Bahia no longer going to the capital but coming to Ilhéus for secondary studies. There was also a business school, and the Ilheenses nursed the dream of a law school. The priests talked about the possibility of founding a seminary to attract more men with a clerical calling in that zone so lacking in religious spirit. There were several private elementary schools, in addition to a city-run one near the beach. On Pontal another elementary school was in operation, and a woman teacher who had been educated in Switzerland was starting a kindergarten, with relative success.

Some time ago doctors had discovered that the fever, which killed even monkeys, was typhus. And although it had not been eradicated in the interior, in the city it had almost completely disappeared. Besides the old hospital, there were now two large hospitals and an out-patient clinic. To be sure (as Ilheenses would admit in their more candid moments), the hospital in Itabuna was superior to any in Ilhéus. But that was the only one in the neighboring city, while in Ilhéus a patient had a choice of places to go for treatment.

Center of a country and of a zone of monoculture, Ilhéus was a city with a high cost of living, perhaps the highest in Brazil. Vegetables cost a fortune, meat was absurdly expensive. Every product, even the barest necessities, came from outside—except for vinegar, produced from the substance exuded by soft cacao, and the chocolate manufactured there. Rents were also very high: however fast new streets were added to the city, demand for housing still exceeded supply. Living was expensive, but money flowed freely.

The chocolate factory was small, and its distillery, where vinegar was made from cacao syrup, constituted Ilhéus's sole industry. The actual number of industrial workers was not large, merely those in the chocolate factory, the dockworkers, and the craftsmen who repaired shoes or stitched sacks in the export houses. Even the distillery normally hired workers who alternated between harvesting cacao and manufacturing vinegar. The regional Communist Party organization, which had its headquarters in Ilhéus, united in its fold—in addition to an agronomist, drivers, a white collar worker, a cobbler and a professor—workers from the chocolate factory, the docks, and the railroads and trucking companies. They were strong cells, capable, brave and combative, but they had not succeeded in winning over the plantation workers, whose ignorance was such that many didn't know whether Brazil was a monarchy or a republic. Some thought that Emperor Pedro II still reigned. No peasants' cell had ever really functioned, despite the leaders' ardent desires. One of them had once spent six months wielding a hoe on a plantation and had with extreme difficulty managed to recruit four or five members. But as soon as he left, the cell ceased to operate. Those men who could neither read nor write, who had survived the battles for control of the land, many of them a cross between peasant and assassin, were largely apathetic in face of the misery that bent their backs like slaves. Only one word aroused their interest: land.

Besides the Communist Party (which, because it was strictly illegal, was never counted among the existing parties), there were the government party and the opposition party—identical with the sole difference that one was in power and the other desired power—and the Integralist Party. This was the fascist party, allegedly supported by the exporters. The Ilhéus group was one of the strongest Integralist centers in the country.

Violent death had long since become a rarity. Only occasionally was there news about a murder. The intellectuals of the area referred in speeches to those times of death and fighting as something lost in the past, distant and a bit legendary. It was true that some of the colonels who had been part of those struggles still walked the streets of Ilhéus, talking about "the good old days." But no longer were there gunfights in the middle of town or crosses beside the roads, where today fast cars sped by. All that had remained was the tradition of courage cultivated by Ilheenses, with their hereditary disdain for a coward. The Ilheenses sincerely believed that the killing over land would never return.

The old market had yielded its place to a new one, a modern and hygienic building where people came to buy their food. The only thing unchanged in the environs of the market was the shanties that had sprung up upon the arrival of boats with their cargo of immigrants. They were the same miserable shacks, the same skinny, unhappy folk who had come from the impoverished land of the north in search of work in the rich cacao country. That old epithet of Dr. Rui's (who had died drunk in the middle of the street, during Carnival, while making a speech to a group of revelers) had become a classic, used by one and all when referring to the area by the docks where the immigrants put up their shanties while waiting to find a work contract: the "slave market." Then they would ride second-class in the trains to Itapira, Itabuna, Pirangi, and Água Preta, the tenuous hope of a new life on their thin and melancholy faces. In general they went with the idea of retracing their steps a year or two later with money in their pockets, of returning to the land they had left behind and planting it when the rains brought better times. They never returned. They would spend the rest of their lives, scythe on their shoulders and machete at their sides, filling sacks with cacao, pruning fields, drying the beans in sheds and kilns, never getting ahead, always owing the plantation store. Once in a while one would run away, be apprehended and handed over to the authorities in Ilhéus or Itabuna. There was never a single instance of a fugitive being acquitted, despite the agitation stirred up by the communists in some recent cases. They were sentenced to two years in prison, and when they later returned to some other plantation, demoralized and without hope, they had completely given up the idea of flight. There were also a few cases of workers who killed colonels. They were sentenced to thirty years in the Bahia State Penitentiary.

The intellectual life of Ilhéus was not what one might call the most imposing. There was the poet, who was considered Ilheense despite having been born in Belmonte. The rest were incorrigible sonneteers like Rui Dantas, racking their brains with rhyming dictionaries. The Commercial Employees Association had a literary society, where white collar employees read their compositions and love poems to one another. The colonels' sons, the first generation of Ilheenses, for whom their parents harbored grand futures, lounged around nightclubs and cafés, graduates in law, medicine, or engineering—lawyers without clients, unrespected doctors. One or two found a few clients, but work held little appeal. They had money, extensive plantations built by their fathers. They loafed, spending their time in brothels or courting the richest young women, thus uniting two family fortunes by marriage. The Revolution of 1930 had shattered the old political molds, and the struggles which broke out in the nation between left and right disoriented the colonels. They were used to the old routine of government parties and opposition parties, both underwritten by the colonels, in which young men made a name for themselves. Now they saw the parties had less impact, as the masses joined either the left or the right. Faced with this transformation, the colonels didn't know what to think, and so buried themselves in their plantations, working day and night, men who grew old shouting orders at their workers. They felt panic when a politicized worker yelled an insult at them in the streets of Ilhéus. To them it seemed the end of the world was at hand. The end of the world that the bishop had announced from the pulpit of the Cathedral of Ilhéus during the festival of St. George. The colonels' sons would kill time in cafés, and one drunken night the attorney Rui Dantas had defined them with a phrase that the poet Sérgio Moura had deemed his only intelligent and correct one: "We are a generation of failures . . ."

The poet disagreed, however, with the second part of the phrase: "But at least we know how to drink, which few people do . . ."

Sérgio Moura said that drinking rum in the company of prostitutes was clearly not knowing how to drink. The truth is that the poet didn't like those college-educated young men, sons of colonels, about whom he had once written some harsh epigrams.

Besides the Commercial Employees Association (which held very successful monthly dances), the Ilhéus Commercial Association occasionally brought together in its halls the city's "high society." In the Arts and Trades Society the workers and craftsmen talked about politics. It was a building near Unhão Hill, where for years the society was dominated by anarchist elements. Then the communists and socialists fought for political power in the Arts and Trades, as it was known. The Commercial Employees Association, although not Integralist in toto, did provide a large part of the following of that fascist party. All three associations sponsored social events, but the most chic dances were those given at the Ilhéus Social Club, an exclusive club that admitted only the wealthy men of the area. It was an attractive modern building at the end of the beach, surrounded by coconut trees, with tennis courts and an excellent dance floor. According to town gossips, the colonels held orgies there when no party was going on.

Business was intense—large warehouses, large stores, a multitude of traveling salesmen in the extremely expensive hotels, several banks, the grand Bank of Brazil building, countless speculators. The life of the city of Ilhéus was a life of work, political struggles, and struggles for money. In its narrow streets, teeming with people, one saw new faces daily. There was a time when everyone in the city knew each other. But that time is long past; now only the most important people are known to all. The ships bring in newcomers, men and women in search of the easy gold growing on the cacao tree. The fame of the "Queen of the South" has spread throughout Brazil, a fame inseparable from old tales of death and gunfights, or from newer tales of cacao as the finest crop in the country. In the belly of ships, on the rapid wings of planes, in trains heading for the backlands, the fame of Ilhéus travels onward, the city of money and cabarets, of dauntless courage and dirty deals. Not only in the big cities—Rio, São Paulo, Recife, Porto Alegre—were businessmen taking interest in and talking about that land of cacao. Even blind musicians, in marketplaces in the northeast, were singing of the city whose luxury dominated the south of the state of Bahia:

> *"She's the Queen of the South,*
> *all dressed in precious stones . . ."*

> *"She has cars, she has banks,*
> *She has cacao and money,*
> *A land of splendid grandeur!"*

The Peasants

1

Antônio Vítor advanced in long strides, and, even before arriving at the small cleared area in front of the house where a few chickens were scratching, yelled to summon his wife.

"Munda! Oh, Munda!"

He stopped beside the door of the adobe house, which was higher on the right side than on the left, a low, hasty construction which had later been expanded in the rear. He looked toward the sky, happiness stamped on his backwoodsman's face.

"Munda! Munda, c'mere!"

"What is it, for heaven's sake?"

"C'mere, now! Run!"

The house had never been whitewashed, and holes were visible in the adobe between the wooden strips. The roof had once been covered with thatch and coconut palm fronds to keep out the rain. But João Grosso, who manufactured bricks on his land, had repaid a debt to Antônio Vítor with a load of roof tiles, so now these rather than thatch covered the house. It had become a "tile-roof house," and Antônio Vítor often talked of building a new house, one made of brick and with a floor. He had even begun saving for the construction but, receiving little encouragement from Raimunda, had given up and used the money to buy a piece of land which was now a small cacao grove.

Antônio Vítor takes his eyes from the skies and looks toward the house: What the devil's taking Raimunda so long?

"Munda! Hurry up!"

His eyes linger on the house. In real bad shape . . . Through a hole in the wall he can see inside, but he doesn't spot his wife. A house with holes in it, a miserable house . . . The first profit will go to build a house. No, not the first, 'cause then how'll they buy the electric kiln to dry cacao when the heavy rains won't let them use the outdoor drying frames? Rain . . . He looked at the sky once more, yelled again:

"Munda! Where the devil'd you get to? Munda!"

Raimunda came to the door, cleaning her hands on her chintz dress. She has aged greatly, her mulatto's hair is white, she is overweight.

"What is it, man? What's got into you?"

Antônio Vítor took the woman by the arm and drew her beside him. He pointed to the sky with a thick finger.

"Look . . ."

Raimunda looked, placing her hand over her eyes. She searched for what her husband was indicating, and when she discovered it her face lighted up in a smile. A kind of beauty came over that plain and aged face, that angry expression that she had never lost. Her eyes were almost damp, and when she spoke, her voice was heated:

"It's gonna rain, Antonyo!" She had never learned to say Antônio, pronouncing the *i* as *y*. "It's gonna rain today."

Antônio Vítor laughed, patted her shoulder with his callused hand. Raimunda laughed too. Clearly, both would like to show greater signs of joy but did not know how. They stood there, laughing that wary and timid laugh to one another.

"It's gonna rain . . ."

"Yes it is . . ."

"And it'll be today . . ."

And they turned back to look at the sky. A blue sky in which only an experienced eye could spot on the edge of the horizon the black speck of a cloud coming from the direction of Ilhéus. A cloud anxiously awaited at the beginning of that new harvest. If it delayed a few more days the early crop would be ruined, and the early crop was approximately a third of the total yield. They seemed to lack the strength to take their eyes from the incipient cloud slowly advancing over the fields. And they laughed toward the heavens.

Before the couple, the cacao trees stirred in the breeze. Anyone seeing them, green and leafy, would think the lack of rain at the start of the year could have no effect on their production. The beautiful, puissant trees were in flower, apparently indifferent to the sun, without a single scorched blossom. Only the grass was parched, with large patches of bare soil where chickens scratched. But Antônio Vítor and Raimunda knew that if it did not rain, the cacao trees would drop their flowers, all of which would die before becoming fruit. And the few that became fruit would wither before attaining their full growth. The cacao trees would still be as lovely, as leafy and green, but unless the rains came that very week, they would bear no fruit that year. Already a few flowers, victims of the sun, had fallen to the ground. This is why Antônio Vítor longs to say something, to speak in longer sentences, to—if it were only possible!—reach out his hand to Raimunda and caress her. She too, despite her angry face, feels like expressing her happiness with something beyond the smile with which she greeted the cloud. But they don't know how, just as they didn't know how when their two children were born, first Joaquim, then Rosa. On those occasions also they had said nothing, standing beside one another without words or gestures, timid and impotent.

They had been the same when they celebrated twenty-five years of marriage. They had gone to a luncheon at the home of Dona Ana Badaró (they had never gotten used to saying "the home of Captain João Magalhães"; to them it would always be the Badaró house), who also was celebrating her silver wedding anniversary that day. It had been a splendid luncheon, reminiscent of the days when the Bardaró fortune was discussed far and wide. The luncheon featured many courses, there was wine on the table, and even the remaining crystal made an appearance. Raimunda went to help in the kitchen and insisted on serving the meal. Dona Ana would not hear of it, and despite the large number of guests, despite the presence of the doctor who was engaged to Dona Ana's youngest daughter—despite all that, Dona Ana had Raimunda and Antônio Vítor sit at their table and eat with them. That day the captain and Dona Ana were especially attentive to each other, they kissed during the luncheon in sight of everyone, and when the doctor proposed a toast, Dona Ana leaned her head on the captain's shoulder and he stroked her hair. She wore a sweet and contented expression.

Antônio Vítor and Raimunda felt that they had the selfsame reasons for a joyous gesture, but they lacked the means of expressing them. They returned home that night, following the road, silent and grave, each in his own world, without speaking. It's true that he possessed her that night, but it was just like many previous nights, their bodies tumbling in the second-hand bed (which they had bought from a Syrian), followed by a heavy sleep.

And now, staring at the sky where a dark rain cloud is swelling and coming nearer, they feel the need to tell each other words they do not know, to caress each other in unknown ways, and that often-revealed impotence intimidates them, making each ill at ease before the other. Raimunda's face is frowning again, that same angry face of so many years before, now an old woman's face worn by the sun of thirty harvests. Her mulatto's mouth has lost the smile which graced it when Antônio Vítor pointed out the cloud. But so great is the joy in her heart that she once again opens her thick mulatto lips, summons to them that difficult smile, takes her eyes from the sky, and turns to the backwoodsman.

"Antonyo!"

"Munda!"

He is looking at her, waiting. Raimunda shares his desire for words and caresses, for some way to talk about and celebrate the coming rain. The two look at each other, knowing no words, knowing no caresses, devoid of comments, unable to rejoice. They look at each other for only a second. She repeats:

"Antonyo!"

"What is it, Munda?"

For an intimate period of time a certain anguish, born of the inability to speak, shows in her face. But she quickly smiles again.

"It's gonna rain, Antonyo!"

"Yes it is, Munda!"

"It's gonna be a big harvest!"

"Real big, Munda!"

They say nothing more because they know nothing more to say. They look again at the sky. The cloud has grown; soon it will cover their field. This year they may bring in over thirteen thousand kilos of cacao. Maybe even more, who can tell? Maybe . . .

2

The thirteen thousand five hundred kilos of cacao that they hoped to harvest in that crop was the result of twenty-seven years of daily effort. Antônio Vítor and Raimunda's effort. The piece of land that the Badarós had given Raimunda as a wedding gift was forest. Until the end of the fighting over Sequeiro Grande, where he had acquitted himself with great effectiveness, Antônio Vítor did not tend to the land. Raimunda remained in service at the plantation house until the night of the fire. It was only when the fighting ended and Sinhô, who had suffered a bullet wound, gave orders to let the hired guns go, that Antônio Vítor gave any thought to the piece of land he owned. He threw together a crude shack and began to clear the strip of land. Previously it had been the large wooded area of Repartimento plantation, next to Sequeiro Grande, and from its land had emerged the best of the Badarós' fields. The only part still to be cleared was that small piece that Raimunda, the goddaughter, had received as a wedding gift. Sinhô Badaró had transferred the title to Antônio Vítor and Raimunda's name.

The first year was terrible, worse than any Antônio Vítor could remember. In the snake-ridden forest they hastily built a hut barely large enough for a pallet and the improvised oven of stones where they cooked the beans and meat that constituted their lunch and dinner. He and Raimunda began to fell the large trees. Half the week they worked in the Badarós' fields to get money for food and clothing; the other half they dedicated to their own land, to cutting down trees. The work progressed slowly because there were only the two of them. Raimunda, though strong and healthy, was after all a woman, and soon pregnancy began to take its toll. She miscarried in the fourth month, while helping Antônio Vítor saw a tree trunk. She nearly died, and Antônio Vítor had to borrow money from João Magalhães to pay the doctor who came to treat her.

That was a day of anguish. Raimunda's belly was large, and Antônio Vítor watched her out of the corner of his eye when she moved before him, waiting for him to finish his work with the ax on the tree to be felled, so she could help with the heavy saw that would complete the task. At that very moment Antônio Vítor was thinking that soon Raimunda's pregnancy would prevent her from helping him. He didn't know what he would do when she could no longer hold up under the work. This work in the forest was too heavy for a woman . . . It was rough even for a man, much less a woman carrying a baby in her belly . . . The work on the Badaró plantation was still more or less bearable; since the family was in Ilhéus, there was nothing to do in the plantation house, so Raimunda had to work in the fields alongside the other wives and daughters of the hired hands. Her job, for twelve hours at a time, was to split open the cacao pods as the men shook them from the trees. The children gathered the pods, and the women and older girls split them. It was dangerous, for a badly aimed stroke, one with a bit too much strength behind it, would send the heavy blade through the pod and cut the hand that held it. Was there any worker's wife without deep cuts in her hands as the result of her work? Some lost fingers to the sharply honed knife. The cacao beans were collected in an enormous pile, then carried on muleback in special baskets to the molds.

Even so, it was light duty compared to the work in the forest, felling trees to make open spaces where they could set fires to clear the land. That day Antônio Vítor was thinking such thoughts, wondering how much longer Raimunda could stand that exhausting labor of cutting down trees. It'd be hell once she gave out . . . He barely made enough money working on the plantation to support the two of them and allow them to devote the weekend to their work in the forest. Where would he get the money to pay a helper?

As soon as he started sawing from his side, each of them at one end of the crosscut saw, the miscarriage began. It happened there in the woods; blood drenched the soil. Since there was danger of hemorrhage, he had to get a doctor from Tabocas. Captain João Magalhães, who was on the plantation, lent him a horse and some money. Less than a month later Raimunda was back at work in the forest and in the fields. By the end of the year the trees had been felled; around Christmas they set the fires to clear the land.

The following year Raimunda did not return to work in the Badaró family's fields. On the other hand, Antônio Vítor worked there every day, earning a bit of money to buy the cacao seedlings he needed to plant his piece of land. Raimunda worked their land, planting manioc and corn, raising chickens and turkeys. That year they planted a small cacao grove, and by the following year the trees, rising amidst the cornfield, already had branches and leaves.

When the manioc had reached a good size they harvested it, and this marked the beginning of Antônio Vítor's good relations with Firmo. The two had not gotten along since the period, still fresh in memory, of the fighting over Sequeiro Grande. Antônio Vítor had been part of a group of men who invaded Firmo's fields and stirred things up. But Firmo was the only small grower with a gristmill on his land. The large mill belonging to the Baderós had burned in the fighting and never been rebuilt. Firmo's was small but the manioc Antônio Vítor had harvested was a trifle, enough for a few sacks of flour. Antônio Vítor had someone feel out Firmo, who put his mill at the other man's disposal. They agreed that a third of the flour would be for Firmo, who was to provide two men and a woman to help Raimunda with the furnace, the press, and the scraping of the manioc. The work took only two days. And so Antônio Vítor sold his flour at the outdoor market in Itabuna, using the money to buy cacao seedlings. They planted them in another small patch of the forest, then the corn that brought in money for everything else.

In the four years that followed, they continued to work for the Badarós, Raimunda stooping over the soil planting manioc and corn in the space between the young cacao trees, picking the yellow ears of corn, making flour, taking corn, chickens, and turkeys, as well as stalks of bananas (they had planted a clump of trees near the hut) to sell at the market in Itabuna, where she had established a regular clientele. Antônio Vítor now assisted Firmo with his harvests, in expectation of the favor being returned when his own cacao put forth blossoms and bore fruit.

On Sundays he devoted himself to erecting an adobe house. He made the frame from poles, sank it into the ground, then added a roof made from palm fronds. Then he mixed clay with dirt, cow manure, and a little sand and water until it was like cement. Other Sundays were spent on the task, almost like play, of throwing the clay against the wood frame, the "slaps." It was situated in the middle of the land and had a door and a window; they moved in. Where the hut had been, he began to build a small drying frame for cacao. But that task was not only more difficult but also cost a lot of money. He planed the boards for the floor of the frame, managed to buy the zinc for the roof, but suspended the project because he lacked money for the rails. When he got the money together, he hired a carpenter to assist him. Now, his frame ready, he waited for his fields to bloom.

One morning, after the long months of idleness during which Joaquim, their oldest child, was born, while Antônio Vítor was taking Raimunda's place traveling to the Itabuna market to sell flour, corn, and bananas, they awoke to a festival of cacao trees in bloom. Antônio called for his wife;

she came and the two of them stood, with tears in their eyes, gazing at
the first flowers of their cacao trees. In that crop they harvested three
hundred and seventy-five kilos of cacao.

He still remembers the day he walked into Zude Brothers & Co. to
sell his three hundred and seventy-five kilos of cacao. He had had to
go to Ilhéus and made use of the trip to sell the first fruits of his fields
to Zude, who paid the best prices. Maximiliano Campos made a point
of receiving him in his office, treating him in a very friendly manner.
Antônio Vítor felt like a colonel. Such friendliness touched him. A man
like Maximiliano Campos, manager of an export house, offering him a
drink in his office. Antônio Vítor drank his glass of liqueur in a single
gulp, without the slightest idea that it was an expensive liqueur meant
to be drunk slowly, in small sips savored with clicks of the tongue.
He thought old Maximiliano's way of drinking odd, and imagined
him drinking sugarcane rum with all those refinements, choking on
the potent alcohol, burning his tongue. Antônio Vítor smiled timidly
in the office, looked at Maximiliano in fear that the Zude manager
could read his thoughts. But the old man was as friendly as ever and
went on talking with him.

When Antônio Vítor arrived to make that sale, three hundred and
seventy-five miserable kilos of cacao, he almost trembled. It was possible
that an important firm like Zude Brothers & Co. wasn't interested in
buying such a small amount. He walked into the offices ill at ease, his
hands shaking, his hat still on his head. When he said what he had
come for, the clerk behind the counter left without saying a word, and
Antônio Vítor didn't know what to do. He took the clerk's action as
a sign that the firm was uninterested in the purchase, so uninterested
that the employees didn't even bother to say no, just left him standing
at the counter. His voice tremulous, all he had a chance to say was:

"It's just that it's my first cacao . . ."

The clerk turned his head, smiling, and Antônio Vítor thought the
young man was making fun of him. Embarrassed, he was about to
leave, when the young man returned, accompanied by Maximiliano
Campos. Antônio Vítor knew him by sight, having seen him more than
once, some years before, in the presence of Sinhô Badaró. Maximiliano
Campos shook his hand, called him "sir," and asked him into his office.
Only after he was in the office did Antônio Vítor remember that he was
still wearing his hat, and removed it, feeling very confused. A young
woman working at a desk smiled, and Antônio Vítor knew nothing to
do but return her smile, fiddling with the hat in his hand.

They went into the office of Maximiliano Campos, who opened a
cabinet, took out a bottle of liqueur and two glasses, and served.

"To your prosperity!"

Antônio Vítor swallowed the liqueur. Maximiliano asked about him, who he was, where his farm was. "It's not much of a farm, Mr. Maximiliano . . . A little piece of land Sinhô Badaró give me when I got married . . ."

"Did you work for Sinhô?"

He told the story of his life. Fighting beside Juca, Sinhô and even the captain in the last stages of the battles for Sequeiro Grande. When he finished his narrative, Maximiliano commented on the current decline of the Badarós:

"A sad thing, Mr. Antônio . . . A sad thing . . ."

Then he assured Antônio Vítor that he was certain to do well and would one day be a rich colonel, for after all hadn't many others started out the same way as he? Antônio Vítor felt awash in happiness. Maximiliano made a grand gesture. Cacao was at twelve thousand nine hundred that day, and Maximiliano gave him thirteen thousand, since it was the first crop from a new farm.

"That's so you'll remain our customer, Mr. Antônio. So you won't sell your cacao to some other house . . ."

He took the money in trembling hands. He went out into the street unable to see anything, neither the blue sky nor the passersby laughing at such a big man, money in one hand, hat in the other, bumping into people with an idiotic smile on his face.

When he regained his senses, Antônio Vítor was in a store buying presents for Raimunda, cuts of silk, a pair of shoes.

He went back to the farm with happiness swelling his chest. For the first time in his life he traveled first class, hoping to talk with the colonels on the train. Some, who knew him, did in fact say hello and inquire about unimportant matters, but none engaged him in conversation. They were rich colonels who wore riding breeches, worsted jackets, and leather boots. Antônio Vítor was wearing poor clothes of blue denim, cheap shoes, a tattered hat on his head. In the net above the seat were Raimunda's presents. Abandoned in the train, in the three hours he spent amid the colonels' indifference, Antônio Vítor thought about how happy Raimunda would be when he gave her those gifts. A pretty pair of shoes, a piece of silk cloth, a swaddling cloth for their little boy . . .

In Itabuna, Antônio Vítor felt, also for the first time, the need for a good pack mule. What plantation owner or small grower didn't have a mule in harness to take him back and forth from the fields to Itabuna? He needed to buy one, now that he was owner of a farm, and would one day have a plantation. Thinking these thoughts, he took off his shoes to trudge through the eighteen miles of mud between him and his land. He would arrive at night, when the kerosene lamp was already casting its reddish light in the adobe house.

Not only did Raimunda show no happiness with the gifts, she grumbled
for almost a week about the expense, when there were so many things
they needed for the farm. They needed scythes to harvest the cacao,
which should amount to close to a thousand kilos the coming year.
They needed to build a trough for the soft cacao; they couldn't go
through another year of drying it in kerosene crates . . . She went on
about all those useless expenses. Why silk? She couldn't even get the
shoes on her wide feet, with their splayed toes. The only thing she didn't
complain about was the swaddling cloth for their son. It was the only
thing that made her feel happy, the only thing for which she was truly
grateful.

But Raimunda was that way, querulous and angry, a woman of few
words who hated the parties and dances, with their harmonica and guitar
music, held now and again in the houses of workers and small growers
in the vicinity. When she did go, she refused to dance, remaining off in
a corner and complaining that her shoes hurt her feet; she would end
up taking them off right there in the dancing area. These dances, in
fact, where few women showed up in shoes, their faces painted with
dye from red paper and a ribbon in their mulatto hair—these dances
always ended with everyone in their bare feet, those feet that could not
stand shoes. In that, Raimunda was no exception. But in her antagonism
to dancing she was, turning down the men who asked her and making
herself disliked, since the number of women was very small compared
to the men dying to dance. The women said of her:

"She always was stuck-up . . . Ever since she lived with the
Badarós . . ."

But it wasn't because she was stuck-up. She didn't like it, and that was
all there was to it. What she liked was the land—working it, planting it,
harvesting the fruit the land produced. There she was the equal of a
man in output. Whether it was picking and splitting open the cacao
pods, dancing over them in the drying frames on sunny days, removing
the *visgo* or mucilaginous pulp from the trough, she could do it all like
the best worker on the plantations. And there she felt happy, among
the cacao trees, waking at dawn, going to bed at dusk for the deep
sleep of weariness. Captain João Magalhães was in the habit of saying,
when Antônio Vítor's name came up, that he owed his prosperity to
Raimunda. Antônio Vítor himself agreed. He had great respect for
his wife and always listened to her opinion. That's what happened
when Antônio Vítor was thinking about building a better house and
Raimunda opposed the idea. Her opinion prevailed, and they bought a
small piece of land instead, where they planted more cacao. By then
their daughter Rosa had been born, a mulatto with a smiling face like
Antônio Vítor's.

Their son had taken after his mother. Joaquim revealed his relation
to Raimunda from an early age. He was just like her. The same dour and
energetic face, the same goodness hidden under a façade of grumbles and
murmured words, the same obstinacy. At thirteen he ran away from home
and went to work on a distant plantation, but that lasted only a short time,
and he went down to Ilhéus, where he found work in a warehouse that
sewed sacks, which he left for a position as driver's assistant, learning
to drive and repair automobiles, and one day he signed on as a sailor,
vanished for two years only to reappear in the streets of Ilhéus (they said
he'd been in prison) and take a job as bus driver, which is where he was
today. Antônio Vítor didn't get along well with him. Whenever they saw
each other there was friction, the farmer thinking that his son wanted to
boss him around. Joaquim had learned much that Antônio Vítor didn't
understand, and he lived among suspicious people, as Carlos Zude had
once told him. Antônio Vítor couldn't understand his well-spoken son,
who wanted him to give better pay to the few workers who helped him
with the harvest, who told him he was robbing them. The day Joaquim
told him that, at dinnertime during a visit to the farm, Antônio Vítor hit
him in the mouth so hard that it drew blood.

"You callin' me a thief, you whelp?"

Joaquim got up to leave. Raimunda cleaned the blood running from
his lip and went with him to the highway. She said nothing to him
later, but this was the first night Antônio Vítor ever saw his wife
unable to sleep. She was crazy about Joaquim; the two understood
each other without words and enjoyed being together silently, close to
each other. Antônio Vítor talked a lot; it was his daughter that he liked,
who was as talkative as he, had numerous acquaintances throughout
the neighboring farms and plantations, and never missed a dance. She
enjoyed dressing up, a rose in her hair, a ribbon on her calico dress,
a fake ring on her finger. His daughter did business with the itinerant
Syrian peddlers, from whom she bought trinkets.

Truly, what created the real conflict between Antônio Vítor and
Joaquim was that the father had never forgiven the boy for not remaining
on the farm to help him. Antônio Vítor didn't understand how Joaquim
could leave, go to the city, sail on ships like a sailor, drive trucks and
buses like a driver—when his father owned a piece of land that needed
hands to till it. If Joaquim were in the fields it would be one less worker
to pay, and Antônio Vítor constantly bemoaned his son's lack of interest
in the land that was his. How could he find the courage to leave when they
owned that land? What the devil was he going to do? Nothing good, that's
for sure; even Carlos Zude had once told him that Joaquim was involved
with suspicious people and he should be careful. And the gall of the
boy to say that he, Antônio Vítor, his father, who deserved Joaquim's

respect, underpaid his workers, exploited them, robbed them . . . There was nothing for such audacity but a slap in the mouth, and that's what Antônio Vítor did. Like everyone, Antônio Vítor paid five mil-réis to the few workers he hired at harvest time. Firmo also lent a hand and he paid him by doing the same during his harvest. The large plantation owners had no need of that. They had many workers, not only for the harvest but during the lull as well, when the only work was pruning the fields, cleaning, and building new drying frames. Antônio Vítor let his workers go during the lull. He paid them their balance, when they had a balance, and sent them away till the next harvest. And Joaquim said he robbed them . . . He didn't even have a general store on the farm like the great colonels. It was the stores that really *did* rob them, with their absurd prices. Of course, Antônio Vítor would have liked to be able to open a store on his farm, to sell to the eight workers he hired for the harvest. That way he wouldn't end up owing them five mil-réis a day . . . It would come out cheaper . . . But he lacked the capital for it, and what he had was barely enough to pay off the men. Pruning the fields and buying groceries would eat up the year's profits. Besides which, for some time he had been increasing the size of the fields with new cacao seedlings as the money came in from the first trees he had planted. Everything he earned was sunk into that piece of land. His hard-earned money was transformed into cacao trees. His farm . . . What pride he felt as he said it!

And Joaquim grumbling that he robbed his workers . . . Only a slap would teach him to respect his father! After all, Antônio Vítor had been a worker himself; that was how he'd begun thirty years before when he first came to these lands in the south. He had never gone back to Estância, but he dreamed of doing so one day. He must have a child there, Ivone's child; maybe he'd turned out better than Joaquim . . . Joaquim took after his mother . . . Not that there was anything wrong with Raimunda. Antônio Vítor hits his hand against his mouth to drive away the thought. Raimunda is good and a hard worker. Joaquim got his stubbornness from her, his brusque ways that also made him seem a little like the Badorós. In fact, it was possible that Joaquim had some Badaró blood in his veins, since they said that Raimunda was old Marcelino Badaró's daughter. In any case, Joaquim was the great disappointment of Antônio Vítor's life, and since the day he slapped him, he hadn't returned to the farm. As if by some kind of tacit agreement, neither Antônio Vítor nor Raimunda spoke of their son.

By contrast, they spoke often of their daughter, Rosa, who had married the overseer on Colonel Frederico Pinto's plantation. The truth is that if not for Raimunda there might have been no marriage. Rosa had been born the same year as the death of Sinhô Badaró, the year of the big rains, when the Sant'Ana plantation was split up. Antônio Vítor and Raimunda suffered at the subdividing of their old boss's plantation as if they had been its coowners.

Antônio Vítor had shed his blood for those lands, killed for them. Now he saw people who weren't Badarós taking over the fields and building other plantation houses. In the town there was talk about Olga, Juca's widow, saying that she had run off to Bahia and was spending money like mad. Raimunda had become even more taciturn, and not even her large belly could make her give up her work on the land. Rosa was born amidst those disappointments, and brought happiness to the adobe house. While still a girl she was helping with the field work, and when Joaquim ran away it was she who drove the two donkeys that carried soft cacao to the trough. From an early age she liked to beautify herself and paint her mulatto face with red paper. She ruined herself with Tibúrcio one night at a party. She gave herself to him in the woods and became pregnant. Antônio Vítor beat her when he found out; Raimunda dragged from her the name of the man responsible, went there, and raised a scandal. Perhaps more than anything else it was the reputation of Antônio Vítor, who had killed so many men during the fighting over Sequeiro Grande, that convinced Tibúrcio of the need to get married. The wedding took place in Itabuna, with a priest, and the two went to live on Colonel Frederico's plantation, where Tibúrcio was overseer and earned two hundred and fifty mil-réis a month. Now and then Rosa would come visit her parents, accompanied by Tibúrcio, and talk of the plantation. The colonel's wife liked Rosa, and her son was being brought up in the plantation house.

This year Antônio Vítor hoped to harvest thirteen thousand five hundred kilos. If cacao brings twenty mil-réis, that's eighteen thousand. There should be something left over for a trip to Estância. Thirteen thousand five hundred is something, and his farm is worth forty thousand. Maybe more, despite the few improvements, the small size of the drying frames and troughs, the lack of an electric kiln, despite their house that in no way differed from that of a worker.

Despite everything, now it's going to rain; it's a good year. Others were bad years, difficult years; at times all appeared lost. Once he had had to borrow five thousand at high interest when drought wiped out a crop and killed the recently planted cacao trees. The only reason he didn't go under was that with the boom of 1914 he was able to pay off the debt and even make a little money. He also remembers the flood that carried off the new plantings and washed away part of the house.

But all that was in the past, all that was behind him. Now he was going to harvest thirteen thousand five hundred kilos of cacao. He could build a better house, hire more workers, make Raimunda take a rest from working in the field. She really needed it. She was old and worn out, her hair was white, and at night she moaned with the pains of rheumatism. Now she could rest, in a new whitewashed house, one with a floor. She deserved a rest; she had been working like a pack mule. She seemed more like a tree of that land, planted there with deep roots, her feet wide and black, than a woman who had once been young. She was like an old tree of that land.

She too needed the rain, which had seemed destined not to come this year, to blossom in a few rare smiles. Ever since the threat of drought, Raimunda had been irritable, sour, pessimistic, saying they were going to lose everything. Like the cacao trees, she needed rain. Now the rain clouds were approaching over the hill. It's going to rain, the trees will blossom from their trunks to their branches, the workers' feet will sink into the mud, the cacao pods will turn yellow—the color of gold. To Antônio Vítor there is nothing prettier in the world than a cacao farm when the yellow of the cacao pods lights the shade of the trees. For Raimunda too, there is no lovelier sight. She too will be reborn with the rain, her face will wear less of a frown, her feet will sink into the pleasant mud, her toes open and penetrating into the soil: more a tree of the land than a woman. A tree of that land of theirs, land they had planted, twenty-seven years merged with it, sleeping upon it, eating upon it, giving birth and making love upon it. Planted in the earth, trees that are beginning to age.

3

With difficulty, leaning on his gold-headed cane, Colonel Horácio da Silveira walked to the veranda of the plantation house. Before him, the cacao fields stretched in endless succession. The colonel stopped at the door opening onto the veranda; the sunlight was painful to his age-racked eyes. The old black man removed his hat in respect when he saw him. He didn't help him because all the workers knew the colonel couldn't stand being helped. Leaning on his ancient cane, squinting, his face at times contorted in pain, he half dragged himself; but he would not tolerate their taking his arm to help him walk. He cursed those who tried, and, despite his later apology, could not stifle that initial burst of anger that made him lose control of himself. He was almost blind, but he denied it, claiming he could see perfectly well. When someone came to visit him, he would let the other speak until he could recognize him by his voice. Then he would talk freely, recalling the past and discussing the present, the price of cacao, the possibility of a boom, and politics.

Politics remained his great passion. He still held the leadership of one of the traditional parties in the zone, now back in power. Stuck in the plantation house of his immense plantation, semiparalyzed by rheumatism, and nearly blind, he was the owner of the cacao land, making and unmaking figures of authorities, lord of thousands of votes, incalculably rich, filthy rich, as they said throughout those counties. Of late almost no one saw him, and on the streets of Ilhéus Colonel Horácio was an almost legendary figure, near yet distant, celebrated in the popular poetry sold in the markets, as a person from the past but present in every important decision.

When Colonel Horácio reached the age of eighty, sixty years of which had been spent in those lands of Ilhéus, he was honored with grand festivities in Ilhéus and Itabuna, despite his being in the opposition

that year, fighting the government. He had been in the opposition
since the victory of 1930. For some years he remained loyal to the
deposed regime and was among those who took the longest to fit into
the new governmental machinery. He had been slow to relinquish a
certain anger at those who had overthrown the system of government
so much to his liking, under which he had built his fortune and of which
he was one of the most powerful mainstays in the south of Bahia. At
one point his opposition to the succession of interventors in the state
government appeared to be a rich old man's whim, and his fellow
partisans thought seriously of removing him from the party leadership
because his obstinate fidelity to the deposed government prevented any
negotiation or possibility of agreement with the administration.

"He's crazy . . ." they said.

As proof they cited the answer the colonel had given a group of
young men from the Integralists who, courting his prestige and fortune,
had sought him out in hopes of bringing him into the fascist movement.
Having already won over Horácio's son, they now hoped for the colonel's
backing as well.

Confidently, they made the trip to the plantation. They wasted more
than an hour on explanations to the colonel: what fascism was, who
Mussolini was, the genius of Hitler, the progress of Italy and Portugal,
the danger of bolshevism, what the Integralists planned to accomplish in
Brazil, the reasons for the need to have Horácio lend his prestige to the
new political movement and be one of its chiefs. Upon entering, they had
greeted him with two cries of "*anauê*" as if he were a great fascist leader.
Colonel Horácio listened to the entire story, without doubt somewhat
flattered by the young men's attitude and praise, and finally asked if
one of their goals was to maintain opposition to the administration until
Washington Luís was restored to the presidency and Vital Soares to the
state government.

"If it's to put Dr. Washington back in, you can count on me . . ."

The leader of the group explained that this wasn't exactly what they
had in mind, that their leader was someone else, and said in praise of
him: "a genius, a man enlightened by God." When he then spoke his
name, the Integralists stood up and saluted with four "*anauês*." Horácio
told them he couldn't, that he was for Dr. Washington; he was "a man
of his word, not a turncoat."

In the celebrations honoring his eightieth birthday, much mention
was made of "his work," of the progress he had made possible in
the zone. He was called the "builder of civilization." But Horácio
was terribly offended when, on the pretext of giving him a rest, they
tried to hand the party leadership to a younger man, a lawyer new to
the zone, a young man of great ability and greater ambition. Horácio,

in his retreat on the plantation, was informed of the maneuvering and knew it would all come to a head at the birthday celebration. The explosion would come at the large banquet in Ilhéus, the final event of the festivities. Horácio listened in silence to the speeches saying wonderful things about him, a showering of fancy words calling him everything laudatory that could be said of a man; he only perked up when a journalist (a young man originally from Bahia, where he had lived in poverty, who had worked for his newspaper in Ilhéus) proposed that, as a birthday gift, they give the colonel the right to rest from the political lists and leave to younger hands the task of faithful continuance of his "great work." Other speakers followed, and someone proposed the name of the lawyer—Josué Santos as new party leader. Maneca Dantas looked at Horácio, studying the face that he knew so well and finding it the same as those many years before, on the day he had discovered Ester's unfaithfulness. The same. The same narrowed eyes, the twisted mouth, the furrowed brow.

Maneca Dantas had been invited to join the conspiracy against Horácio. Josué had shown him all the offers from the administration, which was eager to gain the support of Horácio's fellow party members. Maneca Dantas could be mayor of Ilhéus again if not for the colonel's stubborn and stupid—"stupid," the lawyer repeated emphatically—allegiance to something that no longer existed: the Old Republic. Because of this they were suffering an unnecessary ostracism, since the government itself had approached them so insistently. In the entire country there was no longer anyone who held such a violent position against the victorious revolution. Even among the most fervent sympathizers with the fallen regime, not a single one refused anymore to cooperate with the new government. Revolution? Not a chance. Hadn't Colonel Maneca seen the São Paulo uprising of '32? It had been the last. And hadn't even its leaders since made common cause with the government? What could Horácio be thinking? Josué concluded, decisively:

"It's senility, Colonel, senility . . . And we can't allow ourselves to be led by a *détraqué* old man."

Maneca Dantas didn't know what *détraqué* meant, nor did he ask Josué. It was only when he got home that his son—at that time a law student—explained to him, in words equally difficult, the exact meaning of the term. Maneca Dantas confined himself to offering a warning to Josué Santos:

"You don't know my friend Horácio, counselor. If you did, you wouldn't get involved in this . . ."

Josué shrugged and went ahead with his petty conspiracy. Maneca Dantas, at the banquet table, heard the speeches, studied Horácio's face, and ran his eyes over the people around them. Horácio was apprised of everything; many had made their way to the plantation to spread the tale, and Maneca Dantas himself had told him of Josué's proposals and explained the meaning of the word *détraqué*.

"It's French, my friend . . ."

"I never did take to the kind that puts on airs by talkin' in some foreign language . . ." said Horácio, and Maneca knew he was referring to the late Virgílio.

Later, as Maneca was about to leave, Horácio warned his friend:

"Let the young fella be . . . I'll show him a thing or two. Leave it to me . . ."

And now there he was, in the leading hotel in Ilhéus, with close to two hundred at the banquet table. The best people in the area, people from both government and opposition, businessmen and planters, exporters, doctors, engineers, and agronomists—all celebrating the colonel's eightieth birthday. Food and drink, expensive drink, champagne and kegs of beer—something new to Ilhéus—had been brought especially for the banquet. Outside, a small crowd pressed against the windows to see Colonel Horácio da Silveira, known to most only by hearsay. It was rare for the colonel, who stayed more and more within the boundaries of his lands, to come down from his plantation.

There they were, and Maneca Dantas was becoming increasingly worried. None of those present knew Horácio da Silveira as well as he, who had been his partner in the fighting over Sequeiro Grande, where they had both grown rich burning the forest, planting cacao, and killing people. Thirty years had passed, and now some youngsters were trying to replace Horácio in the party leadership, remove him from politics. They thought he was too old, senile, *détraqué* . . . He looked at Horácio, who was hearing the name of Josué Santos—"the brilliant advocate," in the speaker's words—proposed as new leader of the party. While the young man was speaking, Maneca Dantas remembered the days when Horácio had been state senator. He slept during the sessions, never opened his mouth except to grunt his support, never failed to take his revolver to the senate as if he were heading for a gun battle. He squandered money in the cabarets with prostitutes. When he came back, he found his plantation somewhat neglected and gave up his seat in the senate. As replacement, he had seen to the election of Dr. Rui, who shone brightly in great speeches. And he never again accepted parliamentary office or political posts. He contented himself with being the head of the party, the big boss. He made the mayors of Ilhéus and Itabuna, the judges were his men, and he hoped that his son, upon graduation, could make use of these positions and rise quickly in his profession. Actually, the boy had been elected state deputy as soon as he graduated, but the revolution had come and he lost his seat. Now elections were approaching again and Josué Santos wanted the right to support the government while there was still time, to choose the candidates, maybe make himself state deputy, or perhaps federal deputy. The young man finished his speech; by now the banquet seemed more dedicated to Josué than to the man whose birthday was being commemorated. Perhaps, alone among all those present, only Maneca Dantas expected a reaction from Horácio. The rest were convinced that he would thank them for the tribute and pass the party leadership on to the "brilliant advocate" seated at the other end of the table and smiling modestly at the words of praise.

It was time for Horácio to offer his acknowledgments. He had had Maneca Dantas's son write a speech and then had it copied in very large letters which he could see and read without difficulty. But when he rose, amidst applause, he did not take the piece of paper from his pocket. He opened his tired eyes a bit, looked at all those people, the journalist who had spoken, Josué, smiled at Maneca Dantas and Braz. His voice was strong, even though it now quivered a little. But his voice did not quiver—it seemed a young man's voice—when he said:

"This doesn't seem like a birthday banquet. It seems more like the burial of a rich man with his relatives fighting over the inheritance . . . That's what it seems like . . ."

And he sat down amidst the surprise, mingled with fright, of those present. Everyone sat in silence, not knowing what to say, not knowing what to do, their glances going from Horácio, who once again appeared to be sleeping, to Josué, who attempted to smile beneath the paleness that was overcoming him. And thus, in this atmosphere, ended the banquet that was the "golden clasp" (as the *Afternoon Journal* had written) on the commemorations of Colonel Horácio da Silveira's eightieth birthday.

Six days later Josué Santos was assassinated in Itabuna, shot as he left a Masonic meeting. The assassin got away, and word quickly spread through that city and Ilhéus that it had been at Horácio's orders. Maneca Dantas explained to a group of young party members, among them the journalist who had given the speech:

"You don't know my friend Horácio. You only know him by name, from hearing about him. I know him personally, intimately . . ."

The crime caused a great furor, for assassinations in the civilized streets of Ilhéus and Itabuna were something long forgotten, things of the past living only in the memory of blind musicians in street fairs, stories that mothers told their children instead of nursery tales. And, suddenly, that past had returned, and a lawyer lay riddled with bullets in front of the Masonic building. Because of the case, the newspapers recalled the ancient battles, the times of struggle for possession of the land, the forest of Sequeiro Grande. An inquiry was begun, but nothing came of it because Horácio finally decided to support the government. That was the last time anyone spoke of removing him from the leadership of the party.

The truth, however, was that despite his passion for politics, Horácio no longer understood it very well, in those confusing times after the victorious revolution of 1930. He was deeply confused by this "modern politics," as he called it, of communists and Integralists. His son was in with the Integralists and wore a green shirt. His friend Braz, already an old man, for the last few years had taken to wearing a revolver again, to safeguard rallies for the leftists, saying that foreigners wanted to take his lands and that he wouldn't give them up. Braz still backed Horácio but used words the colonel had never heard before; there were even some who called him a communist. It was Braz who sent Horácio's son scurrying during an Integralist rally broken up by leftists. Horácio told himself: *Never saw the likes . . . Who can understand it!*

No, he definitely didn't understand this kind of politics, so different from the old kind, with men voting instead of fighting it out in the streets. Horácio viewed both communists and Integralists with suspicion. There was even talk about "workers' rights"!—which for him was inconceivable. He felt his son was acting stupidly in wearing a green shirt, saluting, shouting *anauê*. But he didn't get involved; he let it go, trying to think about his son as little as possible, so as not to think about Ester. She was to blame for all of this, a timid woman with no will of her own, who was afraid of everything except cuckolding him. His old age was embittered by these things, especially by the son with whom he felt not the slightest solidarity and to whom he devoted almost no affection. Silveirinha, attorney and ex-deputy, did nothing beyond spending money in Ilhéus. He had turned out timid, had inherited Ester's fear, and couldn't hear a gunshot without turning pale. He hated the cacao fields and spent as little time in them as possible. They had told Horácio that the boy had fled during a political altercation, some time earlier in the streets of Ilhéus, and the fact upset the colonel for days. Horácio preached courage above all virtues and felt pity for the son who had taken after his mother, frightened of everything. At times Horácio and Maneca Dantas talked, complaining of their shiftless and unfit sons, who had graduated from college and then spent their time staggering around the streets of Ilhéus and spending money on prostitutes. It was for their sons that they had worked, going into the forest, killing people, planting cacao. So that one day their sons could be important men and not the bums they were—unfit and useless. Horácio blamed it on Ester, the fear that had lived inside her and was passed on to Silveirinha. His old age was embittered by these things, and more and more he restricted himself to his plantation. Of late he didn't even go to Ilhéus but stayed in the plantation house, directing the harvests, fighting with the workers, showing care only with the mulatto woman Felícia, who had never left him and who had taken Ester's place in the colonel's bed for as long as he had been able to make love.

Horácio possessed one of the largest fortunes in the cacao zone. His plantations extended far beyond Ferradas and included the greater part of Sequeiro Grande. The boundary between the counties of Ilhéus and Itabuna ran through his fields. He harvested more than six hundred thousand kilos of cacao, owned innumerable rental properties in Itabuna, Pirangi, and Ilhéus, and had a great deal of money on deposit in the bank. But he still lived the same frugal life as always: no luxurious plantation house, penny-pinching economies as if he were poor, and complaints about the small fortune spent by his son. He personally inspected the work in the fields and had ordered the beating of an overseer who had tried to rob him.

That day, after lunch, he dragged himself to the veranda. He was going to take some sun, warm the gigantic body that was now bent, listen to the conversation of the blacks. The area in front of the plantation house was empty. Some workers were passing through on their way to the fields, completing some unfinished pruning. Horácio could feel the sun's heat on his wrinkled skin. The old black man greeted him. The colonel turned his eyes toward him.

"That you, Roque?"

"It's me, yessir . . ."

"Pretty hot, eh?"

"Real hot, yessir . . ."

Horácio thought about the drought. If there was a drought, the crop would be ruined, there'd be no profits that year, he wouldn't be able to buy more land, acquire new fields.

"Maybe it's not goin' to rain . . ."

The black man looked at the sky, where he had already seen the rain cloud approaching.

"It's gonna rain all right, boss. Don't you see the cloud?"

Startled, Horácio looked at the sky, where he saw nothing.

"You think I'm blind?"

"Oh no, no, sir," said the black man, frightened. "It's just that you ain't said nothin' . . ."

Horácio looked again, and still saw nothing.

"It's a rain cloud all right . . ."

"And it's a-growin', boss . . . It's gonna rain today, 'round nighttime . . ."

Rising, Horácio went to the railing of the veranda.

"Go get Chico Branco . . . Move!"

The black man left in search of the overseer. He found him at home, having lunch. From the veranda, Horácio sensed him coming by the sound of his footsteps. He knew Chico Branco's heavy steps; he was a fat mulatto, violent with the hired hands, who knew how to get a day's work out of a man.

"Hello, Colonel."

"You seen that it's goin' to rain?"

"I saw it. I was just about to come talk to you . . ."

"You didn't see anything. Nobody sees anything I don't. Nobody cares, that's why I've got to keep after them. I knew since yesterday it was goin' to rain; I saw the cloud this mornin' . . ."

"But, Colonel . . ."

"No buts . . . It's just the way I said! I saw it before anybody . . ."

The overseer fell silent; what good was it to argue? Horácio thought a bit, then ordered:

"Have them stop the prunin'; no need for it anymore. Have them work on the dryin' frames, clean the troughs, get after the people from Ribeirão Seco. Hire workers . . ."

The overseer left. Horácio remained silent for some minutes, then could no longer resist. He asked the black man:

"Roque . . ."

"Yessir?"

"Is the cloud growin', Roque?"

"Yessir, it is."

Horácio smiled. He would see one more harvest with the cacao trees full of fruit. He should go to Ilhéus and do some business with Schwartz. At the end of the harvest he would buy more fields. And one day, he thought with a certain sadness, all this would belong to his son . . . It was a pity one had to die . . . He so enjoyed seeing the cacao bloom and bear fruit. So enjoyed buying land, yelling at his men, doing business . . . Fortunately he had only one son, and that assured him that his plantations would not be divided, like so many others, like the Badarós' . . . Colonel Horácio da Silveira's plantations would never be divided. They would always be his . . .

"Is the cloud growin'?"

"Yessir, it's already big."

"Will it rain today?"

"Yessir, it's gonna rain. 'Round nighttime . . ."

The sun warms Colonel Horácio da Silveira's body. But what he feels on his shriveled skin is the imagined and longed-for caress of falling rain washing the land and penetrating to the tree roots, bringing strength to the cacao trees.

"It's goin' to be a large crop."

"Yessir, it sure is."

The cloud covers the sun, and a shadow falls over the colonel.

4

The parrot pierced the silence of the front yard with its screech, repeating the phrase memorized years ago:

"Careful with the cacao, you damned nigger!"

It had heard this for years from Teodoro das Baraúnas. When he fled during the time of the fighting over Sequeiro Grande, the parrot had been left in the Baraúnas plantation house and the Badarós had adopted it. They had first taken it to Ilhéus, but when they had to sell the house in the city and Dona Ana came with Captain João Magalhães to their remaining lands, they brought the bird back once more to the cacao fields. He was a small parrot, one of the most talkative varieties. They named him Chico, and he repeated his own name throughout the day:

"Dona Ana," he would say, "Chico's hungry . . ."

He wasn't hungry at all; he just wanted to talk. By Dona Ana's calculations the parrot was over forty years old. The workers said the parrot was the bird with the longest life, living more than a hundred years. When he came to the Badarós, Chico was a past master in profanity, which Teodoro had patiently taught him. From the plantation house veranda he insulted workers and visitors in equal measure. Teodoro had laughed in amusement. In his new home Chico did not abandon his old habits and acquired new ones such as laughing the ringing guffaw of Captain João Magalhães, an effusive cackle that the wind swept up and scattered in the fields. He also learned, with Dona Ana, to call the chickens, ducks, and turkeys for their feed of dry corn.

This was one of his favorites pastimes. Upon escaping from the cage in the kitchen, where he lived, he would walk to the veranda in his sailor's gait, there to insult the blacks working at the drying frames. When he tired of invective, of goading the hired workers with his screams, he would start calling the poultry in the front yard, imitating the sound

86

Dona Ana made with her lips, doing a marvelous imitation of the sound of corn in a can. The birds, chickens, turkeys, ducks, and geese would come running from every corner of the yard, gathering in front of the veranda in expectation of their ration of corn. Chico would continue calling until all were there. And then he would laugh Captain João Magalhães's guffaw. It was because of this that the captain said that Chico had inherited more from Teodoro das Baraúnas than just dirty words and orders shouted at workers; he also had his perverse nature.

Chico's latest acquisition as far as phrases were concerned, an acquisition of which he was so proud that he repeated it ceaselessly, was João Magalhães's shout when, returning from Ilhéus, he dismounted at the entrance to the field, at the start of the boom:

"Dona Ana, we're going to be rich again!"

That day the captain appeared not to know any other words and repeated the same ones in every manner from that initial yell that had rung through the plantation house, reached Dona Ana in the yard, and made Chico's feathers stand on end in the kitchen—to a tender murmur, almost in Dona Ana's ear, as they sat in the hammock on the veranda, where Chico walked before them on the railing. He also told Chico, who was perched attentively on his finger:

"Chico, we're going to be rich again!"

He scratched Chico's head, and the parrot closed one eye in what seemed an ironic gesture. So often did he hear the phrase, not only that day but in the days that followed, while cacao was going for absurd prices, that he memorized it and yelled it at everybody—the workers at the drying frames, the cook in the kitchen, the chickens in the yard, Captain João Magalhães, Dona Ana, even to himself when he was alone:

"Dona Ana, we're going to be rich again!"

Then he laughed that delightful guffaw of João Magalhães. He laughed till exhausted, repeating the phrase endlessly:

"Dona Ana, we're going to be rich again!"

Then he shook his wings, ruffled his feathers, and spread his tail in a great green fan.

$$5$$

$\mathbf{D}$ ona Ana Badaró (despite all that had happened, despite the poverty and decadence, no one remembered to call her Dona Ana Magalhães) heard the parrot's screech and the delightful and repeated guffaw that followed. It all seemed like a caricature; the bird's artificial voice deformed the words and made them almost metallic, lacking the warmth of the captain's voice. But even so, Dona Ana smiled at hearing the phrase, her face lighting up with hope:

"Dona Ana, we're going to be rich again!"

It was no longer for herself, nor even for the captain, that she wanted to be rich, to return to the old times when the Badarós were lords of the land whom everyone greeted on the street, to whom clerks at the doors of shops bowed their heads in respect. It was for her children, the girls who had modest marriages and whose husbands needed help. Her doctor son-in-law spoke of leaving Pirangi, practicing in the capital and applying for a university position. If she became rich again—if those lands, the rest of the forest still to be planted, a remnant of the days of affluence, were to once again abound in cacao—then her daughters' dreams might come true. Is it really her daughters who harbor dreams, or Dona Ana who dreams for them? They still owned a piece of the forest; for thirty years those trees had awaited the money to pay for cutting, burning, and planting of new cacao seedlings. Dona Ana had never allowed the captain to sell that piece, a strange outlook in those lands of southern Bahia heavily planted in cacao. They had received good offers, and more than once the captain had been inclined to sell during one of their several financial binds. But he always encountered the unshakable will of Dona Ana:

"That forest is our daughters' future . . ."

Now she spoke of their grandchildren. It was for them that she thought of planting the lands and recouping the Badaró fortune. And in the silence of her room she dreamed of one of her grandchildren using the name that would otherwise disappear. There was no male left in the family, and in their decadence the captain had not kept his promise to Juca, to adopt the Badaró name. The promise had died with the burning of the plantation house, at the end of the fighting when Horácio became total master of the situation. The Badaró name had disappeared with Sinhô's death, living on only in Dona Ana. The grandchildren had other surnames, those of people recently come to the cacao lands. People without roots there, unlike her, Dona Ana Badaró . . . New people in the land, people no one knew, arriving daily, attracted by the gold of the cacao trees. Of those old-timers who had tamed the land and planted the fields few were left, old and worn out. Still, Dona Ana thought, that land belonged to them by right—the right of conquest, sealed with blood, much blood spilled in the forest, especially the forest of Sequeiro Grande.

Dona Ana lives amid dreams of a better future for her daughters, sons-in-law and grandchildren, and the remembrance of the splendorous past. What has become of that shy dark woman of old, shy even under the impassioned eyes of João Magalhães, yet as bold and decisive as the most courageous man during the fighting, the battles and the blood? Thirty years have swept over her and today her black hair is white, her beautiful eyes are faded, her firm flesh is softer. Thirty years of poverty break a person. But in Dona Ana resided a pride that sustained her from within and, despite the aging of her body, kept her dreams intact. In a trunk that was never opened lay the most cherished mementos of the days of the Badarós' prosperity. Her bridal veil, the Bible that Sinhô had read before beginning any undertaking, two revolvers: one that Teodoro das Baraúnas had given João on their wedding day, and one that had belonged to Juca, her unforgettable uncle, "the most gallant and accomplished conqueror of the land, who had stepped over bodies to plant cacao." Who had written that? Dona Ana also kept the newspaper clipping. A man who had been looking into the happenings of thirty years ago had done some stories for the papers and had written that about Juca. Dona Ana had added the clipping to the relics hidden in the trunk, with a secret pride. That secrecy was undone, however, by the verses of blind singers in the markets that recounted the struggles for Sequeiro Grande. Sometimes, when Dona Ana went to market in Itabuna or Pirangi, she could hear the guitar player asking for alms as he sang the frightening story for the curious new arrivals to the cacao lands. At such times she felt mixed emotions: the desire to draw close and immerse herself in the tales of her father's and uncle's courage (she herself is mentioned in one such popular poem), coupled with the desire to flee, shamed by her current poverty. The blind man's voice, shrill yet perfect for that simple, primitive chant, brought the fierce battles between the Badarós and Horácio to everyone's notice. It was never long before someone recognized her and surreptitiously pointed her out to the others:

"That's Dona Ana Badaró. Sinhô's daughter . . ."

"They say she could shoot like a man . . ."

And she would flee in sudden revolt against those people who raised up her dead and made them seem foolish. But that feeling was short-lived. Truthfully, she was glad that her father and uncle, and she herself, could be heard in the mouths of blind guitar players on the roads of the cacao country and the backlands. It had been like that for thirty years, since the black man Damião had gone mad, missed when he fired at Firmo, and taken to wandering from field to field repeating the prophecies of Jeremias, the sorcerer of the forest.

She never spoke of those times, however. Her son-in-law the doctor sometimes pumped her for details, asking for accounts of the deeds in his thirst for heroic stories. She refused, answering in a voice suddenly harsh:

"That's all over and done with, son. Those people are all dead, it's a sin to meddle with them . . ."

It was João Magalhães who told their son-in-law the stories, making up what he didn't know, giving them the flavor of poker-table anecdotes and appearing as the major hero in each one—he who had fought only because he had no choice, at the very end of the battles.

But not a day goes by that Dona Ana doesn't remember those times. The recollections give her strength to dream of a less mediocre future. And, though she doesn't speak of the past, it is Dona Ana who watches over that tradition and keeps the Badarós' story alive, who keeps everything from rotting in these new times. If not for her, wouldn't João Magalhães have borrowed money from Horácio himself—their mortal enemy, the man who had won the struggle, burned their plantation house, sacked the fields, ordered Juca and so many of the Badarós' men killed? It had been she all right, and the captain had grumbled a lot about her foolish pride, the pride of a pauper. Captain João Magalhães didn't understand. It wasn't so much pride; Dona Ana was attempting to keep intact the reality of thirty years ago, even the enmities. She had been very unhappy when Antônio Vítor made his peace with Firmo, despite both having been secondary players in what took place. She had complained to Raimunda, as if she were still the lady of the house and the other her servant. Today they were almost equals, each harvesting nearly the same amount of cacao. But the reality of those times was so alive in Dona Ana that she followed with great interest the petty struggle in which Josué Santos attempted to remove Horácio da Silveira from the party leadership. And when Horácio ordered Josué's elimination, she breathed more easily, relieved and satisfied. At the table where they had lunch, upon hearing the news she told the captain, her daughter and the doctor, at that time her fiancé:

"That's a real man . . ."

The captain's chin dropped at hearing his wife praise their unforgivable enemy. Dona Ana explained:

"I don't like him, but it was wrong for them to take away what he won. It was his by right. What are these young fellas nowadays compared to a man like Horácio? I don't like him, but the wretched man did the right thing . . ."

That's what Dona Ana Badaró was like, although today she was not even a dim reflection of the beautiful dark young woman who carried both the litter of the Virgin in processions in Ilhéus and a gun in the fighting for Sequeiro Grande. Dona Ana Badaró, a young woman whose name and fortune were legendary in the cacao groves, desired and feared by every young man who came to those lands in search of a living. Won by a gambler, to the envy of all the other adventures of the time. Today she is old and broken, but her heart is young, living in another world much more beautiful than this, a world where the business of cacao was settled with bullets on the roads and not, as now, in offices with phone calls and telegrams.

The tireless parrot shouts its phrase. Dona Ana smiles, looking at the rain clouds gathering in the sky. When the captain arrived he had brought two pieces of news: the boom and the rain. He had never changed: always vibrant and happy, optimistic and full of plans. Almost always he was content to make plans, to imagine. But this time Dona Ana is inclined to force him. This time she won't remain in the idle recollection of the past. This time the forest will be cut down, cacao planted, the Badaró fortune recouped. And once again Dona Ana will stroll through the streets of Ilhéus before the respectful gaze of all, and the Badaró name will signify not just the past but the future.

The parrot screeches, and Dona Ana looks at the rain clouds:

"That's right, Chico, we're going to be rich again . . ."

Her smile brings to mind the gentle and resolute smile of Sinhô Badaró.

6

I t was on an intensely sunny day, during the hard work in the final stage of harvesting the fields, that Beanpole got the idea. The last cacao pods had been cut down, yellow as gold, already threatened by the violent sun that announced the lull. Beanpole was extremely thin and tall, thus the nickname that had permanently replaced his real name at some distant time in the past. No one knew where he was from. He had worked at many trades: he had shined shoes, sold lottery tickets, worked on the docks in Ilhéus, who knows what else. It's possible he might have once been a thief, as was whispered on neighboring plantations. In any case, Beanpole currently owed a lot of money to the plantation store. He had a worse case of syphilis than a prostitute and had spent nearly three months lying in a bunk, without working, running up such a bill that Capi, who shared the house with him and had much experience on plantations, said:

"You gonna die workin' and never quit . . ."

But Beanpole had no desire to die working, much less die doing heavy work in the cacao fields, work with no future. Why he had brought his skinny hide here not even he himself knew. He had come on the train one day to Itabuna. It occurred to him to take a look at the plantations. They hired him during a dire shortage of workers (the rains had returned to Ceará), and he stayed, captive of his debts to the store. Colonel Frederico Pinto said he had never seen a worker as bad as Beanpole. Lazy and no-account, he avoided work as much as possible. But who could avoid work when Tibúrcio, the overseer, was on top of you yelling:

"Faster . . . faster . . ."

Faster and faster, that's the law of hired workers on cacao plantations. "Faster," shouts Tibúrcio from his horse, the rawhide whip in his hand, the whip that sometimes strayed from the animal's haunches to the back of any man who protested. "Faster," he shouts, adding:

"You're lazy good-for-nothings. You don't know how to work, you steal the money you get, you're a bunch of thieves . . ."

When Tibúrcio's voice crosses the fields and falls upon the men, Beanpole's face twists in anger. Beanpole doesn't remember ever hating anyone in his life. Not even Rosa, who abandoned him in the streets of Ilhéus, causing him to take the train to Itabuna. But if he could just meet up with Tibúrcio some night on the road, with nobody but the two of them . . . Thinking about it, Beanpole even manages to smile. It was during the last days of the harvest, before the pruning got under way, that he had the idea for the mummers group. A group of Wise Men for the celebrations at the end of the old year and the beginning of the new one . . .

The idea first arose merely as a function of the celebrations. Someone said that Christmas was coming and Beanpole remembered the mummers group. Why not put together a group? But Tibúrcio's voice continued above them with its curses and threats:

"Don't steal the boss's hard-earned money . . ."

And that was when Beanpole linked the idea of the group to the idea of fleeing. How many times had he planned to run away, leave those lands, light out into the wide world far from this work among cacao trees? But, like all the plantation workers, he always remembered the beating that Ranulfo had suffered when he tried to run away. He had been caught in Ferradas and whipped in front of all the workers, assembled especially for the purpose. Colonel Frederico was there too, and Tibúrcio's riding whip went to work on the man's back. Afterwards the colonel said:

"Let this be a lesson to all of you not to try to rob other people . . . Workers in debt got to pay up 'fore they can leave . . ."

Who wasn't in debt? Ranulfo was constantly shaking with malaria and on reduced pay; the fever prevented him from producing like the others. His bill continued to grow, and it was in the delirium of his illness that he fled. Since the beating he keeps to himself in a corner, speaking to no one, his head hung, brooding over things. Capi has said that Ranulfo might do something stupid and ruin himself for life. For all his cynical cheerfulness, Beanpole also feels something strange in his head sometimes, his eyes cloudy, a bitter taste in his mouth, and the shotgun tempts him. It would be great to see Tibúrcio stretched out on the road. They all hate the overseer more than the colonel. The colonel is untouchable, sacred, while the overseer was once a worker just like them. But he went up in the world and now he's worse than the boss himself.

Beanpole made the connection between the two ideas. With the group going from field to field, from plantation to plantation, on festival nights, he could escape without being noticed. He knew the roads leading to the backlands, and nobody would catch Beanpole, who knew how to travel fast. Nobody was going to apply a whip to his back.

He certainly wasn't about to stay at that job. His bill at the plantation store was growing. It was huge, over a thousand réis. How could he pay? It was impossible. The voice of Tibúrcio interrupted Beanpole's reflections.

"Faster . . . faster . . . Don't steal the boss's money!"

Beanpole ran his eyes from the mounted overseer to the men, yellowed from malaria, bent over in the fields, their machetes striking low as they harvested the pods from the trunk, their scythes on long poles harvesting the pods from the higher branches. During the pruning they will cut away all the shoots that sap the trunk's strength, strength the fruit must have to grow. They will remove the green branches that clash with the golden color of the fields, branches that are born in the tree crown and climb heavenward. All of that is of no use to the cacao tree; it is the tree's "vanity," as the workers say. All these tenuous green ornaments must be removed so the cacao tree can devote its full energy to the pods, inside which the cacao beans are covered with *visgo* that will spill through the openings in the troughs onto the men's feet.

The cacao fields are the work, the home, the garden, the cinema, often the cemetery of the workers. The enormous feet of the hired hands look like roots, bearing no resemblance to anything else. The *visgo* of cacao sticks to their feet and never comes off, making them like the bark of the trunk, while malaria gives them the yellow color of nearly ripe pods, ready for picking. Thus the song that Black Florindo sings as he harvests cacao:

> "*My color it's cacao,*
> *I'd give my love to you,*
> *But listen good, my li'l brown gal,*
> *I'm yellow, swollen now,*
> *The fever does that too.*"

Black Florindo is only twenty and was born in these lands. He has never been off the plantations. He is Beanpole's friend, and the mulatto is thinking of taking him along when he flees. Black Florindo has the strength of an elephant and the goodness of a child. All he knows how to do is laugh and sing, nothing else. The day Ranulfo was whipped, Beanpole and Capi needed all their strength to hold him back and prevent his throwing himself onto Tibúrcio with the stub of a knife in his hand.

He sings as he works in the fields. His powerful and sad voice penetrates the cacao trees; then, swept by the wind, it flees, telling of the life of these men of cacao. The lives of many people revolve around the cacao trees. There are the exporters, some of whom have never even seen a plantation. There are the large growers, the owners of the land, courageous and rich. There are lawyers, doctors, agronomists, inspectors. There are the overseers, the meanest people in the world. And there are the workers, those who pick cacao, who dry the beans, who prune the fields. They are the poorest of all, the hired hands, those who never come out ahead at harvest's end. The voice of Black Florindo recounts the life of these blacks, mulattoes, and whites who stoop in the fields. The song is anonymous; no one knows who wrote it or where it comes from. After the last of the land was conquered and the workers lost any hope of winning a plot of land to plant, the song appeared and became popular throughout the plantations:

"*I plant cacao from sun to sun,*
I work my fingers to the bone,
But listen good, my li'l brown gal,
I never take no money home,
I never take no money home . . .

My fate, my life—how sad they are,
The fate of workers in the fields,
But listen good, my li'l brown gal,
Because you know of my ordeal . . .
Because you know of my ordeal . . ."

Beanpole stops working for a moment to listen to Florindo's song. What songs will they sing in the mummers group? Beanpole never heard of an Epiphany group coming from a cacao plantation. It's possible that nobody knows entirely even one of the parts for the shepherdesses' dance. He himself doesn't. The songs of this cacao land are new songs, born here and telling of misfortunes and killing over land, work songs that, like the one Florindo is singing, help with the harvesting. The overseer jerks him from his rest with his voice of authority:

"Faster . . . Faster . . ."

Children gather the pods cut from the trees. The copperish red sun climbs in the sky, burning the naked backs of the men. They have been there since 6 A.M. It is early morning, and the birds are still trilling, the sun is still mild, and Beanpole holds a scythe and machete, cutting down cacao pods in harvest season, pruning trees in the lull time. Tibúrcio rides up on his horse and shouts at them: "Faster, faster. Those men are stealing the boss's money." The sun climbs in the sky, climbing up

Beanpole's back as well. And it burns, no longer the soft early morning sun, when dew dampens your feet. Now the earth burns; naked backs gleam under the rays in summer, rain runs off them in winter. You have to be careful of the numerous snakes of various species, each more poisonous than the last. The rattlesnake is easy to spot from a distance, because it shakes its rattles, but who can foresee the arrival of a *jaracuçu* or a *pico-de-jaca,* or the presence in a cacao tree of a coral snake, which looks like a vine among the branches? Sweat runs down Beanpole's face, and on the face of Florindo, who is black, the drops glisten like diamonds. Beanpole cuts cacao pods and thinks about the mummers group. He'll invite Florindo, invite Capi and Ranulfo, invite Astério who's married and has two daughters. They're still little girls— the older one is twelve—but so what? With their mother they make three women, and three women mean a lot in a farm workers' festival. Women are still going to be the biggest problem. In these lands anyone with a mate, anyone who's married or living with somebody, doesn't take chances with his woman because someone might steal her. On cacao plantations women are a rare and precious thing. They are few in number, and those few are in the fields working to help their husbands. They split open the pods gathered into large piles by the children—so young! The children earn five hundred réis for a day's work. They're naked, and their enormous bellies make them look like pregnant women. Bloated children. Bloated from the earth they eat, good-tasting earth that takes the place of the food they lack. All of them—black, white, and mulatto—are the same yellow color, resembling the leaves of cacao trees. In a few years they'll be workers just like Beanpole or Florindo, without a scintilla of difference. To the yellow of ingested earth will have been added the yellow of malaria—if they don't die first, of dysentery or typhus. A lot of children die on these plantations—God's little angels, as Dona Auricídia, Colonel Maneca Dantas's wife and a pious lady, calls them. She says they all turn into angels in heaven, with hummingbird wings. Those who don't become angels become workers, soaking up the noonday sun on their naked backs, like a lash. Faster, faster, calls the overseer's voice, don't steal the boss's hard-earned money. Beanpole hears the order and works faster; the fruits fall from the trees, the children carry them away, running. The women split them with a sharp blow of the machete. Sometimes one cuts her hand with a miscalculated blow, then covers the wound with earth and spreads cacao *visgo* over it. The wound closes; stopping work is out of the question. Don't steal the boss's hard-earned money.

Florindo's voice lightens the work with his song in which floats a distant and vague hope:

"One of these days I'll have some land,
And plant cacao for me,
But listen good, my li'l brown gal,
Just when's it gonna be?
Just when's it gonna be?"

At noon, when they broke for lunch, Beanpole told Capi and Florindo of his idea for a group:

"It'll be real pretty!"

They discussed the subject and made plans. Black Florindo laughed with satisfaction: an Epiphany group.. Capi wanted to know if it was going to be folkloric or a shepherdess group. He remembered an Epiphany group from long ago, in a faraway city, when as a young lad he had gone out as King Herod ("King Herody," as the shepherd girls had said in their chant). Those were happy days, days that Capi hadn't recalled for a long time. But where could they find women, single and beautiful girls, to make up a shepherdess group?

There wasn't much time to talk. They had to return to work, as fast as possible. The overseer yells their names: get to work! And they remain on the job until the sun has completely set. Just as night falls they suspend the harvest and return to their houses. The children run home; how can they have the strength to run? The women are tired, slow-moving, silent It seems absurd even to call those people women. No one who ever saw a city woman, as Beanpole has, with makeup and perfume, well dressed, beautiful, made for love, could ever believe that these black and mulatto rags, panting with fatigue as they return from the fields, are women. They are nothing but the remains of people, and even so they sleep with their men, they kiss and bear children who will eat earth.

The evening of that workday, Beanpole, Florindo, and Capi had their heads filled with thoughts. A mummers group . . . An Epiphany group for the January festival. Black Florindo laughed with happiness . . .

They came down the road talking about it. The idea of the group will fill up the days till the new harvest. There are plans, conversations, tasks to be accomplished. Capi prefers a shepherdess dance, while Ranulfo favors the folkloric. Only Florindo has no opinion; to him it's all the same, it's all happy and good. And the black man laughs his clear guffaw.

Then night comes, and it is a weary night, a short night. They eat beef jerky and manioc mush, drink a swallow of coffee. Some—very few—have women. They are tatters of people, black tatters, mulatto tatters, with flaccid breasts that hang to their navels, with ugly faces and dirty, injured legs, with a malodorous sex. But—they are women!

And so few are they that the greatest happiness is to have one to sleep with! Sighs of love are rare in the workers' adobe houses. And many are the crimes of passion, killings over women, for each scrap of a woman is worth more than the most expensive woman in the greatest city in the world. Never was any woman more ardently desired, and by so many men, as the least of these black and mulatto peasant women with their worn faces, legs covered with cacao *visgo,* callused hands, and sagging breasts! Whoever has a woman must be a brave man to defend her with knife and rifle from the desire of all the others, those who toss in their bunks, shuddering at the contact of their own hand. A weary night, short and sad, is the night of workers on cacao plantations.

But for Beanpole, Capi, and Florindo, and for Ranulfo too, this was not a sad night. When Capi put away his small guitar and Florindo stopped singing in the yard in front of the house, when they extinguished the wick of the smoky red lantern, each was thinking his own thoughts, imagining the Epiphany group. It would go out on New Year's and visit nearby plantation houses. It would go out again for Epiphany, the night before and during the day itself. With the lights of its ingenuous lanterns it would illuminate the cacao fields, and the workers' lives as well. From the bunk, Capi asks Beanpole:

"What we gonna call it?"

7

What *were* they going to call it? Capi's question confused Beanpole's thinking. They needed a name—who ever heard of a mummers group without a name? Beanpole recalled groups he had seen in other lands, in cities of the north. He remembered names: Santos Dumont's Balloon, a funny name, a group that had gone out in Aracaju; Sinhazinha's Bumba-meu-Boi, which took place in Juazeiro, organized by an old woman. A name . . . It wasn't so easy . . . Unless they gave it the name of the plantation: the Tararanga Group. It had a nice sound to it. But then he remembered the Perfect Love Group, which he had seen in the streets of Maroim. The Perfect Love Group: now there was a snazzy name . . . It's true there were certain advantages if they used the name of the plantation. It might be the colonel would help out with a little money. Ten or twenty mil-réis; it was something. The name of the plantation would make things easier.

It'll have the plantation's name, Colonel . . . The Tararanga Group . . .

The Perfect Love Group was so pretty . . . Rosa would like it if she heard about it. The memory of Rosa troubled Beanpole's lonely nights. Cynical and mocking, he had been a mulatto Don Juan among the servant girls, nursemaids, and cooks in several cities. He could whisper a jest better than anyone, knew how to cultivate the tender hearts of nursemaids, and had become absolute master of the dark-skinned mulatto girls in domestic service in the city of Ilhéus. Until Rosa came along. She came on the scene, none knew from where, in her print dresses. With her oblique eyes, prominent cheekbones, and long loose hair she seemed like a gypsy. Months of love on the runways of the docks, on deserted rafts, in train stations. Rosa lived on Conquest Hill, though Beanpole never found out just where. Rosa lied a lot: sometimes she was married, sometimes the

daughter of violent parents, sometimes she worked in the richest homes.
It was never possible to place any credence in what she said. She was
the biggest liar in the world. Now and then she would disappear, and
three or four days would go by without anyone seeing her. Beanpole
would go crazy and comb the city of Ilhéus from top to bottom. He
would knock on the door of houses where she claimed to work:
   "A girl named Rosa work here?"
   "Not here . . ."
   At one house they had a servant by the name of Rosa, but she was
a toothless old woman, and when Rosa learned of the story she almost
died laughing. On other days she would become sad, neither speaking,
singing, nor lying. When they made love, on those days that Beanpole
hated, she was cold and apathetic, appearing to be lost in some distant
world. But nearly always she was cheerful, and talkative; he had never
seen a woman who chattered as much. She was the loveliest thing in
those lands, and many had their eye on her! How many fights must
have erupted because Rosa dispensed smiles at passersby who looked
at her with wonder and desire. Beanpole wished she would be serious
and give up that forwardness of hers. But Rosa smiled, incapable of
seriousness; she really was crazy, as crazy as they come. But, oh!, when
on nights of love her voice rose from the abandoned rafts to the starry
heavens, then Beanpole forgot everything and gave himself totally to
gazing at Rosa, her wonderful face, her small white teeth, her sweet
oblique eyes.
   One day she went away and did not return. That day she was serious
and her voice was different. In the morning, when she got up from the
raft, she warned:
   "I'm going away, Beanpole. It was good, real good . . . I'll never
forget you . . . But I have to go away . . ."
   He asked, fought, humbled himself, begged. She said nothing more.
She gave him one last kiss and left. Again, Beanpole roamed the city
of Ilhéus from end to end in search of Rosa. There was no house on
Conquest Hill where he didn't look for her. He never saw her again. It
was only in Itabuna, where his senseless anguish had dragged him, that
he learned that she was living with Martins, the manager of the Zude
import house, with a job stitching cacao sacks. The pain was killing.
Beanpole went to the cacao lands and fell into that wretched life, but
Rosa is still in his thoughts. Day and night Beanpole thinks of her, of
her eyes, her breasts like young cacao fruit, her loose hair. How often
has he spoken to his housemates and fellow workers of his days with
Rosa? Capi, Florindo, and Ranulfo all know the story in every detail.
And when syphilis overcame him, laying him in the bunk for weeks,
he spent the time recounting to Florindo, in a repetition of which the

black man never wearied, every word of Rosa's every gesture, every sigh of love.

The Perfect Love Group. Rosa would like that. But what does the name matter, Perfect Love or Tararanga, if what Beanpole wants is to flee, make his way to the backlands and later follow the roads back to Ilhéus? He would avoid meeting up with Colonel Frederico and would look for Rosa wherever she was. Who is this Martins who gave her a job? Beanpole has a knife that he has never used except to cut some tobacco to smoke in a straw cigarette, but he might very well stick it in Martins's throat if he doesn't leave Rosa alone. Not that Beanpole hates him the way he hates Tibúrcio, but if Martins doesn't give up the woman who belongs to him, then . . .

The important thing is to flee . . . Get out of there, take the most difficult trails through the forest, sleep in the woods, reach the Baforé Mountains, then the backlands. Then later he would come down the Conquest road, hide out in Itabuna, hop a truck heading to Ilhéus. In Ilhéus Beanpole was absolute master . . . And at that point another problem enters his head and steals his sleep: should he take Florindo or not?

Florindo sleeps in the bunk beneath his. Even in sleep the black man is smiling. Is he thinking about the mummers group, dreaming about it? Black Florindo is indeed dreaming of the Epiphany group, something he has never seen. He imagines the figure of the ox, is frightened by the hobgoblin. But what he sees with eager eyes are the shepherd girls, so beautiful, and all of them Rosa, Beanpole's Rosa who has found a place in the black man's heart also. Perhaps Florindo loves her even more than Beanpole himself. Through his friend's narratives he has become accustomed to her, to her memory, and has imagined her in a thousand different ways. First she looked something like a blonde prostitute that he saw in Palestina, on a street in the red-light district, a woman who would get incredibly drunk and then raise a scandal on the streets where respectable people lived. She looked like porcelain, and the police ran her out of that small town; and often Florindo pictured Rosa as looking like her, with blue eyes, a small mouth, and hair the color of gold. Later, when Ranulfo got hold of an old magazine discarded on the porch of the plantation house, with a photo of an almost-naked film actress wearing only a brassiere and panties—a dark woman with a perfect body—Rosa became like her in Florindo's nights. But, more modestly, she was also like the daughter of Jesuíno, the overseer at Maneca Dantas's plantation, a spirited young mulatto woman who enjoyed courting. She was like a black prostitute with whom Florindo had slept in Pirangi and who had given him a loathsome disease. There were several Rosas in Florindo's dreams, but whoever she was, in the painful moment of orgasm he would repeat in his solitary love the words that Beanpole had attributed to her. Rosa lives in Beanpole's heart, but she also lives in the callused hand of Black Florindo those nights without women on Tararanga plantation.

Now he dreams of Rosa, dressed as a shepherdess in the Epiphany group. There are many of them and each is Rosa, Beanpole's Rosa. There is the blonde Rosa, with her small mouth and blue eyes, cursing the married women, so drunk she can't keep her feet. There is the seminude Rosa, in bra and panties, a dark, pretty film actress. There is the mulatto Rosa, with restless eyes, her face painted with dye from red paper, her hair slicked down with pork lard. There is black Rosa, who has thick thighs marked with injuries, a coarse laugh, and who spits copiously. And Black Florindo laughs in his dream, seeing himself dancing in the mummers group, dancing with Rosa. How pretty the group is!

Should he take Florindo or go by himself? Beanpole can't solve the problem. It's best to consult Capi, a man with many years' experience on these plantations. Capi had never tried to flee despite the homesickness that he harbors deep in his heart. Capi is from Ceará and came in a drought year when the fame of the lands of southern Bahia spread through the sun-drenched northeast. Never since has he been able to leave. He came alone; his wife and children stayed behind in the blazing land, and he had set out for a short time, just long enough to get some money together. He owed the plantation store. In Ceará his wife looked after their piece of land, the cow and the goat, and would send some money as soon as she could. Capi would pay off the plantation store and leave. Such have been his hopes for years. Now and then a letter comes from his wife, written by the teacher at the school near Capi's piece of land; in it his wife says that she's getting money together to send. But it is money accumulated penny by penny, and it takes time. Capi waits patiently, meanwhile doing everything in his power not to increase his debt.

That night he dreams too. In his uneasy dream he recalls an Epiphany group with which he had gone out—so many years ago!—dressed as Herod. In a mixture of Bible passages and old mystery plays, they acted out the story of the birth of Jesus. He was Herod and it was to him that the shepherdesses sang those unforgettable verses. On his bed of bare boards, Capi moves in a desperate effort. The shepherd girls have paused in their singing and it's his turn to answer. Just how did the verses go? It was many years ago, Capi was still single and didn't even know of the existence of these lands of Ilhéus or of cacao trees, but he knew the verses of the shepherdess group and the steps to the pastoral dance. It was in that group, on those wonderful nights, that he met Susana, his wife. She was one of the shepherd girls and sang:

"O King Herody,
Show respect to the child
Who is our God . . . "

And he, King Herod, answered. Capi made a desperate effort to remember. Before him stands Susana as a young girl, dressed as a shepherdess and singing. There are beads of sweat on Capi's forehead; he moves in the bunk, his dream becomes a nightmare.

Beanpole closes his eyes. Should he take Florindo or not? Let Capi decide; he's more experienced than anybody. Now the mummers are about to leave, with Beanpole at their head, and the road leads to the backlands. He runs, the group behind him, their lanterns swinging as they sing a well known song:

"I plant cacao from sun to sun,
I work my fingers to the bone . . . "

The group falls farther and farther behind. On the trail through the woods Rosa comes toward Beanpole. She comes laughing, talking, lying. Behind her, come from the cacao fields, are Martins and Tibúrcio. Beanpole searches for his knife. Rosa is laughing: who can flee a cacao plantation? Not Ranulfo, and now he is being beaten. The whip rises in Tibúrcio's hands and descends on Ranulfo's back. And Beanpole flees but they all come together in front of the plantation house: the laughing Rosa, Martins in pursuit of her, Colonel Frederico shouting, Tibúrcio holding the whip, Ranulfo being beaten . . .

Ranulfo opens his eyes and looks around. His eyes are used to the darkness. It's taken a long time for Beanpole to get to sleep tonight . . . Ranulfo has been waiting for a long time. He raises his head a bit and hears Beanpole snoring. He gets up a little at a time, avoiding the slightest noise. If anyone wakes up he'll say he was going outside to urinate.

He opens the door held by a wooden latch and slowly slips outside. Now he is at the road and can leave in search of love.

The sky sprinkles stars, the night is warm, desire rises from the earth in hot waves. Who can sleep on a moonlit night? However tired Ranulfo is from an entire day harvesting in the fields, how can he sleep when the night is so beautiful, the heat is like a curtain, and desire wells in his chest? Fireflies blink in flight. In a distant house a guitar moans; someone else who can't sleep in the warm night. On such nights the bunks creak and no one is surprised or scandalized. In these nights of desire, without women, all that remains to the workers is the caress of their hand on their sex as they imagine bodies making love. It is a tragic imitation of love, like a caricature.

Only a few have a woman; the others have only their right hand for love. But Ranulfo, yellowed Ranulfo, felled by malaria, the runaway who was whipped in the sight of everyone, the most wretched worker on the cacao plantations—he has a love. And this is why he waits for the men to get comfortable and fall asleep in their bunks so he can go out into the starry night. He has a love, a love that grew slowly, whom he conquered little by little, who is, despite everything, the only thing of value in his worker's life.

Walking along the road toward their meeting place, he thinks about his love and a smile crosses Ranulfo's swollen face. What does it matter if the others laugh at him, if they murmur disdainfully in corners? He will run his hand along her neck in a caress and make love to her on that night of desire. Love is everything in the lives of men: when it appears, it is as if the world were transformed, as if everything were covered with roses, as if the atmosphere were perfumed, as if men themselves became better. They all think about their loved one during the day, while they work. Whether it be the millionaire who makes rivers of money with a simple phone call, the clerk pecking away at a typewriter in an unimportant office, the revolutionary awaiting death in a concentration camp, the idler who sleeps till noon and still has nothing to do in the afternoon, the fisherman crossing the waters in his boat—all think about their loves for a moment, with happiness, and this brings relief from the millions, from the typewriter, from imminent death, from the uselessness that hangs with equal weight. Ranulfo, too, sometimes thinks of his loved one, with a mixture of affection and disdain, swearing that he'll never see her again, never. And then he leaves to meet her. Before it was only the boys, just beginning to fathom the secrets of love, who possessed her in their sexual anxiety. But Ranulfo discovered her and conquered her. Now she waits for him every night by the pasture fence.

The night sprinkles stars and desire. Ranulfo hums softly along the road, moving carefully so no one will see him, with an excuse ready if he runs into anyone. The night is lovely, that night of so many stars when the men dream about the Epiphany group and the rains that should be on their way to make the cacao trees bloom. The heat rising from the earth, the cloud cutting across the sky are signs that the clouds will soon burst and tomorrow the roads will be covered with mud. Ranulfo hums softly, totally overcome by desire, the desire for a female to lay.

He arrives. The mulatto Ranulfo, broken by malaria, his back marked by the whip, knows no pretty words like suitors in the city, those sweet words of affection uttered to loved ones in the moonlight. But the moon shining on Ranulfo is the same romantic moon of suitors and lovers. He jumps the fence, and the semidesiccated pasture grass scratches his legs.

"C'mere, you sweet black gal!"

It is all he knows how to say, but there is a world in those words. A world of tenderness, of grateful love. The words contain all the words invented by poets, the most beautiful and most romantic, the most affectionate.

What does it matter that she's only a black mule, a four-legged animal, and that this love is abnormal, degrading, and dirty? To Ranulfo, a worker lost in the cacao plantations, none of that matters; he knows no moral code or law but that which prevents him from fleeing the plantation as long as he owes the store. To him the black mule is like a beautiful woman and the moment of love that she gives him is truly wonderful. The coupling of man and animal at the edge of the cacao fields holds the same intense desire as in the most refined lovemaking in the cities he has never seen. Such is love on the cacao plantations.

Shaking and suddenly disgusted, Ranulfo takes the road back. But rain begins to fall in a sudden downpour that washes the earth, the cacao fields, the animals, and the men. Tomorrow there will be mud on the roads.

8

The frames for drying cacao beans resemble ships about to sail off through a sea of golden trees. They stand side by side near the plantation house, five in all, where the workers dance over the beans as they dry in the sun. Farther on are the troughs, to which donkeys carry the soft cacao. Through openings in the boards drains the sticky substance that covers the beans, which the colonels use to manufacture homemade vinegar.

Perhaps because the frames resemble ships, there are songs in the cacao lands that speak of the sea and voyages. A desire to flee, perhaps, in those men, many of whom arrived there by sea, in search of wealth:

> *I want to be a sailor,*
> *And go to other lands . . .*

The tin cover of the frames burns in the sun. In case of a sudden rain, it's only necessary to slide the cover over the rails of the frame and the cacao will be safe. Then it won't turn "musty" and become merely "standard" cacao, with the difference in price to be deducted from the workers' wages. Above the ground, which appears as if waxed, the cacao from the troughs is drying, turned by the feet of men who dance upon it in a dance of their own invention, singing a song equally their own. It recalls another dance that blacks in other times danced on the covered decks of slave ships, and the music speaks of the desire they harbor of becoming sailors one day, of leaving in the belly of ships for other lands. But these frames, which recall cargo ships ready to plow the high seas, are anchored beside the cacao fields and, however strong the south wind, will never depart:

106

A ship that never sails,
A ship captive of the earth.

However strong the south wind bending the pasture grass, filling the cacao fields with yellow leaves, they will never depart. Nor will these blacks and mulattoes, who sing songs that tell of seas and voyages—nor will they ever depart, sailors on the cacao drying frames held fast to the rich black earth!

In the sun, the drying cacao beans become burning coals, and on these coals men dance, turning them so the cacao can become "superior" cacao rather than "good" or "standard." Because the difference in price will go on the worker's bill, and even after ten years he won't come out ahead. "Careful," yells the overseer, "don't mess up the cacao, don't rob the colonel." They sing and dance; the cacao beans burn. At first they leave marks on the toes, but later the feet become accustomed to it.

The hotter the sun, the better, and the better the cacao will be. It will have the same mulatto tone of the men's faces and will give off the smell of chocolate. All these workers know of chocolate is the similar smell of cacao.

Beanpole dances quickly, his feet moving in a strange ballet. Black Florindo laughs, dancing better than anyone. Capi is in the troughs thrashing the beans. His feet are covered with sticky *visgo* which no amount of water will wash away and which will remain for the rest of his life. Florindo breaks out in the sailors' song, his voice joined by a chorus of workers:

"*My boat's about to leave,*
The wind it is a-blowin' . . .
A boat without a sail,
Or even oars for rowin' . . . "

Farther ahead, white from a recent coat of whitewash, is the kiln. It looks like the most innocent of houses. Nevertheless, the workers look upon it with horror. The electric kiln is a small white house with a single entrance more like a hole than a door, through which the men squeeze to enter the inferno. During the unhappy rainy days of winter or when, as at harvest's end, the amount of cacao picked is too much for the frames, the beans are dried artificially with electric heat. In the winter, when the rains of July come, the frames are useless. The sun is not to be seen and the tin roofs are pulled shut and the beans taken to the kiln. The electricity is turned on, or the nonelectric kilns are stoked with wood. Inside, the heat is infernal, and one has to hold out for six hours turning the beans, for the kiln is dangerous and can, with frightful ease, ruin hundreds upon hundreds of pounds of cacao. And if they are ruined, the workers must pay. The overseer warns them as they enter: "Careful. Be careful. Don't ruin the cacao." Many have died of congestion when they left the kiln and rain fell on them outside. One day one of them died because when he came out his throat was dry and he eagerly devoured a piece of watermelon. He died an ugly death, his eyes bulging, his mouth twisted, right in the door of the pretty, white kiln.

"He jist up and dropped dead," they said.

Many have dropped dead and the workers fear the kiln with a mortal dread, looking upon it as an enemy. It kills people, and it burns the colonel's cacao. When cacao burns, the workers pay for the loss, which is taken from their wages, and their debts rise in the illegible books of the plantation store. But if a man dies coming out of the kiln, no one pays anything; he is buried right there in the fields, and it's been shown that he makes good fertilizer. When a man dies it's because his time has come, and it's even better to die suddenly, to drop dead, than spend months in bed, thin and yellow, dying a little at a time. Such are the women's comments when someone gets rained on leaving the kiln and drops dead.

The unknown musicians of the plantations have composed songs for the enemy, for the kiln that burns cacao and kills men—infinitely sad songs to accompany the deceased:

> *Maneca died in the oven*
> *Just as sundown came . . .*

On Colonel Frederico Pinto's plantation there was only one electric kiln, which was located near the drying frames and the plantation house. The motor wasn't very powerful, only enough for the kiln and lighting the colonel's house and two bulbs in the house of Tibúrcio, the overseer. The other two kilns, on the edges of the plantation, were wood powered. In that year's end preceding the great lull before the boom, when the rains were late in coming, the electric kiln was put to work because there wasn't enough space in the frames to dry all the cacao. It was the day after the end of harvest, when Beanpole could think of nothing but the Epiphany group, that Ranulfo died—dropped dead. The others were at the drying frames and troughs, and he had gone into the kiln to turn the cacao beans in their drawers to prevent them from burning. Rain clouds had been gathering since the night before, and now and then, despite the sun, there were small cloudbursts. "The fox is getting married," the women would say when it rained while the sun shone.

As Ranulfo was leaving at the end of his time in the kiln, the cloudburst hit before anyone could say a word. His mouth twisted, his body shuddered, and he fell in the doorway. Capi saw the scene from the troughs:

"Ranulfo dropped dead . . ."

The men left their work and came running. The overseer shouted to Beanpole:

"Go get the colonel . . ."

When they arrived, Ranulfo was already dead. Inside the kiln the cacao was sizzling. They stood around the dead man.

"He looks bad," said Irineu's daughter, who was eighteen and desired by all the men.

Colonel Frederico Pinto appeared. At the door of the plantation house stood his obese wife and their brood of children. The colonel gave orders:

"Turn off the motor, the cacao's frying. Quick, Mr. Tibúrcio . . ."

From inside the kiln came the sound of cacao burning and the colonel listened, frowning in annoyance. "That batch is ruined . . ."

And only after hearing the sound of the motor silenced did he turn to the dead man. The workers backed away, and only Irineu's daughter stood her ground, smiling at the colonel. Dona Augusta, Frederico's wife, appeared and asked:

"What happened?"

"Ranulfo dropped dead . . ."

Colonel Frederico Pinto looked at the dead man, at his open mouth and spasmodically contracted hands.

"Why the devil didn't he wait for the rain to stop?"

The cloudburst was over now and no one answered the colonel. Dona Augusta crossed herself, placing her body between her husband and Irineu's daughter, who moved away, her head hung.

"Uppity little nigger gal," she grumbled.

She felt sorry for the dead man, but her thoughts were on the mulatto girl with the firm breasts—Rita, Irineu's daughter. She knew what the girl was after: she wanted to throw herself at Frederico, sleep with him, have him set up a house for her in Pirangi.

"A piece of trash," she grumbled again.

Ranulfo's body was still where it had fallen. Tibúrcio returned on the run, and the colonel took his eyes away from the dead man.

"Take care of the cacao right away. Maybe it can be saved . . ."

Tibúrcio and two workers went into the kiln. Colonel Frederico Pinto told the workers:

"Back to the frames . . . This is no time for a wake . . ."

The men retired slowly. Capi looked behind and saw Ranulfo with his bulging eyes. Tibúrcio and the pair of workers came out of the kiln.

"The cacao's safe . . . Only a little burned . . ."

While the two men, with the help of Irineu's daughter, took away
the body, the overseer went to turn on the electric motor. He shouted
to Beanpole:

"Get in the kiln . . . Careful with the cacao . . ."

Colonel Frederico Pinto reiterated the caution:

"Careful with the cacao . . ."

The dead man was in the distance, carried by his arms and legs.
Suddenly, everything fell silent for a long minute. Then, from atop
the drying frames, the voice of Florindo rang through the fields in the
kiln-song lament:

> *"The oven did him in,*
> *The oven killed a man . . .*
> *Maneca died in the oven,*
> *It's all part of the plan . . ."*

Colonel Frederico Pinto turned, nimble and nervous. He ran his
handkerchief over his forehead and told his wife:

"Fortunately the cacao's safe . . ."

Florindo's voice lost itself among the cacao trees:

> *"Maneca died in the oven,*
> *Poor man, it happened all a-sudden!"*

9

Lunch was being served in the plantation house. Dona Augusta had rounded up all her children—except for the three boys and one girl who were studying in Bahia. Four of them were at the table. The black women brought in the platters from the kitchen. Colonel Frederico Pinto looked at his wife, thinking about Lola Espinola. There was a time—long past—when Dona Augusta had been a pretty and elegant girl. Over twenty years ago. Frederico had begun getting rich when he married her. Augusta's father had died, and she brought some lands with her to increase Frederico's capital. But the very first birth ruined her, and Dona Augusta started putting on weight, eventually becoming the monstrosity that contrasted so with her husband, who was small and wiry. Besides being fat, Dona Augusta was jealous, and it was her jealousy that had brought her to the plantation. When she was still living in Ilhéus, in one of the best houses on the avenue, all she could think about was her husband running around loose on the plantation, taking advantage of every young mulatto girl at an age to be ruined. She ended up coming to live on the plantation to keep an eye on Frederico and put an end to his debauchery with the workers' daughters. Colonel Frederico Pinto took little notice of his wife's attacks of jealousy. There on the plantation, napping in the afternoon in hammocks strung on the veranda, eating all the delicious food the black women could prepare, Dona Augusta became even fatter, a mountain of flesh repugnant in the colonel's sight.

At the table, eating stew, Frederico amuses himself thinking of the furor Augusta would raise if she knew he was sleeping with Lola. But his wife suspected nothing, knowing only vaguely of Pepe's existence, and for her it was nothing but gambling business; she knew that Frederico was crazy about a poker game, and she didn't mind.

"While he's playing he's not with other women . . ."

111

But if she should find out—what a scandal! It'd be horrible. She'd never stop talking about it, baring her soul to the servants, complaining to Tibúrcio, whimpering at night. It was a good thing she'd come to live on the plantation; that way she was removed from those evil tongues in Ilhéus, those old women with nothing to do but gossip and make life hell for other people. Not that Colonel Frederico Pinto really cared. Augusta could go to hell if she found out; he was not going to give up Lola. What a thought: give up Lola just to satisfy that elephant . . .

Ever since he had seen an elephant in the circus Frederico had never been able to think about his wife without recalling that strange animal. What restrained the colonel and prevented him from taking Lola for himself, setting her up with a place of her own and spending all his time with her, was the children, both those who were studying in Bahia and the young ones still at home. There were eight children; there had been twelve, but four had died while still small, with the exception of Carlos, who had succumbed to typhus during a vacation. Carlos was fourteen when he died, the eldest of them all. If it weren't for his children Frederico would do something crazy, such was his indifference to what others might say . . . And it was enough to sleep one night with his wife to make a child . . . Augusta took no precautions and in reality had no desire to avoid the children that came every year . . . Now it was they who kept the colonel tied to his home and to his wife, who prevented him from breaking off with everything and taking Lola away from Pepe.

Dona Augusta eats in silence. She too is mulling over thoughts. She thinks about Frederico, the children, the plantations. She thinks about Rita, the drover Irineu's daughter. The stupid little thing was throwing herself at the colonel; anyone could see that . . . And he was naturally encouraging her . . . Irineu was no doubt helping things along, dying to see his daughter in bed with the colonel, money flowing, the family moving to Pirangi, extra money every week in the drover's account . . . She was throwing herself at him; anyone could see that . . . Those pointed breasts, that straightened hair, that coquettish smile . . . Dona Augusta is angry; her food won't go down. The children fight at the table, each claiming a better piece of meat. Dona Augusta complains angrily. Why is Frederico laughing?

Finally she can no longer contain herself and says:

"You think I don't know?"

A slight start disturbs the colonel's thoughts. Does she know something?

"Know what?"

"Everybody's talking about it . . . That daughter of Irineu's . . ."

"Drop it, woman . . ."

"Maybe you haven't noticed yet, but . . ."

"But what?"

"All that's missing is for her to rub up against you. And naturally you encourage it . . ."

Frederico laughs.

"Drop it . . . You and your damned jealousy . . . I haven't even looked at the woman . . . Drop it . . ."

At the living room door Rita, Irineu's daughter, appears. Dona Augusta's face contorts with rage.

"What do you want?"

The girl smiles shyly.

"I wanted to know if the colonel's wife could lend us two candles to light at the feet of the deceased . . ."

For the first time, Frederico looks closely at the young girl. If it weren't for Lola it would be worthwhile to spend some time with Rita. She wasn't all that bad looking. But he had a beautiful and refined woman and had no need to go back to mulatto girls from the fields. Dona Augusta's voice is harsh:

"We don't have any candles . . . Black people don't need candles or coffins . . . What a strange idea . . ."

"It was for the wake," said Rita, surprised. "Nobody ever begrudged a candle for a dead person."

Only then did Dona Augusta remember the dead man with the bulging eyes. A sudden shudder runs through her fat body.

"Go away . . . I'll send Esmeralda with the candles in a little while . . ."

Rita smiles.

"May God reward you . . ."

Dona Augusta turned to Frederico:

"Didn't I tell you? She invented that business with the candles just to come up here . . ."

The colonel laughs again.

"Drop it . . . She came for candles and you almost denied her the charity . . ."

He thought for a moment, confused thoughts.

"Charity never hurt anybody . . . We ought to do good to the poor . . ."

Dona Augusta tried to make excuses:

"I'm going to send the candles . . . I just didn't want to give them to that little flirt."

Tibúrcio came to the door, begging their pardon:

"All the cacao is safe, Colonel . . ."

Frederico turned to his wife.

"Send a bottle of rum to the wake too. They might not have the money to buy any . . ."

10

The shade in the fields is soft and sweet, like a caress. The cacao trees enclose themselves in large leaves that turn yellow in the sun. The branches seek out one another and embrace in the air, seemingly a single tree climbing and descending the hillside, its topaz shadow going on for hundreds and hundreds of yards. Everything in a cacao field is a shade of yellow, where, at times, green violently bursts forth. The tiny ants covering the tree's leaves, destroying the blight that threatens the fruit, are blondish yellow. The flowers and new leaves, which the sun dapples with burnt yellow, are a faded yellow. Yellow are the early fruits that withered from the excessive heat. The ripe fruits recall golden lamps in ancient cathedrals, shining with brilliant resplendence in the sun's rays as they penetrate the shadows of the fields. A yellow snake—the *papa-pinto*—lies in the sun on the path worn by the workers' feet. And even the earth, clay that summer has transformed into dust, has a vague yellow tone that sticks to and colors the naked legs of the blacks and mulattoes who work to prune the cacao trees.

From the ripe pods spills an uncertain golden light that softly illuminates small corners of the fields. The sunlight filtering through the leaves sketches yellow columns of dust that rise in the air toward the branches and are lost above, beyond the highest leaves. The kinkajous, monkeys that plant cacao, leap noisily from branch to branch, staining the gold of cacao trees with their dirty, lackluster yellow. The *papa-pinto* awakens and stretches its yolk-colored back, looking like a flexible metal bar. Its covetous yellow eyes stare at the happy and frolicsome band of passing monkeys. Drops of sunlight fall through the trees. They explode into rays on the ground, and where they fall upon puddles of water, turn the color of a tea rose. As if a rain of topazes were falling from the sky, turning the ground of burning dust into tea rose petals. In the tranquillity of morning in the cacao fields can be found every shade of yellow.

And when a light breeze blows, that entire sea of yellow sways, the tones blend together, creating a new yellow, the yellow of cacao fields, the most beautiful in the world! A yellow that only the people of Ilhéus see during the days of the summer lull. There are no words to describe it, no image with which to compare it. It is a yellow beyond compare, the yellow of cacao fields!

The Rains

1

Carlos Zude stopped in front of the poet, who was alone in the meeting room of the Ilhéus Commercial Association. He extended his hand, smiling his friendly smile.

"Good evening, Mr. Sérgio."

"Good evening."

Carlos Zude could feel the poet's pride like something tangible. It hung there almost visible in the air of the room, hurting like a pinprick. It was curious how that bothered Carlos Zude, despite the total disdain he felt for Sérgio Moura. Sérgio was beyond doubt a good executive secretary and always kept his work in order, but there were dozens of young men like him, all capable of doing the same service for a good salary. It did not occur to Carlos Zude that his pride came from his verses, since to him verses were worthless. Carlos Zude considered every kind of art a useless invention of the idle. He was suspicious of anyone who wrote, painted, or sculpted. It wasn't the same ignorance held by the colonels, so easily transformed into respect. The colonels disdained artists until they gained recognition. Then they began to respect them and admire them from afar. Carlos Zude was beyond the concept of recognition. He had a set idea about art: "a waste of time." Only recent revolutionary events, in which so many writers were involved, led him to consider that perhaps it was a dangerous waste of time. But he exempted poets from his idea of dangerous. They were just bums, worthless bums. And since Sérgio Moura was a hard worker and always kept the association's paperwork in order (Carlos Zude was president of the Ilhéus Commercial Association), Carlos never remembered that Sérgio Moura wrote verses that were published in the papers in Rio. He thought he was more of a dilettante. A weakness of the executive secretary. He disdained Sérgio with the same natural disdain that he had for anyone who worked for a salary. But this disdain did not prevent Carlos Zude from being the friendliest person in the world with his subordinates. He was incapable of raising his voice, of shouting, of making a violent complaint. But he still disdained them; they belonged to another world. His world was that of great businessmen, of exporters, of large plantation owners, a world that granted admission only to the managers who owned stock in the firms.

Why then did he feel the poet's pride hitting him in the face like a slap? He felt it, that was all. It was there, filling the room, in Sérgio's hieratic attitude, as he stood there, his face serene as he awaited the exporter's orders. It was such a concrete thing that Carlos didn't know what to say; he felt annoyed, and to some extent angry. Still, there was nothing to be criticized in Sérgio's attitude. He stood before Carlos, looking at him, the papers for the meeting on the table. Maybe it was the flower, a rosebud that the poet held in his right hand. That struck him as an insult. Why an insult? Confused, Carlos doesn't know what to do with his hands. To top it off, Julieta invited this guy to their party tomorrow. An exclusive party for a small group, only their closest friends—and she invites Sérgio . . . What the devil could she see in him? Women are really impossible to understand. Nobody in the world can understand them . . . The poet twirls the rosebud in his hand; he really is insufferable. Carlos Zude opens his mouth to speak—his wish was to say something sarcastic and cutting—but the phrase doesn't come out. He says nothing; Carlos is the negation of irony. Why the blazes did Julieta invite the guy?

The entrance of Schwartz, who managed the interests of an export house with German capital, was greeted by Carlos with such exaggerated joy that it startled even Schwartz himself.

"My dear Schwartz! How are you? It's been so long . . ." And he gave him a strong embrace.

Schwartz said hello to Sérgio:

"And the poet, how is he? And those verses?" He spoke in a tortuous style, and besides that, had never read a single verse of Sérgio's. Schwartz didn't read anything published in Brazil, though he read widely in German—poets and nebulous philosophers. His favorite author was Nietzsche, and the German often said that Nietzsche helped him bear life in Ilhéus. A well-groomed and still-young man, he had been in the city a relatively short time. He had come directly from Germany to replace the Jew who had previously administered the firm.

Only then could Carlos Zude ask:

"Everything ready for the meeting, Mr. Sérgio?"

The unbearable poet raised the rosebud.

"Everything, even the whiskey."

"Very good, very good," Schwartz said happily. "Whiskey is more necessary than anything . . ."

What Carlos wanted to know about was the reports he had sent from his office. They were there, on the table, in the spot that Carlos would occupy, the head. The poet pointed with the rose. It was enough to provoke a fight. Carlos Zude made an effort to control his nerves; he needed every ounce of calmness for tonight's meeting. The two Rauschnings arrived, followed immediately by Reicher. Antônio Ribeiro was the last to arrive. Schwartz filled the blue-tinted glasses with whiskey.

They seated themselves around the large table. It was a solid group of men who above all else gave the impression of cleanliness. Their suits were of heavy cashmere, their shoes were expensive, their shirts were silk. They gave the impression of power. Pencil in hand, the rosebud resting on the papers, Sérgio Moura was seated at the other end of the table, opposite Carlos Zude. The latter looked at the rosebud that colored with blood the whiteness of the paper where the poet would jot his notes. After a short silence, Carlos turned his gaze, looked at Reicher, the least powerful of the exporters, and said:

"I called you here, gentlemen, for a matter of utmost importance—"

"Should I take notes?" the poet interjected.

Carlos had to turn to look at him, and the rosebud pursued him once again. That was something he hadn't considered: should the proceedings of the meeting be written down? No, they shouldn't.

"No . . ."

He looked at Reicher again.

"First, however, I want to advise that I represent here not only my own thinking but that of Karbanks as well . . ."

The exporters exchanged glances. One of the Rauschnings tapped his brother on the knee to call his attention. Sérgio also leaned forward in a gesture of interest. Carlos stretched his legs under the chair; the sensation of uneasiness provoked by the poet's pride was beginning to dissipate.

"I believe we can speak frankly," he said, and the sensation of discomfort left his chest entirely. The poet was once again in his place as an insignificant employee. Carlos at first had thought of asking him to leave; they wouldn't need him at the meeting. But now he preferred that Sérgio stay, so he could realize Carlos's strength, see what he represented and what he was capable of. He merely advised:

"Don't take notes, Mr. Sérgio . . ."

"Fine." And the poet again picked up the rosebud and twirled it in his thin white hand.

Carlos Zude spoke in measured tones. His impression was that he was murdering Sérgio.

"Karbanks and I have come to the conclusion that we should raise the price of cacao."

He paused, waiting for the reaction that his words should produce. But they sat silently, except that one of the Rauschnings nudged the other in the stomach. Finally Antônio Ribeiro, speaking for everyone, asked for further explanation. He frankly didn't understand the reason for an increase in prices.

Carlos Zude first stretched out in the chair, then sat erect, with the air of one about to say definitive things or give a lesson. Without knowing why, he looked at the poet and spoke to him.

"You gentlemen are aware that the crop in the Republic of Ecuador was destroyed by blight . . . And you also surely know that after the Gold Coast and Brazil—"

"Ecuador is the largest exporter of cacao . . ." Reicher interrupted.

Carlos took his eyes off Sérgio and looked at Reicher with a certain disapproval.

"Not only that . . . There's a more important fact to note in Ecuador's lost crop . . ."

"What's that?" asked Antônio Ribeiro.

The Rauschnings were following attentively, and Schwartz was making an effort to penetrate the hidden meaning in Carlos Zude's words. What could be behind all this? Was this Brazilian, with unmistakable vestiges of black blood in his thick lips and his cheeks, trying to put one over on them, get them involved in a deal where only he and the American would show a profit? Carlos Zude refused the São Félix cigar offered by one of the Rauschnings; he didn't smoke. He cleared his throat and began to talk.

"All of us are in cacao up to our necks. That's our business, and that's where our interests lie. Isn't that right?"

The Rauschnings nodded. Schwartz, intrigued and wary, made no gesture at all. Reicher grunted in agreement. Only Antônio Ribeiro spoke.

"That's for sure."

The poet sniffed the rosebud. He too was intrigued and remembered at that moment Joaquim's dramatic gesture, and in his ears rang, like some tragic verse, the word the driver had flung into the room: "Imperialism!"

Carlos's hands (who can control a poet's fantasy?) began to turn into dragon's claws. They multiplied themselves above the reports and the data—figures, figures, and more figures in front of the exporter. Carlos Zude raised himself higher in his chair. Now his legs were no longer extended. Just the opposite; his trunk bent over the table and his words seemed to move over it—or at least that's how the poet saw them. Carlos continued:

"Since this is an established truth, I now ask you: what security do we have?"

Carlos seemed like a professor, a young professor, for his attitude had rejuvenated him, and the others were somewhat confused. The poet (the only one Carlos wanted to crush) thought that Zude was doing a bad job of explaining. Sérgio had already begun to penetrate Carlos's thinking but felt that the others still hadn't caught on. Despite his attitude, the exporter was himself confused and didn't know how to explain.

Carlos repeated the question emphatically:

"But what security do we have?"

"What do you mean, security?" Reicher asked.

Schwartz closed his eyes; he was also beginning to understand and felt more at ease. He too had been thinking of such things but had thus far lacked the courage to bring them to fruition.

"Yes," Carlos said, "what kind of security? We buy cacao and sell it abroad. Some of our firms are themselves foreign, and that's where their capital comes from. And what does that capital rest upon? Where's our security?" He took his eyes from the poet and looked around. The poet sniffed the rosebud, and Carlos Zude would have liked to call him effeminate, even though he wasn't, just to insult him and burst that air of superiority.

"It so happens, gentlemen, that our security, our capital, our money"— he repeated—"our money, all depend exclusively on a handful of colonels and some yokels who own a few fields . . And that they take care of those fields and plantations as they should. In case you gentlemen aren't aware of this, I'm here to inform you . . ."

He removed some newspaper clippings from among the papers:

"These are from Buenos Aires. A bit old, but no matter. What's important is the information . . ." He was undecided for a moment, not knowing whether to ask the poet to translate the clippings. Finally he decided not to give him the satisfaction. "I don't need to have them translated, since I know what they say. This first one"—he held up a newspaper clipping glued to a sheet of paper—"tells of the bankruptcy of the largest exporter in Ecuador." He dropped the paper on the table and looked at those present. "The loss of the crop, the lack of business, having to absorb the plantation owners' losses, bankruptcy . . ."

He held the other clipping in his hand and tried to read a name.

"Sr. Julio Remigez—another exporter—committed suicide. At the start of the crop he had bought a large amount of cacao against future delivery, tens of thousands of kilos. He didn't receive the cacao. He put a bullet in his head . . ."

Antônio Ribeiro whistled; he was frightened. Reicher also felt a bit uneasy. The Rauschnings exchanged glances; they too were beginning to understand. This Carlos Zude was a genius . . . Schwartz felt calm now, not even noticing Carlos's thick lips and prominent cheeks, features recalling the black blood that must run in his veins. The poet saw the dragon growing, filling the room once again. Now the men around the table began to form a single body, the monstrous body of some fantastic animal.

"Gentlemen, I think—and Karbanks shares my thinking—we should raise prices . . . From what I've learned, the Gold Coast crop won't be large this year either. Drought has hurt the trees there, and there's going to be a shortage of cacao. It's an excellent year to begin raising prices . . ."

"But—" said Antônio Ribeiro, who didn't understand.

"Speak up," ordered the voice of Carlos Zude.

"But . . . a boom does us very little good. Between the prices we pay the growers and what they pay us in New York, our share is almost the same; the profit difference is minimal . . . In addition, we'll be tying up a lot more capital . . . I don't see the advantage, or what it has to do with the question of security . . ."

Carlos Zude looked pityingly at the exporter. Then he looked at Schwartz and the Rauschnings. Those foreigners surely understood; they weren't stupid like Antônio Ribeiro. Seeing that the Germans did understand and approve, he smiled with satisfaction. The poet saw the dragon smiling, a lethal smile. Carlos spoke in the same calm voice:

"It's self-evident . . . The boom will doubtless entail a great investment of capital . . ."

"The plantation owners are going to get rich; they'll be even stronger . . ."

"That's true. The plantations are going to appreciate tremendously. That's what we should hope for. Because afterwards . . ."

He paused before speaking the words:

"Will come the bust . . ."

The elder Rauschning couldn't resist; he applauded. Antônio Ribeiro still didn't fully understand. He was a man who had been lucky in business and opened an export house; he was just starting out in commercial life.

"I don't really understand . . ."

Then the elder Rauschning, a white-haired man with soft blue eyes, took the floor and began explaining, slowly and calmly, giving examples: a plantation producing, say, fifteen thousand kilos is worth so much today, and the boom will make it quadruple in value, and with the bust it'll be worth eight times less. He provided numbers; it was all so clear that there was no way to misunderstand. Antônio Ribeiro felt an unusual joy.

"How far do we raise it?"

"However far we have to," said Carlos. "And we'll lower it as far as we have to . . ."

Then he asked:

"Are we all in agreement?"

Everyone agreed, and they hailed him enthusiastically. Carlos Zude looked at the poet Sérgio Moura, his flower abandoned, having wilted over the hours. Carlos couldn't resist; he gave a half smile of victory. It was only then that the poet sensed that immense wave of hatred. But he merely reddened slightly and bit his lower lip. He no longer saw a dragon but a man laughing, which was even more hateful. Carlos accepted the whiskey that Schwartz poured into his glass.

"And when the exporters are also plantation owners, we won't be dependent on whether or not the colonels decide to prune their fields or whether or not the small growers have the money to do so . . ."

Schwartz confirmed with a curt, sharp gesture.

"We'll bring some order to this," and he lifted his glass in a toast. The poet saw their faces through the blue glass of the tumblers; they looked like strange and terrible beings. Triumphant, Carlos Zude dismissed Sérgio, saying in the most friendly of tones:

"Good night, Mr. Sérgio. Sleep well, and don't forget to show up tomorrow."

They all left, but in the room remained that atmosphere of expensive cigars, grave and fine scents, of cleanliness and money. The poet felt it entering his nose with such violence that he took the rosebud and breathed the last of the perfume in the flower, the perfume of a wild garden.

2

When the last bus departed, at 9 P.M., for Itabuna, Marinho Santos left the agency for the Ilhéus Café, where the usual circle was already waiting for him. From there they would go to the cabaret or the bordellos. Except for Martins, Zude's manager, who of late was involved with a woman who stitched cacao sacks; her name was Rosa and she was a real beauty. Reinaldo Bastos, a young employee from the Zude office, was there, as well as Zito Ferreira, a long-haired part-time poet, director of a weekly humor magazine and a chronic sponger. Also present was Gumercindo Bessa, one of the directors of the Commercial Employees Association (Martins was president), an inveterate member of the gang who seldom showed up since becoming an Integralist. He had changed his scene, busy with Silveirinha, and when he did appear it was only briefly, in an effort to lure the others into Integralism through preachments that almost always ended in arguments. Zito, who despite his physical and intellectual decadence, his heavy drinking and his cynicism, preserved a degree of independence, would ridicule him, the fascist movement, and its speeches and rallies. On a certain occasion Gumercindo took offense and tried to start a fight, and Marinho Santos and Martins had to intervene. Since then he had rarely come to the café. The word around the city was that it wouldn't be long before he was manager at Schwartz's, where he worked.

Marinho Santos sat down.

"A beer, good and cold . . ."

The others were already having a beer. The owner of the bus company greeted Gumercindo in particular.

"How are you, Mr. Gumé? Good to see you . . . You're really the big man these days . . ."

Gumercindo opened his mouth to reply, but Reinaldo Bastos was dying to repeat the phrase he had heard that morning from Carlos Zude and was palming off as his own:

"They're like frightened children . . ."

"A good image," repeated Zito Ferreira. (It was the third time he had repeated his praise and he made a mental note to increase the bite he was planning to put on Reinaldo from five to twenty mil-réis.)

"Who?" asked Marinho Santos. "Who's innocent in this land of know-it-alls?"

"We were talking about the colonels, the plantation owners . . ." clarified Martins. Conspiratorial and fearful, he revealed another secret: "The exporters are united . . . There's going to be a price increase, a big one . . ."

Marinho Santos put down his glass of beer. His eyes widened.

"That's what I thought . . ."

"Today we're closing at nineteen and a half, against future delivery. Tomorrow we'll close at twenty . . . Later, who can say? I don't doubt it'll hit twenty-five . . ."

Marinho Santos asked for details:

"Explain it clearly . . ."

"Certainly . . . Mr. Carlos arrived from Bahia today. He came by plane. He'd been talking with Karbanks. He was happier than a troupe of clowns. As soon as he arrived, he raised prices. Then he set up a meeting of the exporters for today, at the Commercial Association . . ."

"The one who ought to know what's going on is Sérgio Moura," said Zito.

Hearing the hated name, Gumercindo grimaced in disapproval.

"Don't mention that bag of pus in my presence . . ."

Zito laughed.

"You're really mad, aren't you!"

Seeing no further opportunity to repeat "his" great phrase, Reinaldo Bastos felt vaguely displeased and drank his beer joylessly.

"So prices are going to go up?" Marinho Santos repeated the question, but now only to himself. He was making plans to buy another bus, maybe some trucks. "There's going to be money all over the place . . ."

Reinaldo Bastos was looking for the chance to repeat the phrase. It wasn't his, true, it was Carlos Zude's, but nobody knew that. Not even Reinaldo Bastos himself remembered, at the moment, that the image didn't belong to him. He had carried it around in his head all day, turned it over, changed the word order—"frightened children, that's what they're like"—even replaced the word "frightened" with "innocent" but didn't like the result and ended up using the phrase just as he had heard it that morning from the boss's mouth. He chose his moment well, when a large group was present. It was a success. Zito Ferreira had waxed enthusiastic:

"Yes sir . . . What an image!"

Now Reinaldo waits impatiently for another opportunity.

"It's going to be a big crop . . ." said Martins. "The rain is on its way . . ."

Marinho Santos looked at the sky, craning his neck toward the door of the bar. Clouds were accumulating. They ordered beer.

"The colonels will have money to burn . . ." said Zito.

Reinaldo was about to use the phrase but Gumercindo cut him off.

"There's nothing of frightened children in them. They're sharks . . ."

"Sharks?" Reinaldo Bastos's mouth dropped in surprise.

Zito Ferreira swallowed his beer and said:

"Whether they're sharks or frightened children, it's to them that we owe the progress of this zone. They conquered the land, planted cacao, killed people, built cities . . . They're our heroes . . ."

Gumercindo shouted angrily:

"Heroes . . . Progress . . . If you say they're responsible for the backwardness of Ilhéus I'll agree. It's the truth."

"Responsible how?" asked Zito.

The others were interested, even Reinaldo Bastos. An argument between Zito and Gumercindo ("a couple of real brains," as Reinaldo would say) was something worth hearing.

"They're men without culture, even when it comes to cacao," Gumercindo began explaining, his voice still rather angry. "They're backwards in politics, demo-liberals"—he emphasized the word—"and don't even know how to take care of their own plantations. You want to know something? Colonel Horácio harvests his seven hundred and fifty thousand kilos of cacao, right? I know because he's our customer." (He said "our" as if he were a partner in Schwartz's firm.) "Seven hundred and fifty thousand kilos—"

"That's a devil of a lot of cacao . . ." Marinho Santos interrupted.

Gumercindo Bessa assumed an air of triumph.

"And do you know how much he could harvest if he took good care of his fields technically, using modern methods?"

The others waited.

"At least a million two hundred thousand . . ."

"You're kidding . . ." said Zito.

"The gospel truth. Just the other day Mr. Schwartz was explaining it to Silveirinha. Point by point . . . A million two hundred thousand, twice the present amount . . ."

"In any case," Zito replied, "it wouldn't be either Schwartz or

Silveirinha, who as you know is a weakling, to tame the wilderness and plant cacao in the wild old days. It was people like Horácio, my friend, who had the guts . . . Heroes . . . What you say about the current production of the fields may or may not be true; I have no way of knowing. Let's say it is, for the sake of argument . . ."

"Not for the sake of argument. It's true . . ."

"Fine. Let's say it's true . . . But, who conquered the land, who was it that shed their blood for the progress of Ilhéus?"

Without waiting for an answer, he continued:

"If there were any gratitude in this world, they'd have already erected a statue to the colonels, to the great colonels, to Horácio, my friend, to Horácio . . ."

Zito could feel the admiration around him. He was beginning to get drunk, as well as sentimental; this always ended with him declaiming his verses.

Marinho Santos was worried about the price increase.

"So cacao's going up, is it? Yes sir, it's going to be a serious matter . . ."

Colonel Maneca Dantas, who had arrived that evening from his plantation, was passing by in the street. He still had on his mud-caked riding boots and was strolling about the city, alone and with an abstracted air, looking at the menacing sky. He was half laughing as he went, his hat in his hand, his head almost totally covered with white hair. He dragged his feet a bit, talking softly to himself, doing some calculations about the crop. Gumercindo pointed to him.

"There's one of your heroes . . . Looks more like some crazy man . . ."

Reinaldo Bastos thought this was the time:

"They're like frightened children . . ."

"A good image . . ." (*I'll take him for at least twenty*, Zito thought.)

Marinho Santos suggested:

"Shall we go to the cabaret? To celebrate the news of the increase . . ."

At the end of the street, Colonel Maneca Dantas looked to see if he could spot his son, Rui the attorney. He hadn't seen him since he arrived, and he wanted to speak with him. The group passed by the colonel.

"Good evening, Colonel . . ."

"Good evening . . ."

And, looking at the sky:

"It's going to rain, isn't it? The crop . . ."

But the others were already in the distance, and he muttered the rest to himself.

3

The group split up at the cabaret door. Gumercindo went off in search of Silveirinha, with whom he had some political matters to discuss. Martins went after Rosa, who must be waiting for him. He had a woman of his own and thus no reason to be there. Besides which, Carlos Zude wouldn't like his manager to be seen frequenting a gambling house.

"A manager has responsibilities . . . He's not just any employee."

Reinaldo Bastos went in with Marinho Santos and Zito but, not finding the opportunity to make use of his great phrase, soon left. He preferred to go to the avenue, where he might run into his girlfriend strolling with other young women—a new public for whom the image was still fresh. He promised to return shortly. But just to be on the safe side, Zito got the twenty mil-réis from him:

"I'll double it at roulette . . ."

On the avenue, where elegant young people strolled, couples courted, and groups of friends talked, Reinaldo Bastos did not find the young woman he was looking for. He walked the entire length of the avenue, needing to tell his phrase to someone, anyone. And by a coincidence that would unsettle his entire life, Reinaldo Bastos told it to Julieta Zude.

He was walking rather glumly along the avenue when he met Julieta, who was talking with Guni, sitting on one of the marble benches by the sidewalk. Both were yawning, having run out of conversation, and Julieta was still filled with neurasthenia and fatigue. She had come to the avenue in hope of seeing Sérgio strolling by; the poet was in the habit of walking alone along the beach, dispensing rare greetings and enjoying the sea air. Only after she was already on the avenue did Julieta remember the exporters' meeting. Sérgio would be there, acting as secretary. He would be directly across from Carlos; the thought amused her. That's how Guni found her. The two sat there talking but the subject quickly exhausted itself. Guni, who was thin and constantly in a state of excitement, ranked the men who passed by. She was the subject of much talk in the city, and it was said that (on a visit with her husband to a plantation) she'd even been to bed with workers. In reality the deep eyes of the Swedish woman revealed a sexual appetite that gave rise to the rumors. Julieta was tired, feeling a weight on her body.

When they spotted the young and athletic Reinaldo Bastos, Guni wanted to know who he was. She bit her lips in a gesture of desire.

"He works for the firm," Julieta explained.

"A good-looking man . . ."

That was why, when Reinaldo passed by and greeted them with a ringing "good evening," Julieta called him over. He stood there in front of the bench, quite awkward at first, then more at ease. Julieta encouraged him and laughed; anything, she thought, would do as a distraction. Guni eagerly flirted with Reinaldo, but he had eyes only for the boss's wife and imputed a special meaning to each of her smiles, to each innocent sentence. Reinaldo had an extremely low opinion of all those rich women and was sure, albeit a bit frightened by the thought, that Julieta was interested in him.

Dragging his feet, Colonel Maneca Dantas appeared on the avenue, his smile unwavering, his eyes on the heavens that were darkening with clouds. A cold wind, heralding rain, came from the sea. When the colonel said, "Good evening, Dona Julieta," Reinaldo glittered with the phrase:

"They're like frightened children . . ."

"Who?" Guni asked.

"The colonels . . ." And Reinaldo mixed what he had heard from Zito and Gumercindo into an explanation that the women listened to smilingly.

A vendor passed by and Reinaldo offered them ice cream, fumbling awkwardly for coins with which to pay. For Julieta it was all a diversion: the timidity mixed with desire on the part of Carlos's employee, the sentences with their double meanings, the desire to show off, the deliberate choice of long words . . . Guni saw none of this, only an athlete standing before her, with a young body made for love. But Reinaldo never took his eyes off Julieta.

There was a moment when Julieta became uncomfortable with the situation. In front of the group passed young men and women, colonels and businessmen. All were walking along the avenue to take advantage of the breeze from the ocean. They looked at the young man standing before the bench, proud of being seen with Julieta Zude and Guni Gerson. Now and then a spiteful comment punctuated the dialogue of

passersby. Reinaldo smiled at those he knew; tomorrow he would have
much to recount at the Commercial Employees Association dance. But
a group of young women came by, among them Reinaldo's girlfriend
(almost his fiancée; all that was missing was the formal proposal). Her
name was Zuleika and she thought at first that her boyfriend was there
explaining something, at Julieta's request. She passed by at just the
moment when Reinaldo was explaining his theory about the colonels,
and he didn't see her. Zuleika bit her lips when Caçula, a friend who
was with her, affirmed:

"He didn't see you . . . He's really wrapped up in his conversation . . ."

They returned from the midpoint of the avenue. This time Zuleika
said in a strong voice:

"Good evening . . ."

Reinaldo was startled, and Julieta grasped the situation immediately.
It amused her. The group stopped a little way farther along, Zuleika
apparently thinking that Reinaldo was going to talk to her. The young
man was uneasy and lost his train of thought. That was when the ice
cream vendor approached:

"Don't you want to offer us an ice cream?" Julieta asked.

"Oh!" He called the vendor in a loud voice, afraid he wouldn't
hear.

The young women in the group whispered and laughed. They remained
where they were, waiting. From the group someone called:

"Ice cream man, over here!"

They were silent for a minute. Julieta and Guni ran their fine tongues
over the small container of ice cream, the Swede smacking her lips. The
vendor returned and spoke with Reinaldo.

"The young ladies said you'd pay . . ."

Julieta laughed, and Reinaldo turned red, again searched for coins,
but found none. He attempted an explanation, but also found none. The
women in the group laughed, vaguely sensing a scandal. Julieta wasn't
enjoying it and was mildly put out; the neurasthenia was coming back,
the impression that all of this was silly and ridiculous. Guni had no
idea what was happening.

"Your girlfriend is angry . . ." Julieta said.

She's jealous, Reinaldo thought, happy at the idea that Julieta would
feel jealousy over him. He began to explain that there was nothing
between him and Zuleika, nothing important, when Julieta interrupted:

"We have to go . . . We don't want to cause a fight between you
and your girl."

They got up, said good-bye, and left. Reinaldo watched them go,
elegant and superior, women from another world. He was happy; Julieta's

last sentence had struck him as little short of a declaration of love. *She'll look back*, he thought as he waited for her form to disappear at the door of the mansion. She didn't, but he found an explanation for it in the fact that in Ilhéus people talked about everything. Only then did he go over to Zuleika's group, ready to make a scene:

"So you can't even talk with a lady? What backward people we have in this land . . ."

But as he approached, the group left, in long strides, turning their backs on him. Reinaldo stood there, ill at ease. The ice cream vendor complained:

"Where's my money?"

Afterwards Reinaldo was alone, with his brilliant phrase and the image of Julieta. "I might as well go to the cabaret," he grumbled to himself. Colonel Maneca Dantas was coming back down the avenue with the dragging footsteps of an old man:

"It's going to rain, young man, a big crop . . ."

4

The lights of the city shone, electric bulbs tearing through the water that now fell in a heavy rain, in large downpours. The rain had begun falling at 10:30, announced by thunder that growled from behind the hills. The last stars disappeared from the Ilhéus sky, and the droplets began like small, intermittent stones. The men who were talking in the street ran for home, bars, or cabarets. The rain got heavier, a violent torrent washing away the detritus of a working day in the city of cacao. The floodwater that formed beside the walkways swept along the most sundry things: pieces of receipts, empty matchboxes, cigarette butts, a small ladies' handkerchief with its edges upward, floating like a white boat.

In the downtown area, on the avenues by the sea, on the dockside streets lined with bars, there was plenty of lighting; the shafts of light pointed the way for those who were rushing indoors. But as the city made its way toward the hillsides the lights became fewer, the posts more distant one from the other, and they were no longer those elegant, powerful, polished steel posts with three electric bulbs that graced the avenues; they were tall wooden poles with a single minuscule light on top. They barely lighted a yard on either side, pools of light in the blackness made even darker by the rain. From the hillside descended recently formed streams of dirty red water that soaked the slopes leading up Conquest Hill, where the factory workers' houses swayed. Identical streams descended Unhão Hill, where washerwomen and maritime workers lived. And beyond all that was Snake Island, where the poorest of all lived, those who couldn't afford even a shanty on Conquest or Unhão. Snake Island, with its straw shacks, its adobe walls, a place where the people of Ilhéus never took the tourists who flew in with an interest in learning about the cacao culture. It was the lowest area of the city, as well as the poorest. And because a part of the nearby hill had been removed to make room for the new streets of the modern district next to the railroad, Snake Island had no defense against storms. The residents used to say that in the rainy season the district was totally cut off from the rest of the city. Thus it had been given the name Snake Island. It not only was surrounded by water but flooded as well, with the water inside the houses making it island and lake at the same time. All the water that flowed through the city ended up there, flooding Snake Island. And it dragged with it the red clay left over from the demolished hill; the tortuous streets became a viscous sea of mud, terrible to cross. A few poles illuminated that dirty red orgy, a strange color that many of the inhabitants of the clean city didn't even know existed. A scattering of electric bulbs shone inside a few shacks. In most, however, the flickering red light of lamps cast more shadow than brightness on the walls. Here, in Snake Island, lived highway workers, many railroad workers, some from the chocolate factory, porters and stevedores from the docks. In a speech someone had once called Snake Island the "red district," a reference not to the color of the houses and ground but to its dwellers' sentiments. No Integralist would dare set foot in Snake Island, even during the day. There was a famous story: once, at the beginning of the Integralist movement, the Green Shirts had decided to hold a rally on Sunday afternoon for the workers of Snake Island. A speaker, a journalist, had come from Bahia, and the Integralists entered the district marching four abreast and singing their anthems. In their green shirts with the sigma emblem they stopped in the small square in the middle of the island, raised their hands and shouted *"Anauê."* The workers gathered and surrounded the improvised rostrum. The rally began, but got no further. The chronicles tell that they left in a forced march ("a frenzied flight," said the poet Sérgio Moura) minutes later, the majority without their green shirts, while the mud-stained few that still wore them hastily tore them off. A few were left wearing only their undershorts. The truth is that the workers had taken over the entrances to the streets leading to Snake Island once the Integralists had passed. And when they started catching it at the rally and tried to retreat to the city, they found to their surprise the workers guarding the entrances to the streets, armed with brooms ("the weapon you use to shoo chickens," Joaquim had said). They say that Black Roberto, a stevedore who had once been a sailor, with every swing of the broom against the head of an Integralist shook Snake Island with his shout: "Down with Integralism!"

The poet Sérgio Moura also related that on that day, which marked the beginning of fighting in the streets between leftists and fascists, he ran into a young Integralist, an acquaintance by the name of Nestor, much given to reading, still running like crazy through the downtown area. His shirt was gone, his pants stained with red clay, and there were broom marks on his face, not to mention an expression of enormous fright. With some difficulty the poet managed to stop him and ask, with his usual thirst for anything new:

"What's going on?"

The Integralist took a deep breath before explaining:

"They're killing the young people of Ilhéus . . ."

Sérgio wasn't satisfied with the answer and pressed for details. The young man told him what had happened. (Later the Integralists would call him naive, since according to them it was Sérgio who planned and prepared the reception, which in fact wasn't so.)

The half-dressed Nestor narrated the dramatic details, broomsticks turning into rifles and dozens of workers changing to thousands of murderers. Sérgio expressed his distress and disapproval, then wondered:

"But why didn't you stay there, fighting for your ideals?"

The Integralist, according to Sérgio, replied:

"I can't die. I know a lot of Brazilian history!"

It may be that this anecdote, which circulated throughout the cacao zone, is nothing but a fabrication of the poet Sérgio Moura. It may very well be. But the truth is that the Integralists, shooed away by brooms, never returned, not in groups, much less singly, to Snake Island. Not even on those days when the police penetrated the district to make arrests. Not even when Joaquim and sixteen others were hauled away in a truck transformed into a "paddy wagon" and the police considered Snake Island rid of extremists. Not even on those days of terror for the district did the Integralists dare to venture into those streets. In their rallies, held downtown, they always recalled that "heroic date" when, as they told it, "a small group of patriots was attacked by hundreds of killers." Once Nestor himself gave a lovely speech on the subject, in which he, as a connoisseur of Brazilian history, compared the date to the most glorious in the country's past. In Snake Island, in commemoration of the date and the event, there had remained a green shirt covered with red clay, which had been hoisted onto a pole where it still stood, transformed into a colorless rag flapping in the wind.

Some of the seventeen taken by the police were still serving time in the penitentiary in Bahia. Joaquim had been sent to Rio. But most returned to Snake Island, bearing on their backs the mark of the rubber hose. The people of Snake Island, like any good inhabitant of Ilhéus, took pride in the fact that those taken prisoner had not said a single word; the police had never been able to discover those responsible for the two bombs that exploded one night in the Integralist headquarters. It was said that the prisoners from Ilhéus smiled as they were beaten.

Such traditions clothed Snake Island in a certain lively and exciting mystery. But more real than any other tradition, one that endured through time, was the mud in the streets. It rained so much in winter, so much water collected there, that not even the harshest summer could dry up the mud completely. There were also puddles into which one's feet sank. On a certain occasion a reporter from the *Afternoon Journal,* at Sérgio Moura's urging, published a sensational photographic coverage of the streets of Snake Island. It asked the mayor to take measures, but the *Ilhéus Daily* came out against it, proving that the city needed highways more than "paving urban streets." It also raised certain questions about the morality of Snake Island inhabitants, calling that sordid district a den of thieves, bums, con men, hoodlums, and extremists. A committee of workers went to the *Afternoon Journal* to protest these accusations. The photo was published in the paper, with a story below. In the foreground stood Black Roberto, and that newspaper clipping is still stuck to the wall of his shack with a straight pin. The *Ilhéus Daily* returned to the theme, citing statistics furnished by the police: many thieves and a few extremists actually had been arrested in Snake Island. Black Roberto himself was among the extremists arrested. The matter did not bear fruit because Joaquim, without doubt the most well-thought-of person in the district, feared that it might result in a large-scale provocation. So the streets were not paved, and mud continued in abundance everywhere, including inside the houses. Through that mud, through the rain that never stopped all winter, the men left in the morning for the chocolate factory, for their jobs at the port, for the highway. The women left too, some for the market to sell the peppers they grew in their yards, limes, tangerines. In this way they helped to stretch their meager income. Others worked in the chocolate factory, but most spent their days in the cacao warehouses, stitching shut the opening in the sacks that the men filled with beans. During that time the whole of Snake Island belonged to the children. They were many, black and mulatto, looking at first glance like the children on the plantations. But only at first glance, since in reality these were two different kinds of poverty. The plantation children were the color of earth, their bellies enormous and their sex, accustomed early to contact with animals, prematurely developed. These of Snake Island were also yellow, but a different yellow, more toward the green; they had no bellies, and their sex was always small. The skin hung on their bones; they were emaciated and frightfully cunning. Their great point in common with plantation children, the children of farm workers, was the ease with which they died. While they were still small they wallowed in the mud of Snake Island, and as if that weren't enough, spent part of the day fishing for crabs in the nearby swamps. They would return with feet black from the ocean mud, a few crabs dangling from an improvised cord made from vines. At such times the crabs would be a family's supper. When they grew a little older they would spend the day in the city, playing soccer on the beach, and all would become part of a gang of petty thieves who dedicated themselves to stealing slices of codfish and pieces of beef jerky from business establishments. Sometimes they also ran away with the receipts, but that was rare. Some continued in the profession, thus the *Ilhéus Daily*'s statement about thieves being arrested in Snake Island. Most, however, as soon as they turned seventeen, went to work building highways or at the port.

In summer, when the sun reigns supreme, the way to Snake Island is still bearable. A fresh breeze even blows through the district, coming from the sea and losing itself on the hillside. But in winter, when rains rule the day and the night, those Ilhéus winters when the sun is never seen, only those who live there can stand to cross the quagmires surrounding the roads of Snake Island. It is always there that the typhus epidemic begins which yearly threatens the city of Ilhéus. From there the sick are taken to hospitals, the miserable coffins to the common burial trench at Vitória Cemetery. At such times the inhabitants of the city avoid Snake Island; some even think the dwellings of the hollow, so favorable to illnesses, should be destroyed. A municipal councilman once offered a bill to that effect, to which the Communist Party responded with a flyer asking why, instead of destroying the workers' homes, didn't the city bring sanitation to the district? The newspapers debated the matter, and everything remained as it was before. Doctors went there unwillingly; on many days automobiles couldn't make it through the mud holes and the doctors had to trudge the rest of the way on foot. They would arrive filthy and grumbling, but in reality their mood mattered little because in general the sick had no money for the costly medicine.

Nevertheless, just as on the plantations, just as in the rich homes of colonels and exporters, so also in the miserable shacks of the dwellers of Snake Island happiness is reflected on every face this night when the first rains fall. For the rain guarantees this year's crop, and so there will be work in the port, ships and more ships to load, there will be work in the cacao warehouses, there will be work in the chocolate factory, and labors will continue on the roadways. For Snake Island, the refuse of the "Queen of the South," the "latrine of the city," as Nestor said in his address—it too is a function of cacao. Snake Island too is bound by the chains of cacao.

5

In little more than an hour after rain began to fall, the streets of Snake Island were impassable. Joaquim guesses that by now the water has already penetrated most of the houses, turning everything inside to mud. Joaquim has a raincoat and pulls it up around himself. On meeting nights he always exercises caution and never goes home through the busier streets. When they meet, like tonight, he usually goes by way of Conquest Hill, as if on his way to visit a friend or look for some mulatto girl to sleep with. He goes completely around the hill, emerging in the uninhabited area on the far side of Snake Island. He comes that way and enters the house through the backyard planted in pepper bushes and guava trees. But tonight, with all the rain, these are needless precautions. The streets of the city are deserted, with only the bars packed with people. The orchestra at the El-Dorado, one of the city's cabarets, accompanies Joaquim part of the way with strident jazz, good for dancing. Joaquim walks carefully; the soles of his shoes, made from old tires, slip easily. The shrill notes from the jazz band's clarinet die in the rain as Joaquim crosses Sebo Street, where cheap prostitutes live. One calls him from the window and he quickens his step. Almost slipping at the corner, he resumes a slow pace. At this hour, close to midnight, others like him are crossing the wet streets and quagmires to reach Edison's house at the exact time of the cell meeting. Joaquim thinks that in many cities of the world, possibly at that same moment, other men are walking, in the rain or under the stars of a clear sky, to their cells, to help change the destiny of the world. A joyous emotion fills Joaquim's chest whenever he thinks about the Party. Joaquim loves several things in the world: he loves old Raimunda, who looks like a tree and lives hunched over the earth, planting and harvesting cacao. He also

139

loves, in spite of everything, the backwoodsman Antônio Vítor, who threw him out of his house and understands nothing. He loves Jandira, a mulatto girl who works in the kitchen of the foreigner Asfora and walks along the beach with him on moonlit nights. He loves the sea of Ilhéus on nights at the docks when he talks on the piers with the stevedores. He loves bus and truck motors, loves the cacao trees that make up the vision of his childhood. But he loves his Party in a different way. The Party is his home, his school, his reason for living. Few know that Joaquim once thought of committing suicide. Perhaps that sharp sensitivity came to him from old Badaró, who according to what was said in Ilhéus had slept with his grandmother. Perhaps it came from a more remote ancestor, one of those Dutchmen who had emigrated to Sergipe after the defeat in Pernambuco and there mingled their blood with blacks and people of mixed race, with the result that some of the men were tall, like the mulatto Antônio Vítor. Perhaps it came from some black music maker, some black man longing for Africa.

Joaquim fled the farm at an early age. The anxiety for new worlds that had torn Antônio Vítor from Ivone's arms on the piers in Estância and had thrown him onto the cacao plantations, repeating rifle in hand— that same anxiety had torn Joaquim from those plantations to the docks of Ilhéus. He learned to drive automobiles and to repair trucks; he made friends in Snake Island. One day he embarked as a sailor and traveled to other lands. When he returned he knew of things that he had never thought possible, had learned mysteries that would resolve the fate of the world. It did not make him feel self-important.

Before sailing, a certain day, his heart was heavy with sadness and bitterness, as if all the misery of Snake Island weighed upon him. It was anguish without a solution; he neither knew from where it came nor how to solve it. He decided to kill himself, accepting the sea's insistent invitation. It was then, in the Flower of the Waves Bar, that he met that Swedish sailor who spoke Portuguese. When he left the bar the next morning he no longer wanted to kill himself. It was as if a man with a heart shriveled by suffering had suddenly found love. As if, after the most terrible of winters, spring had one morning suddenly arrived. He embarked as a seaman, and when he found someone patient and kind who was willing to teach him, his joy knew no bounds. But his education really only grew in the months in prison, in Rio. He had been arrested in Snake Island, and a note attached to his file read "dangerous." So they sent him to Rio, where the prisons were full. There, in his terrible thirst to know, he studied not only politics and economics but also the most elementary things: grammar, geography, rudiments of French. He had a lively and clear intelligence and an amazing facility for learning. The others saw how useful the youth could be and didn't waste their time with him. When he returned to Snake Island he was the same quiet and affectionate Joaquim, friendly and modest, but he was also a man, a man who knew what he wanted and what he must do.

Now he follows the way from the railroad to Snake Island. Where the hill once was, are streets with fine houses. Colonel Ramiro's mansion stands out among them, near the pier jutting out over the sea. Behind these houses begins the true swamp of mud. No more cobblestones, only loose clay that becomes a sea of mud at the slightest rain. Joaquim walks carefully; the wind pushes at him, and the mud is slippery.

A man appears in the distance. Well dressed and walking slowly, avoiding the mud puddles. Joaquim stops. Who can it be? Then the light from a pole falls on the familiar face of Martins. *He must be coming from Rosa's house*, Joaquim thinks. He steps aside for the other to pass.

"Good evening . . ."

Martins has no wish to be seen; he desires to keep his affair as secret as possible. Joaquim laughs and continues on his way. But now his conversation with Sérgio Moura that afternoon disturbs him. Martins reminded him of Carlos Zude and Carlos Zude reminded him of the price increase. How can he explain to the waiting comrades the workings of the entire capitalist machinery? Joaquim thinks of his comrades with fondness. They are few in number, poor and weak, many of them uneducated; some can barely read—but they propose to change the destiny of the world, turn it "inside out," as Lefty used to say back in prison. It is a huge and unprecedented task, demanding the entire life of each of them. Joaquim feels a certain pride that makes his heart beat faster.

He stops suddenly, looking at the man in front of him. He is about ten yards ahead, and Joaquim stands still, his heart almost stopping too. It's a cop, it has to be. Who but a cop on the trail of a thief or revolutionary would venture out into these mud holes on a night of torrential rain? What other well-dressed man (except Martins, who was already on his way home) would come to Snake Island tonight? Only a cop. Is he looking for some thief or is he trying to find the meeting? Joaquim tries to get control of himself and regain the necessary calm.

In the distance he observes the man as he passes under the light pole. He can't make out his face, but he notes that the man is wearing good clothes, a gabardine coat, something Snake Island dwellers don't own. At no time did Joaquim think of turning around or fleeing. What he thinks about is getting to Edison's house ahead of the cop, warning the comrades, preventing any of them from being nabbed. Turning back, climbing Conquest Hill and then coming around the far side is impossible. He'd be too late. The only alternative left is to risk it, walk quickly along this same route, overtaking the cop and, upon entering the first streets of the district, pick up speed. Luckily, the cop, also afraid of slipping, is moving slowly too. Joaquim yanks off his shoes, rolls up his pants legs, and closes his raincoat about his chest. He looks like a worker on the way home. He leaves his shoes near the railroad tracks, where he'll be able to find them tomorrow. But what if the cop recognizes him? Or decides to use him as bait?

Then Joaquim will have to grapple with him, and unless the policeman shoots him, Joaquim will win, since he's as strong as a bull, accustomed to lifting one hundred and thirty-pound bags of cacao. The detective moves ahead, and Joaquim quickens his pace. He walks down the middle of the street, his feet sinking into the mud, the red water sloshing quietly. The brim of Joaquim's hat has already collapsed under the violent rain. Who could have informed on them? Several thoughts cross his mind as he strides rapidly, resolute and almost perfectly calm.

The man is moving slowly, fearful of slipping in the mud. He has also raised his pants legs so as not to dirty them. And when he passes under the next pole, Joaquim sees that his shoes are soaked with mud. The sound of puddles of water under Joaquim's bare feet resemble the quacking of a duck. The resemblance diverted Joaquim's attention for a moment and took him back to the cacao fields. At this hour Raimunda would be sleeping, and early in the morning she would leave for her work in the plantings. She could never imagine that her son was following a cop, might have to fight with him, might be arrested—who could say?

Faster. If the cop recognizes him, he'll jump him, not give him time to pull his revolver. He neither could nor should kill the detective, for it would bring about brutal reprisals. Terrorism solves nothing. He remembers the things he learned in prison, the violent scenes he witnessed. The men beaten, the scars of cigarettes put out on their backs, the fingernails yanked out. It's better to fight with the man. He'd go to jail, but at least he'd prevent the meeting being discovered, the collapse of the cell, the wiping out of the organization. Joaquim walks faster and faster, closer and closer to the man. Whatever else, the cop has courage to venture out to Snake Island on a night like this. In Ilhéus there have never been any secret police, just detectives from the locality, policemen that everyone knew. For political police they brought in people from the capital. Joaquim will jump him . . . It's the best he can do . . .

His steps splash the water from the small puddles: splat, splat. The cop proceeds with great care, his hands holding up his pants, already spattered with mud. His hat is slouched down over his eyes, his coat pulled up around his neck. Joaquim reviews his plan. First he'll yank on the policeman's hat, covering his face and blocking his vision. Then he'll lay him out flatter than a pancake. He advances, his foot splashing noisily in a deep puddle. The man turns around, startled. Luckily, they're almost beneath a pole and Joaquim recognizes Sérgio Moura. The poet is visibly frightened; the noises had already been preying on his mind. It might be a worker, but it could also be a thief.

"Mr. Sérgio!"

The poet exhales in relief:

"What a scare you gave me, Joaquim . . ."

Between poet and driver there is a certain respect that impedes complete intimacy between the two. Nevertheless, they esteem and admire each other. But there is still something, which even they can't define, that doesn't allow them to open up. Joaquim treats Sérgio with great respect, giving importance to what the poet does, and was for a long time unwilling to express an opinion about his poems. Once, however, at the poet's strong urging, he asked why he wrote revolutionary poetry in language no worker could read. Sérgio had spent weeks worrying about the problem, and it was due to that observation that he now sought more popular rhythms, at times fruitfully.

He stands in front of the poet, not knowing what to say. It may be that Sérgio has come looking for some woman from around there, some tryst, so Joaquim doesn't mention the subject. It was the poet who said:

"I came to look for you . . ."

"For me?"

"The meeting today, you know? The exporters . . ."

The rain is too heavy for them to talk in the middle of the street. Joaquim ponders. In the deepest reaches of his being there are prejudices against such intellectuals. At Edison's, the comrades are gathered. They are the most capable, the most responsible. But Sérgio is so sincere in his excitement, narrating parts of Carlos's speech, that Joaquim smiles and says:

"Come with me . . ."

From some house or other in Snake Island come sounds of a guitar. Now and then a pole shines light on the puddles of water. In a small adobe-walled room, at the rear of Edison's house, the lantern illuminates the tired faces of a few men.

Sérgio feels a strange emotion, as if things had taken on new and profound meaning. The men look at him suspiciously until Joaquim explains:

"Comrade Sérgio is going to make a report . . . It's of the utmost importance. We're going to listen carefully and then discuss it . . ."

Then the shoemaker Edison, who presides over the meeting, raises his voice, a voice as sweet as a child's, and says:

"You have the floor, comrade . . ."

Sérgio is standing; the black porter makes room for him on the bench and smiles. Then the poet loses all his fear of words, of attitudes, and feels calm and assured. He begins to speak.

6

From the door of the house Carlos Zude saw the car enter the garage. The avenue was now silent and deserted. Only an occasional couple slipped along the beach, that accomplice of vagrant love. Carlos felt like a victorious general. He had in his hands the exporters' unanimous backing for his plan for a price increase. And, even if someone had opposed it, what did it matter? Together, he and Karbanks would wipe out anyone who dared dissent from the undertaking, calculated in detail and examined with love and knowledge. Dark clouds had been accumulating since late afternoon. At night rain fell in torrents, and from the door Carlos Zude looked out at the wet sidewalk. The couples were scurrying to take advantage of the dry moment for the act of love on the damp beach. Carlos Zude observed everything with sympathy—the avenue, the houses, the black clouds, the couples, and the sea. He felt a vague desire to sit on one of the benches on the avenue and make a flippant remark to a passing woman, maybe go and tumble with her in the sand. He had the impression that tonight nothing could resist him, nothing would be denied him; it was a great day in his life.

Before him is the sea, where the waves beat on the shore in a ceaseless tossing. On his nights of calculations and meticulous commercial research, Carlos Zude hears that constant rumbling of the sea, that endless agitation. But behind, beyond the city, the river and the hills, lie the cacao fields. Carlos Zude has almost no idea what they're like. He has made a few quick visits to the plantations of colonels with whom he is friends, customers who invited him to celebrate weddings and baptisms. Then his city-bred eyes stared at that infinity of cacao plantations, heavy with yellow fruit, the golden fruit that made the land's fortune. On such days Carlos Zude felt tiny and tentative, without roots in the land, adrift in the air, easily swept away by any storm.

145

What were they, the exporters, in that world of cacao? Go-betweens, men who bought and sold, with no tie to the land except immediate profit. And they were at the mercy of contracts that the colonels broke as soon as the slightest increase was announced. Profits were large, but the eternal specter of losses and insolvency hovered over them. Small exporters went through hell when the colonels broke contracts for the sale of cacao through some well-staged dodge and left them suddenly facing poverty. They had no roots there; they arrived after the cacao trees, planted in blood, had grown and begun to yield their fruits of gold. They were upstarts, with no roots in the black, fecund land. Carlos Zude thought it essential to possess the lands. Only they could provide a document of citizenship in the cacao zone, only they were a sufficient guarantee for his business dealings.

Maximiliano Campos, in the days when Carlos was an adolescent concerned only with women and vice, managed to keep him at home with his narration of astounding tales of Ilhéus, of gunfire and fighting, of killings and burning when, at the turn of the century, the colonels, the Horácios and the Badarós, conquered no-man's-land to plant cacao. Carlos had fallen in love with those stories, just as in childhood he had been seduced by the books of Jules Verne. From early adolescence onward, the image of black cacao lands red with blood had occupied a place in his imagination. Today he knew that the revolver and repeating rifle, the hired assassin and burning, no longer worked to conquer those lands. They were no longer no-man's-land, haunted forests untouched by human hands. Now they were cacao fields, delimited by barbed-wire fences, registered in notary offices, with titles to the ownership of the land. The lands had owners, rich and powerful colonels, who also owned voters, homes in Ilhéus, governmental positions, highways, and luxury automobiles. They were the owners of Ilhéus because they were the owners of the land . . . Their feet were buried in the mud of the fields, along with the bodies of fathers, sons, brothers, friends, and hired gunmen. They had roots there, these owners of the land! Carlos and the other exporters were recent arrivals, come to reap a part of the profit as intermediaries in the sale of cacao. The winds of any storm could sweep them away, into poverty, bankruptcy; they had no roots sunk into the soil.

Carlos Zude smiles, though not at the couple running from the beach because the rain has started falling again. He smiles at Maximiliano Campos, at the baroque language in which he recounted the struggle for possession of the forests. Now Carlos Zude, leading the exporters, undertakes the conquest of those lands, and it too is a struggle to the death. In the furthest depths of his being, the dwelling place of the adolescent who went from reading Jules Verne to listening to the stories of Ilhéus,

Carlos regrets that it was not a heroic struggle, with rifles, ambushes, and hired gunfighters. It was a struggle of offices, stock markets, boom and bust—a very different struggle. Perhaps it was petty, thought Carlos, suddenly sad. There was the poet Sérgio Moura, the rose in his hand already wilting, a smile on his lips. But it wasn't petty! It was heroic in its way, in the way of Carlos Zude, cacao exporter.

The rain was falling in heavy sheets, the wind hurling droplets into Carlos Zude's face. It was a struggle that demanded intelligence and calculation, vision and tact. What did it matter if the poet smiled and sniffed that wilting rose as if the room where the exporters met smelled of pestilence? What did the poet, an insignificant clerical employee, know about all that, what did he know about great negotiations, about a plan that would take five years? There were no battles in open country, what Maximiliano used to call a "certain loyalty." Loyalty? What about the moonlight ambushes? It was like one immense ambush, thought Carlos Zude, smiling.

The rain fell on his shoulders and face. Not a form was to be seen on the deserted avenue. Nothing but the electric lights reflected on wet asphalt. Carlos Zude opened the door and went in.

In the bedroom was Julieta, abandoning her uninteresting book, sad and restless, that unexplained pressure on her beautiful breast, the deep yearning for something never revealed. Carlos flashed her his triumphant smile.

"It's an ambush . . ."

"What?" said Julieta vaguely, not expecting a reply.

But Carlos sat on the edge of the bed with its immaculate white sheets and began to explain. He started at the beginning, the beginning of everything, when the land belonged to no one, a forest of century-old trees, unexploited. He told of the fighting, of the deaths in ambushes and skirmishes, of dodges, of the land planted in cacao bringing forth its fruits of gold. Julieta listened, her eyes wide with interest; it was like a fairy tale, brutal and moving.

The land . . . Without it, nothing did any good—neither the large offices nor the great transactions with New York and Berlin. Who were they, the exporters? Who was she, Julieta, so different from the women here? They were newcomers, without roots, not firmly planted in the cacao soil. Only by possessing the land could they become the masters, truly people of Ilhéus, owners of Ilhéus. And he began to reveal the plan, feeling the need to open up and, in a type of vanity not peculiar to him, praise himself, feel all the greatness he had imagined, the full strength of his personality. To Julieta it was like a dream. Her husband never spoke to her about business, a world that didn't exist for her. All she knew was that profits were large and allowed them to maintain the luxury and the jewels, the trips and the dresses. But she knew nothing of the mechanics, and the revelation of the exporters' plans, plans envisioned by Carlos, conceived and nurtured by him, suddenly gave her a new concept of her husband. There he was, sitting on the bed; he had aged, his eyes were a bit dim, and he had wrinkles. There was something of the great man about him, Julieta could feel, but at the same time it was a greatness that did not attract her. During that unexpected conversation she came to admire him as she had never admired anyone. But she also felt more and more distant, as if she must decide between Colonel Horácio and Sinhô Badaró on one side and Carlos Zude and Karbanks on the other. She recalled Reinaldo Bastos's phrase (never imagining it was Carlos's): "They're like frightened children." They were men of the revolver, of armed struggle; what would they do faced with those intellects, those calculations, those commercial mysteries, faced with this new breed of man like Carlos and Karbanks? Julieta felt they were different kinds of greatness, as if she could take that of the colonels in one hand and that of the exporters in the other and weigh them. Carlos closed his eyes as he explained the plan in minute detail. Within five years the land would change hands; it would have new masters. She admired him. A certain strength ran through her husband's face, a certain decisiveness, even a certain heroism. Yet there was something that disturbed her, and if she had a rosebud, even one wilted and almost dead, Julieta would breathe it in search of a wild perfume that would pluck her from that closed and gloomy atmosphere.

But she was moved when Carlos, ending the commercial description that in his impassioned voice had taken on an almost epic tone, placed it all at her feet in his constant renewal of their love.

"And then we can go live in Rio, travel to Europe, we'll have nothing to fear . . . You'll have everything, everything you want . . ."

Julieta took his hands and saw that he was tired. He was a great man, she thought. A great man whom she did not love, whose greatness did not tempt her. But he was a great man who loved her, who placed his greatness at her feet. And he was tired.

"You're tired . . ."

She felt his cashmere clothing.

"And you're wet all over, you poor thing . . ."

She helped her husband, brought his silk pajamas, went to get a glass of vermouth. When she returned, Carlos was looking out the closed window at the rain falling outside. He drank in small sips and said:

"It's going to be a large harvest, the first of the boom . . . One day the bust will come, Julieta, and then the land will be worthless and we'll become its owners . . ."

Julieta again recalled Reinaldo Bastos's phrase. And she said, almost unwittingly:

"It's going to be terrible . . ."

"Terrible?" he asked, and at once understood.

There was a brief silence while the two thought. Julieta had understood what it was that separated her from the greatness she sensed in her husband. And Carlos thought it was sad that it must be that way, a frightful and petty struggle. But the colonels had done the same and felt no guilt. He said:

"Nothing in life is easy . . . We're always walking over others . . . That's how it has to be, unfortunately . . . That's how it has to be . . ." he repeated, attempting through the phrase to ward off melancholy thoughts. He was not only tired; he was sad as well.

Then Julieta took his arm and led him to the bed. And she opened her body to him, held him and gave herself to him, but it was out of pity, to console, to make him forget, like the gesture of a friend; it was not out of love. The rain lasted the entire night, and so did sleeplessness.

7

The rain fell on the cacao fields, shaking loose the leaves burned by the sun. The snakes fled to their hiding places, the kinkajous leapt restlessly about, the spectacled owl hooted in the night. On the highway, the first puddles on the red clay foretold the sea of mud that the roads would become in the months ahead. Rain that would guarantee the crop. That would guarantee the blooming of the trees, the growth of the fruit. Later sunny days would come and the green fruit would take on the color of gold. Those lands gave fruits of gold that illuminated the fields and filled men's hearts with dreams.

When the months of the lull came, the eyes of men and women throughout the south of Bahia turned toward the sky in a single anxious question. Would the rain necessary for the early crop, the June crop, fall during those torrid months—or would drought hit the fields, attacking everything, killing the flowers and the young fruit, turning only the leaves to gold? Not that the droughts there were like those in Ceará, which killed cattle, people, grass, and forest animals, and dried up the wells. In the cacao zone such droughts were known only through hearsay, in the stories that people from Ceará told when they came to the plantations, driven by the devastation in their far-off land. But if rain didn't fall at the proper time, that was enough to kill the cacao flowers so there would be no fruit, thus ruining the early crop and endangering the entire harvest. Since the last of the great forest land had been cut down and planted, the rain in the lands of Ilhéus was less constant and abundant. The men, well versed in any indicator of rain, any indicator of drought, looked at the sky and interrogated the horizon. There were those who could tell the coming of heavy rain when not a single cloud as yet broke the clear southern sky. They could tell by the wind that came beforehand. They could tell by the smell of the grass. At the same

150

time as the animals in the fields, the birds and monkeys, the men knew rain was coming. And then all of humanity in the lands of cacao was happy, bursting forth in smiles like the flowers that days later would burst forth in the fields.

On the first night of rain, when he suddenly saw the initial cloudburst, the mulatto Antônio Vítor went to the door of his house and smiled. Raimunda came and stood beside him. They said nothing, but merely watched in gratitude, an emotion recurring every year at the time of the lull. The rain fell on the fields with a grave and solemn sound. The couple of small growers held an almost religious attitude toward the waters that tumbled from the heavens. Antônio Vítor said:

"It took a long time but it came . . . Praise God!"

Raimunda said nothing. But she smiled her rare smile and took a step forward. She too let the rain fall on her face.

Captain João Magalhães was euphoric. To him the arrival of the rains was tied to the news of the price increase. With expansive gestures he explained to Dona Ana, his bursts of laughter accompanied by the parrot walking pedantically back and forth along the railing on the veranda. Beyond the fields fed by the rains, still unexploited and virgin, lay the rest of the forest that they had never been able to plant. Now Captain João Magalhães's eyes turn toward it. In it lies all their hope for the future, their resurgence, their return to the old days. Once that forest was felled and planted, they would be the rich and powerful Badarós of old. This piece of Repartimento forest was perhaps the one only left for planting in all those immense cacao lands, unparalleled for growing cacao. Land as good as Sequeiro Grande . . .

Colonel Frederico Pinto hears the noise from the workers' houses. It comes from Ranulfo's wake: the workers talking about the mummers group and the rehearsals, making plans as they stand around the body. Frederico thinks about bringing an electrician from Ilhéus to examine the kiln. The colonel is the rich man of this zone. There's no comparison between him and João Magalhães or Antônio Vítor. His fortune is among the largest in Ilhéus: field after field, adjacent plantations, land that the colonel conquered, cleared, and planted, fields that he bought later, as well as some taken from small growers in well-executed dodges. Even in bad years the colonel harvested some 225,000 kilos. He was one of the "nobles" of that land, belonging to the caste that frequented the Social Club, spent money in the cabaret, played poker at Pepe Espinola's, and built mansions in Ilhéus. The "nobility," as it was ironically called by Sérgio Moura, who liked to confer titles upon the colonels: Duke Horácio, Baron Maneca Dantas. It was to this group, the largest plantation owners, that Colonel Frederico Pinto belonged.

His wife is sleeping. Today he had to satisfy his wife's desires, thus calming her jealousy. Now, in his pajamas, he watches the falling rain. He'll be able to buy more land . . . And lavish jewels on Lola, expensive dresses, imported French perfume. For Colonel Frederico Pinto the rain represents liberation. Fear of drought tore him from the seductive arms of the Argentine *rubia* and brought him anxiously to the plantations to advance the pruning so that something could be saved even in a drought. Now the rain was falling and he could return, sleep in Lola's arms, plunge into her mysteries of love. The drumming of the falling rain arrives at the veranda of the plantation house. Colonel Frederico Pinto is nervous. The memory of Lola Espinola has brought with it an overpowering desire for a woman. He wishes he could leave immediately, order them to saddle a horse, gallop the three leagues to Itabuna, take a taxi and, in the morning, knock at his lover's door. Pepe would be in the cabaret, gambling. He would sleep happily. He knew every detail of his lover's body and recalled them one by one. His nervousness increased, and he began pacing back and forth. The noise of the wake was an insistent invitation. Colonel Frederico went to the living room, put on a raincoat over his pajamas and an old hat on his head, and headed in the direction of the workers' houses. He wasn't sleepy that night.

Colonel Horácio da Silveira awoke with the first rain. His sleep was the light sleep of the old. The ancient bed, now falling apart, creaked when Horácio got up. He wore a nightshirt as he had for thirty years. With flowers embroidered on the chest. But now his gigantic body was bent and skeletal, the weary body of an old man. The rain, coming in the window, wet the sheets and sprinkled drops on Horácio. His octogenarian eyes could discern very little. He felt for his cane (it had a gold handle in the shape of a cacao fruit), leaned on it, oriented himself by the entering wind, and walked to the window. Outside was the diffuse light of early morning. Colonel Horácio da Silveira's eyes were a confused fog. But he could feel the rain on his face, sweet as a caress, and had no need to see it. There was silence in the fields, broken only by the sound of rain and the fall of dead leaves. Just beyond the window of the colonel's bedroom lay a cacao field. The wind ran through the leaves; the colonel heard and distinguished, one by one, each of the sounds, however subtle, that broke the silence of the night. He was as content as a cat when it is petted. He murmured to himself, smiled his hard, wary, and intimidating smile. The rain wet him, and his body itched; his wrinkled hand went from chest to legs as the wind and rain brought back the pains of rheumatism. He knew he was alone; everyone else was asleep. He could groan softly amid the happy words he muttered. Damned rheumatism. It came back with the rains, racking Colonel Horácio with violent pains. What does that matter, if the rain falls, if the cacao trees don't lose their recently born flowers, if the fruits turn golden and the crop is a big one, the biggest ever?

In the cities of Ilhéus and Itabuna a few lament the fact that Colonel Horácio da Silveira, the richest man in the cacao lands, the all-powerful master of politics, lives a lonely life on the plantation. No one takes care of him; he has no friend at his side, no wife, no lover, not even his own son, whom he dislikes. "It's a sad old age," they say. The pious churchwomen, who know the stories of bygone times, add that the colonel is paying for his sins, which are both numerous and great. Even in the old days, when men tore at the earth with axes and scythes and felled others in their conquest of the forest, then too they were saying things about Horácio. Today they speak with commiseration admixed with a certain element of hatred. They feel sorry for him but also judge it fitting that he is alone and abandoned, suffering. Horácio knows what they say, as he knew thirty years earlier of the stories told in sacristies and cabarets. But he also knows he is not alone. He is with his cacao trees, his fields, the animals that live on them, even with the last of the snakes and wildcats. He is in the middle of his world, a part of it; he is not alone and unhappy. If he were in the largest city in the world, with thousands of electric lights, the sounds of music and beautiful women, amidst friends and comfort, the colonel would be alone and unhappy, for he would be away from his cacao fields.

What does it matter that the rains bring on his rheumatism? What does it matter that no one is beside him? He hears, senses, feels, and knows every sound of the fields where the rain is falling. He mutters happily while the rain smoothes the wrinkles from his face. He holds out his hands so the raindrops can fall into them. Morning is coming; the colonel's weary eyes distinguish brightness breaking through the fog of night. And he distinguishes, one by one, the voices of birds warbling, greeting the rain in the cacao fields.

"It's a-rainin'," said Capi.

Everyone ran to take a look. They stood there watching. It was no longer the afternoon cloudbursts but the long-awaited rain that would go on for days and days. The earlier downpours, infrequent and uncertain, were insufficient to eliminate the workers' doubts. Were they just clouds that the wind would blow away, or would they turn out to be the rain needed for the crop?

The rain tumbled down over the cacao trees, the grass, the red soil. Rain enough for many days. A light went on in the plantation house.

"The colonel's awake . . ." said Rita.

"He's happy . . ."

In the small workers' house the corpse had been left unattended. It would be buried right there, in the fields. Ranulfo was the most heavily indebted of all the workers. He was up to his teeth in debt, and the colonel wouldn't give any money to bury him in town. Nor would he—now that the rains were here—let two workers off to carry the dead man away in a hammock. If tomorrow were Sunday they could arrange for a hammock, borrow a few coins, and take Ranulfo to a cemetery like a human being. But in the middle of the week it was difficult . . . The dead man remained there, turning green, his eyes bulging from congestion. Already the bottle of rum is half empty.

Rita, the first to return, looked at the dead man. He was a good guy, that Ranulfo. When she would come back from the river or the fields, he used to look at her like a tame dog. It was rumored that Ranulfo was shacked up with a mare, the only female he knew. But that was common among the workers, who from childhood were accustomed to having relations with animals: goats, sheep, later donkeys and mares. Many became addicted, and were pointed out by the spiteful.

What made Ranulfo ridiculous in Rita's lively eyes, eyes that held an invitation to love, eyes that constantly offered the girl's still-preserved virginity, was the memory of the beating he had received. A man who had been beaten . . . It's true that the same whipping had put an end to the overseer's chances with Rita. She had distanced herself from Tibúrcio, who had been courting her, after seeing him, lash in hand, whipping Ranulfo. Both of them lost out in her eyes. One had been beaten with a whip, his back marked; it was as if he had been castrated. And the other had whipped a defenseless man tied to a post.

Ever since she left Tibúrcio standing in the grass the night the overseer had tried to possess her, things had gone badly for her. The overseer had begun to persecute her father, and she turned to the plantation house for protection. But Dona Augusta was jealous, and the colonel took no notice of her. Rita looks at the dead man. Ranulfo, who meant nothing to her, had messed up her life . . . The candles light the enormous feet of the deceased. With the heat of the kiln the sticky coating of cacao *visgo* had turned into a crust, resembling a crude shoe. Rita's feet have that same dark covering, darker than her skin. In her baths in the river, using soap for washing clothes, she has often tried to remove it completely. Impossible. People from Ceará who had been on these plantations and later returned to their lands upon news of rain there, and were then once more forced back to Ilhéus by droughts years later, said that the *visgo* of soft cacao never comes off the feet of anyone who steps in it. Rita sits down on the bench. Everybody says she's pretty, some say she's the prettiest girl in the cacao fields. Maybe pretty is an overstatement. Her body is well put together, slim, the body of a young mulatto girl, but her face isn't beautiful, with its large nose and small, exciting eyes. A man's feet, which have never worn elegant feminine shoes, hands rough with calluses from using a machete, muscular legs from long roads. But her breasts were firm, her belly flat, and her thighs rounded. She wasn't worn out like the rest of the workers' women. Nor was she a shrinking violet like the few young women who hadn't married or shacked up. She liked to color her cheeks with red paper and straighten her hair. She was desired for leagues around, and the demon of desire lived in her body as well. But she knew how to preserve herself; she knew, from what she saw and learned from life on the plantation, just what a woman was worth. So she fended off the constant attacks from the workers. She hoped to marry an overseer or a small grower, or— who could say?—even to sleep with the colonel, with the wonderful possibility of a house in town, of a better life without work.

The rain-dampened men returned. Rita's father, an old worker who

has been a widower for many years, is the plantation's drover. Beanpole
and Capi act as hosts. Workers have come from all around, bringing
rum. The colonel also sent a bottle.

The dead man is merely a pretext; the wake is virtually a party. They
talk about the mummers group; news has spread, and only the coming
of the rains could turn their attention from such an important subject.

Rita will prepare the lanterns, and her father will buy tissue paper in
Itabuna when he takes in the herd. It's already certain that four young
women will come, who, along with three little girls, will make seven
shepherdesses. Capi will be the ox. Someone will lend the chintz sheet,
and there are skulls of dead cows in the countryside. Beanpole will be
the hobgoblin. All he needs to do is wrap his skinny body in some kind
of drape made from old flour sacks.

"What about the verses?" someone asks.

Nobody knows the verses, and that problem draws everyone's eyes
to the body. He died in the kiln, dropped dead. Nobody knows the
verses. Capi knows a few isolated bits, but that's not enough. Nor
is there an orchestra, just two guitars. But Beanpole is prepared to
surmount all difficulties. They'll arrange for empty kerosene cans
and, as a last resort, sing songs of the cacao fields. The important
thing is for the group to go out, make its way through the plantation
and its neighbors, get as far as possible from the plantation house.
Beanpole will be able to flee and take Black Florindo with him,
and they'll be free of the cacao plantations forever. Florindo appears
removed from all this, divided between the terrifying sight of the
dead man—the creator of ghosts—and the coveted body of Rita.
He is sitting beside her, and no one can drink rum like him. He
raises the bottle in enormous gulps and feels Rita looking at him
in admiration. But the corpse holds him there; perhaps the black
man is the only one who feels a bit of fear this rainy night. Fear
of the dead man's bulging eyes, of the green of his malarial face,
of his fingernails dirty with earth. The conversation goes on about
the mummers group, and the rum bottle passes from hand to hand.
Old Celestina was there at the start of the evening to say strange
prayers. Then she left; she is too old to bear an entire wake. And
no one present knows a prayer for the dead . . . Possibly one, Capi
perhaps, knows the entire Lord's Prayer. But those pretty prayers for
the dead that really perk up a wake, prayed in a resonant voice, only
old Celestina knows. When she was younger a wake was really done
right. The old woman led the prayers, indicated when it was time to
drink, enforced respect. When she dies it'll be even worse, because
then the bodies will be buried without any prayers at all. For now, she

still comes, dragging herself along the road, with her staff and black shawl, to murmur confused Hail Marys, her magic hands removing evil spirits from the face of the deceased. And when she dies?

A' awful land, thinks Black Florindo. That's why he wants to leave with Beanpole. A land where a man drops dead and there's nobody to pray for his salvation at his wake. The candle evokes ghosts before Florindo, but the bottle drowns his cares. Rita is interested in the talk about the group. Florindo looks at her legs.

Agitated and persuasive, Beanpole explains how beautiful the group will be. "Fantastic," he says, and everyone forgets the dead man, skinny green Ranulfo, in their thoughts about the group. An idea is in Beanpole's head as he sees so many people there: "There's enough for a practice." But out of respect for the dead man he says nothing; it could be considered disrespectful. But it wasn't really; it'd be like a party for Ranulfo. Ranulfo had been enthusiastic about the group, so enthusiastic that he talked about it that day, making suggestions— Ranulfo, who never talked, silent since his beating. Why not rehearse the group right there next to him, so the poor man wouldn't be buried without seeing the group dance? Beanpole looks over the others; what will they say?

Capi's guitar is on top of his bunk. With it they'd have all they needed for the practice. The rum bottle passes from hand to hand, raised to thirsty mouths. Black Florindo drinks more than anyone else, and is the only one to look at the dead man, his color greenish from malaria. There are both men and women, a good practice. Beanpole suggests, rather ill at ease:

"What if we . . ."

They turned toward him. Beanpole was respected on the plantation as a man of initiative.

"What?"

Black Florindo is thinking that what Beanpole wants is to ask the colonel to give two men the next day off so they can take Ranulfo's body to town.

" . . . if we had a practice for the group?"

"Now?" Rita's father was surprised.

There was a silence, and they all looked at the dead man, as if waiting for him to decide. But Ranulfo, dead and indifferent, wouldn't answer.

Rita, who liked the idea, is anxious. Capi thinks it's irreverence to the dead, a lack of respect. A wake is a serious thing. God might punish them. Florindo is both tempted and fearful. He thought Beanpole was going to suggest something else: for them to take the dead man to the cemetery early in the morning, to speak to the colonel, ask for a day off for the two of them . . . The group is nice, the practice is a happy affair, and he could get to dance with Rita, famed for her rounded buttocks. Ranulfo doesn't mind; he has never noticed anything around him since he was whipped. Beanpole explains:

"It's for him. What good's it do if there's no prayin', or a woman to lead the prayers? Well, there ain't, an' there he is, like a devil . . . He never talked, he was sufferin' the pain of the whip. Who don't know that? But when I told him 'bout the group, he even laughed. An' he talked an' it was like he was another man . . . Ain't that right, Capi? Ain't it, Florindo? He was like another man . . . He talked, he even argued. He was gonna go out, it was all arranged. There's no woman to lead the prayers, there's no prayer, so the practice's for him, so he can go happy, watchin' the practice . . . There ain't no prayer, so we'll hold the practice for him. It ain't the same, but what's wrong with it?"

That Beanpole knew the darnedest things . . . That smooth-talking mulatto sure could talk, say things, convince people.

"He's even smilin', sayin' it's all right . . ."

Then Rita gets up, extends her arms and almost shouts:

"Then let's do it . . ."

"Let's do it . . ."

"Capi, get your guitar . . ."

Capi grumbles that he's never seen a wake like this one. But he goes to get his guitar, fingers the cords, tuning the instrument. Now all of them are on their feet, and only Black Florindo looks at the abandoned Ranulfo, his enormous feet, an ugly liquid coming from his mouth. *A' awful land.*

And the rehearsal begins, right there in the room, beside the corpse.

"What're we gonna sing?"

Nobody knows any songs for Epiphany groups. Capi knows a few isolated bits, but not enough. The only thing is to sing songs from around there, those unhappy work songs.

"Sing, Florindo . . ."

The black man begins:

> *"Maneca died in the oven,*
> *Just as sundown came . . ."*

Rita takes the lead, Beanpole gives instructions, and the dance begins to take shape. On that very spot, next to the corpse that appears to be watching with interest.

"Didn't I say he'd like it?"

Capi's guitar sobs. Wakes weren't like this in Ceará. All dance, men and women, and suddenly form two parallel lines and dance facing the

bed where the body lies. It is like an homage, like the missing prayer
for the dead, the one Celestina did not pray.

> *"The oven did him in,*
> *The oven killed a man . . .*
> *Maneca died in the oven,*
> *It's all part of the plan . . ."*

Capi had never seen a wake like this one. Nor had Beanpole, Florindo,
or Rita. But they are no longer afraid, and they sing to the dead man,
dance for him, so that Ranulfo can leave happy, forget the beating,
remember only the mummers group. Rita holds the candle, first at the
dead man's feet, then in her hand. "Every group's got a lantern," she
says. Ranulfo had no prayers, but now he has song, now he has a dance
in his honor. This was the nicest wake he'd ever seen, Capi thinks.

The colonel's footsteps approach. They stop singing and dancing,
and the candle returns to Ranulfo's feet. A respectful silence surrounds
Frederico Pinto. Sitting on the wooden bench, he offers Rita a place
beside him. And he asks with interest:

"Where's Celestina?"

"She already left . . ."

"Weren't you praying?"

The workers exchange glances, hoping that Beanpole will answer.
Only he can explain to the colonel:

"Don't you see that there wasn't no prayers for him? Colonel, sir,
we was about to bury him like some animal, some outcast. The colonel
knows how quiet he was, ever since . . ."

He spoke softly:

" . . . since he got beaten . . ."

Frederico waits to hear the rest.

"So we decided . . . we're gonna have us a group . . ."

"A group?"

"A' Epiphany group . . . We're rehearsin' for him to see it, for him
not to be buried unhappy, rememberin' the whippin' . . ."

Frederico looks at the dead man. He'd had him beaten to set an
example. Frederico feels a distant remorse, the desire to explain to
the men why he did it. It wasn't for pleasure, and he wasn't a cruel
man; it was to set an example.

"What did he have to run away for?"

They nodded in agreement.

"What'd he have to run away for?"

What could he do but order Ranulfo whipped when they caught him?
He didn't do it because he enjoyed it. And anyway, who did anything

on the plantations because they enjoyed it? Just imagine if he patted
the head of every runaway trying to escape his bill at the plantation
store. There wouldn't be a worker left, and no plantation owner would
be able to tolerate it. He had to maintain respect. It was an unwritten
law going back many years, and all were familiar with it. And whoever
broke that law had to be punished as an example to others. It wasn't
Frederico's fault.

He made himself comfortable on one end of the bench, put a foot
on top, and looked at Beanpole. Rita came near him with her warm
virgin body.

"He ran off because he wanted to; nobody forced him to."

Beanpole took advantage of the opening:

"Colonel, we was thinkin' . . ."

To Frederico any type of conversation at that moment was comforting.
"What?"

He thought he knew what they were going to ask, and he was inclined
to grant it. They would ask for money to bury Ranulfo in town and a
day off for the two men who carried the body away in a hammock.
It wasn't much money, but the men would be needed in the fields
now that the rains had come. Even so, he'd say yes; it was a way of
squaring accounts with the dead man.

"We'd like to ask for . . ."

"I know, Beanpole. You want to bury Ranulfo in town . . . As if the
land there was any better than here . . . But all right."

Florindo laughed. He knew that wasn't what Beanpole wanted. He
wanted help for the Epiphany group, that's what. They stood there not
knowing what to say. No one remembered the dead man any longer,
their thoughts on the group. Only the colonel and Florindo looked at
Ranulfo. Rita leaned closer against him. Frederico could feel her body.
Beanpole spread his arms, looking like a scarecrow. Frederico didn't
understand. His nervous hand slid around Rita's waist and touched her
rounded buttocks. Then she spoke:

"It's just that we . . ."

A flash of desire shot through Frederico. He touched the mulatto
girl's flesh and thought of Lola Espinola. Florindo was following the
scene, as offended as if he were Rita's owner. Much that was happening
that night offended Black Florindo. *A' awful land.*

"What is it?" smiled Frederico, now fully against Rita, feeling her
arm on his, her round thigh against his body.

"We was hopin' for a little help for the Epiphany group . . ."

And everyone forgot the burial of Ranulfo, taking advantage of the
colonel's good mood to explain. Rita made a special effort, smiling,
and when Frederico spoke he touched her warm flesh. Outside, the rain

was falling. Only Florindo looked at the forgotten dead man with his enormous feet; the candle was burning out. Capi takes up his guitar, smiling softly. Florindo wished he were a fast talker, like Beanpole, so he could get into the conversation and discuss the burial.

"All right," said Frederico. "I'll help . . . But you only go out on feast night and holidays. I don't want any loafers around the fields . . ."

Rita was so happy that she clapped her hands. The candle lighting the dead man went out.

"Hey, where's a match?"

Even in the dark, Capi fingered his guitar. Whose voice was that?

"We gonna rehearse?"

"It's really for the dead man, so he can see it and travel happy on that long journey . . ."

"He was so good, poor thing. He's goin' to heaven . . ."

"Don't talk 'bout the dead. It's a sin . . ."

"Let's practice. Is that okay wi' you, Colonel, sir?"

Frederico was using the opportunity to pinch Rita's breasts, her hard virgin breasts. The light from the match illuminated Florindo's face.

"Colonel, sir, I'll take 'im to the cemetery myself . . . I'll put 'im in a sack . . . Alls I need is money for the gravedigger . . ."

The candle once more lit the dead man's feet. Frederico let go of Rita, thinking again of the beating Ranulfo had suffered. Hadn't he already given permission for the group, hadn't he promised money? Florindo was standing, and he was not smiling. He was sad; nobody remembered the dead man. Frederico raised his eyes and stared at him, speaking in a tired voice as if he had just come from a battle:

"You can take him . . . Two of you better go . . ."

It's not my fault, he thought. Why the hell wasn't he in Ilhéus, in bed with Lola, far away from all of this? Beanpole asks fearfully:

"What about the group?"

The colonel made a gesture of assent with his hand. He stood up, tugged on the brim of his hat, which he hadn't removed, and left. The rain tumbled on the cacao fields. The rehearsal began again around the corpse. At the bend in the road Rita overtook him with some lame excuse. She was offering herself, laughing and showing her white teeth. Frederico pushed her away with his hand and continued on his way.

9

The next night the violent rain continued. During those twenty-four hours the sun came out for a few moments, and at times the rain turned to drizzle. But such moments were brief, and it quickly began raining heavily again. The people of Ilhéus looked at the sky and knew there was rain for many days, one of those downpours at the beginning of the crop that flooded everything and made roads impassable, washing away houses on the hills and in Snake Island, sweeping the mud to the streets by the railroad and port as it descended from Conquest and Unhão. But they also made the cacao trees, which had begun to wither in the sun, burst forth in flowers. Nothing but blessings were heard about that rain from everyone in the cities of Ilhéus, Itabuna, Itapira, Belmonte, and Canavieiras, and in the small towns from Guaraci to Rio de Contas, as well as on the plantations and farms.

That second night of rain began with a benediction at six o'clock, delivered in the Cathedral of St. George by the bishop. It was a gloomy twilight, with the electric lights barely breaking through the persistent rain. Candles burned at the altars, burned at the feet of the warrior saint who symbolized so well those lands recently emerged from the battles of conquest, burned in gratitude for the rain that had come. The benediction had been commissioned by the Ilhéus Commercial Association, in the name of the plantation owners and exporters. They were thanking the patron saint for the rain that made possible the flowering of the fields, the ripening of the fruits, just as later they would give thanks for the sun that permitted the drying of cacao in the large drying frames. The bishop prayed his Latin phrases, the girls from the convent school sang in the church choir, while Sister Maria Teresa de Jesus played the organ donated to the cathedral by the firm of Zude Brothers & Co. The turnout of men was not great. Practically all those in the church were women; the

162

colonels and exporters were content to pay for the service. They were on their plantations or in their commercial establishments taking care of the business that the certainty of the crop made possible.

The bishop raised his hands toward heaven, casting the benediction upon the bowed heads before him. Then he prayed for the well-being of his flock, for good harvests and the spiritual uplifting of the people of Ilhéus. His deep voice filled the church and vanished under the vaults. The organ sounded once more. The old women, and a man or two as well, went out into the rain. The next day the newspapers carried the story of the ceremony on page one.

That benediction was not, however, the only religious celebration that night. While colonels and exporters were lighting candles at the altar of St. George, black stevedores from the port, loafers who lived off the scraps of cacao, black cooks and fishermen were holding a celebration to Oxosse, the St. George of black people. It was in Olivença, on Pontal Island, home of Salu, the *pai-de-santo*, or priest, of the blacks' fetishistic religion brought from Africa.

Around them the coconut trees bent in the wind. Coconuts dislodged by the strong south wind buried themselves in the sand. In the middle of the coconut grove was Salu's *terreiro*, the meeting place in Olivença for such rites. Olivença was the remains of a town almost totally destroyed in a struggle before the fighting over Sequeiro Grande, when cacao first began, when parties won elections at riflepoint, those long-ago years when for three days gypsies ruled the city of Ilhéus. They said that on the floor of the small chapel, now worn smooth, you could still see bloodstains from the eighteen corpses laid out there at the end of the fighting. Almost completely destroyed, Olivença never rose again, yielding its place to Ilhéus. It was a few minutes from the Pontal district, half an hour on foot, six minutes by car. In that land, where everything gave the impression of growth, progress, and life, Olivença was decadence, ruin, and death. The only ones living there were fishermen who set out to sea in their fearless balsa rafts. There were two or three shabby stores, and the wind blew in through the windows and cracks of what had once been the finest houses in the entire zone, when Olivença, in the days of sugar mills, was the center of life in these lands. Before cacao, when sugarcane was Ilhéus's green crop, when rudimentary mills made the fortunes of the rich. Now the fishermen lived in the houses abandoned by their owners, and from there dominated the entrance to the sandbar and the seaward side where enormous waves broke against the palm-lined beach. The balsa rafts rested in the rain; on the verandas of the houses hung fishing nets. And in the most remote part of the settlement was Salu's place of worship, established in honor of Oxosse, St. George, the lord of Ilhéus and of cacao.

The worship site, or *candomblé*, of Oxosse was what kept Olivença from dying altogether. On feast days (in April it was the entire month), at night the blacks and mulattoes of Ilhéus would set out for Olivença and come pray to the saint. On April 23, St. George's Day, a celebration was held that brought people even from distant plantations, black women in the clothes they wore for feasts, black men in red shoes and starched white pants. In the sand of the beach, which was the only road, were the footprints of dozens of pilgrims. And the atabals echoed, audible all the way to the port of Ilhéus when the northeast wind blew. In years when drought threatened, when the first rains came there was also a large celebration in Oxosse's *candomblé*. The rich prayed to St. George in the Cathedral in Ilhéus, the bishop's white hands raised in benediction of the year's crop. The poor prayed to Oxosse, also St. George, in Salu's *candomblé*, his black hands raised in gratitude.

On the second night of rain the atabals had been hammering their relentless beat since early evening, summoning black people to the celebration. From the port of Ilhéus canoe after canoe set out with mulatto and black women dressed in celebration garb, with black men from the docks, sailors from the ships, idlers from the bars. Through the rain-soaked sand, all marched toward Olivença.

A few whites have come also, curious to attend the blacks' religious celebration. Rui Dantas, who was courting Lola, has come and brought the pair of dancers, who had expressed interest in the barbarous rhythms. The lawyer explains to Lola and Pepe, rather inaccurately, details of the African mysteries.

Rosa, Martins's lover and object of Beanpole's desire, also came. She is an *iaô*, a priestess, and dances in the middle of the site. She spins, doubles over, and her buttocks rise, thrusting toward the eyes of the spectators. She isn't a woman but a pair of buttocks that whirl through the room reaching men, women, and the gods, as well as the coconut trees and the seas. The Yoruban songs and the music of the atabals and cowbells are deep like the calls of death and love. No one drank, but all are drunk from the drumming; the saint is with each of them, and now they dance with their arms, arms like serpents, on all sides of the site, coming from the floor and the roof, from the walls and bodies. Pepe Espinola is interested. He is thinking how successful that dance, stylized, would be on civilized stages. The arms that move to and fro, that approach and withdraw, to the sound of the bracelets of the Bahian women. Inside Salu's body, Oxosse rides around the site on that rainy night. It was Oxosse who sent the rain so that his black people would have work. And this is why they give thanks to him.

Oxosse announces through Salu's voice that this year there will be much money, even some for the poor. It won't be cacao that comes forth from the earth; it will be gold. Ah! Oxosse is a good saint who is going to send gold to them all, even to the poor!

They dance into the advancing night. Rui Dantas composes madrigals to Lola Espinola. The Argentine woman feels the music calling to her body. It isn't like the tango, with all its degradation. It's primitive music, of unequivocal desire. Rosa dances, they all dance into the advancing night. Dancing with their arms, dancing with their buttocks. Rui Dantas makes propositions. Pepe is indifferent to everything. Rosa will be a success on stage. The rain falls heavily.

In Olivença the drumbeats celebrate the coming of rain; the black women sing and dance in honor of Oxosse, god of cacao's poor. The music spreads into the sea.

$$\boxed{10}$$

"**N**ow," Carlos Zude said, "let's hear some music." He put the record on the victrola.

The atabals of *candomblé* music echo in the lighted living room of the Zude mansion. Guni, the Swedish woman, breaks out in a smile when she hears the music, at once barbarous and religious. It was a song of Oxosse that had been recorded, the drumbeats of atabals in their ceremonies, that now echoed in the elegant room. First they moved their feet. Even Aldous Brown, the cold and melancholy Englishman, felt the call of the music make its way through his body. It was barbarous and primitive, without a doubt, but it was also powerful. Guni moved her thin, well-formed buttocks, moving her body in sensual sways, rolling her eyes, seemingly in need of a man. Julieta joined her at once; in her the black dance was more natural, even if it was more an invitation to possess her than the homage paid by blacks to their African gods. The whites who had already taken everything from them now were finally taking their religious music as a means of arousing their own desires. The men and women joined the line that was dancing in the living room, gyrating their buttocks, shaking their breasts, flinging their legs. As they passed, Julieta grabbed the poet Sérgio Moura by the hand and pulled him into the dance. The poet's hands rested on her hips, moving up and down in accompaniment to the motion of her buttocks. The Swedish man gave a harsh scream, thinking it to be the way the blacks screamed in their rituals. As the drums accelerated, the bodies in the room sought to keep pace with the rhythm of the music.

It was a "select gathering." The Zudes had invited only their intimates to the birthday party: Colonel Maneca Dantas, who had come in that day from the plantations and whose friendship was of great interest to Carlos; the Swedish couple; Brown; two English engineers from

166

the railroad; the still young Mrs. Bastos, whose husband had died of fever; the young agronomist from the Cacao Experimental Station who was Carlos's godson; Dr. Antônio Porto, an M.D.; his wife (a pretty mulatto woman, daughter of one of the richest plantation owners in Itabuna); and his two sisters.

Schwartz, Reicher and his wife, and the Rauschnings and their wives were there also. It was a group almost entirely of foreigners, and Colonel Maneca Dantas's eyes widened in reaction to the free talk and spicy stories of the women, who minced no words. The poet was also present and had brought the orchids as promised. Julieta had pinned one to the neckline of her dress, just over the breast, while the others rested in a vase hanging on the wall.

Sérgio had come with some misgiving. He wasn't accustomed to these high-toned parties, whether it be the large plantation owners taking their families to the Ilhéus Social Club or the large exporters and their exclusive gatherings, with fox-trot music playing till early morning and scandalizing the elderly ladies on their way to five o'clock mass. Feeling shy, he decided to adopt an ironic, biting mien. But that attitude was short-lived because the truth is that the poet was the *clou* of the party. Julieta introduced him as "our great poet . . ."

Almost all the men knew him, and the women were extremely friendly. Sérgio was surprised to learn that the Swedish woman was a great admirer of his and was familiar with his popular poems. She didn't leave his side throughout the beginning of the party and only let him go when Julieta came to bring him a cocktail. At the start everyone was rather quiet. Carlos was talking with Rauschning and Schwartz about the crop and the price increase. The others were spread around the room, chatting. Guni wanted Sérgio to tell her about the blacks, about witchcraft and voodoo. She laughed hysterically, clapped her hands in enthusiasm, did everything but devour the poet with her eyes. Women came over to hear Sérgio's explanations, with excitement and delight in their eyes. Sérgio introduced deliberate ribald notes, feeling a strange excitation from the unfamiliar atmosphere. In another group the young agronomist was making a hit by reading the women's palms, telling the future, present, and past. He read the palm of Julieta, whom he called godmother, without even trying to disguise the interest she aroused in him. But Carlos Zude did not consider him dangerous in the least. He was too young and too unsophisticated to interest a woman like his wife. He could see that Julieta attached no importance to him and noted a wrinkle of boredom above her lip. The agronomist predicted love affairs for Julieta, with a cynicism that disturbed Maneca Dantas.

"Godmother, I feel sorry for my godfather . . ."

Dr. Antônio Porto's wife, a country woman who had been suddenly cast into that world and had quickly acquired the defects of that crowd but nothing else, asked:

"Tell us everything . . . Don't hold back a thing!"

The agronomist asked Julieta's permission:

"Is it all right to say it, godmother?"

"Go ahead . . ."

Maneca Dantas pricked up his ears. The agronomist intoned:

"I see a great love affair . . ."

Those standing around laughed. Dr. Antônio's wife asked for details.

"What's he like?"

"Young, a good appearance, intellectual, refined . . ." The agronomist thought he was describing himself, but Julieta saw the poet Sérgio Moura down to the last detail.

"What else?" someone asked.

"Poor godfather . . ." the agronomist repeated.

Later he read other palms, and Julieta went to look for Sérgio. Servants brought drinks. One of the elegant touches at the Zudes' was that the servants wore a kind a waistcoat, like English servants. After the drinks, the atmosphere became considerably more spirited. Sérgio began to notice the married women's flirtations. Reicher and Dr. Antônio Porto's wife were surreptitiously exchanging signals, and in a corner he took her hand. Guni approached Sérgio when Carlos began putting records on the large victrola.

"Want to dance?"

They danced. Guni clung to him, her small breasts touching his chest, her cheek against his. On one of the turns Sérgio noticed Julieta looking jealous and felt happy. When the fox-trot ended he went over to her. But she was aloof, and he had to make a few flattering remarks to get her to smile. When they played the next fox-trot he danced with her. The agronomist looked at them, seeming to understand. That was why he decided to go after Guni. First, however, he whispered to Aldous Brown: "Godmother is really scandalous with that would-be poet." Sérgio, enraptured by the dance, said nothing; now and then Julieta's hair brushed his cheek. He wished he could kiss her at that moment.

Around the room, the conversation, the flirtations, and the discussions went on. Schwartz, who didn't dance, was discussing cacao with Reicher, along with politics. Reicher, a Jew, the son of Bessarabian immigrants, was attacking Nazism, which Schwartz vehemently defended. The agronomist went from woman to woman, finally pausing with the fat wife of the elder Rauschning, who laughed at his feeble jokes in a graceless titter. She wore large diamonds on her small, fat fingers. Aldous yawned in the company of the widowed Mrs. Bastos; the word in the city was that they were lovers. Maneca Dantas continued to drink and feel scandalized. His white hair fell over his forehead, and at that moment he was thinking of his son, who must be in the cabaret or gambling at Pepe Espinola's house. Maneca Dantas felt himself abandoned there, lonely, in the middle of something he found alien. The only time he really talked, and then at length, was when he told Guni about the battles over Sequeiro Grande. The Swede almost fainted at the details.

It was when they all had a few drinks in them that Carlos played the *candomblé* music. It looked like a madhouse. Only Carlos, standing beside the victrola, and Maneca Dantas, staring wide-eyed, took no part in that high-society Afro-Brazilian ceremony in which, under the pretext of doing a religious dance, they gave vent to all their repressed desires. They lined up one behind the other, their hands on the waist of the person ahead of them. Sérgio's hands slipped from time to time and stroked Julieta's buttocks. At times the line contracted, and Julieta leaned her body against his, leaned against him tightly, pressing. Suddenly they all broke apart and began dancing separately, face to face. Julieta looked him straight in the eye, then bit her lip in a gesture of strong desire. They leapt about like savages; the agronomist jumped up and down, as did Aldous. Carlos Zude watched with his expressionless eyes; Maneca Dantas had never seen the likes of it.

Later Antônio Porto's wife asked if they knew how to play the "sweethearts game." They said no, but Julieta and the agronomist, and possibly others, were lying. They decided to play it. Mrs. Porto directed the game. Maneca Dantas tried to beg off but she wouldn't hear of it. The men and women went to one room, while the doctor's wife remained by herself in the other. She called the wife of the younger Rauschning and Carlos and explained: "This is the living room of a house where everyone—parents, brothers and sisters, even the servants—is away. The only ones there are the daughter and her boyfriend, sitting on the sofa." She had them sit down. Then she asked them:

"What do you think they would be doing?"

They took each other's hand. Then one of the women was brought in, another explanation, and she placed the heads of the couple together, narrowing the distance between them. Then she had to take Mrs. Rauschning's place beside Carlos. A man came in, heard the explanation, and placed Carlos so he was kissing the woman's hair. He took Carlos's place. And so, one by one, they came in. When Maneca Dantas's turn came he had to hold Guni on his lap. She smiled, draped over his legs. His flesh, that of a virile old man, quivered. When he got up, replaced by Sérgio, his legs were shaky and sweaty. With Guni in his lap, Sérgio was gripped by arousal. Julieta came in, placed Guni's hand around Sérgio's

neck, and brought their faces together; she knew she was to take the
other woman's place. And when she did so, as they waited for Reicher
to arrive and make new changes, she slowly stroked his neck. Sérgio's
lips were flush with Julieta's face. Around them everyone was laughing,
finding it a delightful prank. By now Carlos's expression was morose;
he suggested that they dance instead of playing that silly game.

The party lasted till morning. In the living room with its smoked glass
they did not hear the rain outside. Guni danced a scandalous dance in
which she raised her skirt. Aldous had lipstick on his face, and Mrs.
Bastos's lipstick needed refreshing. Carlos put more records on the
victrola; the agronomist repeated the same vapid jokes, successfully in
the case of Mrs. Rauschning. Julieta and Sérgio talked on the sofa. She
would phone him the next day.

Sérgio left with Maneca Dantas. The high-society party had shaken the
colonel's long-held ideas about the family. He had read, he didn't know
where, about the crisis facing the family, the danger of its dissolution.
He had also heard the bishop's sermon on the subject, a very eloquent
sermon. But tonight he had seen it for himself. He was astonished, and
he summed up his astonishment in a phrase:

"It's the end of the world, Mr. Sérgio, the end of the world!"

"And it's going to end in a new flood, Colonel. Just look at the
rain . . ."

But Colonel Maneca Dantas was speaking seriously. There was
amazement in his voice and his eyes were popping at what he had
seen:

"It's the end of the world . . ."

The Boom

1

The boom lasted three years. It began unexpectedly, after the rains, giving the impression of having come in the belly of the black clouds that filled the skies over the city and countryside at the end of that year. For three years Ilhéus and the cacao zone swam in gold. "Money lost its importance," Colonel Maneca Dantas had the habit of saying some time later. Ilhéus and the cacao zone swam in gold, bathed in champagne, slept with French women recently arrived from Rio. At the Trianon, the most chic of the city's cabarets, the aforementioned Colonel Maneca Dantas lit cigars with bills of five hundred mil-réis, repeating the gesture of all the country's rich plantation owners in earlier booms—coffee, rubber, cotton, and sugar. The prostitutes— even the worn-out and decadent ones—received gifts of necklaces and rings; ships brought to Ilhéus, Itabuna, and Itapira, to the port of Canaveiras, to Belmonte and Rio de Contas the strangest cargos: jazz bands and expensive perfumes, hairdressers and masseurs, gardeners, agronomists, and seedlings of European fruit trees for the orchards, adventurers and luxury automobiles. It was spectacular, much like a carnival procession.

The boom got its start at the beginning of the rains that saved that year's early crop. Captain João Magalhães gained a reputation as a man of vision because, according to several people who had been with him on a bus trip, he had seen the coming of the boom before anyone else. For many years cacao, as in these sad days of the present, had hovered around an average of fourteen to fifteen mil-réis per fifteen kilos, with a maximum of nineteen in good years. Even so, it was an excellent crop that brought appreciable profits and made the colonels wealthy. Suddenly it began to climb dizzily. To tell the truth, at first no one sought an explanation for the unexpected boom.

It was only some months later that the communists launched their first flyers denouncing the cacao exporters' action. In the first months there was general astonishment, quickly supplanted by greed. In one month futures of fifteen kilos of superior grade cacao went from nineteen to twenty-eight and a half. Two months later they rose to thirty. Every glance betrayed the lust for profit, as ships began bringing new things to the port of Ilhéus. Stevedores had more work than they could handle. At midyear cacao shot up headlong once more and by the end of the harvest was selling at thirty-five. "There's money to burn," the attorney Rui Dantas would say, sitting in the bar over a glass of gin. Like that of all the inhabitants of the cacao zone, his life had undergone an abrupt transformation with the boom. When cacao hit thirty-five, everyone thought the boom had peaked out. The price would not go any higher. Only Joaquim and his comrades knew that this was the beginning of an economic adventure that would not only change the lives of a few men but would transform the whole of the cacao zone. With the new harvest came new surprises: cacao rose to forty-two mil-réis. In time it reached fifty, fifty-two at its peak. On that occasion, at the beginning of the third year of the boom, no one was any longer surprised. Anything was possible in those wondrous lands. In the final year the price of cacao at no time fell below forty-eight and gave the impression it would never fall. Afterwards events happened quite rapidly and ushered in the era of those the poet Sérgio Moura was to call the "beggar millionaires."

There is a photo of the port of Ilhéus, still published today by the newspapers in the state capital when they print some noteworthy fact about the "Queen of the South," a photo shot during the boom. It was taken from the peak of Conquest Hill and shows eight ships of various types and sizes jamming the small port, almost on top of one another, three planes on the ground, motorboats, barges, and sailboats. It also shows crowds scurrying through nearby streets toward the docks. It was an exceptional day, perhaps, but the entire boom was exceptional, like one long, strange festival. It was during those years that the city government took serious notice of the long-standing problem of the port and began thinking about building new piers in the part of Ilhéus facing the sea, thus freeing the city from dependence on the small port and the difficult and hazardous sandbar.

Another reason was that it was during the cacao boom that the *Itacaré* disaster occurred. This was a passenger yacht that ran aground on the bar one stormy morning, resulting in a large number of deaths. It was overloaded like any of the ships entering that magical port in the splendid times of cacao at forty mil-réis. It was carrying a jazz band, prostitutes, colonels, students, and lawyers. It was also carrying immigrants, and the band was playing just before the shipwreck. Among the street poetry dealing with the disaster was one that went:

> 'Twas August twenty-third,
> The clock had just struck nine,
> Ilhéus got the word
> Of shipwreck in the brine.
> All by the tempest toss'd,
> The Itacaré was lost,
> And yet no cry was heard.

The event rocked and horrified Ilhéus. But, still, how to deny, short of lying, that the magnitude of the drama engendered a feeling of pride in the inhabitants, who were becoming accustomed to seeing everything in Ilhéus in large scale: the fortunes, the scandals, the construction, the dodges, the festivals, and now disasters also? It was a month with no sensational news for the dailies, and even the papers in Bahia and the major ones in the south—Rio and São Paulo—gave a great deal of coverage to the event. One of them even flew in a reporter, who interviewed survivors and took pictures. The street poetry called the day of the shipwreck a "holiday" in Ilhéus.

The reporter, in the several stories he filed, noted the agitation of commerce, the excitement running through the city and the cacao zone. The wreck of the Itacaré did not dissipate the nervous happiness that possessed the inhabitants like some hitherto unknown fever—neither the wreck of the Itacaré nor the subsequent scandals that rocked the city one after the other as the boom ran its course.

Years later, when business had returned to normal, when Ilhéus once more awoke to balanced prices for cacao, after the great boom and the great bust, a foreign university professor doing research in economics in the northeast of Brazil (he later published a book in his own country) spent a few days in the cacao zone, studying its characteristics. He had been recommended to a local merchant by a mutual acquaintance from São Paulo. The open wounds left in the life of the city and surrounding towns by the frightful bust, recently ended, were by then beginning to heal. But no one blamed the bust. They all blamed the boom.

The foreign professor, with his wire-rim glasses and his air of a precocious boy, eager for statistical data, economic details, and numbers, turned to the merchant who was acting as his guide and who struck him as well informed, took out a small notebook and a pencil (they were in a bar), and asked:

"What facts characterized here the cacao boom?" His Portuguese, learned from a grammar book prior to his departure, was hard and metallic and contrasted with his air of an ingenuous boy.

His informant thought a bit and soon answered:

"The scandals . . . Ah, sir, frightful scandals . . . There'd never been so many, and one right after the other . . . The men acted like they'd gone crazy, women too. Family responsibility disappeared. Father fought with son, husband with wife, daughter-in-law with mother-in-law . . . Naked women—naked as a jaybird, sir, believe me—walked down these very streets. Respectable men left their families for fancy women . . . It was the thing for married women to have a lover . . ."

The economics professor from the foreign university opened his mouth rather foolishly. His informant dropped his arms, still impressed with the memories of those years:

"I never expected to see so much, and if they'd told me I'd have said they were lying. But I saw them with these very eyes that I'll take to my grave . . . It was horrible, sir, horrible . . ."

He summed it all up in a difficult word, one with which he intended to show the foreign professor that he was no ignoramus as he might think:

"It was a pandemonium, sir, a pandemonium . . ."

The professor was wide-eyed behind his glasses, making him look like a scared child. He did not succeed in getting a single statistic from the merchant, but he heard, throughout that long and whiskey-filled night, the most appalling stories ever heard by a professor of economics.

With the boom came feverish construction, not only in Ilhéus but also in Itabuna, Pirangi, Palestina, and Guaraci, in the cities and small towns. Land came to be worth a fortune, second in cost only to Rio. Colonel Maneca Dantas sank five hundred thousand in building a mansion in Ilhéus, a present for Dona Auricídia's old age; during the bust he sold it, with great difficulty, for a hundred and twenty. New streets were opened. In Itabuna a small radio station came into being, with loudspeakers in the squares. Before long Ilhéus had one of its own. The growing rivalry between the two cities expressed itself through the newspapers, the soccer teams, and the year-end festivals.

The colonels suddenly found themselves with wads of money in their hands and didn't know what to do with it. They had spent their entire lives conquering and planting the land, buying fields, harvesting cacao, spending the profits from harvests on maintaining their houses, their sons' education, and the plantations. Now there was money to burn. And as there was no more land to conquer—much less any to buy— the colonels didn't know what to do with the money. They gambled in cabarets, playing roulette, baccarat, and cards, but since that wasn't enough, they played the stock market. It was an exciting game, and they gambled heavily in it, with the same unflinching courage that had always characterized them, and with unflinching ignorance as well. They understood nothing of that game but thought it worthy of them and of the times in which they were living.

The appreciation of the cacao plantations far surpassed anything even the elder Rauschning had imagined. The value of the fields did not quadruple as he had predicted: it increased tenfold. Anyone who owned land would not hear of selling it. Offers to buy came from all sides. People came from north and south looking to acquire a cacao plantation. When Dr. Antônio Porto had to sell his fields and move to the south, after the dreadful scandal involving his wife, who had run out of the house after her lover, half naked through the streets of Ilhéus at noon on a business day, he received impressive offers. They paid him a fortune per square yard of land planted in cacao, but there is no record of any other fields being sold during the boom. Cacao was synonymous with gold, the best crop one could wish for, the best use of capital. The inhabitants of Ilhéus said this with great pride.

If the number of new faces in the streets of Ilhéus had already been large, the boom brought to the cacao zone a multitude from all parts. People looking for work and fortune, adventurers seeking only to exploit the moment. It was during this period that the red-light districts of Aracaju, Bahia, and Recife emptied out, with ships and small sailboats arriving packed with women—white, black, and mulatto, foreign and Brazilian—all thirsting for money, disembarking with huge grins plastered on their faces and drinking champagne at night in the cabarets, where they helped the colonels at the roulette tables.

Five cabarets filled the sleepless nights of Ilhéus with noise. The Trianon, on a first floor near the sea, was a luxurious cabaret of unbridled gaming where virtually no one but the colonels and the exporters was admitted. It was where the most expensive prostitutes hung out, the French and Polish women who had come from Rio de Janeiro, ready to teach their generous planters the most refined forms of vice. The Bataclã was the most democratic, though there was still a predominance of colonels there, crowding the gambling rooms. It was on Unhão Street, facing the port. In the dancing rooms, however, one could find students on vacation, merchants just starting their careers, employees from the business establishments. It was an old cabaret and the only one to survive the bust, continuing in existence through the years. At the El-Dorado, on nights of partying, the white-collar workers gathered. It was lively and almost familylike in its modesty, featuring beer and local women. The Far-West, on Toad Street, attracted overseers from the plantations, small planters, stevedores, and seamen. The owner banked the card games, which were played with greasy decks in the back room. Sometimes there were disturbances and the police would intervene. It was closed down once but quickly reopened. The dominant figure in the Far-West was Wasp-Waist Rita, she of the immense buttocks who sang sambas and danced on top of a table. She was introduced by a thin and effeminate cabaretier as the "great vedette of the samba," despite this being the first place where she had ever engaged in that profession. She had come to Ilhéus as cook for a wealthy family. One day an overseer, drunk and in love, shot her in those buttocks that tempted him so. At the Bataclã there shone another celebrated woman, Agripina. Slim and vice-ridden, she murdered tangos and drove romantic students wild with passion. They nicknamed her the Vamp because of her languorous gaze, and a student wrote a sonnet dedicated to her. The poorest people frequented the Retiro, a sordid cabaret at the edge of the docks, where beer was a luxury. They were factory workers, field hands who came down to the city, loafers, bums, and thieves. There was a blind man who played the flute and now and again some customer would play the guitar. There was a time when upper class young men, well-heeled students on vacation, would go to the Retiro in search of the picturesque. Truth be told, that only happened when Rosa, abandoned by Martins, made her debut there as a waitress. They went because of her, an incredible beauty amid the sordidness of that poorest of all cabarets. It was from the Trianon, on days when they really hung one on, when Karbanks was in town and enlivened everything by his presence, that the Ipicilone Group set out. This was the most extravagant of all the things brought about by the cacao boom in the city of São Jorge dos Ilhéus. It consisted of men and women, intoxicated, taking off their pants and skirts and, in the early hours while the city slept, marching seminude from the cabaret to the street of prostitutes, singing the group's official song:

> I won't go to your house,
> 'Cause you don't come to mine.
> You've got a big bottom
> That my mullet fits just fine.

They would wake up the lightly sleeping old maids, and sometimes even scandalized the pious churchwomen heading for five o'clock mass, who would carry to the bishop's ears the echoes of such horrors. From their pulpits the bishops and priests would condemn with flaming words the evil life of the people of Ilhéus, promising that the fires of hell awaited those disgraceful revelers. But work on the new cathedral got a shot in the arm with the boom, its steeples rising heavenward, an architectural horror that the people of Ilhéus declared would be the grandest church in the southern part of the state.

The boom also promoted the growth of the spiritualist centers that left back streets to thrust themselves upon the civilized heart of the city in a chain of "séances." The boats brought well-known mediums, seers, and miracle workers. When the colonels weren't in the cabarets it was because they were at "séances," where they went to ask the spirits' advice on how to play the market. There was also a significant rise in the influence of the fascist party, the Integralists, whose leaders began a major fund-raising campaign. Wearing their green shirts, they held parades in which they announced the demise of liberal-democracy.

The city government built a large stadium (which the local press, as it had in reference to the high school, said was "the best in the north of the country"), where teams from Itabuna came to play hard-fought soccer games. It opened and paved new streets, cutting down the few remaining coconut palms along the coast. Intellectuals came from Rio de Janeiro to give lectures. Someone, welcoming one of them and alluding to the incredible number of traveling salesmen with the most varied products who disembarked in Ilhéus, dubbed them "the traveling salesmen of culture." They came in every boat, bringing everything and managing to sell it all. There was money; the only problem was finding something to buy with it. Planes and ships arrived fully loaded and left fully loaded. Doctors and lawyers arrived and spread into the farthest outlying towns. Highways were extended farther and farther, and swift buses came and went without an empty seat. They carried Syrians with their suitcases on their backs, highway peddlers, future small town merchants. Fortunes were born, and the colonels spent money like water. Suddenly they were seeing the result of all they had done for thirty years, since the period of the conquest of the land. It had been worth the sacrifice, the deaths, the bloodshed. The conquered land yielded fruits of gold.

When, one day the poet Sérgio Moura attempted to characterize the boom years, he uttered the following phrase:

"It got to such an astounding point that they even opened two bookstores in Ilhéus! . . ."

2

The scandals the merchant mentioned to the foreign professor began with the "badger game" perpetrated by Pepe Espinola on Colonel Frederico Pinto at the start of the boom. A cabaret was proposed as well as a group to establish the Trianon, and Pepe needed money. The Argentine saw the chance to get enough money for the rest of his life. It was incredible how he was dreaming more and more of a peaceful house (he imagined it as being just like his parents') in a district outside Buenos Aires, perhaps Chacaritas. A house for an old bachelor, money in the bank to cover expenses, and his city, which already seemed lost to him. Her tangos, her theaters, her cabarets, the countless lights in the streets—all that he had left behind now beckoned him. Perhaps in that idea of an exclusive chic cabaret, with gambling, champagne, and women from Rio, lay the fulfillment of his dream, so fearfully difficult to attain.

The twenty thousand mil-réis that Colonel Frederico Pinto had given Pepe to pay for his return to Argentina were sunk into that business, and all of Ilhéus found the matter amusing.

Pepe left Rui Dantas at the Bataclã around eleven o'clock and headed home. At dinnertime he had mentioned that he wouldn't be back before morning. Colonel Frederico Pinto had eaten with them, praising the fish, looking forward to an evening of love in Lola's arms. They knew Pepe's night-owl habits; Lola had complained bitterly about them, amidst easy tears, when the comedy began: whenever he went to the cabaret he never returned till the wee hours of the morning. There was no need for warning. The colonel got in bed with his lover, without a worry in the world. He didn't even notice Lola's melancholy excitement, a certain shame that made her divert her eyes.

When Pepe came in unexpectedly the colonel became nervous. It was not fear, for Frederico was a man tested in fighting, accustomed to shoot-outs where blood flowed. It never even entered his head that it could all be an act. When he saw Pepe's fury and desperation he became so nervous it was pitiful. Pepe knew it wasn't fear. It was shame for the betrayed husband, a certain remorse, and a certain sadness. Pepe also knew it would do no good to try frightening the colonel. If he tried, he'd ruin everything because Frederico would react. Therefore he opted for pathos, a scene he had rehearsed at length. He opened the door, stood looking at them both, covered his face with his hands:

"They told me, but I didn't believe it . . . *No lo creí!*"

It was a heartrending cry, a sob that filled the bedroom. The colonel felt it in his chest and was ashamed. Pepe dropped into a chair, attempting to speak Portuguese, hurt and querulous:

"Colonel, I never expected this of you. I trusted you like my mother . . . I never expected it . . . Not from you and not from her . . ."

Frederico looked at him. Pepe had tears in his eyes, a creature reduced to nothing. Colonel Frederico Pinto felt humiliated at what he had done and didn't know what to say. He felt the desire to console Pepe, felt that he liked him. The Argentine went on:

"I thought she loved me . . . and you were my friend . . . I never expected . . ."

He turned to Lola, a sudden rebellion in his voice:

"You bitch!"

Only then did the colonel speak, to say that it wasn't Lola's fault. He got up from the bed, small and nervous, a comic sight in his nudity in the middle of the bedroom, defending the woman. Pepe felt like laughing his head off as he let the tears stream from his eyes. Lola had hidden beneath the covers, and Pepe could imagine it was her heroic effort to hold back the laughter that moved the sheet over his lover's breasts. Colonel Frederico Pinto was quite agitated and was trembling. Pepe forced tears from his urge to laugh.

They easily arrived at an understanding. The colonel would give them twenty thousand so they could return to Argentina ("trips abroad are very expensive," Pepe had explained) and start life anew. The important thing was that he would not abandon her, as he had threatened to do.

"That is what I should do, Colonel. I do not because of you."

"It was an act of madness by us both . . ." Frederico explained.

Pepe would have the money the following day. The colonel put on his clothes in Pepe's sight, very abashed, and set a meeting for the next day in the bar. Frederico was still apologizing—"I lost my head." Pepe wiped his eyes. Beneath the sheets Lola was gasping, a part of her naked thigh visible. From the bedroom door the colonel looked back and saw the white flesh. He shook his head sadly and left. The door to the street closed, his steps faded into the distance. Pepe lay down on the bed and stretched out his arms:

"I'm tired . . ."

But he raised himself to a sitting position because now Lola's sobs were louder, her face still hidden by the sheet. Pepe uncovered her:

"*Qué pasa*? What's the matter?"

Lola's voice emerged through throttled sobs:

"He loved me, Pepe. He loved me . . ."

"They've all loved you, you silly girl."

"No. This one really and truly loved me. I feel sorry for him, poor man! So good . . . Like a child . . ."

She turned her large liquid eyes to him and said:

"Pepe, I don't know how I stand this life. It's so dirty, so miserable . . . If I didn't love you, I don't know . . . I think I'd kill myself . . . Yes, I'd kill myself . . . I'm dirty, Pepe, all the way to my soul . . . Dirty . . ."

Pepe took the woman's hand. He remembered Dandy. He reached out his other hand, found Lola's blonde hair. He caressed it softly, sweetly, with infinite tenderness:

"One must have character!"

The sheet muffled her sobs.

3

From the rustic, impassioned hands of Colonel Frederico Pinto, Lola Espinola passed to the soft, versifying hands of the lawyer Rui Dantas. Pepe threw himself into the business of the cabaret, went off to hire women in the south, for behind the gambling and dancing at the Trianon was the house with its imported women, its main business. It was only then that Ilhéus fully realized Pepe's true profession. The house where he pimped for the whores was frequented by exporters and rich colonels. It was easier to fool with almost anything in Ilhéus than with the "Love Nest," the name Karbanks had given to the half-hidden bungalow. Which is why Colonel Frederico Pinto's efforts to enlist the mayor and police chief in a move to run Pepe out of town came to naught.

"Nobody forced him to act so stupid," they said on the street corners of Ilhéus by way of commentary on the scandal. The event was savored in every way possible, and even a venomous epigram circulated about the affair, one that began:

> Lola was a married woman,
> Or so thought Frederico Pinto . . .

They told the colonel that the epigram was penned by Sérgio Moura, but then many things in Ilhéus for which he was not responsible were attributed to the poet. Sometime later Frederico learned that the epigram was by Zito Ferreira, to whom he had told the story the night of the "badger game," while drunk and still thinking of himself as a homewrecker.

After the scandal the colonel spent some time at the plantation. But before long he was back, recounting in bars his adventures with new dark-skinned mulatto girls, conquests achieved in the fields: he had set up one of them, by the name of Rita, in her own place in town. But he would permit no one to speak of his affair with Lola; that drove him out of his mind and he would reaffirm his intention to have his revenge against "that thieving foreigner." The truth is, however, that when the colonel returned from his plantation almost no one was any longer talking about his affair. "The topic of the day," as Reinaldo Bastos, consumed with jealousy, put it, was Julieta Zude's brazenness with the poet Sérgio Moura. Taking his revenge for the epigram that he still believed to be of Sérgio's authorship, Colonel Frederico Pinto went from one group to the next, from bar to bar, commenting on the spicy deed. Everywhere he met with a ready reception, a very ready reception, for the spiteful commentary. Many disliked Sérgio Moura. As for Julieta, haughty and distant, they had no tolerance for her and felt an instinctive suspicion toward her. This was especially true on the part of the married ladies, the churchgoing old maids, and the marriageable young women who secretly envied her. She was like a foreigner and had nothing in common with them. Instinctively they placed her on a par with Lola, on the same plane, greeting her with respect only because she was the wife of Carlos Zude, one of the biggest cacao exporters. Julieta smoked, wore shorts on the beach, walked down the avenue in slacks in the morning, spoke freely with men, and had few and distant dealings with the local society women. They talked about her manner and her clothes at the Ilhéus Social Club dances, and she bordered on being a permanent scandal. Rumors about those exclusive parties at Carlos Zude's house, with Englishmen and Swedes, Germans and Swiss, would arrive in distorted form to barroom tables and the bosom of families. Reinaldo Bastos, who, ever since he had spoken with Julieta had been living in expectation of a glance from her, a summons to her bed, and who now saw she had fallen for the poet, was consumed with anger. He spread the word that he had caught her buying books by Freud in one of the local bookstores. And to those who asked for explanations as to who this Freud was, he whispered in confidence:

"He writes pornographic novels . . ."

Which led Zito Ferreira to give him a lecture on psychoanalysis that cost him a bite of fifty mil-réis. When Julieta crossed the streets of the business district, replying with a curt, dry nod to the effusive salutations of the customers of Zude Brothers & Co., satirical smiles preceded the malicious comments. Some took upon themselves the task of counting the number of times she passed by the Commercial Association, the times that Sérgio came to the window, the exact number of smiles they exchanged.

"A disgrace," they concluded.

But the house of Zude Brothers & Co. paid the highest prices for cacao and everyone wanted to be their customer. They would bow when Julieta, knowing nothing of the scandal she was causing, appeared in the street, serious and beautiful with her Spanish face, languid eyes, and dark hair. And sometimes, happy and carefree, she would casually visit the Commercial Association, startling the stenographer and the accountant.

It was said that more than once she had bedded down with the poet on the couches at the Association. Rui Dantas, whose literary differences with Sérgio Moura went back a long way, had attempted to substitute the word "association" in the local speech for "rendezvous" or the slang term "love nest." Whenever he headed for a brothel he would inform those around him:

"I'm going to the Commercial Association . . ."

This joke was a huge success in the bars of Ilhéus and was widely repeated. Bit by bit, however, other scandals began to diminish the local interest in Sérgio and Julieta.

Truthfully, the first time that Sérgio Moura possessed Carlos Zude's wife actually was in the Commercial Association. She had arrived at the end of the afternoon and was going through an agonizing day. That was why she had come, without fear of evil tongues, like a desperate person who, disillusioned with doctors, turns to a faith healer, caring little what people will say.

They exchanged their first kisses in the meeting room. Julieta did so seeking in the sexual novelty of the man the cure to her crisis. *I'll never see him again,* she thought as he kissed her slowly, first on the eyes, then on the cheeks, and nibbled her ear. The poet sat in the president's chair, the same chair where Carlos Zude had laid out his ideas to the other exporters, and Julieta sat on his lap. Sensing like some small wild animal the exciting smell of the nape of the woman's neck, the poet buried his nose in her dark hair, where he could distinguish nuances of perfume, the smell of washed skin mixed with that of expensive scents. She clung to him, forgetting everything in the unalloyed excitement of the flesh, in her need for a man. She closed her eyes; perhaps afterwards the sadness, the anguish, the "neura" might be greater and more terrible. But in that twilight, everything went away—the senseless anxiety, the unexplained pain, the total emptiness that was killing her.

Evening was falling over the city and the room was darkening rapidly. Sérgio had not turned on the lights. He pushed aside Julieta's dress and kissed her left shoulder. She shuddered voluptuously, and that first possession was violent, like a black man covering a mulatto woman on the sandy docks in a hurried and dangerous coupling. He dragged her to the couch, raised her clothing; she stifled a sigh. When they finished, Julieta took Sérgio's hands, feeling the need to say something:

"Do you love me?"

It was a necessary piece of playacting, she thought. She owed him that for not feeling nervous anymore. She would have liked to come, go to bed with him, and leave—cured, lightened, finding the afternoon as the sun set beautiful beyond description, without having to say anything, without having to pay.

But she thought that was impossible, and gave herself to the task of playacting:

"Do you love me?"

Sérgio, however, wanted her; she was something his pride desired. It was necessary to conquer her, he was well aware of that. And he did not answer. He understood, with a certain subtlety, that if he answered they would both be playacting and Julieta would never return.

And he spoke of different matters, spoke of art and poetry, told stories, marvelously ingenuous stories of birds and flowers that he had gathered among men of the countryside during his research into folklore. He allowed his rich and wild imagination to roam loose in a kind of wandering that captivated the woman. He was proud of having possessed the beautiful woman, young and desirable, and desired to keep her. Possibly it would take some time for him to understand Julieta entirely, but he perceived her like one who divines a light among trees by the halo emanating from it.

Perhaps—almost certainly—at that initial moment, before the first possession and the long, half-crazed conversation that followed, the interest on the part of the rich and neurasthenic young woman in the poet, a man she felt to be different from the others in the city, was destined for the same short life as the sentiment that had tied her to previous lovers. Perhaps she would not have loved him for long; she had had other lovers before, at least two, and when she had given herself to them she had been driven by the same need to forget the sadness that seized her, to fill that anguished time. The only thing greater than that desperate anguish was the spasm of love that made her forget everything, that let her rest and brought her a sudden tranquillity. But the interest was short-lived, and immediately afterwards the man no longer satisfied her, became just like Carlos, the same routine, powerless before the terrible anguish. There was nothing left.

But it was no longer that way when, after the violent and primal possession, he spoke, crazy and smiling, in a torrent of lively words, of diverse and seductive matters. For Julieta Zude it was another world, a world about which she had never even suspected, of whose existence she had been completely ignorant. And it was a beautiful world, one of values previously unknown to her, of daring values. All the values that till then had represented to Julieta the essence of life—money, luxury, business, cocktails, parties—sank before the disdain they elicited from Sérgio Moura, to be replaced by other values that Julieta Zude suddenly saw in the Ilhéus twilight, one day at the beginning of the boom. Birds and books, flowers and verses, phrases, people, feelings that he evoked with words that blended happiness, insanity, and irony. She was a bit startled but infinitely happy. And then she asked questions. She asked all sorts of things and he answered every question. She felt like someone who, traveling through a fog, finally succeeds in breaking through and sees the truth of meadows, crystalline waters of rivers, the colorful gaiety of the landscape, life itself unfolding.

Sérgio was talking like that because, timid and aggressive in his timidity, he was constantly ill at ease among men. He had once said that conversation between men was always a struggle, with a hidden meaning in every word, and almost always a bad one. It was a battle of words in which each sought to prevail. The only time he had not felt this was in the meeting of the communists where he had come forth so spontaneously. With women, though, he dropped many of the masks he used to hide his timidity, and then there was no divergence between him and his poetry, sweet and rebellious, almost for children. He became jovial and a bit irresponsible, lost the shyness that made him aggressive with men, the timidity that led him to scandalize Ilhéus with his garishly colored clothes.

At that moment what he felt for Julieta was merely desire. Desire for a beautiful, civilized, sensual woman, desire for the wife of Carlos Zude, the exporter, who symbolized everything that Sérgio detested, and desire also—yes, also!—for a woman, just a woman, nothing else, more capable of understanding him than men. Desire to be who he was, for some minutes at least. And desire to conquer her so she would return and he could have her again and talk afterwards. Julieta laughed.

"You're crazy . . ."

She looked into his eyes. They were so childlike! She saw the desire shining in them, believed it was love, and that belief completed the feeling of enchantment and joy that had welled up inside her. And then all the enchantment grew into desire, compelling and new. No longer was it that anxiety to forget anguish in the act of union, in the heat of the man. It was the desire to give herself fully to one who was both her love and her friend, one who was like a part of her own self. It was all pure joy; Julieta felt herself led by an impulse she had never felt before. And she kissed the poet with the gentleness of innocent courtship. Sérgio opened her dress, took her breasts in his hands, kissed them with burning pleasure, which to Julieta was the height of tenderness. He brought orchids when she took off the last of her clothing. Orchids red and white, violet and spottled, all those that had sprouted amid the rough cacti in the Association's garden. Scattered them over the woman's splendid body.

The voluptuous and almost childish game described in one of Sérgio Moura's most beautiful poems is the re-creation in verse of the free-flowing rhythm of that early nightfall, when the mysteries of sex held for Julieta Zude a meaning of peace that she had never before found. One verse speaks of the "serpents of your tongue spearing the sex of orchids," while another says that "orchids were born in the white lands of buttocks." In that game, almost a child's game, so refined in the vice of love that it was almost pure, they spent the melancholy hour of twilight. When he said "daybreak" instead of twilight, Julieta understood because that was what she felt. And when night came, filtering stars through the platbands of the windowpanes over the woman's naked body, that long and almost painful possession completed for Julieta the image of the man she had waited for and recognized. He was a sorcerer or a god, his gentle head was filled with thoughts, and she smiled in the fatigued serenity of love. In the poem, Sérgio Moura speaks of "tongue venomous like orchid petals," and of "tongue wise in all the lore of love," but only in that twilight did Julieta feel the tongue capable of achieving miracles in creating worlds from words, worlds more real than the sad and poor world of riches in which she lived. And she said so when she read, in later times, the poem he had written, that poem like a lullaby, entitled "An orchid was born in the Land of Cacao." And it was only then that he understood Julieta fully.

The second possession was long and almost painful because of its subtlety, as birds trilled attempting to keep pace with the wounded rhythm of the sighs of love in the meeting room. And when they stretched their tired bodies and lay side by side in the newborn night, she pleaded, yearning for the magic world that the poet possessed:

"Talk . . . Talk, I want to hear you . . ."

4

For the first year of the boom Antônio Vítor thought only of Raimunda's well-being. Since there were no more lands to buy, Raimunda thought they should put the profits in the bank. Raimunda was one of the few people in the entire cacao zone who was suspicious of the boom from the very first. If they asked her why, she had no answer. She had not seen Joaquim during those months, so it could not have been her son who warned her. Her gloomy air, gloomier by the day, contrasted with Antônio Vítor's joy. Antônio Vítor thought of two things immediately: building a new house on the farm ("the plantation," as he now put it, excited by the appreciation of his land thanks to the boom), and going to Estância for a visit after the harvest. He had other, smaller projects: hiring a greater number of workers so that neither he nor Raimunda would have to return to the hard work of harvesting or to the drying frames.

He never expected Raimunda to react the way she did. There was no way to make her understand that it didn't look right for the wife of a "plantation owner," a "man of money," to work the harvest like the wife of some hired hand, trample cacao in the troughs like some black person. Raimunda shook her head, looking at her husband as if she feared that the boom had driven him crazy. The boom upset the normality of their life. It had been a difficult life at first; they had worked hard, but when the boom came times were already good, for they had enough to live on, with their land planted and their cacao producing. By bringing new value to cacao, the boom upset all that. Raimunda was afraid. She looked at her husband, who dreamed of absurd projects, and felt she barely knew him. Now he had the harebrained notion that she shouldn't work the harvest, that they should take on more workers. Without even saying no, the next day she went

189

out to the fields, the machete blade tucked in her waistband. Antônio
Vítor saw her leave and had no alternative but to go himself, the
scythe on his shoulder, his feet unshod. He had thought about not
going barefoot anymore, of never removing his boots. That's what the
plantation owners did. He shook his head in disapproval of "Munda's
backwardness." He would like to see her resting, reaping the profits of
the land in that year when the fruit of the cacao tree was more valuable
than gold dust. In Ilhéus the price of cacao was climbing sharply.

He began building the new house. He wanted something good.
Raimunda was against it but Antônio Vítor was unyielding. They
had an argument that involved few words, and he stalked out in a fit
of rage. After that she did not interfere again. From the adobe house
she could see the other one rising, the bricks laid, the masons preparing
the mixture of lime and sand. First they had dug deep trenches for the
stone foundation, after which the walls began to go up. Raimunda felt
an unexplainable hatred (or was it fear?) of the new house. One day
the roof tiles arrived, brand new. Raimunda was summoned by Antônio
Vítor's shouts:

"Munda! Oh Munda!"

She replied from the kitchen:

"What is it?"

"Come see the roof tiles for the new house . . ."

Raimunda did not want to see them. Only late in the afternoon, when
she had finished the last of the day's tasks, did she lay eyes on the
"French" roof tiles. Small and shiny, they were different from the others
and must have cost a fortune. Raimunda shook her head in disapproval,
wandering through the house and grumbling under her breath.

There was a party the day the roof ridge was raised. For Raimunda
there was no doubt that this business of the boom was addling Antônio
Vítor's head. He wasn't in his right mind anymore, that was for sure!
Else how could he—right in the middle of the harvest!—give the
workers half a day off so they could come to the party? The roof
ridge beam was decorated with paper streamers. The openings where
later the doors and windows would go were covered with palm fronds.
Great quantities of rum were distributed. The only one who didn't
show up was Raimunda. Firmo had come, as well as other nearby
small farmers and the hired laborers.

Antônio Vítor was beside himself with happiness. At that same
moment, alone in the fields, with her sharpened machete blade
Raimunda was cutting open the cacao pods gathered by the workers
that morning.

And things got worse with the arrival of the expensive furniture he
had purchased in Ilhéus: armchairs for the living room, a soft mattress

and a bed with a wire frame, a cupboard, dishes and glasses, and to top
it off, a radio that ran on batteries—"things of the devil" that Raimunda
had already seen one day in Dona Auricídia's house. Antônio Vítor was
out of his mind, as anyone with half an eye could see. All of that was
something only a crazy man would do; the boom had left him not right
in the head. Such were Raimunda's thoughts as she helped him open
the crates containing the varnished items of furniture.

The day came for them to move into the new house. It was attractive,
encircled by verandas, whitewashed on the inside, painted blue on the
outside (just like Colonel Maneca Dantas's house, which Antônio Vítor
had always thought was very pretty), furnished, with no gaps in the
floor, which was made with new boards. They brought whatever could
still be used from the old house. From now on, workers and pack
drivers would live there. They were already on the site, waiting for
Raimunda to leave so they could bring in their poor belongings. But
Raimunda hesitated. She did not know how to pull herself away from
that house where she had spent thirty years, where she had given birth
to her children, where she had slept with her husband every night. She
walked about the house with a pain in her heart, feeling empty inside, an
uneasiness that she could not explain, a premonition of misfortune.

In front of the house, the workers with their few pitiful bundles
waited for her to leave. The ones who were going to live in the
house were happy. It had a kitchen, a bedroom and a living room,
and in spite of everything it was a better dwelling than those one-
room shacks with an oven made of four rocks on the bare earth.
Raimunda hesitated. She looked at the nooks and crannies of the
house, thinking that if it had been up to her, Antônio Vítor wouldn't
have built the other house. He'd sunk a fortune there to no good purpose
at all. They'd always lived in the adobe house, why these highfalutin
things now?

Antônio Vítor came looking for his wife.

"Let's go, Munda. The men're waitin' for you to leave . . ."

"I'm comin', Antonyo . . ."

She looked at everything once more. She shook her head, her face
took on even more of a pinched expression, and she walked to the
door. But outside, Antônio Vítor was so happy, waiting to take her to
the new house, that she dredged up a smile from the heart and brought
it to her lips, as he said to her:

"The radio's turned on, Munda. There's a little man talkin' like
nothin' you ever heard. You'd a-think it was witchcraft . . ."

"Are you happy?" she asked.

He laughed, and she said:

"Let's go then!"

But she never got used to the new house, its iron stove so different from the clay one in the other house, its comfortable furniture, its delicate glasses that broke at the slightest touch. She would walk through the rooms like a stranger. She would sit on the edge of the armchairs, look suspiciously at the radio, only feeling at ease when she sat on the veranda, resting on the long wooden bench that they had brought from the old house. Their daughter came to spend a few days with them and fell in love with the house. Raimunda couldn't even get used to the bed. She had difficulty falling asleep on the soft mattress. She would lie awake at nights, and the next day, when she went to the fields, she was tired, ever older, her face showing more and more annoyance. But now a certain sadness was mixed into the ugliness of her features, a mute sadness filled with foreboding. Her daughter remarked to her, just before she left to rejoin her husband:

"Ma, with that look on your face you're goin' to bring bad luck on yourself."

"God forbid," Raimunda replied.

5

Talk about Sérgio and Julieta was beginning to die down, having become something of a perennial scandal, when Ilhéus was rocked by news of a struggle between Colonel Horácio da Silveira and his son, Silveirinha the lawyer. It was a scandal with enormous repercussions. Horácio da Silveira, almost unknown physically to the younger generation, which seldom caught sight of him, was legendary in the city. People spoke of him as one would of somebody distant who nevertheless influenced virtually everything that went on, not only in Ilhéus but also in the neighboring cities of Itabuna, Pirangi, Guaraci, Palestina, and Ferradas, and throughout the cacao zone. Master of hired gunmen, ballots, voters, immense landholdings, city governments, police stations. His name was spoken with respect; by many, with fear.

Silveirinha was already well known on the streets of Ilhéus, where he would stroll wearing his green shirt, frowning, unfriendly, and taciturn. Every afternoon he could be seen in a bar with Gumercindo Bessa, talking politics and playing dice. Later he was often spotted in the company of Schwartz, with whom Colonel Horácio had severed relations because he considered him among those responsible for his son's attitude, if not the sole responsible party. The dispute was the subject of comment for months, the trial attracting the passionate interest of the population of both cities, with wagers on the outcome and even fighting in the streets on behalf of father or son. The lawyers were making money hand over fist, and there was talk of dodges on top of dodges. Horácio's hatred for the Integralists stemmed from that struggle. And since at that time he belonged to the ruling party and had the mayor of Itabuna in his pocket, he took advantage of the chance to block some Integralist rallies and order a few Green Shirts roughed up. This won him the opposition of the local judge, who sympathized with the fascists and prejudiced the colonel's interests in the settlement of the inventory of Ester's goods.

By striking at Horácio, the exporters, acting through Schwartz, who was financing Silveirinha's lawsuit, were striking at the most powerful planter, the wealthiest colonel, the symbol of the feudal lords of the cacao region. But almost no one, except Sérgio Moura, who discussed the matter with Joaquim, realized the true significance of the struggle. For most, it was an impassioned question of legal rights, recalling old lawsuits from the days of the conquest of the land. And when they woke up, it was already too late, for the bust had changed once again the way of life in the cacao zone.

It all began because Silveirinha the lawyer replaced a merchant marine captain as head of the Integralists in Ilhéus. No one was surprised by the enthusiastic (if less than unanimous) election of the young attorney, and everyone said it was because of his father's fortune. With Cacao at an all-time high, who better to lead the fascist party than the son of the largest plantation owner? There were some who said the "men with brains" in the party were laughing at Silveirinha behind his back. Be that as it may, he was elected and they gave him a personal guard, four husky Integralists with their pockets full of money who never left the cabaret. When the "greens" began their fund-raising campaign, Silveirinha was first on the list, pledging fifty thousand mil-réis. He did not, however, have that amount in ready cash. The inventory of Ester's goods (half of all that Horácio possessed) had never been carried out; the colonel administered everything. He had easily convinced his son:

"You're goin' to end up with all this anyway, so why pay lawyers to do an inventory now?"

Nor had Silveirinha ever felt any necessity for an inventory, for money, or for land. He had whatever he wanted; it's true that sometimes Horácio grumbled about what he called "throwing away money," but he always ended up signing the checks. From time to time Silveirinha traveled to Bahia, and Marta's cabaret would go wild.

Silveirinha pledged fifty thousand and went to talk to Horácio, to ask for the money. It was the first year of the boom and cacao was around twenty-eight mil-réis. As he saddled up in Itabuna, Silveirinha felt the difficulty of his mission. He went reluctantly.

He and his father barely spoke. Silveirinha had always been terrified of the colonel, especially since that day, when he was a freshman law student in Bahia, that another boy from Ilhéus, in an argument, exposed the entire story of Ester and Virgílio, declaring that he, Silveirinha, was not Horácio's son. That made Silveirinha even more timid and embittered, more distant from everyone, bearing a silent hatred inside. He never got to the bottom of that story, for he never wanted to talk to anyone about it. Thus he never found out he really was Horácio's son and had been born before Ester met Virgílio. He was certain he was the son of adultery, felt he had none of his father's characteristics, despite the fact that physically he reminded one of Horácio during his youth, when he was a pack driver who prodded donkeys through recently opened cacao roads. But he was not as courageous as his father, or as audacious or as capable of daring accomplishments. He was already afraid of Horácio, who bullied him, but now he came to fear him much more. He lived in terror of Horácio one day telling him he supported him merely out of pity, that he was the son of an adulteress, and sending him away in one of his fits of rage.

As regards the memory of his mother, Silveirinha's thoughts were several and contradictory. He believed she was right (when he thought about Horácio), that she had done well to betray the colonel, saw the maternal adultery as a kind of before-the-fact vengeance for the brutalities that Horácio inflicted upon him. His mother had avenged him. At such times he came to feel a certain sympathy for Ester (whom he did not remember and of whom he had not a single memento); he forgave her and was all but certain that his father had had her killed, that the illness had been merely a subterfuge. But on the other hand, when he thought of her separately from Horácio he hated her. She struck him as an adventuress, and he held her responsible for all that he did not have and all that he was not. For the courage that he had been denied, for his timidity, for the lack of understanding between him and Horácio. He hated his father but also admired him, though he would never admit it. And he wished he were like him and thought he was not because Ester, fleeing from her obligations, had sought another man for the father of her child.

Thus, from an early age, hatred had come to fill his heart. In the plantation house the only one he had loved in his abandoned childhood was the black woman Felícia, the only person who had treated him kindly. Horácio had paid no attention to him. Colonel Maneca Dantas would come by now and then and take him on his lap, but it was a gesture without affection. Perhaps if Dr. Jessé hadn't died he would have had a friend, for the doctor at times treated him with kindness and was gentle with him when Silveirinha was ill. But Jessé had died many years ago and the boy was orphaned of affection of any kind. At boarding school he had made no friends. At college, after revelation of the incident involving his mother he had avoided everyone. Inside there was only hate, an unsatisfied and hidden hate that revealed itself in small acts of evil. But it was also a fearful hate, for Silveirinha had inherited all the terror with which Ester, cast into the terrifying wilderness, had filled her heart. They spoke of the time he struck an old man living on the plantation who had been wounded in the leg during one of Horácio's battles. He was no longer fit for work and had lived there, doing nothing, ever since the fighting over Sequeiro Grande. Silveirinha had given him some order or other and when the old man refused to obey, struck him with his arm, knocking the crippled man off his feet. Horácio was on his way home and witnessed the scene. He quickened his pace. He was already past seventy, but his hand was still heavy and the colonel's fingers left their mark on his son's face— a young man of nineteen.

Perhaps what had led Silveirinha to fascism, more then any political conviction or sympathy for the ideas espoused by the party, was the bloodbath the fascists promised would follow their coming to power. The poet Sérgio Moura said that Silveirinha had his own list of people he would order shot when the fascists triumphed. And that, when he was elected regional leader of the cacao zone, he had expanded the list to include various fellows from his own party, Integralists that didn't like him. Possibly none of that was true, mere inventions of the scandalmonger poet. But it fit Silveirinha so well that people quickly believed and repeated it.

Silveirinha arrived at the plantation at lunchtime. Horácio wasn't expecting him. He greeted his son with a few grunts and began to eat. Silveirinha sat down; Felícia went to get a plate for "my little attorney." She loved him, had watched him being born, and when Ester died it was she who took care of the boy and raised him. For her, Silveirinha had no shortcomings, and for his sake she would argue even with the colonel himself. Silveirinha also cared for her, but in the way one cares for a dog, distantly.

They ate in silence. Horácio asked only about the price of cacao and about Maneca Dantas. When they finished lunch Horácio went to take the sun on the veranda. It was a pretty day; from the veranda they could see the cacao in the drying frames, the workers dancing a dance of their own invention over the coal-like beans. A few words of their song drifted to where father and son sat, on the same bench but distant from each other, at opposite ends. Horácio said nothing, probing the floor with a dead branch from a guava tree, trying to discern his son's movements by the noise he made. Silveirinha was looking for a way to begin the conversation. They remained like that for some minutes, in the sun, silent like two enemies about to hurl themselves upon each other. Finally Silveirinha spoke:

"Did you know, father, that the national leader is coming to Ilhéus?"

At that time Horácio still had a vague sympathy for the Integralists, to which his son's recent election contributed. Therefore he replied with a certain show of interest:

"When's he comin'? They say he knows how to talk . . ."

"Maybe next month. He's coming because of the fund-raising drive . . ."

Horácio was not pleased with the reason. The Integralists had already gotten a lot of his money, in contributions wrested from him on several occasions.

"Those people are always after money, aren't they? What do they do with so much money? . . ."

"It's for the campaign . . ."

"Huh! Campaign . . . My good friend Braz told me the money goes to support a bunch of bums . . . It might just be . . ." he grumbled.

Silveirinha stood up; Horácio could tell by the sound.

"Braz is a communist! . . ."

His son's voice was irritated. Horácio felt him near, the young man's shadow projecting over him. The colonel looked at the floor, where he thought he could distinguish Silveirinha's pointing finger in the confusing shadow. He thought: *can that pup be threatening me with his finger?* He looked toward the place where his son ought to be, and raised his head:

"Braz is a pal, a friend. You say he's a communist but I don't believe it. They say the communists want to take away people's land, and how's my friend Braz going to hand over his lands? You're a fool, you were always a fool . . ."

He thought his son's finger was pointing at him and so he insulted him. He spat his phlegmy old man's spittle, as if to reinforce his words. Silveirinha could no longer contain himself:

"A murderer . . ."

The shadow was upon Horácio and now the colonel was certain that his son's finger was extended. He stood up.

"Maybe he's a murderer. But when he killed people it was together with me, and if you have any money today it's because me and my friend Braz killed people. He's a killer and so am I, if you want to know . . . But it's from these killers that your money comes . . ."

He sat down, holding his aching kidney.

"I want you to know that in my house no one says anything bad about my friend Braz." He was suddenly angry. "And lower that finger that you're pointin' at me. Or I'll learn you some respect . . ."

Silveirinha sat down also. Things were off to a bad start.

"I'm not pointing my finger . . ."

"And a good thing too."

He had irritated the old man, making matters more difficult. Still, he was in a hurry, wanting to return to Itabuna that same day (he hated sleeping at the plantation), and he couldn't wait for Horácio's anger to pass . . .

"I need some money . . ."

"You already spent the five thousand?"

"It's not that. It's just that I pledged some money for the party's fund-raising campaign. I'm the regional leader, so I was first on the list."

"How much was it?"

The answer was slow in coming.

"Fifty thousand . . ."

Horácio was shocked. He had already given money to the Integralist movement. From time to time they managed to get some out of him, but it was on the order of five hundred. The largest amount he had given at one time was two thousand, and then under protest. He asked again:

"How much?"

"Fifty thousand. I'm the regional leader . . ."

Horácio got up again; his kidneys were aching, as well as his shoulders. He located Silveirinha; he spat out the words:

"You think I'm made of money? Or maybe you think I'm as big a fool as you are and that I'm goin' to give that gang of no-goods fifty thousand? Tell me somethin': are you crazy or just drunk?"

Silveirinha did not answer, wishing only that he could kill the old man. But he trembled before the octogenarian who shook his hand in his direction, his eyes searching for him and his mouth spitting these words:

"If that's what you came for, you can saddle your horse and turn around . . . Fifty thousand!"

He repeated in an ironic tone, like someone repeating an absurdity:

"Fifty thousand . . . Only a fool like him . . ."

Leaning on his cane, he went inside, lay down in his bedroom on the same ancient bed where he had slept with Ester some thirty years ago. Silveirinha watched him walk, half dragging himself, his staff feeling out the way. He muttered in his hatred:

"Cuckold . . ."

And that gave him a sudden satisfaction and he repeated the curse two or three times more, feeling almost avenged:

"Cuckold . . . cuckold . . . cuckold . . ."

But his satisfaction was short-lived. He thought about the Integralists. What would they say? Silveirinha harbored no illusions and was aware that he had been elected because of money, knew there were those in the party who laughed at him and his lack of ability as a speaker, knew that Nestor had said of him at the time of his election:

"This cow's going to give a lot of milk . . ."

But he also knew that through the party there were possibilities of one day giving vent to the hate that filled his heart, which was his reason for living. What would they say now? What he would give to be like

Horácio, capable of killing, of removing from his path anyone, whoever he might be, who got in his way. And thinking of that, he thought of Ester. It was her fault, that mother of his who'd been a lawyer's lover. It was her fault that Silveirinha, so he thought, was not Horácio's son. If he were, he'd know how to resolve the matter with the old man, force him to give him money. He remained a long time on the veranda, deep in thoughts nurtured by hate. He drove away the old black man who had come to talk with him, drove away Felícia when the black woman asked if he wanted anything. Then he went inside, where Horácio was sleeping stretched out across the bed. He did not have the courage to wake him. He mounted and left for Itabuna.

6

Karbanks contributed but asked that his name not appear on the list. He did business with everyone, and though he praised the patriotism of the Integralist youth ("very sensible ideas," he told Gumercindo Bessa), it did not look good for him to appear as one of the sponsors of the fund-raising campaign of the Integralist Party in southern Bahia. This attitude was more or less general among the cacao exporters. All gave money, but only Antônio Ribeiro, who had joined the Integralist movement and wore a green shirt and dragged all his employees into the movement—only he had put his signature on the list, where it preceded the figure of five thousand mil-réis, his contribution. He wrote *pd.* in front of the figures and went to get the money from his safe. The rest, except for Reicher, who was Jewish and refused to contribute, gave but did not sign. Gumercindo Bessa, who was proving to be a real diplomat and an extremely useful element to the party, told them he understood and that it was only fair that it be that way. He laughed unconcernedly when Carlos Zude, after handing him the check, praised liberal-democracy:

"Say what they will, Mr. Gumercindo, there's no system like liberal-democracy . . . Look at England and her great empire!"

And he laughed his pleasant laugh at the young man. Gumercindo laughed also.

"It would be true, Mr. Carlos, begging your pardon, if there weren't so much corruption. But it's liberal-democracy that'll lead the world to communism . . ."

Carlos raised his hands.

"Could be . . . As for me, I like the liberal climate. I was brought up in it. I heard Seabra's great speeches, Mr. Gumercindo . . . Ah, what an orator! But you're right too . . . We've been too liberal . . ."

The colonels were less understanding than the exporters. It's true that the boom, with money flowing freely on all sides, simplified the tasks of those charged with fund-raising. But at times it was necessary to threaten . . . Gumercindo threw numbers at the colonels, large numbers that demonstrated the growth of the Integralist Party, its imminent and inevitable rise to power.

"We have our roll of honor, but we also have our blacklist . . ."

The heralded coming of the national leader (which never materialized) also contributed to the success of the campaign. More than anything, however, more than the number of followers, more than the opinions of eminent men throughout the country regarding the green creed, more than the sensation caused by the approaching visit of the national leader—what helped was the much publicized rumors that "the communists are growing in strength and are about to take power." To the colonels the word communism held a tragic significance. They saw their daughters as prostitutes, their lands taken, unimaginable chaos. And the Integralists exploited the fact admirably by spreading frightening news: the communists were going to take over everybody's land the way they did in Russia and make the colonels work the soil; General Luis Carlos Prestes was in Brazil, hiding out somewhere, plotting the communist revolution. However absurd the rumors, the colonels accepted them without question. They had heard vague stories about the communists, and sometimes they read their flyers asking better pay for the workers; they knew that in Snake Island there were men capable of anything. It was a horror. And they gave money to the Integralists, even when they belonged to the traditional political parties of government and opposition. Because all of them—planters, exporters, priests, businessmen—agreed about one thing: it was necessary to fight communism. It was the only thing the colonels feared in that first year of the boom, when Ilhéus was being transformed into an El Dorado and cacao into the best crop in the country.

It happened that, at the same moment when the Integralists were launching their fund-raising campaign, the Communist Party was fighting for a raise for the plantation workers. Flyers were distributed not only in the cities but also in the countryside, and their effects were beginning to be felt, if still quite slowly. The flyers said that the farm workers' life was "worse than that of the former slaves." They further declared that "while everything is floating in gold in Ilhéus, cacao workers are dying in darkest poverty."

Gumercindo Bessa carried copies of the flyers in his briefcase. More than any other argument, his showing them to the dumbfounded plantation owners convinced them of the necessity of helping the Integralist Party.

About three months after the violent scene between Silveirinha and Colonel Horácio, the lawyer and Gumercindo were talking in a bar at midday. Gumercindo was discussing the success of the campaign:

"A success . . . A huge success . . . We're going to raise over a million . . . Even people who were attacking us before are giving money . . ."

They were both wearing their green shirts, and Gumercindo was looking for a way to ask Silveirinha about the fifty thousand with which he had headed the list. Silveirinha thought especially highly of Gumercindo; perhaps he esteemed Schwartz's young employee more than any other of his fellow party members. He had been the chief backer of Silveirinha's election as leader, fighting the group that wanted Nestor, an intellectual. He was more open with him than with anyone else. They played dice every day at the Ponto Chic, where they discussed party business. Gumercindo knew how to lead Silveirinha, to plant his own opinions in him, later to be launched as Silveirinha's own. In that way he fostered in him the illusion of being the one who thought and decided. An ability possessed by few. And he would applaud heatedly every time Silveirinha came forth with an idea that he had put into his head little by little.

"Yes sir, a very fine idea . . . That's just how it is . . . I'm with you . . ."

The campaign was nearing its end; contributions were coming in from Itabuna, Itapira, Pirangi, Ferradas, from everywhere. The only thing missing was Silveirinha's fifty thousand. Gumercindo tried talking around the subject.

"I think within a month we can send off the money . . . We need to prepare a big celebration. A commemoration . . ."

They discussed the plans. Gumercindo suggested:

"That's where you could formally deliver your contribution. It's the largest one, the leader's . . . What do you think? Not a bad idea, eh?"

Silveirinha was thinking. And he spoke openly with his comrade. The old man refused to give any money. He was senile, more cantankerous than ever; there was no way to reach an agreement with him. The only thing he did was hurl curses. Gumercindo had already heard rumors about the matter, as Horácio had told Maneca Dantas about the fight with his son. He asked for details, and Silveirinha recounted the scene in broad outline, his eyes downcast and embarrassed before his friend. But Gumercindo immediately took his side, speaking ill of old men in general: "a generation incapable of understanding the ideas of young people."

"What can we do now?" Silveirinha asked.

Gumercindo, at that initial moment, saw no solution to the problem. It was too bad, but it looked like an impasse. They ended the conversation with the vague hope that the colonel would die soon, a hope expressed by Silveirinha which to some extent shocked Gumercindo.

"Anyway, he's near the end . . . He won't last long . . ."

Seeing that Gumercindo was shocked, he felt obliged to explain:

"He never treated me like a father treats a son . . . If I said I was sorry, I'd be lying. I don't give a damn if he dies . . ."

He clenched his teeth on the hate-filled words. Gumercindo looked at him for a time, finally getting used to the idea.

Well now, he thought, *in that case maybe something can be done.* "The colonel really can't live much longer. He's already eighty, isn't he?"

"Eighty-three . . ."

"It's a real fix . . ."

They said good-bye. But around the middle of the afternoon Gumercindo went looking for Silveirinha. He found him in the bar, talking with a group of Integralists. He took him aside to a table, with a mysterious manner. He leaned his head close to the leader's.

"Tell me something: the inventory of Dona Ester's goods was never made, was it?"

"No . . ."

"Why not?"

"The old man wouldn't allow it . . ."

Gumercindo laughed triumphantly.

"There it is . . . You're asking your father for money, like a slave, humiliating yourself, when the money's really yours. You have a fortune of your own, the inheritance from your mother . . ."

Silveirinha was not encouraged by this piece of shopworn information.

"What good will it do? The old man'll never permit it . . . You don't know my father . . ."

"But his consent isn't needed . . . You have the right, and that's all there is to it. He's obligated by law . . . I believe it should already have been done; it's past the legal time limit . . ."

He remembered that Silveirinha had a law degree.

"But of course you must know about that better than I do; you're a lawyer . . ."

Silveirinha made a gesture as if to say that he knew nothing about the law. And he asked for more details. Gumercindo had told him all he knew. He thought for a few moments and finally decided to speak:

"Why don't you have a talk with Mr. Schwartz? He's a foreigner but he understands a lot about the laws here . . . A well-educated man."

Silveirinha answered, offended:

"Did you talk to him about the matter?"

"Yes, I did, but don't take offense. You know he's been very helpful to us. Now that you're regional leader you have to be aware of something: Mr. Schwartz has been one of the mainstays of the party here. I spoke to him about the matter. He knows your father well because he buys cacao from him. But he's willing to help you. He even said he'll advance you the fifty thousand if you like . . ."

This last item weighed heavily in Silveirinha's decision. All that he wanted was not to lose face with the other Integralists. And the possibility of arranging to borrow the money from Schwartz, to be repaid with interest after Horácio's death, struck him as an excellent solution. Better than that complicated business of the inventory . . .

But what Schwartz wanted to talk about was precisely the inventory. In fact he seemed to be expecting him, since he had drinks waiting in his office. Silveirinha had been there several times, but always on business—delivery of cacao, settling of accounts. Now he saw that the German, in private, was quite different from the businessman with whom he was acquainted. He laughed and joked, was a likable person, fully interested in Silveirinha's cause.

"These are acts of an old man used to having his way . . . But right is on your side . . ."

The entire story was discussed once more. Silveirinha proposed a loan. But Schwartz had much more to offer him:

"You can quadruple your fortune . . ."

And he outlined for Silveirinha an immense business plan. The young man, ambitious and a failure, felt the pull of so much action, such a future, so many possibilities of being someone and achieving something. Schwartz would finance his suit against Colonel Horácio, the inventory. It would be a relatively small expense because the colonel had no case. Silveirinha had the law on his side, so there was no place to hide. Afterwards, if Silveirinha so desired, he could become a partner in Schwartz's export house; there was much yet to be done. The exporting of cacao was a great business. Especially if one had roots in the land, one's own plantations . . .

The German served whiskey and talked. His rough tongue found soft tones as he described the business. Gumercindo opened his mouth in rapt admiration. Silveirinha was impressed.

They went into details. Schwartz advised Silveirinha to return to the plantation and ask the colonel to divide the lands, hand over to him those that were his. Silveirinha was taken aback.

"Anything but that. I won't go there. The old man is capable of anything, you know him. He knows very well what he's done . . . He'll be howling mad; he might even have me killed . . ."

Schwartz smiled at the young man's fear and interrupted:

"Then the thing to do is start the lawsuit. Hire a lawyer . . . Unless you, as a lawyer yourself, want to handle it."

"No. It's better to get somebody else. The old man's going to become my enemy . . . He might do anything . . ."

They said good-bye. Schwartz opened an account for Silveirinha with a large line of credit. As he left, he grasped his hand warmly in a gesture of understanding and sympathy. But when the office door closed behind Silveirinha, Schwartz's face filled with contempt. He murmured something in German, something that might be verses from some classical poet.

7

And the lawsuit began. The lawyers saw it as a spectacular source of income. Ilhéus, upon learning of the affair, was shaken. Street corners seethed with groups looking for news. In the bars they talked about nothing else. Even the cacao boom, the incredibly rising prices, seemed secondary to the petition that Silveirinha's lawyer had filed, requesting an inventory of the goods of the late Ester Silveira, wife of Colonel Horácio da Silveira. The newspapers were full of sensational facts, with headlines about international conflicts, talks in the League of Nations, huge strikes in some parts of the world, revolutions in China, and passive resistance in India. About the trial, not a word. But Ilhéus and the entire cacao zone forgot the newspaper headlines and talked exclusively about the inventory of Ester's goods. Old stories were revived, long-forgotten names were cited once again. Virgílio and Margot, Dr. Jessé and Rui the lawyer. At night in the bars, where Gumercindo Bessa no longer appeared, Marinho Santos, Zito Ferreira, and Reinaldo Bastos recalled the old times. Zito, spreading his hands, declared:

"You could write a novel about it . . ."

When Maneca Dantas, who had gone to take the news to Colonel Horácio, arrived in Ilhéus upon returning from his friend's plantation, he was almost mobbed in the streets. He had to repeat the account a hundred times, in bar after bar, on corner after corner. And it expanded in the telling, grew; it was said that Horácio threatened God and the world, swearing he would have Silveirinha killed. The latter thought it best to leave for Bahia while the suit was in court. And despite the fact that the initial trial and the one that followed were long, arriving at a settlement only years later, despite the fact that other scandals took place in Ilhéus during the cacao boom—even so, at no time did interest in the struggle between Horácio and Silveirinha disappear entirely. Perhaps it

was the almost legendary figure of Horácio that imbued the trial with
that aura of vivid emotion. Perhaps it was because, more than any other
fact, the trial demonstrated that the struggle between the cacao growers
and the exporters was coming more and more into the open. For didn't
everyone know that behind Silveirinha stood Schwartz and his firm?
That it was he who was advancing the money for the initial stages of
the lawsuit?

Maneca Dantas set out as soon as he heard the news. He could imagine
how this would affect Horácio, who had a visceral love for his lands, for
whom dividing them signified something worse than death. He went
to take the news, like one who tells a woman of the unexpected death
of her husband. Before leaving, he spoke with his son about the legal
aspects of the case. Rui was pessimistic:

"It's a lost cause, father. Silveirinha is right and there's no way the
colonel can wiggle out of it . . . If he tries to fight it, drag it out in
court, he'll just be wasting money . . ."

But Maneca Dantas knew Colonel Horácio da Silveira well. "Knew
him intimately," as he liked to put it. He raised objections:

"My friend isn't goin' to divide his fields . . . I know him . . ." and
he muttered threats against Silveirinha.

"Listen, father," Rui said, "the days when everything was settled
with rifles are past . . . That was a long time ago . . . When Hector was
a pup . . ."

Maneca Dantas grumbled that those were better days, when a son
didn't rise up against his father. Nowadays that's all you saw—son
against father, ruination. It caused the old colonel pain. He had seen
Horácio struggle, weapons in hand; he had helped him, they had crossed
forests and cut down woods, and all to what end? He looked at Rui as
if he too were guilty, as if the lawyer also wanted to divide his lands.
Rui shrugged his shoulders at his father's angry words.

"I don't have anything to do with that . . . I don't even like Silveirinha.
But what I can't do is say he has no right. It's in the codes, Father!"

Maneca Dantas relented. He loved his son above all else in the world
and it pained him not to see him excelling, a great lawyer, rising in
politics. He hung around women, spending money, pleading a few small
cases in mediocre fashion. But when all was said and done, he was still
his son, the one in whom he had placed so many hopes. And he wasn't
a bad son; he would be incapable of turning against his father. Maneca
Dantas smiled at Rui, put on his riding boots, and went to catch the bus
to Itabuna.

As was his custom, Horácio was sitting on the bench on the veranda,
with one foot on the seat and his chin resting on his knee, trying to
distinguish the sounds of the work going on around him. They talked,

while outside the men picked the cacao fruit from the heavily-laden fields. Cacao was going up, raising prices. Horácio was unusually effusive.

"What a boom, my friend! What a boom . . ."

Maneca Dantas stated the facts of the case. Horácio listened in silence, his nearly sightless eyes peering outward, where the fields that he planted so many years ago must be. Felícia appeared and brought Colonel Maneca rum. And coffee for Horácio, who slowly stirred it while he listened. Maneca Dantas's voice was a monotone as he told of the suit and of Rui's opinions.

Afterwards there was silence between the two old men. "Cacao is a fine crop," sang one of the workers as he brought down the yellow fruit. Finally Horácio spoke, his voice rising in the tremulous voice of an old man, full of anger:

"You see, Maneca my friend? I'm an old man, worn out. I'm goin' to die one of these days, I can't have much time left. I fought over land, you know that 'cause you fought at my side. You and Braz remember, it was a dirty business . . . I wiped out the Badarós, I made all this, this world of fields . . ."

He paused and asked:

"What did *she* do?"

I wonder why he never pronounces Ester's name, Maneca Dantas thought. He knew that Horácio's anger was more against his deceased wife than against Silveirinha himself.

"Tell me, my friend, just what right does she have? What right? Your son says mine has the right, by law. Tell me, my friend, what right does she have? What did she plant, what trees did she cut down, what bullet did she fire? What right does she have? The only thing she ever did was make a cuckold out of me; she didn't help the least bit. If it'd been up to her we wouldn't have planted cacao or burned away the forest. She was always off cryin' in some corner, whinin' about life. I was fightin', riskin' my life; you know that just like I do, and she was sleepin' with another man . . . And now they're sayin' I have to divide my lands and hand over the part that was hers. What part, my friend Maneca Dantas? Show me the field that she planted, the piece of forest that she cleared! Show me and I'll hand it over. You think it's right, my friend?"

Maneca Dantas did not think it was right.

"But it's a question of the courts, my friend. The law's the law, and the boy will win the case. The inventory should have been made already . . ." Horácio raised his dim eyes and searched for the form of Maneca Dantas.

"I never did pay any mind to that stuff about the law, my friend . . . Or are they thinkin' I'm no good for anything anymore? Let me tell you somethin', my friend: as long as I'm still alive nobody will divide my lands. Not any judge, not any lawyer. I won't allow it . . ."

Maneca Dantas tried to explain to Horácio the legal reasons that obliged him to make the inventory. But the colonel didn't want to hear about statutes or the law. To him, statutes and law, judges and lawyers were always things to be molded to his will, made to serve him.

"Times have changed, my friend . . ."

"Times may have changed, but I haven't, friend Maneca. Leave all this to me . . ."

It was the same determined resolve of old, that force that had dominated Maneca Dantas. If Horácio said it, it must be true.

There was a long silence. Then Horácio asked:

"Where'd he get the money to pay a lawyer?"

"They say Schwartz's company is advancin' it . . ."

"Schwartz?"

"Yes . . ."

"That foreign son of a bitch . . ."

A new silence. Horácio reflected:

"My friend, send your son here, I want to talk to him. I'm goin' to hire him, he's goin' to be my lawyer . . ."

"He said it's a hopeless case . . ."

"Send him here, I'll tell him . . . The boy doesn't know what we know, my friend. He looks down on us because we're old . . . I'll show him a thing or two . . ."

And then he remembered Virgílio. If Virgílio were still alive he would be in good hands. Now there was a first-class lawyer who knew how to pull off a dodge, how to win a case, really confound the other side. The dodge dealing with the Sequeiro Grande forest was well done . . . But Virgílio had died of a gunshot one moonlit night on the road. Horácio had ordered the killing. Virgílio had made him a cuckold . . . Maneca's son wasn't cut out for this business . . . He was always writing verses, chasing loose women . . .

"Virgílio was really some lawyer, wasn't he, my friend?"

"And how 'bout Rui?" Maneca Dantas recalled with a smile. "He could really argue a case . . . Remember your trial?"

And they talked about old times until the overseer came to get his orders and was astonished when Colonel Horácio da Silveira ordered him to mount up and go to Itabuna to buy repeating rifles.

8

Amid the excitement and enthusiasm engendered by the rise in cacao prices, two voices were heard condemning the boom, the sole exceptions in those four years of great business and great scandals. One of them was the voice of the Communist Party. Through Joaquim and other bus and truck drivers, on the several lines that crisscrossed the cacao zone the Communist Party's flyers, explaining the true significance of the boom, were distributed almost from door to door. Many did not read them, others read them but paid no heed, but some paused over those phrases that announced future events springing from the boom, prophesying an imminent collapse, events that in the words of the flyer would "remove the cacao lands from the hands of Brazilian capitalists to those of foreign capitalists."

Another flyer asked for immediate improvement in the wages of plantation workers, who despite the boom continued earning five mil-réis for a day's work. This campaign, begun illegally by the Communist Party in flyers, bulletins, and clandestine talks with workers from some of the largest plantations, gained legality and the support of one of the newspapers in Ilhéus. The state government wished to attract goodwill for the upcoming elections, and the party in power took charge of the campaign. The workers' wages rose first to five and a half, then to six mil-réis. The communists then turned their attention to a massive campaign on behalf of workers on the docks and in the cacao warehouses, directly in opposition to the exporters. Violent bulletins were distributed calling Karbanks "the shark of international finance" and Carlos Zude the "lackey of Yankee capital." Schwartz was singled out as a Nazi agent, a combination of businessman and spy, "the true leader of the local Integralists."

Further, in the morning hours walls in Ilhéus, Itabuna, and Pirangi were covered with painted phrases in large letters. They could be seen on the walls of dockside warehouses, the railroad station, repeated where the highway cut into the side of the mountain:

BREAD, PEACE, FREEDOM

At the same time the Communist Party also sent out a call for the small growers to defend their lands against the greed of the exporters and colonels. It was a widely distributed flyer but the small growers were beyond persuading; they had never seen so much money in their lives. The Communist Party tried to get the planters to form a cooperative to export their own cacao but met with enormous difficulties. It was an idea with a certain appeal, but only when the bust came would the growers realize that it would have been their salvation. When they tried to achieve it, it was already too late.

Besides the Communist Party, only the bishop's voice spoke out against the boom. The bishop sounded the alarm against the invasion of Ilhéus, Itabuna, Itapira, his entire diocese, by women of ill repute, professional gamblers, cabaretiers, and drug dealers. In sermons he termed the boom "temptation by the enemy," saying that "it was the devil who hoped, with his gold, to buy the souls of his spiritual flock."

They tell the story in Ilhéus that Karbanks, when he learned of these facts, took steps against all of them. He persuaded the state government to send a specialist from the political police, a commissioner trained in persecution of communists, who installed himself in Ilhéus with half a dozen cops. Karbanks also took up a collection of forty thousand mil-réis at an exporters' meeting, which he gave to the bishop for the work on the cathedral, promising at the same time (on behalf of the exporters) full cooperation for the founding of a seminary in Ilhéus, "assuming that cacao continues to bring a good price."

9

In the house that had replaced the Badarós' plantation house burned by Horácio, João Magalhães is making plans. Dona Ana nods her head. The captain is proud because he was one of the first to foresee the boom and narrowly avoided selling his cacao at low prices. He had gone down to Ilhéus to close a deal for his crop but then had a suspicion that the boom was coming and returned without selling.

"I felt it in the air," he tells Dona Ana.

When the plantation was divided up, they received the forest lands that were still to be cleared and planted. The others had preferred less land and more cacao trees. João Magalhães and Dona Ana had always dreamed of planting that land. If they did so, they could harvest more than twice as much cacao as at present. They had never been able to do so, as the profits from the crops were always plowed into other necessities. There were expenses for their children, debts left by Sinhô and Juca. Dona Ana had insisted on paying them down to the last penny. When the productivity of the oldest fields began to decline, another small piece of forest would be cleared and planted. The first cacao growers had not followed any method on their plantations, and the cacao trees from that period had a relatively short productive lifespan. In the entire cacao zone, those pieces of woodland within João Magalhães's fields were perhaps the only ones yet to be planted. João Magalhães had a tempting offer for them. He talked it over with Dona Ana and they decided to decline. Now, with the boom, that seemingly endless boom, they could clear the forest and plant new fields. João Magalhães believed that cacao prices, at a minimum, would remain permanently at forty mil-réis per fifteen kilos. If he planted the forest tracts his production would rise from the present twenty-two thousand five hundred kilos to more than forty-five thousand per harvest.

So the profits from the first harvest of the boom period were sunk into the forest. He started cutting down trees, opened clearings, and began the burning. The work recalled other times for Dona Ana, when they had opened clearings in the forests of Sequeiro Grande and Repartimento, when the Badarós, her father and her uncle, were working to amass the largest fortune in Ilhéus. They did not succeed; they fell on hard times; they died for it. Olga and the merchant knew nothing about land. Only she and the captain were left. For them there were no more parties in Ilhéus, the life of the rich. They put up with it; Dona Ana never uttered a word that might reveal the sadness she felt at no longer being greeted in Ilhéus as she had been in those days of the conquest of the land. In those days Sinhô Badaró was the big man of the zone, and she was like a princess; her wedding had been an unforgettable occasion. Sinhô had died later of shame, the Badarós had become poor, and now their name was no longer even mentioned. João had stuck with her. Dona Ana understood that on many occasions he had wanted to leave, take her away to other places, to a life more to his liking. Dona Ana had known for a long time that before he came to Ilhéus the captain was nothing but a professional gambler. But she had not wanted to go; she would not know how to live if she were taken away from her lands. He remained, the captive of her eyes, gave himself over to cacao and became a grower like the rest, only smaller and more indebted.

Now, with the boom, Dona Ana sees possibilities of reconstituting the Badaró fortune. If they plant all the remaining forest land, if they harvest fifty-two thousand five hundred kilos of cacao at the present price, they can have a house in Ilhéus again, and help the career of their son-in-law, the doctor. They can recall the splendor that once was the Badarós'. This is why Dona Ana is so encouraging to Captain João Magalhães. She follows the work in the forest with an anxiety revealed in her questions in the evening, asking when the fire will be lighted for the first clearing, writing the Cacao Experimental Station asking about prices for seedlings. If in this harvest they clear all the remaining forest land, in the next one they can plant it with new seedlings, and in four more years production will begin to increase, and after six or seven years it'll be a large plantation; they'll leave this life of humiliation, of hardships, this life that, more than any bullet, killed Sinhô Badaró.

João Magalhães is also encouraged. He laughs a lot, tells stories, discusses the boom, proves mathematically that the boom is not transitory, that prices are not going to go down. Everything makes him feel good: the birth of a grandchild, the marriage of a worker, stories about Antônio Vítor and Raimunda, who fight over the new house they're building. When he comes from the woods, where he directs the men's work, Captain João Magalhães likes to sit in the hammock, with Dona Ana at his side, and dream about their plans.

Once when he went to Ilhéus he stopped by the Bataclã. He still laughs about it today. They invited him to play poker. He knew all but one player, a newcomer to Ilhéus, a well-dressed young man with good manners. They started playing, and João Magalhães saw immediately that the man was a professional. João Magalhães took great pleasure in the incident. He was playing seriously; he had long ago abandoned as useless his knowledge of tricks and sleight of hand. But that day he put them to use and took the professional to the cleaners. The man was beside himself with amazement. João Magalhães went back to the farm laughing, told Dona Ana, who became somewhat alarmed.

"You're not going back to gambling . . ."

"Of course not . . . I'm not crazy . . ."

What he wanted was to clear the forest, plant cacao, make money, harvest sixty thousand kilos. He already talked about it; all his thoughts and actions centered not on the twenty-two thousand five hundred kilos that he harvested now but the sixty thousand he would harvest in six or seven years . . .

One day Captain João Magalhães returned from the woods. Burning would begin the next morning. Dona Ana asked for details, thought about going with him the following day to the clearing. After dinner they went into the living room. João Magalhães sat in the hammock and removed his boots. Dona Ana remembered something and went out. She rummaged through old trunks in the bedroom. When she returned she was carrying the old Bible that Sinhô Badaró had read every night during the days of the conquest. She sat beside her husband. João Magalhães took her hands, kissed her cheek, and said:

"You're going to be Dona Ana Badaró again . . . When you walk by, people will point you out again."

She opened the Bible and once more her voice resounded in the reading of prophetic verses. João Magalhães closed his eyes and saw Sinhô Badaró seated in the high-backed Viennese chair that no longer existed. He smiled at him.

"Leave it to me . . ."

Dona Ana's voice swept over his dreams.

10

So different, Capi thought, from that other mummers group with which he had set out so many years ago in his distant land, during a good rainy season. It was the rainy season in the cacao lands too; the trees were in flower, the fruits were growing, prices were rising. But this group was so different, it bore no resemblance to that earlier one in his youth when he had gone out dressed as King Herod.

Beanpole's Group had started on its way. It could have had another name, a much prettier one, but that's what everybody called it: "Beanpole's Group." He had been the instigator, had gotten money from Colonel Frederico Pinto, had found four young women and three girls, despite difficulty with their parents, had arranged for tissue paper in town and candle stubs from Dona Augusta. He had spent nights rehearsing, nights when the rum bottle passed from hand to hand. And he had managed to get an orchestra: guitar and ukulele, an old harmonica and a tambourine. If it played out of tune, what mattered was that it was an orchestra and played music to which they could dance, a dance that was merely a repetition of the work dance at the drying frames over the cacao beans. Beanpole had dreamed up the mummers group with the idea of escaping. A farm worker's life was the worst in the world; he had already had several professions and none was like this. But how to escape when the colonels had runaways tracked down and whipped as an example to others? The example on the plantation was Ranulfo, a man with yellowish, sagging skin who had been whipped when he tried to escape to somewhere or other. But he had died afterwards, suffocated in the kiln, a skinny cadaver. He had already died before Beanpole conceived the mummers group as a means of escaping, and the first rehearsal was held right beside the dead man the night of the first rains. The colonel had come, and Rita had leaned

against him, as Beanpole had clearly seen. The other rehearsals had
been better, livelier, with more people. Little by little news spread to
the neighboring plantations; players began to arrive, and the orchestra
took shape. It was a lot of work. Beanpole had conceived of the group
as a means of escape. They would go from house to house, increasing
the distance between themselves and the plantations. It was easier to
escape, make it to the outside, heading for the backlands, then return
later to the docks in Ilhéus. In Beanpole's memory was the pleasant
recollection of Rosa, as pretty as anything, with whom he had slept
a few nights in the city, and who had run off later without a word.
He still had to see Rosa, if only to give her a few slaps, to teach her
not to play games with a real man. With the mummers group it was
easier to run away. But bit by bit, in the daily work of organizing,
rehearsing and making ready the group, Beanpole fell in love. In love
with the mummers group. Black Florindo also wanted to run away, see
other lands, and he was going to take him along. At the beginning they
made detailed plans, had long discussions about the best place to leave
the group and head for the forest. Gradually, however, Beanpole fell in
love with the mummers group. He spoke less and less about fleeing. At
times Black Florindo would bring up the subject:

"What's up? Do we beat it or not?"

"Sure, we beat it . . ."

But he said it without passion, without conviction, only in order not
to disillusion the black man. Beanpole no longer had the courage to
leave the mummers group, it was a thing of his own making; he had
created it and it was pretty.

Capi did not find it pretty. He had seen such groups, as well as folkloric
dances, in Ceará, grand things, things that were worth the trouble! He had
even gone out dressed as Herod in a mummers group; they had sung to
him and Capi had responded. Songs made up especially for the group,
not those sad cacao songs they sang here to dance to:

> *Maneca died in the oven,*
> *Just as sundown came . . .*

Who ever heard of that in an Epiphany mummers group? It was
preposterous . . . Epiphany groups had their own music, talking about
the birth of Jesus, Pilate and Herod, the Virgin and St. Joseph. It was
a story, a beautiful story. That was no group, with music made up right
here, talking about drying frames, kilns, cacao. It wasn't what ought to
be done . . . Capi said as much to Beanpole, with a certain disdain, and
it was enough to get the mulatto mad, looking for a fight and taking out
his knife.

"You're pretty damn highfalutin . . . Just 'cause you was in a group back there in your land . . . But I don't believe it was one bit prettier'n this one . . . If you ain't happy, go ahead an' say so, 'cause I ain't afraid of no man, much less one from Ceará."

But Capi had no desire to fight. He was just sorry they called that thing an Epiphany group. He knew what a real group was. Something pretty, something pleasing . . . This was an imitation, and a very bad one at that. "I ain't lookin' for a fight, I'm just talkin' . . ."

"Well you better not talk an' just keep your mouth shut. Nobody's obliged to go out with the group . . ."

But how could he not take part in the group, no matter how different it was from that other one where Capi had been Herod ("O King Herod," he heard the voices singing), since there was no other source of amusement at that New Year's time anywhere on the cacao plantations? "Beanpole's Group" was the great sensation. Workers had come from far away, from distant fields, to Colonel Frederico Pinto's plantation, just to see the mummers group. Beanpole no longer even remembered that he should run away, that he had invented the group only to escape. But how could he run away now that he had the group? How could he abandon it, leave it without a leader, the women dressed in tissue paper (three were little girls, but no matter), Capi transformed into an ox, the lanterns lit, the orchestra playing . . . How could he run away?

Beanpole's Group brought new stars, poor stars, to the roads between plantations on the days before Epiphany. They went out on Epiphany eve, led by the orchestra, from the house where Capi, Beanpole, and Florindo lived. The orchestra played, then came the seven shepherd maids, their faces painted with red dye from paper, carrying the improvised lanterns. Next came the men, in two columns, dressed as best they could, some fifteen of them. In the middle was Capi, transformed into an ox by means of a cow skull found in the fields and a chintz sheet lent by the overseer. Beanpole was the forest demon. And Rita's father, his cattle whip in hand, took the part of a cowboy, yelling the drawn-out, nostalgic yell of backlands cowherds. Ahead of them all was Rita, no one knew just why. Perhaps because she was the most beautiful and everyone desired her.

It was in this fashion that they entered the plantation house. Colonel Frederico Pinto was in the parlor with Dona Augusta and the children. They had visitors, neighboring plantation owners and friends who had come to see the mummers group. From the front yard they sang:

> *"Can we come in and sing our song?*
> *And can we dance . . ."*

At first the people in the parlor were embarrassed. But the colonel ordered some rum distributed. The orchestra settled onto a bench, the dance began. Beanpole had extinguished the lanterns as soon as they entered, so the candles would last for the entire festival. They danced their poor dance, sang their poor song. Colonel Frederico, mocking Dona Augusta's ceaseless vigilance, cast covetous eyes at Rita's buttocks, which heaved up and down in the dance just as in the dances around the drying frame. The orchestra hit some sour notes, winning angry looks from Beanpole, who was directing everything. Capi removed his heavy costume and danced in the parlor. Rita's father loosed his cattle herd yell, his contribution to the group's success.

It was pitifully poor, as poor as could be, infinitely poor. But even so, it was happy, and Beanpole was in love. In love with the group, the songs, the music, the cowherd's yell. He didn't even see Rita, with her gyrating and much coveted bottom, nor the four women and three girls; all he saw was the mummers group, the lanterns and the orchestra, the dance in the plantation house parlor. More rum was served; they danced again, then asked permission to go:

"Can we leave now?
Can we say good-bye . . ."

Beanpole lit the lanterns, straightened out the shepherd maids, one of whom had snagged her dress. He lined up the orchestra, as it was necessary to take their leave dancing. On the porch Colonel Frederico Pinto tried to feel Rita's firm flesh. Beanpole had forgotten all about Rosa. Next they went to the overseer's house, then to the workers' houses. They made their way back to the road, and everywhere there was rum to drink. Black Florindo had drunk heavily but had also danced a great deal and had not forgotten that they should flee.

Along a deserted road, near the woods of Captain João Magalhães's fields, he took Beanpole by the arm.

"Well, how 'bout it? We gonna light out?"

Beanpole temporized:

"Later . . ."

"This here's a good place to take off . . . It's woods, nobody'll see us . . ."

Beanpole turned his beseeching eyes to him under the starry night:

"How can I take off when there's the group? How can we just leave the group to fate? Who'll look after things if we ain't around?"

And he ran to overtake the group that was disappearing ahead, carrying their poor stars in their unsteady lanterns.

11

Marinho Santos liked Joaquim. More than one person had already told him the driver was a communist. Marinho knew he had been behind bars, that he had spent two years in a political prison. But not only was Joaquim an excellent mechanic, an efficient and capable worker, but also—he didn't know why—Marinho Santos had a certain leaning toward the young man. He had never fired him, despite repeated warnings from friends. Besides, it seemed to him that Joaquim had given up those confused ideas of his. Marinho Santos, for his part, as a young man just starting out in life, had also harbored a certain sympathy for the left. He had even gone so far as giving money to illegal movements, in the days when he was a taxi driver. Later he prospered, managed to buy a bus on installments, and his business grew, till now he owned fifteen buses and five trucks. It's true he owed a great deal, with note upon note coming due at the bank every month, a constant source of concern. But business wasn't bad, and Marinho Santos, when he managed to pay his debts, would be well fixed in life. The worst thing was the continual repairs on the motors, the buses standing idle. That's where Joaquim proved his worth: it wasn't easy to find a mechanic like him. A bus that in someone else's hands would spend a week useless in the garage, Joaquim would have running again in a couple of days. Marinho Santos preferred him to stick to that job, despite his having been hired as a driver and the fact that he enjoyed driving. He had no inkling of the cargo—manifestos, flyers, and propaganda pamphlets—that Joaquim carried beneath the bus seats.

A former driver, Marinho Santos liked to boast of his humble origins to his employees, thereby encouraging them to work harder:

"I started as a driver myself . . . Any one of you can make something of yourself . . ."

He enjoyed good relations with his various drivers and employees, especially with Joaquim. The greatest desire of Marinho Santos, who was practically illiterate, was to appear intellectual, well versed in books and literature. He was constantly picking up the tab for the circle made up of Zito Ferreira, Reinaldo Bastos, Martins, and Gumercindo Bessa, and he paid gladly, just for the pleasure of listening to the discussions. It was for the same reason that he enjoyed talking with Joaquim, who knew a great many things, who sometimes showed up with books under his arm. The driver did not open up with him, but from time to time would tell him things, speak to him of distant countries, mainly Russia. Marinho Santos listened, somewhat perplexed. He bought books that he never read, books that would end up in the covetous hands of Zito Ferreira. When Joaquim was "moody" (which did not always happen, to Marinho Santos's profound displeasure) he would begin talking about things of that other land so far away. Marinho would inject comments, spouting literary concepts heard the night before in the bar. But he respected the driver, and nothing in the world could make him fire him. Nevertheless, at the end of the conversation, he offered some advice:

"Get all that out of your head, Joaquim. You can get in trouble . . . Everybody says it's no good . . . And even if it is, how can it work out?"

Joaquim smiled his brief smile that reminded one of Raimunda.

"I'm just saying what's in any geography book . . ."

Marinho Santos winked, as if to say that he wasn't fooled, and left. Such camaraderie allowed Joaquim a degree of freedom on the job, gave him leeway to devote more time to party affairs. Whenever he wanted to leave, Marinho did not stand in his way.

"You can go, but don't take too long . . ."

One day Marinho Santos showed up at the garage with a worried look. Joaquim felt that he wanted to talk to him but hadn't made up his mind. What could it be? The entire morning, as he dispatched and checked in buses and trucks, Marinho wandered about the area where Joaquim was repairing the ailing engine of the company's oldest bus. He couldn't find the courage to speak. Finally, at noon, as Joaquim was taking his lunch from his lunch pail, Marinho came up and sat beside him on the running board of the bus.

"So, Joaquim . . ."

"How's it going, Mr. Marinho?"

"You're a driver, I'm the owner, I got fifteen buses and five trucks. But I used to be a cab driver and thank God I'm not ashamed of what I was . . . That's the truth . . ."

"Working is nothing to be ashamed of . . ."

"I'm worried . . . I'm talking to you because you're more a friend than an employee . . . And I can't keep it in any longer . . ."

Joaquim stopped eating to listen more attentively. Marinho said:

"Maybe it's nothing. But yesterday Martins, Zude's manager, you know, that thin guy who keeps a woman in Snake Island . . ."

"Rosa. I know her . . ."

"A knockout . . ."

"Yes . . . I also know who Mr. Martins is."

"Fine then. Yesterday he told me he heard my name mentioned in Mr. Carlos Zude's office. They were talking—him and the American, Mr. Karbanks. Martins came in and they were talking about yours truly . . ."

He waited for Joaquim's comment, a comment that was not forthcoming. He continued:

"My ears pricked up. Martins said they stopped talking when he came in. All night I was mulling over in my mind what it could be . . . To tell the truth, I didn't get much sleep. You know: I'm not much more than a driver myself, why should rich people, cacao exporters, be mentioning my name? So . . . Today, as soon as I got here, the first thing I found in my office was this letter."

He showed it to Joaquim. It was an invitation from Carlos Zude asking Marinho to stop by his office at three o'clock. "A matter of greatest interest to you," it advised.

"I wonder what it is? I phoned Martins; he doesn't know a thing. I racked my brains all morning but don't have any idea what it can be. It says here"—he read with some difficulty—" 'to discuss a matter of greatest interest to you.' What can it be?"

Joaquim ventured the hypothesis that it might be some exclusive contract for the five trucks to haul cacao for Zude. Marinho disagreed, almost angry.

"Contract my foot! For something like that he'd send Martins here to talk to me . . . And why this conversation with Mr. Karbanks? No, Joaquim, it's something else entirely . . ."

Joaquim admitted he had no idea what it might be, and Marinho left more nervous than when he came, saying he was going to change clothes for the meeting.

"I'm going to spruce up . . . put on my Sunday best . . ."

Joaquim, despite having nothing to do with the matter, was curious. He awaited Marinho Santos's return with interest. Before he left for Zude's office, Marinho stopped by the garage, wearing new worsted clothes, his shoes polished. Shaved and with a silk handkerchief in his coat pocket, he looked like a commercial employee on his way to a party. He asked Joaquim:

"How's it look?"

"Nifty!" the driver said in praise.

"Good Lord, what can it be?" he asked once more, anxiously, then left.

The talk was a long one, because the clock in the garage showed 4 P.M. and Marinho still hadn't returned. Joaquim found himself asking what the devil it could be. He looked at the clock every five minutes, worried. Finally, close to five o'clock, Marinho Santos appeared, beaming. He's been drinking, thought Joaquim, who knew his habits. Marinho came in, locked himself in his small office in the garage; shortly afterwards the young man who kept the company's books appeared, knocked on the door, and went inside. Joaquim heard the key turn in the lock.

It's something serious . . .

When the bookkeeper left, Marinho Santos stuck his head out and looked around the garage, where drivers and oil-spattered employees were chatting. A bus had just arrived and there was still some commotion at the street entrance. Joaquim had finished his work and was washing up under the faucet at the back when Marinho called him:

"Joaquim! Joaquim!"

"Yessir, Mr. Marinho . . ."

"Come over here . . ."

"Coming . . ."

He dried himself. Marinho Santos was waiting at the door.

"Come in . . ."

He remained standing, taken aback by Marinho Santos's precautions. He double-locked the door. Then he sat down in the ancient swivel chair, pulled up another chair, which had lost its cane bottom, for Joaquim.

"Guess . . ."

His face was radiant; he was resplendent. He was also a little drunk. He uncorked the bottle of rum and offered Joaquim a drink.

"No thanks, I don't drink . . ."

"That's silly . . . What good's it do not to drink? You better'n anybody else? Look: what did I used to be? A driver like you, like all those guys out there. I always had my nip of booze, but it never stopped me from working. I bought my buses, paying here, borrowing there, putting up with things . . . And now . . ."

He stopped to swallow his rum.

"Now I'm rich, Joaquim . . ."

"Rich?"

"You know what the men wanted?"

And he told the story. He asked that it be kept strictly between them; no one must know of the fact until the deal was complete. He was telling Joaquim—he explained—because he didn't think of him as an employee but as a friend. Zude and Karbanks had proposed a partnership in the company. Or rather: the formation of a new company. They would pay off all of Marinho's debts, provide the capital to buy new buses and trucks—many buses and trucks—and he would be director of the new company. A fantastic deal . . .

Joaquim pondered it. He was looking for what was behind it, the reason for the proposal. He started asking questions. He ascertained that it would be a joint corporation, one in which all the exporters would invest. What they wanted, they had explained to Marinho, was for the zone to be well serviced with transportation: buses and trucks, especially trucks. They could start a new company but they preferred to make use of Marinho's, which was already in place, functioning and doing nicely. By expanding his firm they would drive the others out of business.

"A corporation?"

"Yes sir . . ."

"What about your capital?"

"The buses, the trucks, the garage, my labor . . ."

"What's your percent of the stock?"

"The majority . . ."

"The majority?"

"Right. Forty percent . . ."

"That's not a majority . . ."

"Sure it is!" Marinho Santos became irritated at that first catch in the deal. "I get forty percent . . ."

"And they get sixty . . ."

"But there's eight of them and just one of me . . ."

"No, Mr. Marinho. You're Mr. Marinho Santos and they're the exporters . . ."

"So what?" Marinho Santos was openly annoyed, his eyes narrow from drink.

Joaquim began to explain, but the other man interrupted:

"That kind of talk has no place here, Joaquim. That communism stuff may be fine in Russia but not here . . ."

"But, who mentioned communism?"

"You think I don't recognize that kind of talk? The exporters, et cetera, and so forth? It's a hell of a deal and I'm going to take it . . ."

"Good luck, Mr. Marinho," Joaquim said, getting up.

But Marinho Santos calmed down and once again treated him with a courtesy and friendliness heightened by the initial stages of intoxication.

"Don't get mad, Joaquim. I'm kinda worked up myself. Don't pay any attention to it. You don't understand business, that's all. What I want is for you to stay on with me. I said that to Mr. Zude and

Karbanks straight off: 'I won't close the deal unless it's guaranteed my employees stay on.' They didn't blink an eye . . . They may be rich but they're good people . . ."

"No doubt they are, Mr. Marinho. I'll work for you as long as you want me . . ."

Marinho Santos poured another glass.

"Ah! You don't drink . . . That's silly, my boy . . . I always had my nip and I've done all right . . . It didn't keep me from getting ahead . . ."

12

Joaquim, standing in front of Sérgio Moura in the entrance hall of the Ilhéus Commercial Association, didn't even say hello. "They want to gobble up everything, Mr. Sérgio . . ." He spread his arms.

The poet looked at the square, where twilight was filling the garden with shadows. He felt satisfied and remained momentarily suspended between his intimate happiness, the driver's heated gesture, and the sadness of afternoon's end. Inside, Julieta was quickly getting dressed. Joaquim had never come by without first calling. However, it was almost always Sérgio who called him, needing to talk with the militant, to put his thoughts in order, ground them in the other man's experience. He always gained something from talking with the driver. He had once said as much to Joaquim, who had replied that he too learned. "You always gain when you exchange ideas with somebody else. And if it's somebody who knows a lot, like you, it's even better," he had explained, and Sérgio Moura had smiled, embarrassed and grateful. Joaquim would come by on a certain day every month to pick up the contribution that Sérgio, a sympathizer, gave to the party. But that afternoon he had arrived unexpectedly, while Julieta was in the poet's arms. When he heard the knocking outside, Sérgio refused to open the door. But Joaquim, familiar with the poet's odd ways (he often locked himself in to write, once the workday was over), shouted his name.

"It's Joaquim, Mr. Sérgio. I need to talk to you . . ."

Only in very serious moments did Joaquim use the familiar form of address with Sérgio. Then he would call him comrade, which gave the poet a certain sense of dignity and was among the things that satisfied him most. There continued to exist between the two of them, despite the repeated contact, a certain distance, perhaps born of mutual timidity. Possibly no one in Ilhéus merited the esteem and respect that

Sérgio Moura held for the driver. He was a man of another time, a future time; it seemed to him that he drew closer to the future every time he saw Joaquim. The driver gave him the impression of gigantic strength and immense faith. He was pure, with a purity that the poet admired despite finding it a bit awkward. Joaquim deserved his special esteem, like certain books that he particularly loved. His Baudelaire, his Whitman. The two understood each other well, but Sérgio felt there was still something between them that prevented their coming together fully and achieving perfect intimacy. They talked of politics, of economics, sometimes of poetry. Joaquim liked to read Sérgio's poems and had had a great influence even on his art, for it had been he who criticized certain of his poems, revolutionary in content but almost esoteric in form.

"A worker won't understand this . . ."

"But poetry . . ." and Sérgio undertook a long explanation.

"All very fine, comrade," Joaquim said, serious. "Maybe everything you say is true. I don't understand it, it may be right, I'm not going to argue. You're the poet. But look: what's this poetry for? Isn't it to help the revolution?"

"Yes."

"And who's going to make the revolution? The workers, the people, the poor, aren't they? How can this poetry help the revolution if the people who are going to make the revolution don't understand what it says? When I read old Lenin I understand everything he teaches, and when I read old Stalin too. I'm a worker, but it's clear and I understand it . . . I think that kind of poetry would be good poetry . . ."

The poet argued at length, not wishing to give in. But later he began a search for popular rhythms, and his new poetics was born of that discussion. Joaquim had been as happy as a child when, sometime after that talk, Sérgio showed him his new poems.

"That's it . . . That's pretty and everybody can understand it," he said, moved. "That's what we need . . ."

Sérgio felt himself fully rewarded.

They talked about politics, economics, even poetry, it's true. Long talks on free nights, but they had never exchanged a word about their lives. Never, however much he might wish to, had Sérgio ever come to Joaquim with a single personal problem. It was not that he wanted to appear better than he was to Joaquim. Once the driver had said to him, in the midst of a heated discussion:

"You'll always be a petit bourgeois . . ."

Sérgio had laughed and added, "Worst than that, Joaquim. Add to the vices of my petit bourgeois origin the vices of the intellectual caste . . . A serious matter . . ."

Joaquim had laughed too, that short and friendly laugh of his.

"Don't take it so seriously, comrade Sérgio. What's important is to be an honest intellectual. I don't understand much of this poetry stuff. But I like yours and I read it to some people, and they like it too. We know you're on our side . . . That's something . . ."

The conversation had ended there, and they had never returned to the subject. Still, Sérgio would have liked to talk to Joaquim about personal things, about Julieta for example.

Julieta had changed greatly in those months. She had found a world and plunged into it like a colonial conqueror avid to cultivate unknown lands, teeming with surprising discoveries. It was the world of books that she had only glimpsed in her disordered reading of novels purchased at random. Sérgio had opened new perspectives to her, a universe of poetry. As if she were floating, she felt light, like clouds freely propelled by the wind. And Sérgio, when he saw what was happening to her, was amazed and dedicated himself to the task of educating her, molding her to his will. It was like writing a poem. He did so with a degree of selfishness, which was another way of avenging himself on Carlos Zude. He had stolen not only his wife's body but her spirit as well; he had constructed another Julieta Zude. She was in the meeting room now, getting dressed, a bit frightened. Sérgio had told her not to be afraid. He had already spoken to her vaguely of Joaquim and she had expressed interest in meeting the driver.

In the entrance hall, Joaquim was trying to tell his story. Julieta approached, ready to leave. Sérgio heard her footsteps, mildly surprised; what would Joaquim say?

"Excuse me," she said.

And she stopped almost directly in front of the two men. The driver lowered his head. But Sérgio Moura made a sudden decision.

"Julieta, I want to introduce you to my friend Joaquim . . ."

He said to Joaquim:

"This is Julieta."

Joaquim extended his hand. The words emerged almost without his being aware of them:

"Carlos Zude's wife . . ."

"What difference does that make?" Julieta said. "Sérgio told me, 'My friend Joaquim will understand. He's capable of understanding everything . . .' Carlos Zude's wife? No, Mr. Joaquim. I'm Sérgio Moura's wife . . ."

"Well. I didn't mean to offend . . ." the driver said. "It just came out . . . on its own . . ."

Sérgio smiled; the lights in the square were coming on.

"Let's go inside . . . We'll talk there . . ."

That Mr. Sérgio, thought Joaquim as they walked to the meeting room. Julieta was flushed; she felt she was talking excessively, that she had offended the young man. Sérgio found the situation both amusing and awkward, but he now wanted to see it through to the end.

They sat down, Joaquim holding his hat in his hands. On the table was a cage where, like a captive prince, a beautiful black bird looked indifferently at those present. Sérgio said:

"Look at the bird there. He doesn't playact. We playact as if we were always on stage. We playact even when we're silent, when we say nothing . . . We're always hiding . . ."

Why's he using big words? thought Joaquim. *What does he want?* Sérgio continued:

"Why playact if we're friends? Take Julieta. People never really know each other. An exporter's wife . . . She has a lover. Of course you already knew that, Joaquim, and even so we never discussed the subject. Playacting . . ."

"It had nothing to do with me . . . None of my business. Why should I meddle in other people's private lives? We talk here, exchange opinions, you help me with some things that I don't know and you do. I learn. Sometimes I say a few things thinking maybe they'll be of some use to you. Your life? It's no business of mine . . ."

Sérgio's voice changed, no longer that of the man of letters amusing himself with the situation. He felt hurt and offended.

"Nobody is a machine . . . Not even the revolution is a machine . . ."

Joaquim looked at Sérgio, then at Julieta. There was disapproval in his gaze.

"It doesn't matter," Sérgio explained. "Julieta is a good person, whether you believe it or not. You can talk in front of her . . ."

Joaquim saw that the poet was unhappy and understood what he was driving at.

"For us every man has worth. He is worth more than anything, comrade Sérgio. The capitalists have money and buy everything: the law, police, priests, government, everything. We have just one kind of capital: the comrades . . ."

"And so?"

"And so? If you were a militant I'd say to you, 'Comrade Sérgio, this is wrong. Her being the wife of an exporter doesn't make it right. If you two love each other, why don't you live together? Why deceive a man?' That's what I'd say . . ."

Julieta look fixedly at Joaquim. Never before had she encountered such candor, such crude candor. Nonetheless, the visitor was likable and she felt no irritation at all. Joaquim noted her almost approving look.

"Excuse me, ma'am. It's just that, if he was a militant, his behavior would be hurting the revolution and hurting him. Then I'd say it. But you, comrade, as a sympathizer have no such obligation. We can't ask of you any more than you already give, which is a lot. Your advice, your contributions, your verses, which are the best of all . . ."

Julieta raised her eyes.

"Do you mean that the right thing would be for me to leave Carlos and go live with Sérgio?"

"That would be the right thing . . ."

"Very well," Sérgio said. "No argument. Looking at it as a whole, it's the best thing. But there are also details to consider. Julieta was born in luxury, with money, in comfort. Foolishness? It may seem so, but it's not. I live on a salary, a salary I'd lose . . . We, Mr. Joaquim, are made of different clay from you militants. Our clay is fragile and easily turns to mud . . . Ah, so easily!"

He was suddenly sincere, totally sincere, and said excitedly:

"That thing which is the party . . . Do you think that we intellectuals who live all around it without ever entering, that we don't love it too? We do love it, greatly! For us it's the certainty of another world, the world we dream of in our art, that we're searching for when we write. It's the certainty that such a world is being built. We're at the door of the party and don't go in, despite all our love for it. We don't go in but stay outside, circling around it like a flock of turkeys . . . Just like turkeys . . . And why? Because we're not made of the same clay . . . We're made of mud . . . Believe me—mud. We live stuck in the mud up to our hair . . . Little things that clutch, hold, deform, and kill . . ."

"Every person tries to better himself . . . And the party helps . . . Nobody is born whole, nobody is born good or bad . . . The party helps, makes you, shapes, straightens . . ."

Sérgio had a formula:

"Better a good sympathizer than a bad militant . . ." he stated.

Joaquim made a vague gesture, perhaps of agreement. Julieta was following the conversation avidly. All this was part of the wonderful world that she was discovering a little more each day. Sérgio's words fell like lead:

"You all speak of the *lumpenproletariat* . . . We talked about that once, remember? Loafers, bohemians, prostitutes, dockside thieves. We're the petit bourgeois *lumpenproletariat* . . . Could I go away with Julieta? Could I really? We're here, it's lovely. The greatest thing in the world . . . She loves me, I love her. Truly, with all my heart, Joaquim, believe me. But if we went away, if she left her husband, if the scandal cost me my job, if we went away, lived on the salary that I could make in a publishing house, where's the beauty? How long would it last?"

"None of it's easy," said Joaquim, suddenly tired. "When a comrade comes to talk to me, he comes with a concrete problem and I solve it. 'Joaquim, things are bad. I don't make enough to eat on. What can I do?' And I say, 'We'll go on strike.' That's a problem, something you can see, almost touch. Now you tell me, 'There's this man's wife; she loves me, I love her. We meet in secret. That's wrong. But we can't go away because we can't take a hard life.' What can I say? I don't know how to solve it. I just don't think it's right, and that's all there is to it."

There was a silence. Julieta was going to say something but checked herself. Joaquim spoke again:

"It's confusing. Once Roberto was crazy about Tancredo's wife, a good-looking young woman. Seems they would get together in the sand dunes. I found out about it and called him in. 'Roberto, this business isn't right. A militant doesn't do such things. If you love the woman, go live with her.' Roberto scratched his head—he's a nervy black man—but he went to live with her. Tancredo was furious, raised a fuss, wanted to fight, but in the end it all worked out. That's it . . . There was another time when everything was complicated. It was Bezerra; you don't know him, he already left. He fell for Elza, Lolô's wife. Bezerra was an honest guy. He didn't lie about it; he went straight to Lolô and explained the situation. He took Elza away with him, but Lolô killed himself. Bezerra went into a depression and was never good for anything after that. It's complicated . . ."

Julieta said:

"It's funny. The two of you there arguing and me thinking silly thoughts. I've heard so often about communists. I thought they were the freest people in the world, in terms of love. Now I see they're just as moralistic or even more so . . ."

"Freedom's one thing; shamelessness is something else . . ."

Joaquim tried to call back the words, but it was too late:

"Forgive me. I don't know how to talk to refined people . . ."

"There's nothing to apologize for. You can speak freely . . . But you didn't understand. I'm glad it's that way . . ." She smiled. "You may not believe it. I wouldn't believe it myself . . ."

Sérgio Moura concluded:

"Enough arguing. Julieta and I are going on. Later we'll see. Who knows what the future holds? Anything can happen . . . I just want to know one thing: will this prevent us from being friends? The three of us?"

Joaquim laughed.

"I'm no puritan . . ."

They stood smiling at one another. Joaquim looked at the couple; they were likable. He liked Sérgio, that complicated man! At heart he struck him as honest. And the woman—God, she was pretty!—also seemed to be a good person. But Carlos Zude's wife . . . Who would have thought it . . . Sérgio said:

"You came here with some news . . . We didn't even let you talk . . ."

"It's all right . . ."

"Tell us . . ."

"Remember what we were talking about the other day? About the boom?"

"Yes . . ."

"Well look, they're going to gobble up everything . . ." He turned to Julieta. "Excuse me, ma'am, I'm going to talk about your husband . . ."

She laughed.

"With Zude and Karbanks leading it, they've formed a corporation with Marinho's company. They kept a majority of the stock. Did you know?"

The poet whistled. Julieta was trying to grasp the significance of the conversation.

"What can they be after?" Sérgio asked.

"A monopoly of highway transport . . ."

"And afterwards . . ."

"If the growers form a cooperative, they can shut off transport. The railroad, you know . . ."

Silence descended over them. Julieta would have liked an explanation but was afraid to ask for fear of appearing meddlesome. Sérgio said:

"Your husband, ma'am, is a thorn in our side. But he's a thorn in everybody's side. He's going to bring unhappiness to everything around here . . ."

She thought with terror: *And he does it for me, to give me what I asked for and no longer want.* But she said nothing.

Joaquim was rising.

"Excuse me, ma'am, if I gave offense. I'm a worker, I don't know fine words . . ."

"You didn't offend me in the least . . . I'm very glad to have met you."

Sérgio went to the closed window, drew back the curtain and looked out through the glass at the illuminated square. The exporters were calmly carrying out their plan. Like soldiers executing a maneuver. Julieta drew close to Joaquim and asked anxiously:

"Do you think this mud, this rotten clay can improve itself someday and be as good as the others?"

Joaquim spoke rapidly:

"No job is hard for someone who's willing to work . . . All soil is good, only sometimes it needs fertilizer . . . Don't be afraid," he concluded.

She smiled. On the table, the bird was watching. Julieta thought it much like Sérgio Moura. In his way, the poet was a prisoner too.

13

When the first harvest of the boom was over and the lull arrived at year's end, a single question was on everyone's lips in the cacao zone, from the port of Ilhéus to the distant town of Guaraci in the Baforé mountains: could prices be maintained? The apparent factors that had occasioned the boom—the loss of the Ecuadorian crop, reduced production in the Gold Coast—would not be repeated. The newspapers carried stories of the large harvest in Africa and elimination of the blight in Ecuador. Would the price of cacao drop? That was what everyone was asking, uneasily.

The colonels had emerged from this first year with profits, albeit less than they had imagined. Despite their spending in cabarets, on expensive women, roulette, and baccarat, the era of limitless squandering had not yet really begun. Uncertainty about the duration of the boom imposed a measure of control on expenditures. Large-scale squandering would only begin from the second year on, when prices stabilized above forty mil-réis. That was when they became aware of the excitement of stock market speculation, gambling on the rise and fall of products with names quite different from cacao. From the second year on, João Magalhães's conviction that cacao prices would never go down became the consensus among plantation owners and small growers.

All those parallel, sometimes intersecting, lives were affected by the cacao boom. Colonel Maneca Dantas began construction of the most beautiful mansion in Ilhéus. He spent five hundred thousand on the house and its furnishings. But he put even more money into playing the stocks. Once he got started, he was no longer interested in any other style of life. It was an easy way to make and lose money. These men who came out of the struggle for the conquest of land, who had lived their entire lives in the forest, who had never been attracted to

233

enjoyment, suddenly abandoned themselves to anything that promised the possibility of new emotions. The majority of the colonels followed Maneca Dantas's example. If there was an exception it was Horácio, locked in legal struggles with his son.

The boom stirred them all—the large plantation owners who tore up money in the cabarets, the small growers who had never seen so much money and so much credit. Nevertheless, there were already signs that something in the city's panorama was changing. From his plantation, where he directed the exceedingly slow progress of the inventory proceedings, Horácio was for the first time encountering difficulties, opposition, and withholding of cooperation. The colonel had always linked his battles to politics, and now he was losing political prestige. The state administration had organized a new political party, bringing together people from the traditional parties; and leadership of the cacao zone had been given to Carlos Zude. They offered Horácio membership on the central directorate, but he declined, offended. When he decided to take stock politically, he saw he was almost isolated. The Integralists had lured away many of his former colleagues. Others, like Braz, had joined the National Liberation Front, which was accused of communism and immediately outlawed. Most, however, were in the new government party. Carlos Zude was "the new blazing political sun," as one local journalist had written. Horácio formed with the opposition the scraps of a party, a still considerable force but one incapable of winning against the government. The opposition boasted of Horácio's joining their ranks, but the colonel wasn't satisfied: as he knew from long experience, winning a lawsuit while in the opposition was never easy.

Colonel Horácio da Silveira could feel power slipping from his grasp but did not understand why. These times were not his times; this struggle was not his struggle. And he dedicated himself to the lawsuit, calling Rui Dantas to the plantation almost every week to give him instructions. He bought weapons and hired gunfighters, lamenting the lack of men like those of earlier days, when he had conquered the land and fought the Badarós. He expected to win the suit. But, just in case, he took preparations to resist the breaking up of his lands. "Not even if I die with a gun in my hands," he had told Maneca Dantas, and the phrase spread immediately throughout Ilhéus.

He had pulled off a master stroke in the course of the suit. When Rui Dantas pessimistically declared that nothing could be done, that it was an open-and-shut case, hopeless as far as the colonel was concerned, the latter summoned him. On the road the young lawyer met the notary from the civil registry in Itabuna, who was also on his way to the plantation, at Horácio's invitation. They arrived together, talking. Horácio was in his room, bathing from a washbowl. The black woman

Felícia was pouring water over his curved back. The bath worsened his rheumatism, but it was a habit of many years standing and Colonel Horácio da Silveira could not do without his cold bath. They waited on the veranda. The colonel appeared, his staff feeling out the way. The notary had no idea why he was there or what was behind the invitation.

"Felícia, bring some rum . . ."

He turned to Rui Dantas.

"You, Mr. Rui, are goin' to make me a rough draft of a will . . ."

The two looked at him, puzzled.

"Done right. Usin' words they used thirty years ago. The rough draft of the deceased's will . . . It'll say that she leaves the use an' fruit for her son. And that he can't sell the lands as long as I'm alive. Use an' fruit, nothin' else . . ."

Now they understood. Rui Dantas was agape at the colonel's wisdom. He recalled the stories of famous dodges, in the old days.

"There's pen and paper inside . . . It's a new pen . . ."

The lawyer went inside. Horácio was alone with the notary.

"Menezes, a long time ago your registry didn't belong to you yet and it was burned down by Teodoro das Baraúnas at the Badarós' orders. I had a claim registered there to the lands of Sequeiro Grande. Later the notary died and I set you up in the registry, isn't that right?"

"That's right, sir . . . I owe it all to you . . ."

"Good thing you remember it . . . You still have those half-burned books there, don't you?"

"Yes, Colonel . . ."

"You're goin' to do a real good job. You're goin' to register Ester's will in one of those books. Then sprinkle flour over it so the writin' looks old. Nobody's ever messed with them, so there's plenty of blank pages . . . There's lots of examples of Dr. Jessé's signature and of my friend Maneca Dantas's. You'll register the will there . . ."

"It's dangerous, Colonel . . ."

"I'm not askin' if it's dangerous . . . I'm tellin' you what you're goin' to do . . . I'll pay you . . ."

"It's not a question of money, Colonel. It's just that, if they find out . . ."

"Haven't you done others? What about the fake mortgages for Pedro Castro's fields, who you think did those? And Nestor Baía's? You're an old scoundrel, Menezes. You'll do it. And I'm goin' to pay you twenty thousand for the job, for the risk. It's worth it . . ."

"But, Colonel . . ."

"Let me tell you somethin', Menezes. I knew your father, he was a good man. He was my friend and I was his friend. That's why I arranged

the registry for you; I gave it to you. I could have given it to somebody
else. But if you don't do what I'm tellin' you, I'll forget you're the son
of old Menezes . . ."

He yelled for his overseer. His shout was repeated across the fields by
the workers at the drying frames. The overseer came quickly. Horácio
ordered:

"Bring Zé Comó here . . ."

The notary watched, filled with fear. Fear of effecting the dodge,
which was a dangerous process, fear of refusing the colonel what he
wanted. The powerful black man appeared, coming down the road with
his repeating rifle on his shoulder.

" 'Afternoon, Colonel . . ."

"I just wanted you to take a look at Mr. Menezes here. Remember
his face, 'cause it might be I'll have you take a message to him in
Itabuna . . . He's a friend of mine . . . Could be . . ."

The black man laughed. Menezes paled.

"It's a deal, Colonel. Send the lawyer with the copy. Who'll sign for
Dona Ester?"

"Leave that to me . . ."

When Rui Dantas returned and read him the draft, in which he
ordered some minor changes, Horácio said:

"Counselor, you keep a woman in Ilhéus, don't you?"

Rui Dantas didn't know what to reply. He had respected the colonel
since childhood and didn't know the purpose of the unexpected question.
Horácio continued:

"No need to be bashful . . . Young men do such things . . . They say
she's pretty, a foreigner . . . That kind of woman likes money. Take
this letter"—he withdrew from his coat pocket an old and yellowed
letter—"and have her study the handwritin' of the deceased . . . There's
a signature . . . Have her imitate it till she can do it right. Then take her
to the civil registry in Itabuna and have her sign . . ."

"Right, Colonel . . . But you don't need to pay . . ."

"It's better to pay, Counselor Rui Dantas. In things like this you
shouldn't owe favors to anyone, whether a friend or a woman. Pay her
two thousand for the risk she's takin' . . ."

Rui Dantas and Menezes left for Itabuna together, both somewhat
dazed. But for Rui his professional self-interest, the victory that he
foresaw by means of the marvelous dodge, overcame his fear and
afforded him a certain ambitious happiness. By winning the case he
would establish a reputation as a great lawyer, besides the fact that the
colonel was paying him royally. For Horácio, money was no object in
this dispute. All his frugal ways, all his pennypinching were irrelevant
to the lawsuit. The old colonel spent money without a second thought.

For him the important thing was to not break up his lands and to teach Silveirinha a lesson.

Menezes commented on the affair. An outrageous dodge . . . But there was no doubt that the colonel was paying generously. Twenty thousand was nothing to be sneezed at. They recalled then the burning of the registry, so many years ago . . . That was also because of one of Horácio's dodges. Teodoro das Baraúnas had come with his men and set fire to the old adobe house. What would happen this time?

"We could really get hurt, counselor . . ."

Rui Dantas was fatalistic.

"Nothing ventured, nothing gained, Mr. Menezes . . ."

Some weeks later, Silveirinha's lawyers were astonished at the appearance of Dona Ester's old will, which took away all the heir's rights except for the profits from the plantation. "The old fellow is quite a man," Horácio's supporters said.

Rui Dantas boasted in the streets of Ilhéus.

14

He boasted in the streets of Ilhéus, but in the office installed in Maneca Dantas's new mansion, the attorney sweated as he searched for a difficult rhyme. Rui Dantas's life had also changed with the boom. From an aimless youth in the city's bars, rich and useless, he was transformed into a well-known lawyer, defending the biggest lawsuit of the day in the zone. He swelled with pride and spent money lavishly. Easy money that Horácio had paid him, even easier than the money Maneca Dantas gave him without a thought. He spent it on Lola Espinola, dressing her in the finest fabrics, offering her jewels, taking her to Bahia for a quick outing. Pepe hit him up for thousands, for he was expanding his dirty business and was now bankrolling the illegal lottery in the city. Lola accepted everything with indifference. Ever since Pepe had worked the "badger game" on Frederico Pinto and opened the cabaret and bordello, the Argentine woman was indifferent to everything. Pepe paid virtually no attention to her, was rarely there, almost as if he came around just to collect. He would take inventory of the jewels, pocket the large amounts of money that he found, say a few kind words to her, and now and then go to bed with her.

Just how Lola had gotten hold of the first doses of cocaine was hard to explain. But she undeniably had, and she abandoned herself to the toxic substance. When Rui Dantas found out, he was alarmed; his experiences in that area were minimal, two or three times in brothels in the capital. He wanted to be angry at Lola, but the Argentine turned her sad eyes to him and stated that it was the only way she felt happy. Rui threw himself into bed with her—he was crazy about the woman—and in the end began sniffing cocaine from time to time. In those days students on vacation, rich young people, snorted cocaine in the cabarets, more from fashion than from addiction. The boom brought with its carnival

of money all that was good and all that was bad to be found in the
large cities. Rui Dantas clung even closer to the woman. He wrote
sonnets for her, in the hope that Lola would leave Pepe once and for
all and be his alone. In his crazed passion for Lola's beautiful flesh
there was always some measure of romanticism, cheap romanticism
to be sure, but even so, capable of touching Lola's professionalism,
and thus saddening her even more. In her long career as an elegant
prostitute, many men had said the same things that Rui told her on
the nights of romanticism mixed with the cocaine they sniffed and the
champagne they drank.

"You weren't born for this life . . ."

That was what made her feel like killing herself. She found the men
to be good, delicate. All those she had met, all those who had entered
her bed to be miserably exploited later, were good to her, gentle, and
treated her with affection. Colonel Frederico Pinto had loved her so
much that she was moved. Rui was too maudlin and hard to take at
times, but he also loved her, wrote sentimental things for her, seeming
more like a gentle husband than a wealthy lover.

But Lola felt tied to only one man, and that was Pepe. She knew
he didn't love her, that for Pepe she was merely a reliable source of
income, but even so she loved him. She was truly happy only when
Pepe appeared and stroked her hair, saying anything at all to her.
When he left, Lola had to turn to drugs, and if she didn't kill herself
it was because she knew that all the businesses in which the pimp was
involved could fail. And then he would need her again

She listened patiently (patience being part of her profession) to Rui
Dantas's long, boring accounts of Colonel Horácio's lawsuit. She felt a
vague sympathy for the colonel, just as she sympathized with Maneca
Dantas, despite knowing that Rui's father was angry with her. Maneca
Dantas had offered her ten thousand to go away, to leave his son alone.
"He'll have to pay a lot more than that," Pepe had said. But Lola would
have done it for nothing if it were up to her. It was she who forged
Ester's signature on the fraudulent will. Pepe demanded five thousand.
On the train, Rui had told her the story of Horácio's wife, and Lola
felt compassion for that woman who had had the courage to flee to her
destiny, the spirit to break with the roots that bound her to cacao. She,
Lola, would never have such courage. Her destiny was Pepe; how could
she abandon him? And Rui saying she "wasn't born for this life" . . . At
times she was furious with him and, on certain nights when he did not
bring her any cocaine, Lola treated him badly. Afterwards she would
regret it; it wasn't the poor man's fault . . . He did everything to make
her happy, from expensive gifts to his carefully scanned sonnets . . .
He had started on the road to drugs, perhaps only to please her . . .

For Rui Dantas the blonde Argentine woman was the definitive passion. A young man lost in the streets of Ilhéus, for him a civilized woman from another land held tremendous appeal. She had accustomed him to champagne, cocaine, and refinements of lovemaking. He could not give her up; he would do anything to keep her. The courtships in which Maneca Dantas attempted to interest him, with rich young women from local society circles, were summarily rejected. He stopped attending parties at the Social Club and made no secret of his liaison with Lola. He took her to the Trianon, sumptuous dinners in the evening, frequented by students on vacation and literati passing through Ilhéus.

And, in the midst of all this, that irremediable calling as husband, fiancé, suitor. He would never be a lover. A calling that made him sweat in search of a sonorous rhyme for his love sonnet. In bed with Lola he would act extravagantly, the two would drink till they fell down, they would plumb the depths of the mysteries of drugs . . . But in his sonnets it was the most romantic of loves, the purest, the most innocent . . .

He holds the pen in his right hand, while with his left he makes a declamatory gesture in the hope of summoning the word. "And they say writing poetry is for loafers . . . A petition is a lot easier . . ." It's because they don't know how hard it is at times to find a good rhyme and apply to it the desired meaning. Rui Dantas has his coat off, his sleeves rolled up, to all appearances a man engaged in bodily combat. Drops of sweat appear on the hairs of his arm and on his smooth brow.

Writing a sonnet is hard work, especially in well-measured alexandrines, but Lola is worth any sacrifice. Besides which there is the success of publication, the congratulations from young men of letters in the city, the comments from acquaintances:

"Well done, counselor! Lovely verses . . ."

Or from the romantic schoolteachers:

"So sentimental . . ."

There were also the colonels, who previously had wrinkled their noses at him, who had thought that, instead of sonnets, Rui Dantas should be addressing himself to juries, attending trials in court. That's what he'd gotten his degree for, not to scribble mawkish poetry. But now they said nothing and treated him with more respect, ever since Rui acted as Horácio's attorney and surprised them all with the discovery of Ester's will. "Good work . . ." they said in praise. In any case, they weren't worth worrying about, and Rui Dantas told the other literati of the city, speaking of the colonels, "They're all bourgeois." The pejorative term conveyed not class feeling but an esthetic distinction.

For Rui Dantas, Zito Ferreira's opinion was much more important, despite his being a professional sponger. He bought him beer every time he published a sonnet, receiving his praise avidly. They would read the product together, or Rui would declaim it in the bar in the presence of the scandalized customers. Rui also read his verses at certain parties, where he would receive looks from the young women who read Delly and Ardel. He thought of eventually collecting his output in a single volume. The *Ilhéus Daily* even announced that "a volume will soon appear, under the title of *Loose Diamonds*, containing the sonnets of our brilliant contributor and the young attorney of this venue, Dr. Rui Dantas." Sérgio Moura had nicknamed the future book *False Diamonds*, a fact for which Rui held a grudge. He never missed a chance to ask people if they understood Sérgio's verses, those hieroglyphs that one needed a "key" to decipher. The problem was the critical praise for Sérgio's poems from writers in the south. Rui Dantas never failed to offer "my congratulations" when the *Ilhéus Daily* reprinted one of these articles. But inside he was consumed by anger. He got his revenge by speaking ill of the poet, his habits, his passion for birds and flowers. Later, when the entire city began murmuring about Sérgio and Julieta, Rui joined in, noising abroad scandalous news: that, during one of Carlos Zude's visits to Rio, one night Julieta and Sérgio were seen at the beach, lying in the sand. And that the next day a pair of woman's panties, with an embroidered *J*, were found on the beach. The panties were exhibited in the cabarets of Ilhéus, and for two days were the sole topic of conversation.

The truth is that Rui considered himself Sérgio's rival in everything: in poetry, where they represented opposite schools and values, in their way of living, and in their positions vis-à-vis the city and its life.

In his office, with its bookcase of thick law books and the portrait of Rui Barbosa on the table, Rui Dantas struggles to compose a sonnet with unusual rhymes. Zito Ferreira had said at the bar, before a large gathering of people, that Rui was a "rhymer among millions." It's true that someone had laughed, finding a double meaning, an irony in the phrase. But Rui did not notice. He takes his time in the choice of sonorous and little used adjectives. His face and arms are sweating; he is sweating almost as much as a porter on the docks.

Under that layer of mediocre intellectual ambitions, Rui Dantas preserved a certain innocence that made his anger short-lived and caused him to offer himself to Lola like a love-struck adolescent. She was a prostitute, a drug addict, and a difficult person, but Rui thought of her almost like a wife. And it was as such that she appeared in that labored sonnet.

The dragging footsteps of Maneca Dantas could be heard in the next room. He comes in, shouting for his wife:

"Auricídia! Auricídia!"

Noise in Rui's office.

"Rui, son. Are you there?"

"Here, Father . . ."

Maneca Dantas comes in, sits down, and only then removes his hat. There's a smile on his kindly face, his customary reaction when he sees his son.

"What are you writing?"

Rui looks at the unfinished sonnet. In the already completed verses, Lola, with a fine dress and a gentle expression, crosses the sun-drenched courtyard of a dream castle. Maneca Dantas would never understand . . .

"A petition, Father, for the colonel's suit . . ."

"Then I'll let you work . . ."

He gets up, goes to the door, turns:

"God bless you, Son . . ."

Rui Dantas bends over the sonnet.

15

At the end of the harvest, the first of the boom, Antônio Vítor went to Estância. Raimunda had stayed in the fields, doing the pruning and taking care of the work. Antônio Vítor filled a suitcase with presents, small remembrances bought from the Syrians in Ilhéus, and boarded a boat. It had been thirty years since he traveled by sea. He felt emotion inside, unaware that it was pride. Thirty years ago he had come third class on one of those Bahiana company boats. He was a young man who knew nothing, homesick and fearful in the moonlit night. On the boat Juca Badaró had hired him. He worked in the fields, did heavy labor. Later he killed people, was himself wounded, and was given a piece of land. He felled trees, planted manioc and corn, later planted cacao. He and Raimunda. Now he is returning first class, wearing squeaky high-lace shoes as he had dreamed, a ring on his finger, good worsted clothes. He was returning as a grower, almost a colonel. He had grown rich on those lands.

And suddenly, on board the boat, he remembered Ivone. He had forgotten her many years ago. The times were long past when he would go to the edge of the forest, when there was still forest, to remember. Later Raimunda came along and he had forgotten Ivone. He had left a child in her belly. What must he be like? Would he be better than Joaquim, who refused to work on the land and was a bus driver and always involved with suspicious people? Antônio Vítor thinks about seeking out that son and bringing him back to the farm. He must be a man of thirty, maybe married, maybe with children. He would bring him, he would be of help on the farm. He would be what Joaquim was not. Joaquim was very much like Raimunda, stubborn like his mother, with her frowning face when confronted with the new house, living there as if by obligation. Raimunda would never change; it was hopeless. She would die working the fields, shabbily dressed, smeared with cacao drippings and with an angry look on her face.

The boat rocks on the waves. Antônio Vítor decides not to have dinner. He stretches out in a lounge chair, covers his body with a blanket. A colonel, napping in the next lounge chair, wakes up and starts a conversation. They talk about the price of cacao, the boom, next year's harvest. Antônio Vítor has never felt so happy.

And upon his return he managed to see Raimunda happy, for a moment. In Estância he had not found Ivone, who had died some time ago. Nor did he find his son, who while still quite young had left for the coffee lands of São Paulo. But he had found one of those Spanish combs that were no longer used nowadays and that Raimunda had always wanted so much to have. For a long time she had worn in her mulatto hair one that had belonged to Dona Ana and was missing a tooth. Raimunda was happy with the gift. All her angry demeanor disappeared when she placed in her hair, already shot through with white strands, the Spanish comb, which was studded with small glass stones. She was so content that she didn't even look so old and so ugly. And even the bad omens fled from her mulatto face with its flat nose and thick lips; she even looked pretty.

16

When the second year of the boom began, a new crop that gave every sign of being enormous, the lives of all these people changed. Antônio Vítor took on the pose of a rich man, indulging in the luxuries of a large plantation owner. Captain João Magalhães plowed money into cutting down the last of the forest belonging to him. Maneca Dantas had built his mansion, Horácio busied himself with dodges, Frederico Pinto seduced young mulatto girls on his plantation and played roulette. They considered themselves the "owners of the land."

In the export houses business went on as usual. The colonel would deliver fifteen thousand kilos.

"The quote today is forty-two mil-réis . . ."

Forty-two thousand to the colonel's account. They deposited cacao and withdrew the money for whatever they needed. For food and gambling, for the family and fast women, for schools and automobiles, for the plantation's expenses and the exciting game of the stock market.

When the first year of the boom came to an end, many colonels appeared at the export companies to settle accounts.

"How's my account, Mr. Zude?"

"Fine, Colonel, just fine. You have credit . . . Make withdrawals whenever you feel like it . . ."

The majority did make withdrawals. A few insisted on a statement of their balance and were amazed to find they had almost no balance; some were even in the red.

"Nothing to worry about, Colonel . . ."

But the boom went on and they once again felt the reality of hundreds of thousands when they sold seventy-five thousand kilos of cacao. The owners of the land.

245

Carlos Zude smiled: "the owners of the land." Once he'd told Julieta that in the near future *they* would be "the owners of the land." He and Karbanks, the Rauschnings, Schwartz, Reicher, and Antônio Ribeiro, the cacao exporters. When they had lands, plantations, they would no longer be dependent on the colonels' cacao. In the thick ledgers of Zude Brothers & Co., as in the other export houses, the colonels' indebtedness grew even as the price of cacao rose. Carlos Zude smiles like a warrior who, assessing a battle, determines that all is well. The plan was admirably designed. And it had been his idea. True enough, he couldn't have brought it off without help from Karbanks and Schwartz, especially Karbanks. It was a year since he had stepped off the plane and called a meeting of exporters at the Commercial Association. Sérgio Moura was sniffing a rose, to all appearances laughing at them. *A poor devil* . . . Carlos Zude thinks. What good were verses? It wasn't only in verses that beauty lay. It was also in the struggle that he waged so victoriously. Few realized it. The colonels had no idea at all. Only the communists spread flyers around, but the police searched them out, and when they caught one clapped him in jail or deported him. Few people knew that he, Carlos Zude, cacao exporter, was a warrior, hero of a terrible battle. But Julieta knew, and that was enough for him.

In his office, Carlos Zude ponders. It's the beginning of the second year of the boom: does Julieta realize what's happening? He had explained it to her one night, an anxious night at the start of the rains. Since then he had felt more happiness in his wife's face; she no longer complained about life there, no longer asked to go to Rio. Gone was the yearning that before had clouded Julieta's listless eyes in the Ilhéus twilight. Carlos noted the fact with joy. It's true he had had little time to devote to his wife's mood changes; in fact, never had he had less time for her. But it was for her that he was working, and if there wasn't enough time, so it must be . . . Carlos feels even prouder. The sacrifice to which business obliged him—not giving his wife all the attention she deserved—is one more measure of how he must struggle, exert himself, to win his battle.

On weary nights, after he did the calculations, after reconciling accounts alone in his office at home, often Julieta was already asleep and he merely kissed her. On other nights, however, he would take her in his arms, seeking in his wife's body the recompense for a day of work. But he felt that in the year just ended he had not shared in her activities as diligently as before. He noticed that Julieta also had distanced herself from many of the things that previously had filled her life. She had not only stopped going with him on his constant trips to Bahia, but had also almost entirely lost touch with the Englishmen and Swedes, her closest relationships. In fact, Guni's husband had been replaced, and the new vice-consul had not established a friendship with them. But Mr. Brown and the Englishmen with the railroad and the consulate were also no longer part of her circle, and they had not left Ilhéus. Carlos, heavily burdened with work, barely had time to notice such things. When he thought about these family details he readily accepted the first explanation that came to mind, both optimistic and pleasant: "She sees me busy, working . . . That's why she makes her sacrifices too . . ."

And he felt like telling her to have some fun, not to worry about him, not to turn into a nun. She'd gotten the habit of reading, always had a book in her hands; she was even getting along with Sérgio Moura. A strange fellow . . . He was conceited, but soon people would see he was nothing but a poor devil. He'd been very awkward at their house, at Julieta's birthday party, as if he'd never been in such a setting before. Her birthday was coming up again . . . He mustn't forget her gift. Last year he'd brought her a pearl necklace and placed it on his wife's naked breasts. What could he give her this year? Now he was not only a cacao exporter but the leader of the area's largest political party. He'd have to celebrate and invite a lot of people to their house . . . Not an exclusive party like last year. Times were changing for Carlos Zude also. It was necessary to convince Julieta. She had new obligations now and should consider her husband's new status. He'd have a talk with her. He needed her help. Julieta should change her attitude toward the people of the city, be more friendly, invite them over, relate to society. He remembered the stories about the colonels. They got along with everybody; they were truly the "owners of the land." There was something to be learned from them. He would talk with Julieta.

Poor Julieta, cast into this small city, she who'd been born for grand parties, accustomed to a different life! But that's how things were . . . It wouldn't be for long. Later—when the battle was over—they could travel, see the world, spend time in the great cities, even live abroad. Carlos would still come to Ilhéus constantly, but he wouldn't have to live there or subject Julieta to the city. He'd repay her present sacrifices with high interest. They'd go to the United States, to Europe. In Ilhéus would be the export company, the plantations. For the new "owners of the land" would not be like the old, stuck in their fields in the midst of cacao trees.

Someone knocks at the office door. Carlos Zude awakes from his dreams.

"Come in . . ."

Reinaldo Bastos sticks his head inside and advises:

"Captain João Magalhães is here . . ."

"Send him in."

The captain came in, holding his hat in his hands, unshaven, wearing his riding boots, a diffident smile on his lips.

"Good afternoon, Mr. Carlos."

Carlos Zude extends his hand, rises, offers a chair.

"How are you? And how's your family?"

"Fine, Mr. Carlos . . ." the captain says awkwardly.

Carlos knows these cacao growers well, and how to deal with them. He allows the conversation to drift from one listless and uninteresting topic to the next. Only after fifteen minutes does he ask:

"What brings you here, Captain?"

Then João Magalhães, having lost his shyness, explains:

"I've been sellin' you my cacao for many years, Mr. Carlos. And my father-in-law did business with Mr. Maximiliano . . ."

"Sinhô Badaró . . . a great man . . . Maximiliano often spoke of him. He died from a gunshot, didn't he?"

"It wasn't rightly from the shot . . . Its consequences . . ."

"Well, I'm at your disposal, Captain . . ."

"It's about my farm . . . I still have a piece of forest, real big. If I plant it with cacao I'll double my yield. Maybe more. I'm clearin' out the trees . . . I started this year but it eats up a lot of money. This was a good year and I was able to make a start. But, you know, a farm has expenses and cuttin' down forest even more so . . . Workers, materials, a real bundle . . . It's all under way but it looks like I'll to have to stop . . ."

"But why, Captain?"

"I've used up the money from the last harvest . . . That's why I came here. This year the harvest looks like it'll yield almost thirty thousand kilos. I'll sell it to you like always . . . But . . ."

"No need to say it, Captain. Do you want an advance?"

"Exactly!"

"But for heaven's sake, Captain, did you need to beat around the bush? You're an old and valued customer. You have rights in this company . . . I'll have a credit line opened for you against the upcoming harvest . . . The usual terms. You draw it out as you need it. The cacao will be quoted at the price of the day of delivery. Is that all right?"

"Thank you very much, Mr. Carlos."

"After all, Captain, do you think I'd let your work stop? For heaven's sake, Captain . . . There's no need for thanks . . ."

He pushes the button on his desk, calling Martins. While he waits, he chats with Captain João Magalhães:

"I was just a youngster and Maximiliano used to talk to me about your father-in-law . . . He wore a long beard, didn't he? And he had a brother also, a tough guy?"

"That was Juca all right. He was shot to death. He was real tough, yessir . . ."

Martins appeared.

"You called, Mr. Carlos?"

"Martins, open a line of credit for the captain against delivery of cacao. Give him whatever he wants to withdraw. The usual receipts . . ."

Martins asked:

"What limit, Mr. Carlos?"

Carlos Zude smiled at Captain João Magalhães.

"No limit . . ."

17

With Rita gone, the mummers group had lost its zest. Rita was in town, pregnant by Colonel Frederico Pinto, with a house of her own, a housekeeper, and silk clothes. Dona Augusta knew about it and yelled at her husband, creating scenes constantly.

Beanpole, on the nights at the plantation, spoke ill of women to Black Florindo. Rosa had left him without a word. Where on earth could she be these days? If he ever found her he'd give her a good beating; that'd show her she couldn't betray a real man. Rita had left the mummers group, chasing after the colonel. Her father was still a mule driver on the plantation, and when he went to deliver cacao he slept at his daughter's house. Beanpole would introduce him to newly arrived workers:

"This is the colonel's father-in-law . . ."

Black Florindo wanted to go away. It had been Beanpole himself who first put the idea in his head. He had planned to flee and convinced Florindo to go with him. But when the time arrived, he had been unable to abandon the beautiful mummers group in the middle of the road. And they had spent another year in the fields, gathering cacao, dancing over the drying frames, going into the deadly kiln. The season for the group was approaching again. Rehearsals had already begun, and Florindo spoke once more of "hightailing it." Beanpole had told him wonderful things about a girl in Ilhéus named Rosa who had been his lover. Night after night he described the woman's beauty: her voice, her smile, her eyes, her hands, her teeth, undressing her in his memory; Black Florindo wanted to see her. Where on earth could she be?

"This time we'll hightail it . . ."

Beanpole made a vague gesture that could have been either yes or no; he himself didn't know which. They were earning a little more for a day's work and were now being paid six mil-réis. From the plantation house the colonel had complained about the increase, saying that it was the doing of the communists. In any case it had helped little, as prices at the plantation store had also gone up: dried meat, beans, a yard of cheap cloth, blue denim pants. Debts hadn't diminished, for that was hopeless. It was that way and always had been that way; it was fate. "Fate is made up above," the old folks would say fatalistically, pointing toward the sky. For them there was a sole, distant hope: the next life, heaven, where the poorest would be the richest. The wage increase solved nothing. Florindo wanted to flee, forgetting that fate is written up above. In any case, with the boom the colonel always advanced a bit more money for the festivals, and once again helped the group, this time with a larger sum. It would really be good if he let Rita come, for Beanpole was readying a banner for this year. If not Rita, who would carry it? It was a pretty banner, of white cloth embroidered in red. A very large cacao fruit, the only thing that Nhá Vitória knew how to embroider. Capi had wanted a Christ Child, but the old woman didn't know how. It had been the cacao fruit, and Capi had complained. But the banner was pretty even so, a pleasure to look at. If Rita came . . . But the colonel wouldn't permit it, nor would Dona Augusta agree to the girl's presence on their plantation. She cursed Rita's father to his face, as if the poor man were to blame.

"You old cuckold!"

Cuckold means a betrayed husband, so how can you call a father whose only daughter is taken away a cuckold? Dona Augusta calls him a cuckold anyway. It's amusing how she snorts when she sees the aged mule driver arriving at the head of his mules, after a long journey.

"You old cuckold!"

She doesn't even seem like a colonel's wife, with her jealousy of a dark-skinned mulatto girl from the fields. And she's as fat as an elephant; the colonel did the right thing. He was getting something out of life . . .

Even if the colonel allowed it, Dona Augusta would never agree. With her large gyrating bottom, Rita seemed like a ship on the high seas, like those Beanpole had seen so many times from the docks in Ilhéus. She also seemed like the tops of the tallest cacao trees when the wind shook them in the sunny afternoon. With Rita gone, the mummers group had lost its zest.

Florindo wants to flee, take off, see the port of Ilhéus, look for Rosa, whose whereabouts are unknown.

"This time we'll light out . . ."

But how can they light out if this year Florindo is going to play the part of the ox in the mummers group? Capi refuses, saying that it's a lousy role, that it doesn't let you dance, and he wants to dance. Last year he complained, considering the group a piece of foolishness, nothing at all like those in Ceará; he had once taken part in one, dressed as King Herod. But afterwards he had danced as much as anyone else, and he had come home drunk as a skunk . . . This year, he said, he only wanted to dance; Florindo could be the ox. What Florindo wants is to take off.

"In the captain's fields we can hightail it and lose ourselves . . ."

Standing in front of the shack, they wait for people to arrive for the rehearsal. They come from far away, from other fields, from the four corners of the plantation. The orchestra has grown and now boasts two tambourines and a pair of guitars. The night stretches out in a silence broken only by the delicate wind over the trees. It whistles pleasantly, and there are those who say forest spirits are loose in the woods . . . The rainy season is approaching. On the road, the reddish light of a kerosene lantern glows in the distance.

"Here comes some folks . . ."

And another lantern on the side trail. And another in the distance, nearly invisible. They are coming for the mummers group rehearsal, almost like a procession of believers carrying out a vow. Pilgrims come from afar.

"Here comes some folks . . ."

Florindo wants to flee:

"You think we can find that there Rosa?"

"Sure, we'll find 'er . . ."

Florindo never tires of the lengthy descriptions. He asks:

"What's she like? She real pretty?"

"You bet she is . . . A real beauty of a woman . . . And then some . . ."

"More'n Rita?"

"Huh! No comparison . . ."

"I gotta see 'er . . . This time we'll take off . . ."

The lantern lights stain the night with red. With Rita gone, the mummers group had lost its zest.

18

Silveirinha's lawyers, up in arms, bellowed in the courtroom:
"It's a bald-faced dodge . . ."

They were trying to prove what everyone knew: that Ester's will was false. But how? There it was, in those ancient, half-burned books, the writing faded and thin, apparently old. There was Dona Ester Silveira's signature, in the handwriting of a schoolgirl, a signature confirmed by the old notary, and underneath it those of the witnesses: the late Dr. Jessé and Colonel Maneca Dantas, who was still alive and had vouched for the authenticity of the will. How could they disavow it? It was the most perfect dodge of recent times, and both in the city of Ilhéus and throughout the cacao zone there was general admiration for the work of the attorney Rui Dantas. The more experienced saw in it the hand of Colonel Horácio, but the majority praised the talent of the young lawyer, on whose work desk a backlog of cases was now piling up.

Silveirinha's lawyers raised doubts about the will, demanded a handwriting analysis, and brought experts from Bahia. Nothing was proved, and the word spread that Rui Dantas had bought them off at great cost. Or perhaps Menezes had done his job so well that even the experts were fooled. This detail has never been clarified, but to this day it's said that the house one of the experts built in a suburb of Bahia, a small house into which he moved his entire family, was paid for with Colonel Horácio da Silveira's money. Silveirinha's sponsors were not disheartened, and when they appealed the ruling of the judge in Itabuna to the state Supreme Court, they demanded a judicial re-examination of the books where the will was found.

While they were awaiting the outcome of the appeal—a slow but momentous struggle was taking place in Bahia centering on the judges, with the lawyers for each side almost living on the street where the court

253

was located—they demanded payment of what, by ruling of the judge
in Itabuna, Silveirinha had coming to him: the profits from his part of
the plantation, profits on almost eighteen thousand kilos of cacao per
year. Horácio summoned Rui Dantas to the plantation and told him
not to contest it, to pay what they asked. It made little difference to
him. He paid gladly, for what he desired was that his lands remain
intact. The lawyers did some calculations in Schwartz's office, while
simultaneously using every means to win the appeal.

Silveirinha received more than four hundred thousand, but the money
went through his hands quickly. He had enormous debts with Schwartz,
and he owed his attorneys; the suit had been a bottomless pit. In any
case, he still had, each year from that time on, the profits from eighteen
thousand kilos of cacao, his share of the plantation. Silveirinha would
have resigned himself to waiting for his father's death—which seemed
to be the best solution—had it not been for Schwartz, who was furious.
He took the colonel's victorious dodge as a personal insult. Had he, an
intellectual who had attended a German university, versed in Goethe and
Nietzsche, later a student of politics, an up-and-coming Nazi leader—
had he come to this barbaric, aggressive, godforsaken city at the end of
the world to be outsmarted by a stupid old colonel, practically illiterate,
a former mule driver, a killer and a lout? Schwartz felt humiliated; it was
a defeat. And he held onto Silveirinha, sending Gumercindo after him in
a flurry of activity. Now he involved himself in the political affairs of
the Integralists almost openly, affording the communists opportunity for
violent attacks in their illegal bulletins. The discovery, in Santa Clara,
of daggers bearing the swastika in the hands of sworn Integralists gave
the communists reason to launch a campaign of disparagement against
the local Integralists, denouncing Schwartz as their mentor and the link
with German nazism. But not even this could stay the growth of the
Integralists' prestige. And it was already known that Silveirinha would
run for mayor in the next election, against Carlos Zude. Even so, there
was not a total break between the two groups. The Integralists used
harsh language in reference to liberal-democrats but never went so
far as complete discord. Carlos Zude prevented it, by never failing
to afford a certain measure of prestige to the Green Shirts' actions.

Schwartz was bringing pressure to bear on Silveirinha. But even the
German himself saw no way of resolving the matter and doubted the
appeal would succeed. It was in a conversation with a discouraged
Gumercindo that the solution suddenly came to him. Gumercindo was
speaking of Silveirinha's conciliatory spirit:

"He says there's nothing left for him to do . . . Now it's just a matter of
waiting for his father to die . . . He can't last long; he's already quite old.
He has a terrible hatred of his father . . . Sometimes he disgusts me . . ."

"Sentimentality . . ." Schwartz interrupted, suddenly interested.
Gumercindo related:

"Could be. But it's a horrible thing to see a son saying that his father
will die soon, that he ought to die right away . . . Damn!"

"So he hates him?"

"And how . . ."

"Very good." His face was serene, with the serenity of one who finds
the answer to a problem that has been bothering him.

That afternoon there was a long meeting in Schwartz's office between
the German and Silveirinha. Gumercindo was not invited. Schwartz was
afraid of his "sentimentality." A few days later Silveirinha's lawyers
brought a suit in court against Colonel Horácio da Silveira, asking that
the old colonel be removed from administering his property for reason of
incapacity and insanity, and that he be hospitalized. And that Silveirinha
be named guardian.

There was incredulous astonishment in Ilhéus. Even Carlos Zude
commented:

"That's going too far . . . It's not a lawsuit . . ."

19

But there was not even time for extended commentaries. Because right away the fight between Colonel Frederico Pinto and Pepe Espinola took place and diverted everyone's attention. It could be called the climactic event of the second year of the boom in the city of São Jorge dos Ilhéus.

The colonel had a mortal hatred of the procurer. He had given him twenty thousand, in the days when he was sure that Pepe was a good man, a failed entertainer, whom he had betrayed and who had opted to bear the affront in silence and leave for his homeland, where he would try to forget and rebuild his life. Deep inside, the colonel still had a sweet memory of all that, a memory that he revives in the bodies of mulatto country girls like Rita or with prostitutes in Ilhéus. In them he would sometimes recognize unforgettable details of Lola and be moved, lightly and tenderly.

He only began to have suspicions when he saw that Pepe forever put off his departure. Later he learned of the company formed for the Trianon, the story of the bordello, and, worst of all, of Lola having become Rui Dantas's mistress. This last piece of evidence came as a shock, for he would never have thought Lola capable of such an act of infamy. From the entire affair, from all that baseness, one thing had remained pure and noble: he thought that Lola truly loved him. Now that memory was dying, faced with the reality pointed out by his friends. A traveling salesman provided the final proof by showing Frederico Pinto a recent clipping from a Rio newspaper, where Pepe, with a number on his chest, and Lola, wearing her hair down, appeared in a photo over an article about the "badger game." The news item told of the arrest of the pair of "Argentine tourists," as the reporter ironically termed them. Colonel Frederico Pinto was indignant:

"That bitch . . ."

He kept the anger inside. The comments around Ilhéus, in those first days, wounded him. He always replied that he had shown Pepe, had taught him a lesson. He would spit to the side whenever he ran into the foreigner, grumbling curses, hoping for a reaction. But Pepe always greeted him in very friendly fashion and continued on his way. Frederico began deliberately to frequent the Trianon, where he gambled huge sums, looking for a pretext to discredit Pepe. But whenever he showed up at the table where the procurer was croupier, he would pass the bank to his partner and retire. Frederico Pinto gnashed his teeth.

One day, however, in the second year of the boom, things exploded. It was in the gaming room at the Trianon. Pepe was banking the baccarat table and winning. Frederico was coming from roulette, where he had lost as usual. He was accompanied by a French woman and planted himself in front of Pepe Espinola, watching his movements. It was never satisfactorily proven—not even at the trial—whether or not Pepe was cheating. The bystanders only heard Frederico's shout:

"Thief!"

He jerked the cards from Pepe's hand.

The Argentine turned pale and stood up quickly. The colonel held up the cards and shouted:

"You son-of-a-bitch foreigner! You think we're stupid?"

Pepe reached out for the cards. Frederico pushed him away. People were pouring in from the ballroom; someone suggested they lynch the procurer.

"Let's beat the hell out of him . . ."

Pepe moved toward Frederico again. The colonel fired, the bullet going wide and lodging in the wall. Frederico raised his revolver again but Pepe fired his automatic from inside his pocket and the colonel fell. Pepe forced his way through the onlookers with the weapon in his hand, descended the stairs, and was arrested the following day in a bordello.

Pepe's trial, instituted in Ilhéus while Frederico slowly recovered from the shot that had hit him in the shoulder, split the city into two camps. Some said Pepe was in the right: Frederico had shot first. Rui Dantas, the procurer's lawyer, moved heaven and earth in an effort to win acquittal. Lola wept desperately, plunging further into cocaine in search of consolation and oblivion each time she came from the cell after visiting Pepe. She roamed about the prison like a madwoman, waiting for visiting hour. She took him fruit and candy, but Pepe lost weight, became saturnine and silent, believing he had done something wrong, something he shouldn't have done. He told Lola:

"A procurer has no honor . . . I should have taken it and said nothing . . ."

Rui Dantas searched for witnesses who could prove that Frederico had shot first, but no one would testify for the procurer against the colonel. Not even Pepe's partner, who tried to reopen the Trianon—shut down by the police—by cozying up to Karbanks and Reicher. The attorney moved heaven and earth; Lola gave him no peace, between pleas and tears, and he kept going. But Pepe's trial proved the colonels were still the owners of the law. The exporters tried to help the procurer. Karbanks liked him, and Lola came to him in tears; they say she slept with him, for the American had made it clear that only then would he do anything. At least that's what was murmured around Ilhéus. Carlos Zude's interest in the matter stemmed from a request by Julieta. Carlos had talked with Karbanks, and the American had said:

"Poor Pepe! After all, he was doing what he could to bring some happiness to the lives of people here, in this desert . . ."

And they took a vague interest, talking with probable jurors when the occasion was propitious. But they didn't take the matter very seriously, and the law upheld the offended colonel. Pepe was sentenced to six years in prison for simple assault. The indictment had been for aggravated assault, and the best Rui Dantas could do was a reduction in the charges.

The trial was a raucous one, so well attended that it brought to mind those earlier trials from the time of the conquest of the land. Newspapers in Ilhéus and Itabuna dedicated front-page columns to it and sent photographers to the courtroom, where Lola was the center of attention.

Pepe, quite pale, ran a silk handkerchief over his shiny bald pate. The prosecuting attorney outdid himself in a speech in which he railed against "that pack of social outcasts and parasites who have made of Ilhéus their paradise." He praised Colonel Frederico Pinto as "an example of an honorable and upstanding citizen, an exemplary head of family, a pillar of the Ilhéus community." It had all come about, he said, because the colonel, seeking respite one night from the fatigue of a harsh day's work by a rare visit to the Trianon, had caught Pepe cheating. In the prosecutor's address the colonel emerged like the angel Gabriel, saving the money of the heads of Ilhéus's families, practically a missionary who stopped Pepe's diabolical actions in their tracks. He also spoke of Lola and Pepe's background, "the dregs of society who besmirch the life of civilized cities."

Rui Dantas's defense was sentimental and pathetic. He tried to take refuge in self-defense, alleging that Frederico had shot first. The prosecution interrupted to point out to the jurors the lack of evidence for the defense's assertions. Rui became disoriented at the interruption and attempted an appeal to sentimentality. He outlined Pepe's agitated life, moving from city to city, a performer with uncertain daily bread and dubious acclaim. This portion of his speech later won him high praise from Zito Ferreira and was the only part of the trial that brought Rui Dantas any joy. He concluded by saying that an unkind destiny had cast Pepe onto the streets of Ilhéus. Both he and his beautiful wife were the victims of unfortunate fate. Colonel Frederico Pinto had fallen in love with Pepe's wife and, spurned, had come to hate her husband. This was the true cause of the incident, of the shots that had been exchanged. Rui demolished the legend of a good head of family with which the prosecutor had cloaked Frederico, caricatured the colonel chasing after Lola (the spectators laughed), offering gifts, trying to "stain that household which, though the poor home of performers, was none the less respectable for it." He concluded by asking the acquittal of "a man doubly the victim of the despotism of another: when the latter attempted to dishonor his home, and when later he sought to discredit him in the pursuit of his profession."

Then came the rebuttal (the prosecutor till then had avoided going into the indecorous details of the case, but decided, now that Rui had brought them to light, to clear up the matter). The entire story of Lola, Pepe, Frederico, and Rui emerged to plain view. The prosecutor told all, what he knew and what people were saying, in detail. Sérgio Moura, present at the trial at Julieta's request, later stated that never before in Ilhéus had so much dirty laundry been washed in public. The prosecutor began with Pepe's background, reading the clipping from the Rio newspaper and placing the old discrediting photograph in evidence. Spectators craned their necks to see something as the clipping passed from hand to hand among the jurors. Next the prosecutor described how Lola tempted Frederico, extracting money from him with sorrowful tales, then laughing at him with Pepe. The colonel—the prosecutor declared gravely—had aided the couple motivated purely by charity, free of ulterior motives. He ridiculed Rui by calling him "that young man, himself a future candidate for the badger game." Maneca Dantas, who was present, left the courtroom in embarrassment. But he returned to hear Rui's rebuttal.

The prosecutor continued: Pepe, using the money lent him by the colonel, set up crooked roulette wheels and marked baccarat decks. Frederico, who had learned the truth at great cost, discovering that the poor, needy performers were mere unscrupulous adventurers, wished to prevent others from being exploited also. That was why he had denounced Pepe in the cabaret, the proof in his hand. And then he had been victim of that "miserable attempt on his life." As for the shot he had fired, he had done so only after being wounded, and even then had fired into the air in order to frighten the procurer. The rebuttal concluded with an appeal to the jurors to find Pepe guilty and thus set an example for all adventurers who would turn Ilhéus into an unlivable city of thieves, gamblers, and pimps. He said that the whole of Ilhéus society, not just Colonel Frederico Pinto, had been struck by the shot fired by Pepe Espinola.

Rui Dantas's rebuttal was simply insulting. In a poetic exaggeration that brought titters to the spectators, he called Lola "a flower of purity" and said terrible things to the prosecutor. The judge had to caution him to moderate his language. Rui lambasted Colonel Frederico as a dissolute old man chasing after a pretty woman, giving her money, trying to buy off her husband, then furious afterwards at the failure of his sordid maneuvers. Spectators were laughing, which Rui took as encouragement. In his rebuttal he no longer dealt with the juridical side of the matter. It was almost an act of personal redress, an oratory of unbridled adjectives. And in his summation he threatened the jurors with the judgment of posterity. "The law," he said, "was made for all. The convicting of Pepe Espinola, an innocent victim, will only serve to demonstrate that which has so demoralized Ilhéus compared with other, more advanced cities: that in this land the colonels are the owners of everything and it is they who make and break. They are the owners even of the law itself."

At 11 P.M. Pepe was sentenced to six years. Lola was taken away in tears. Rui Dantas made a scene in the courtroom by trying to attack the prosecuting attorney, provoking a great stir among the spectators. Only Pepe was calm as he left between two policemen. People gathered around to see him, pointing their fingers at him.

People gathered again three days later when, also with a policeman on each side, he boarded a Bahiana company ship to go to serve his sentence at the penitentiary in the state capital. Ilhéus had come en masse to the gangplank; it was like a festival. Young girls dressed for an outing, men with open umbrellas because of the light rain that was falling. It was a bright afternoon and the rain was a fine mist. They had to open a path for Pepe. His hands were tied with a rope, and one sixteen-year-girl with a doll-like face felt sorry for him:

"Poor guy . . ."

No one else, however, felt any pity for him. They pointed at him and stretched their necks to get a better look. Those in the rear stood on tiptoe. As if only now could they stare at him to their hearts' content, as if during the three years he had spent in Ilhéus they had neither seen nor known him. There was a murmur when he passed, dressed in his best clothes, with his slouch hat on his head and a cigarette in his mouth.

At the gangplank there was one sensational moment. As he began to climb the steps that would take him onto the boat, Lola threw herself into his arms. Pepe raised his bound arms and wrapped them around the woman. He kissed her hair and repeated into her ear Dandy's phrase:

"One must have character . . ."

20

It was midway through the trial, when she still had hope, that Lola Espinola decided to seek out Julieta Zude and ask her to take an interest in Pepe. Someone had told her that Frederico's case was that of all the colonels. It was pointless to ask the landowners. Perhaps the exporters would do something for her lover. That was when she had gone to Karbanks. The American had been casting glances in her direction for some time. He received her with drinks, pinched her arms, and promised to take an interest. But he told her at once that he saw no way of saving Pepe and made reference to a better future for her. After all, what was Pepe except a procurer who sooner or later would leave her to fend for herself? She could, if she chose, have a brighter future . . .

Lola tolerated it all in hopes of help. Karbanks was one of the most powerful men in the land and a request from him would remove obstacles. She left him the names of the probable jurors and agreed to come by the following day for an answer. The next day Karbanks sent her a message: she was to come to his house that night. Lola knew what was going to happen, but she went. She slept there, receiving vague promises in return. Karbanks had spoken to two of the possible jurors and they had promised to show clemency.

"At the very least the lightest sentence . . ."

It was Zito Ferreira, who came to her house with Rui, who advised her to go to Julieta. Carlos Zude, the political leader and great exporter, could easily manage an acquittal. He could even exert some influence with the colonels. The following morning Lola dressed and rang the bell of the bungalow on the street facing the ocean.

Julieta received her at once. Lola stood hesitantly before her, and it was Julieta who extended her hand.

"Please, have a seat . . ."

She looked at her sympathetically. She knew the story and Sérgio had supplied the details. In the magic world of Sérgio and Julieta, bums and rogues, performers and these miserable creatures from the world of prostitution were like victims. The poet felt an unrestrained tenderness for them and liked to tell Julieta that poets had in them something of such people: "We're of the same ilk . . ."

Lola didn't know how to begin. The sea, there outside, was infinitely blue and the morning brightness was also tinged with blue; it was a day made for joyous things, happy and clear. Julieta spoke first:

"Is your husband all right? How are they treating him?"

And Lola began to cry. These were not the tears of her long-running playacting. They were quiet tears, as she huddled in the chair like a wounded animal.

"We're not married, Señora . . ." She was speaking Spanish. "We never have been . . . I saw him, I liked him, I left my husband and went with him. Things a woman does, and later . . ."

Julieta remembered Joaquim. The communist had said: "You two should live together, you should go away." That's what Lola had done. Which is to say, she had done what was right. It was very complicated, and now Julieta understood the bus driver's harshness that afternoon when they spoke at the Association.

"I didn't know then he was . . . what he is. When I found out . . ."

She was going to lie, say that she wanted to run away and couldn't, but she felt that would be to betray Pepe, mistreat him even more than he had already been mistreated.

"When I found out, I stayed . . . He told me to leave him . . . But I stayed. I loved him. Do you understand?"

The tears flowed gently. Julieta extended her small handkerchief.

"And I still love him . . . Yes, I love him . . . If I didn't love him I'd kill myself, since I don't like life, or men, or women, or day, or night . . . I don't like anyone or anything . . . But I love him madly . . ."

Outside was the bright day, blue, a poetic day like something from one of Sérgio's poems, made to hold another world, a world of happiness, the singing of birds, flowers blooming, spring, and happy women. A day that did not enter the living room, that stopped short at the windows without coming in. Julieta was distressed and hoped the woman would finish quickly.

"What is all this to you? What do you have to do with my life? They told me, maybe Zude's wife will ask her husband to do something for Pepe. She's a good person . . ."

"I'm not good . . ."

"I shouldn't have come . . . I know that. You're a married woman, a respectable señora. And what am I? A fallen woman. You were very kind to receive me. But there is one thing that brings me here, that keeps me here to ask you for it. I love him . . . If they take him away I'll kill myself . . ."

"You poor woman . . . I don't know if I'll be able to do anything . . . But I guarantee I'll do everything I can. I'll ask my husband and get him started on it. Don't think that I don't understand . . ."

"You are a good person, they say . . . I have suffered a lot." She had stopped crying.

Now the luminosity of the day began slowly to invade the room, entering through the window. It lighted Lola's face and made her blonde hair seem on fire. A gamut of feelings assaulted Julieta; she was suffering. *She did the right thing, but she paid dearly* . . .

"I don't know what you think of me. Perhaps you're just looking for a favor. And I don't know if you're telling the truth. People lie a lot"— she remembered Sérgio—"spend their lives playacting. But I feel I'm your friend . . ."

She wanted details of the woman's life but felt embarrassed to ask, embarrassed that Lola might think it idle curiosity, bothersome and cruel.

"No. We're not friends. You come from a different part of life. I come from the bad part, the dirty part . . . You have your husband, your home which is more than a house, your good life. I have men, and my man comes and goes, has other women, and we don't have a home; our house belongs to anyone who can pay . . ."

She lowered her voice, and Julieta could barely hear.

" . . . pay for a night with me . . . That's the other side, the dirty side . . ."

She was almost calm; she said everything without hatred or rebellion, like a doctor commenting on a patient's terminal disease. Julieta listened, wishing that Sérgio could be there, and Joaquim too, to bring order to her feelings. She was confused, frightened, and sad.

"So dirty . . . But he wanted something, I don't know what. But I know for certain he wanted something, maybe something for me . . . I don't know what it could be. I'd be satisfied if I could just find out . . ."

"Why didn't you leave it all and go away? If you found it dirty why did you continue?"

"I told you, señora. I love him . . ."

"Forgive me. You gave up everything and went with him?"

Lola looked at her sadly. Even this woman, who had seemed so understanding, also wanted the story of her life, the price of her possible interest in Pepe. Lola would pay, just as she had paid what Karbanks had asked.

"I'll tell you . . ."

But Julieta had understood:

"For heaven's sake, don't tell me anything . . . You're thinking that I'm curious, trying to find out things. No. It's nothing like that . . . It's just that there aren't two sides of life as you think. There's just one side, and it's always dirty, always dirty . . . On your side or mine, it's the same filth always . . . The same . . ."

But she saw, as if he were in the room, the figure of Joaquim. She smiled.

"Maybe there *is* a healthy side. People made of different clay, as someone I know puts it . . . The rest is rotten." She spoke the words slowly.

Now it was Lola who didn't understand. What was all this about? "I'm going to tell you something, my friend . . . I wish I had your courage to leave everything and go away, go hungry, suffer, live a poor life but with *him* . . ." She fell silent, suddenly embarrassed.

And she hurriedly brought the conversation to a close:

"I'll talk to Carlos. I'll ask him and we'll do something. Have no doubts about it. I'll do whatever I can."

She escorted Lola to the door.

"Have courage."

"I do have courage . . ."

The blue daylight enveloped the angular form of Lola Espinola. Her face was furrowed with tears, her famous blonde head downcast where the sun played on it, her hands at her side, unable to look at those who passed by. From the door Julieta envied her, her courage, her suffering, the love she had achieved. That woman was made of good clay, the kind that doesn't turn to mud even in the greatest filth.

If I could only set her husband free . . .

She remembered: "We're not married." That was what Sérgio called dignity.

21

The first serious argument between Antônio Vítor and Raimunda was not over the Vamp. Antônio Vítor wasn't yet involved with her; the fight was about working in the fields. It was a violent exchange of words. Work on the new harvest had begun and Antônio Vítor was adamant about Raimunda not going back to splitting cacao pods as she had done in the past. Not her and not him either. The time had come for them to lay aside the machete and scythe; it didn't look right for them. Raimunda disagreed. What did a new house, the high price of cacao, stylish shoes or silk dresses matter to her? Antônio Vítor ended up shouting:

"You go if you want to, I ain't goin' . . ."

Raimunda looked at him with her angry face. She did not know her husband. She went to the fields and Antônio Vítor spent the day in the house, pacing back and forth, with nothing to do, wanting to go to work also but unwilling to give in.

A few nights later he tried to possess Raimunda. Every week he did so once or twice. But she was tired and woke up in ill humor. When she saw what he wanted, she asked:

"Leave it for tomorrow . . ."

Antônio Vítor took advantage of the pretext: "There it is . . . You worked so hard in the fields, like a pauper, that you ain't even any good for that afterwards. If that's how it's gonna be, I'll have to look for a woman on the side . . ." That phrase, uttered aloud to irritate Raimunda, was in reality only a threat; Antônio Vítor had no intention of carrying it out. Not that he had been faithful to his wife his entire life. At times when he slept in Itabuna he did so with some prostitute or other, but he had never fallen for one as happened with many men.

He only really began to notice Raimunda's ugliness, how old and worn-out she had become, in Ilhéus; he went to bed with the Vamp, following a night of gambling and drinking. The Vamp wrapped herself around him, and when Antônio Vítor returned to the farm he still carried the taste of the woman in his body. That day there was a big fight because he insisted that Raimunda give up working on the cacao trees.

The bad thing, however, was his having met the Vamp in Itabuna, on a Saturday. He always went to Itabuna, to buy supplies and take dried cacao. The Vamp hung out around there, in Fifi's cabaret, and when she saw Antônio Vítor she threw herself at him and dragged him to a table; they ordered beer.

"Are we getting married again today?"

He laughed. She made up a nickname for him: my puppy. She knew how to use words of affection, how to give caresses, how to please a man. Antônio Vítor took no notice of the fact that she was regularly seeing a black-haired student who sat at the next table, smoking in front of an empty glass. During the boom students on vacation played the role of gigolo, strictly as amateurs. Antônio Vítor slept with the Vamp that night and did not return to the farm on Sunday; he spent another night in Itabuna, ordering champagne at the cabaret. Since Dona Ana's wedding day, which was his own wedding day as well, he had not tasted champagne.

He returned to the farm with his head turned. He promised the Vamp that he would be back in Itabuna in a few days. She kissed him.

"I'll be waiting, my puppy."

Raimunda was in the fields when he arrived. He walked about the house, with nothing to do, which suddenly made him feel ashamed. He grabbed the scythe, removed his boots, and went to pick cacao. More than Raimunda, the workers were surprised to see him. At noon he ate his beef jerky with manioc flour, then worked till six o'clock. He returned to the job the following day, but on the third he received a message from the Vamp. An urchin had brought it from Itabuna. The Vamp asked him to go there, saying she was sick. Antônio Vítor saddled his donkey and set out for the city. He told Raimunda it was a summons from a representative of Carlos Zude. The Vamp received him very happily; Antônio Vítor was surprised not to find her in bed.

"Weren't you sick?"

"It was loneliness for my little puppy . . ."

He no longer made excuses when he came to Itabuna and stayed two or three days. He set the Vamp up in a place of her own, withdrew money to pay her numerous expenses, had an account at Fifi's cabaret and at commercial establishments, where the Vamp bought cut after cut of fabric, shoes, perfume and (something that would later scandalize

Antônio Vítor) luxurious ties that she gave to the student.

News spread through the cacao zone with great rapidity. It was not long before Raimunda found out what was happening. And what she heard was exaggerated in the telling: Antônio Vítor was keeping a Frenchwoman in Itabuna, living in a mansion, in splendor. She never said anything to her husband. But she frowned even more than before. Now anyone could see in her face the furrows of tears shed during lonely nights, when she futilely sought sleep in that new bed to which she could not become accustomed. But in the morning, when she went out to work in the fields, she was the same as always, the first to arrive at the piles of cacao pods, the last to lay down the machete with which she split them. In Fifi's cabaret, Antônio Vítor was learning to dance fox-trots and sambas, along with the secrets of roulette.

22

In the middle of the second year of the boom, Martins, the manager of Zude Brothers & Co., fled in a plane. An audit revealed he had embezzled eighty thousand. Nevertheless, when Martins was arrested in Rio de Janeiro he was carrying only seven thousand and swore he had not hidden any money. He confessed to the police that he had spent the remainder and that a woman named Rosa, who formerly sewed cacao sacks and later became his mistress, was to blame for everything. She was somewhat moonstruck, would disappear and then return, but she was pretty enough to turn any man's head. At first glance she seemed very unassuming; she lived in Snake Island. But when cacao began going up, this Rosa—who Martins, like Beanpole, said was quite a beauty—began to disappear, and Martins offered her luxury, a house in the city, servants, and money. Martins's salary was insufficient for such. He supported a large family, even though unmarried; he had a widowed mother, sisters to marry off, and small brothers still in school. At home were eight to be fed, clothed, and educated. And Rosa wanting money, rent higher than in Rio de Janeiro, everything costing a fortune. His salary wouldn't stretch far enough. He had once hit it lucky at the Bataclã, and he started withdrawing a few thousand mil-réis each month from the cashbox, first to help pay expenses, then to win back what he had lost gambling. As the time for auditing approached, he saw he was lost and decided to abscond. His first thought had been of suicide but he felt sorry for his mother, who might die of grief. All he asked of the police detective was not to tell his mother.

She found out anyway, and went with her brood—young girls who looked at the furniture, the layout, and the paintings in the house, who scrutinized Julieta's dresses; young boys silent in their rigid and studied posture—to beg Julieta Zude on her son's behalf. Carlos arrived during

269

the scene and it was he who was moved by the old woman's sobs,
telling her that it had been a bad woman's doing and that her son was
an honorable man. God was witness to that.

Later Carlos explained to Julieta: the eighty thousand was beyond
recovery, so what good would it do to put the young man in jail? He
withdrew the complaint. Martins stayed in Rio, reappearing in Ilhéus
some years later to get his family. He was doing well in São Paulo, and
he disembarked elegantly dressed and speaking with a southern accent;
he seemed not even to recall the incident. To his acquaintances he offered
to be of assistance in the south. And he lamented the desolation that had
befallen Ilhéus in those years following the bust.

"Nobody has any future here . . ."

Rosa ended up in the sleaziest cabaret in town, the Retiro, after
some disquieting talks at the police station. Apparently they slapped
her around a bit, but the Retiro attracted new clientele when she made
her debut, thanks to the furor of the scandal. She didn't last long, soon
disappearing again, perhaps with some man, perhaps merely bumming
along the docks, as had long been her habit after her father had drowned
on a balsa fishing raft and left her an orphan, a street urchin. One day a
painter passing through the city, a modern painter who used scandalous
colors, found her hanging aimlessly around the port. The painter was
with Sérgio Moura and took an interest in the woman. The poet called
her, and Rosa posed for a few days; later the portrait won a prize in
an official salon, the gold medal. The painter had given his canvas a
strange name: *Daughter of the Sea*. Not even he knew why. That was
how he saw Rosa.

A clipping from the *Ilhéus Daily*, with news of Martins's em-
bezzlement and a police photo of Rosa, arrived through Colonel
Frederico Pinto at the plantation where Beanpole was comforting
Black Florindo about the again-frustrated flight. Beanpole read the
news item to Florindo and Capi and showed them Rosa's picture.
Black Florindo stuck it on the wall over his cot. He stared at it and
asked Beanpole:

"What's she like?"

Beanpole thought, recalling gestures and phrases, details of that
unforgettable body and her inexplicable flight:

"What she's really like is the sea."

But Florindo had never seen the sea.

"And what's the sea like?"

23

Colonel Horácio da Silveira had aged greatly in those months. If before he was sick, elderly, and nearly blind, now he seemed an old man with one foot in the grave. It was as if in the first phase of his struggle with his son he had expended the last of his octogenarian strength. The dodge involving Ester's will had drained him. He had spent a lot of money, almost two hundred thousand, but he had kept his plantation intact and still administered that world of land planted in cacao; it was still he who gave the orders, who made the decisions. No boundaries had been specified, only the amount of cacao whose profits belonged to Silveirinha. That mattered little to Colonel Horácio da Silveira. For him the essential thing was that the lands, the plantations that he had built up—stretching across two counties, colossal harvests of almost three quarters of a million kilos of cacao—remain undivided, that no one be allowed to take away any part of his lands. In times past they had belonged to many, unclaimed forest for which he had fought, weapon in hand, at the head of hired gunmen and colonels. Plus small landholdings of small growers, that he had bought or wrested away by deceit, the result of dodges, ambushes, of contracts imposed at gunpoint. A world of plantations running through Ilhéus and Itabuna, each linked to the next, perhaps the largest continuous cacao plantations in the world: Colonel Horácio da Silveira's plantations. His once-gigantic body bent under the weight of his eighty-four years; emaciated, rheumatic and blind, the colonel dragged himself around the veranda, orders emerging in a hoarse and weary voice, raspy from a chronic cold. He was alone on the plantation. In the busy days of the lawsuit there was still movement there: the comings and goings of Rui Dantas, the constant presence of his friend Maneca, the appearance by Menezes, and the fire of the struggle in which the colonel's body seemed to rejuvenate itself to

271

match the strength of a spirit that had not yielded to despondency. But it was all over; he had won the suit, paid the expenses, paid his son's profits. The money had been deposited in the banks. The excitement, the commotion, was over, and the colonel had aged, in body and in spirit. He felt incapable of running his world of cacao trees. He now let the overseer do many things on his own, and responded in occasional monosyllables to questions from the supply worker. After that artificial rejuvenation in the heat of the battle, it was as if he had capitulated to old age, with no desires beyond listening, from the plantation house veranda, to the singing of the workers in the drying frames and kilns. He hadn't even grumbled at the rise in wages; it was a complicated time and he did not understand it. Nor did he any longer offer opinions in the political decisions of his party, which, as the opposition, was seeking to win over voters quickly. He assisted with money and had ordered the roughing up of some Integralists during the heat of the struggle in Itabuna, but he had asked Maneca Dantas to choose the candidates; he didn't want to get involved. His shriveled hands, the enormous hands of old, were nothing but skin and bone, and he would raise them to his dim eyes in an effort to see them, just as he tried in vain to make out the beloved sight of the fields in bloom, the golden fruit hanging on the boughs. He could no longer see, not even when, leaning on Black Roque's arm, he walked among the trees of the nearest fields. His hands, his old and shriveled hands, served as his eyes, feeling the cacao pods on the trunks and branches.

"It's ripe for harvesting . . ."

Black Roque agreed:

"Yessir, it is . . ."

These were the lands of Sequeiro Grande, the best lands for cacao cultivation in the world. The colonel trod the black soil, his hands feeling out the trees as if he were caressing the soft flesh of a woman. From these ever more infrequent walks he would bring back a nearly ripe cacao pod and cradle it in his hand for some time, sitting on the hard bench on the veranda, his leg on the bench and his chin resting on his knee. He looked outward; it was a fog. But he knew that the fog was only in his eyes, that beyond lay the fields planted with cacao trees, fields that he had planted. And that was enough for him in the final measure of his life, at life's end. Almost nothing else linked him to the distant world, to the port of Ilhéus from which cacao-laden ships departed, to Itabuna, which he had helped to build, to Ferradas, which was his fiefdom. His world had as its limits his plantation, but—ah!—in this world he alone ruled, he alone was obeyed, his voice alone carried authority. And it was a beautiful world . . . For Colonel Horácio da Silveira it was the most beautiful of all worlds: that of cacao fields. In his superstitious irreligiosity, his gifts to the church motivated more by politics than by religion, in his belief in the absurd stories of the workers, he never thought of heaven or hell. But had anyone asked him, out of the blue, what heaven must be like, he would surely have answered that it could only be a cacao field eternally bearing yellow fruit, turning golden the shadows where the sun never penetrates . . .

It was thus, in that decrepit final stage of his life, that the news reached him about the new lawsuit instigated by Silveirinha. This time Maneca Dantas came with his son, and the lawyer was truly indignant, feeling that Silveirinha was perpetrating an act of infamy. He even felt a certain responsibility himself, for in the events surrounding Pepe and Lola he had been a bit lax in looking after the colonel's interests. The "insanity" suit was already under way; the judge had appointed a medical commission to examine Horácio.

They talked as the rain fell on the cacao trees. Horácio seemed removed, his present attitude completely unlike the one he had taken when Maneca Dantas had brought word of the first suit, the one over the inventory. Then he had roused himself, taken steps, directed everything. On this rainy afternoon he listens distractedly, his ears turned to the sound of the heavy rain on the cacao trees, as if indifferent to everything. Maneca Dantas had to remind him:

"They say the doctors are comin' this week . . ."

"One was chosen by me, Colonel," explains Rui. "Another by Silveirinha. The third by the judge. He's a young man from Bahia, a specialist . . ."

Horácio listened reluctantly.

"Let 'em come, boy. Let 'em come, my friend Maneca. I'll have 'em all shot. None of them'll get past the gate of this plantation . . ."

"But, Colonel," Rui said, "that's not possible . . . There's no way you can refuse the medical examination. You're not crazy, and the doctors will prove that. You're normal and you're going to win the dispute. The medical report just has to prove you're not incapable of managing your property . . ."

"Boy, not a one of them'll get past the gate of this plantation. I'll shoot 'em . . ."

He listened almost indifferently, hearing the rain fall on the cacao trees. Rui Dantas shook his head and looked at his father in disapproval of the colonel's attitude. Finally Horácio told Maneca:

"My friend, you're a man of experience. Tell those doctors not to come here . . . I'll shoot 'em . . ."

And he turned away from the conversation as if there were nothing further to discuss. For him the matter was closed and not worth any more time. The black woman Felícia came from inside to say coffee was on the table along with cassava and boiled bananas. She too was on her last legs, her kinky hair white, her steps faltering. Rui Dantas thought that these were the remains of people, that Silveirinha was right, despite his revulsion with the methods of Horácio's son.

At the table, Maneca and Rui tried to return to the subject. Horácio mashed the banana in order to swallow it; he no longer had teeth to chew with.

"If you continue in this attitude, Colonel, you're going to ruin everything. They'll use this as a basis for saying you really are crazy . . ."

"Boy, I'm not crazy . . . But I'll shoot any doctor who shows up around here . . . Can't you see I want no part of this tomfoolery? Can't you see?"

He was regaining a certain energy, at least for the moment.

"I'm at the end of my life, and I'm not goin' to put on a show for anybody . . . I'm Colonel Horácio da Silveira, not some circus clown . . . I'll shoot . . ."

And he relapsed into indifference, into inertia, the rest of his coffee undrunk in his cup. Maneca and Rui Dantas said good-bye. Horácio dragged himself to the veranda to listen to them leave. As he embraced Maneca Dantas he told him:

"Maybe we won't see each other again, my friend . . . There's only one person to blame for everything that's goin' on: her, the dead woman. She's the one who's doin' all this . . . Tell the doctors not to come. I'll shoot . . . Good-bye, old friend . . ."

Maneca Dantas felt tears come to his eyes. He looked at the fields, unable to speak. Rui Dantas, already on his horse, urged his father:

"Let's go, Dad. It's getting late . . ."

Maneca tightened his arms around the colonel. He was sure he would not see him again, and it was as if someone had yanked out the deepest roots that tied him to life. As if one era had ended and another was about to begin.

On the road, under the last of the rain that dampened the horse's haunches, Rui Dantas said with sadness and a touch of irritation:

"He's senile, Father . . . I don't know how all this is going to end . . ."

Maneca Dantas looked at his son and allowed the tears to roll down his wrinkled face. He did know how it was all going to end.

24

The letter she had been awaiting for months had not come. She had gone to Bahia, bought fruit, candy, and clothes, and taken them to the penitentiary. But he refused to see her or talk to her. She left the clothes and a note. At the hotel she had wept until Rui Dantas arrived. The lawyer heeded her every desire, but Lola's steadfast loyalty to Pepe wounded him, pained him, made him feel betrayed daily. And now it was he, almost more than she, who gave himself up to morphine and cocaine, abandoning Horácio's defense, the law office, and even his romantic sonnets.

The letter for which she had waited for months, the answer to her desperate note, never came. A prisoner from Ilhéus, recently released on parole, brought her news of Pepe, unhappy news. The procurer was wasting away in prison, morose and distant, losing weight. The other prisoners respected him; he lived isolated from his fellows, lost in melancholy contemplation.

She wrote him again, sent money; there was never an answer. Then she wrote him a final time, a note of farewell comprising only four words of love.

She killed herself early in the morning, shut in her room, the syringe with which she applied the fatal injection lying broken on the floor, her beautiful white hand outstretched. Rui sobbed in despair. The evening before, Lola had mailed a letter to Julieta Zude. Why did she write when she had already decided to kill herself? She still had a gratifying memory of her conversation with Julieta and knew that the exporter's wife had done all within her power, had made every effort to help Pepe. She was largely responsible for the lesser severity of the sentence. Lola had later learned everything about Julieta and Sérgio, and when she had finished writing Pepe she thought she owed something to Julieta

275

and scribbled the note that she mailed. She had decided she would kill herself that evening. But she felt she owed something to someone else, to Rui Dantas. Perhaps the lawyer was tiresome and hard to bear, but he had always been good to her, had granted her every wish, had worked on Pepe's behalf, and Lola fully understood how much Rui suffered to see her still so attached to the procurer even in his final wretchedness. She owed him something, and so she decided to kill herself the next morning; the night would belong to him.

And for the first time she gave herself to Rui with a certain affection. She refused drugs and drank nothing; she was his woman, the wife he had always desired her to be. The house became a home for the few hours of that wintry night. In the morning he left, brimming with happiness. He thought Lola was about to begin a new life. And then Lola killed herself, assured that she no longer owed anything to anyone, that she had squared accounts with life. Her head rolled from the pillow and her long, flowing hair filled the bed with gold.

25

In a corner of the cemetery at Vitória, Julieta Zude was alone as she watched the burial. The men, professionals from the undertakers', removed the coffin from the hearse. Only Rui Dantas emerged from the other car. He had brought an enormous wreath, the largest he could find in Ilhéus, and he was under the influence of drugs, trembling as he accompanied the bier. The gravedigger stood beside the open grave; there were no priests for suicides, no friends, no music, the only words those the men shouted as they lowered the casket:

"Slower . . . Careful . . . Watch out for that rope there . . ."

They covered it with earth, quickly, anxious to get it over with. Rui Dantas placed the wreath, light-headed. Julieta thought he was drunk, not knowing of the drugs. She saw him get into the car and collapse onto the seat. The hearse accompanied the car down the hill.

Julieta Zude walked to the grave, where the earth was still soft from the recent burial. A plaque with white letters reminded:

HERE LIES
JULIA HERNANDEZ
Born in Buenos Aires
Passed away in Ilhéus
Pray for her soul.

Julieta had brought flowers, flowers from the Commercial Association, rare flowers: orchids, tea roses, carnations and violets. Sérgio had picked them at her request. She had not stated her reasons. She spread the flowers about the still-loose clay around the grave. The good clay of which Lola was made. Julieta did not cry, nor was she sad. She said

good-bye to Lola as one would to a dearly loved friend who had left on
a trip but would never cease to be present in her memory, a friendship
that could never be sundered. Though she had seen her only a single
time, she had never had another friend.

She looked around her, at the cemetery, and saw that her world,
her new world, immense and magical, was inhabited only by Sérgio,
Joaquim, and Lola. "Lola Espinola, Julia Hernandez." She had never
been Julia Hernandez; the plaque in the cemetery lied! She had always
been Lola Espinola, Pepe's wife, the woman who had the courage to
follow her destiny, her man, to do what she must. To do what she
must . . . No one would understand . . . Sérgio would nod his head like
a caged bird, the prisoner of a thousand small things. But he had
his poetry and through it could escape to that other world, through
it the purest and most heroic things were his: flowers, birds, the
revolution of which Joaquim spoke. Joaquim would understand. The
driver understood everything. The world he carried within, Julieta saw
without fully understanding, was one he himself was constructing.
Amid pain and struggle, sacrifice and anonymity, illegally, day by
day he was constructing that world for everyone. She had no world
within herself, no open door of escape, like the poet and his poetry. Nor
did she know how to construct it, as Joaquim was doing with his pure
and powerful creative hands, or to pretend like Sérgio with his magical
and fragile artist's hands. She was lost, mired in the mud. On the mud
Joaquim was building the foundations of his world. Sérgio flew above
the mud with invisible wings. True, many threads linked him to that
world; his wings were broken but even so he hovered over the dirt. It
was she who was mired in it up to her eyebrows. She was rotting amidst
the rot on every side. Lola had emerged pure from that rot. Would
Joaquim really understand? Sérgio was a great bird, with an ironic gaze,
mysterious smile, and a heart free of all guilt. But his feet were sinking
into the mud. Julieta saw how millions of threads, each extremely
fragile in itself, joined to form chains of servitude fettering the poet's
feet. Joaquim marched, and Julieta could see in him all the Joaquims
of the world, the men and the women. In the talks that followed that
first encounter at the Association, the militant, no longer distrustful and
past any shyness, had spoken to her of his political ideals, of the future
world he dreamed of, one of brotherhood, equality, and love for all—
the world he was fighting for. Sérgio also dreamed of such a world, but
all he gave to it was his poetry, holding back from total commitment.
His life was not his own; his feet were bound. Julieta was the wife of
a cacao exporter, a neurasthenic society woman who had had highly
experienced lovers, whose husband had educated her in the ways of
sexual perversion, but none of that satisfied her. When Joaquim spoke

to her of the world that was being built, already partially accomplished in legendary Russia and the focus of harsh struggle in the remaining countries, to her, who already soared in the poet's free fantasy, who had already taken flight from her unhappy world but knew not where to head, it was like a sunrise, but a sunrise that she could not reach. Because her partner in the difficult journey was the poet Sérgio Moura, whose feet were trapped in the mud; when he attained that other world it was through poetry, and Julieta needed to march like a soldier, like one who is building something. Her feelings were perhaps the same as if a friend, in the midst of her anguish and desperation, had taken her to a concert and habituated her to true music. But in Ilhéus, a city undergoing a cacao boom, concerts were infrequent; an occasional semifailure of a pianist might come to town looking for a lucrative benefit performance. And the poet, with his political inexperience, and the driver, with his solid militant sense of reality, spoke of the revolution, of tomorrow's world of comrades. The passion and indomitable love with which Joaquim spoke of that world! He no longer seemed to be the taciturn driver, Raimunda's silent son; he was a torrent directed by his faith and no less by his experience in the struggle. Julieta felt like saying: Sérgio, take my arm. Let's pull ourselves out of the mud and leave . . . What does anything else matter?

But she never said anything. She went on living that adventure of love that at least was something, despite Carlos Zude and his daily presence, despite Joaquim who seemed to be waiting for her to decide. But she never said anything.

Now Lola's note is in her pocket, a message from her friend. She saw her only once, but nevertheless she was her only friend. Shadows of twilight fall over the deserted cemetery. *Follow your love if you love him. Follow your destiny. I have always been happy even among all my suffering. Follow your destiny; I who am about to die tell you this. Don't be afraid . . .*

"Tomorrow, Dona Julieta, the world will be better. There won't be any more people like you. The only good thing a person can do today is work toward bringing about that world more quickly. It'll be like a celebration . . ." It was Joaquim's voice.

"And I speak to you of birds; their life is more beautiful than you can imagine. And I speak to you of flowers; what do you know about tea roses? Your navel is pink and could grow tea roses, the loveliest of all roses. Let's forget everything; what matters is that we're here, together, and that I can have you and also be yours. That's all there is and all that matters. And I'll tell you whatever you wish so you'll come back tomorrow." It was Sérgio's voice.

He had his feet mired in the mud. It was so easy to break the innumerable threads that entangled him. It was so difficult to break the chains that bound him . . . So easy, yet so difficult.

Don't be afraid . . .

26

One day at the end of the second year of the boom, despite the persecution its militants were suffering, the Communist Party held a rally at the square by the docks. The communists were attempting to enlighten the people about the true meaning of the boom, to show what the absurdly high cacao prices represented. They now had at their disposal many more elements to present to the small farmers, the colonels, and the people at large. There was the struggle between Schwartz and Horácio (no one said "between Silveirinha and Horácio" anymore, such was the German's influence in the unfolding of events). And there was the matter of the bus companies. With the formation of the new corporation all other companies had been driven out of business, which had not made Marinho Santos unhappy. What he didn't like, however, was quickly finding out that his prestige in the company was virtually nonexistent: the exporters made him break long-standing cacao transport commitments in order to put the trucks to the almost exclusive use of Karbanks, Zude, Schwartz, and the Rauschnings.

Elections were approaching, and the militants felt the need for some kind of action to orient the masses in the electoral campaign. Three probable candidates had emerged for the mayoralty of Ilhéus: Carlos Zude, running on the government party ticket; Silveirinha, for the Integralists; and Maneca Dantas, for the opposition. The Communist Party had decided not to run its own candidate and invited the plantation owners, small growers, and workers to unite behind one candidacy—Maneca Dantas's or someone else's—that could defeat both Carlos Zude and Silveirinha, since both, as the flyer pointed out, "represented foreign imperialism, antinational capitalism, either German or American." They decided to hold the rally as a public protest against the transaction involved in the boom, hoping it would have some effect. Given the impossibility of advertising it, since the police had taken preventative measures, the party set the rally for the time when everyone was getting off work, when the workers from the cacao warehouses and the chocolate factory were leaving their daily tasks. At five o'clock, militants who worked at these places, and on the docks, the railroad, and the ships herded people toward the square.

It was almost opposite the building housing Zude Brothers & Co., and also very near the Exporter. The night before, Joaquim had told Julieta Zude:

"If you want to see something interesting, go to the docks tomorrow at five."

She was at the window in her husband's office and noticed the sudden unusually heavy movement in the square, and a certain agitation among some of the people passing by. Suddenly it began, and Julieta left the window and crossed her husband's office.

"Where are you going?" Carlos asked.

"Not far. I'll be right back," she answered, without even turning around.

It was all very fast. The men arrived in a car that had been waiting at the corner with its motor running. They carried a red flag draped over the radiator of one of the taxis parked in the square. Immediately a stevedore began addressing the crowd. When Julieta reached the throng, squeezed together and shouting support and disapproval, the black man had already launched an attack on the large exporters and the Integralists. "Imperialist lackeys," he shouted. When he shouted Karbanks's name at the astonished crowd, calling him "the greatest agent of imperialism," the militants signified their support. But when he called Schwartz a "filthy foreigner, a Gestapo spy," many who had no connection with what was happening applauded, for the German had become very unpopular because of the Horácio affair. The black man went on to say that the Communist Party at that moment was defending not only the interests of the workers but also of all progressive elements in the cacao zone who didn't want to see Brazilian lands fall into the hands of foreigners. He even defended the colonels, although he demanded higher wages and better treatment for farm workers.

Julieta was caught up in the spectacle. She couldn't hear the speaker's words, or at best was barely able to make out the sense of what he said, but the spectacle moved her; it was a wonderful moment, when men risked themselves to transform the world. She was seeing them in action, and she thought the black stevedore was magnificent; the people shouting, cheering, and booing struck her as capable of even greater feats. The red banner imbued the entire scene with a romantic coloration, and Julieta absorbed the reactions of the gathered mass of people—strong, vibrant, and unspoiled.

Near her, a toothless mulatto growled words of support and threats: "That's right . . . Out with the foreigners . . ."

Julieta smiled at him, feeling a sense of solidarity, thinking him a good person despite his ferocious manner, his unshaven appearance, and his toothless mouth with its red gums. From the window of his building, Carlos Zude watched, wondering where Julieta could have gone, fearing that something might have happened to her. They had phoned the police from his office.

A line of husky men stood in front of the stevedore who was speaking, shielding him. The police and the Integralists would soon arrive, and the self-defense squad was scrutinizing the crowd for probable troublemakers. There were people of every type: workers from the chocolate factory and the cacao warehouses, dockworkers, colonels, clerical employees, waitresses from the nearby bars, and small farmers wearing boots. Rosa was there too, and shouted more than anyone. She shouted without knowing why, simply from the pleasure of shouting, booing, and cheering.

The second speaker had barely begun his talk. It was only then that Julieta saw Joaquim, behind the automobile, and gave him a brief but friendly smile. The new speaker, a professor, was explaining the necessity of forming a voting bloc among the colonels, small farmers, tradesmen—all those threatened by the exporters—for the political and economic struggle. He was about to speak of the cooperative and elections, but the police arrived and began dispersing the rally. The cops came on the scene with shots into the air, led by the special commissioner. The self-defense squad closed with the cops and the Integralists accompanying them. Despite the noise, the orator continued his speech; no one heard. Julieta noted that Joaquim was giving the orders.

They began taking prisoners; the larger group escaped in the car in which they had come. At the last moment before jumping into the car, one of them—the black stevedore—yanked the flag from the taxi's radiator, wrapped it around his arm, laid out one of the cops with a single punch, and then vanished down the street, the car's horn blaring. The intellectual who was speaking was arrested. Julieta, looking for Joaquim, suddenly heard his voice behind her:

"Talk to me naturally, as if we had nothing to do with any of this . . ."

She turned. He was smiling with a certain shyness. They walked toward the building of Zude Brothers & Company. A cop overtook them and was reaching out his hand when he recognized Julieta Zude.

He stood there looking at them. She was talking to Joaquim, laughing a lot, but her hands were trembling.

At the corner of the export house, Joaquim changed directions and headed for the piers, where the lights were coming on. Julieta saw him walking, his pace accelerating. He waved good-bye from the distance. The next day Sérgio confided that Joaquim was in hiding at a friend's house.

She saw Carlos Zude in the window. In her agitation, she smiled at her husband and raised a hand in greeting. Carlos was awaiting her anxiously.

"Have you gone crazy?"

"I wanted to see it . . ."

"Didn't you know it was the communists? They're capable of anything . . ."

She smiled so enigmatically that Carlos Zude, not given to complications, found it strange.

"What's wrong?"

"Nothing . . . You seem afraid of the communists . . ."

"Afraid? You're crazy . . . We're going to squash them. They're nothing but a pack of poor devils."

"Poor devils . . ." she said, and smiled again.

Carlos was upset and asked:

"Who was that young fellow walking with you?"

"Him? I don't know . . . When the trouble started he dragged me away . . . Maybe somebody you know . . ."

"A good thing you weren't hurt . . ." No longer worried, he returned to his business concerns. The police commissioner came into the office and related the events:

"We caught three of them . . . The one who was doing the talking and two others . . . The rest got away, but we're on their trail. The billy club's the only thing for that sort . . . Laid on thick!" he concluded decisively.

Carlos Zude urged him to apply his fullest efforts to the campaign. The commissioner swore not to leave a single communist in Ilhéus, "not even his shadow." But the very next day, in front of Schwartz's export company was a sign covering the entire wall, written in pitch: DOWN WITH NAZISM AND IMPERIALISM.

For Carlos Zude the strangest thing of all was the almost daily discovery of Communist Party flyers on his desk. He looked with suspicion at each employee. Julieta closed her eyes and saw the black stevedore—how superbly he moved!—leap from the car, yank away the flag, knock the man down with a single blow, his arm red, one end of the cloth flapping over his chest.

27

Immediately after these events Carlos Zude went to Bahia to confer with the governor of the state. He and Karbanks returned together. Half the city was at the airport to greet the two exporters, whom one of Ilhéus's newspapers had called "cornerstones of the current progress enjoyed by the zone." That was a glorious week for the cacao zone, for prices rose as never before, reaching the unbelievable level of fifty-two mil-réis per fifteen kilos. Everything else was quickly forgotten in the face of that reality that filled so many hearts. They forgot Pepe Espinola and his scandalous trial; Colonel Horácio and Silveirinha's distasteful lawsuit; Julieta and Sérgio; and Rui Dantas, given to attacks of madness that lasted for days before subsiding. The doctors said it was from the drugs. Everything was forgotten, for cacao was at fifty two. It was unprecedented. Not even gold was as highly prized as cacao beans, those beans seen by the millions in the great warehouses of the export companies.

No one had eyes for anything but the world of money waiting to be made. Captain João Magalhães had already committed the money from this year's crop and well over half of the next, but even so he was smiling as he greeted Carlos Zude at the airport. In Ilhéus looking for cacao seedlings for the first fields to be opened in the forest, he had taken advantage of the chance to welcome back the man many were already calling "the benefactor of the zone." Maneca Dantas, saddened by his son's illness and by what had happened to Horácio, was nevertheless waiting for the plane's arrival. He was one of the wealthy landowners, candidate for mayor, and the doctors had assured him that all Rui must do to be cured was give up cocaine. But as soon as each crisis was over, the boy went back to the white powder, which was all he had left of Lola. Practically all the people of substance in Ilhéus were at the

285

airport, and Carlos Zude felt an inward satisfaction as he left the plane.
He and Karbanks disembarked, shaking hands and receiving embraces.
There were many people, and Colonel Maneca Dantas did not embrace
Carlos Zude until the exporter was already heading for his automobile.
As he sat down, Carlos repeated to Karbanks, who was already stretched
out in the comfortable seat, his phrase about the colonels:

"They're like frightened children . . ."

Zito Ferreira, who was also there to greet them, preparing the way for
future bites, was standing beside the car and overheard. He commented
to those around him:

"They're stealing a phrase from Reinaldo Bastos . . ."

28

The *Ilhéus Daily* poster read: COLONEL HORÁCIO DA SILVEIRA DIES. There were no details, and only later did the public learn how the death of the owner of the largest cacao plantation had occurred. They gathered around the poster, asking each other for details, but the entire story only came to light when the police returned from Itabuna. After that, everything was enlarged, details were invented, phrases and gestures. It was in this manner that those whose only knowledge of Horácio was half legend came to complete his unforgettable profile. A portrait of the colonel hangs in the Ilhéus City Hall, from the time when he was fifty and the great political boss of the zone. One of those enlargements, done in São Paulo, of photos taken in the interior, where every face is pink and all eyes are blue. But no one went to that portrait to recall what the colonel was like. For every inhabitant of the most distant towns of the cacao lands carried in his imagination a picture of Horácio da Silveira, the lord of Sequeiro Grande.

He had received the doctors with gunshot, and the commission designated by the judge returned to Itabuna in a state of panic. The shots had missed, true, but they were enough that no doctor wanted any further part of that painful and difficult mission. The judge, pressured by Silveirinha's lawyers, sent Horácio summons after summons. The lawyers petitioned to have the colonel declared incompetent, holding that his flouting of the law and the potshots at the doctors were sufficient proof that he was not in full control of his faculties. They obtained a report from a Bahian psychiatrist who taught at a university. The final summons stated that if Horácio did not come to Itabuna he would be declared incompetent to manage his own affairs and the judge would name a guardian.

287

Horácio was indifferent to everything. He kept armed men on the perimeter of his plantation solely to keep out strangers. It was these hired gunmen who received the summonses and took them to Horácio. The colonel had his overseer read them to him and then tore them into tiny pieces that he blew away with his lips, making them dance in the air. Sometimes they fell onto his face and he brushed them away with trembling hands. He almost never left his room, where only the overseer and Felícia were allowed in.

Seeing the futility of the latest summons, the judge in Itabuna called into conference Silveirinha's lawyers and Rui Dantas, who had recently emerged from one of his crises. He was leaning toward declaring the colonel incompetent and naming Silveirinha as guardian. But Rui objected, arguing that the colonel had not shown up only because he was unable to travel but that if he, Rui, and the judge went with the doctors Horácio would receive them and submit to the examination. To everyone's surprise, Silveirinha refused under any circumstances to go and to take possession of the fields while his father was still alive and remained there. His terror of Horácio still plagued him. The judge shook his head, unable to find a solution to the complex case. He felt disinclined to accept Rui's suggestion, among other reasons because no doctor was willing to take on the difficult task. On the other hand, Silveirinha refused to acquire possession of the plantation while Horácio was still there.

"A crazy man belongs in an asylum . . ."

"But it's not within my competence to commit him. Why don't you take over the plantations, the property, and take care of your father . . ."

The ruling was published a few days later. This time Horácio took notice. He summoned the court officer who, accompanied by two policemen, brought the paper in which the judge declared him incompetent to administer the plantations that he had put together during a lifetime. When they entered the plantation house, the colonel was snoring in the old double bed. They stood at the door. Horácio opened his eyes, sensing the presence of strangers.

"Who's there, Felícia?"

It was the overseer who answered:

"It's them men the colonel asked to call . . . from the police . . ."

"Huhn!" He raised his body from the bed, feeling for his slippers with his feet. The court officer stepped forward.

"No need to disturb you, Colonel. It's just to let you know . . ."

But Horácio was already on his feet.

"That the land belongs to him . . . I already know that, young man. Tell him to come 'cause I'll be waitin' for him . . ."

His strength deserted him and he sat down on the bed. But his message was not yet complete.

"Do me a favor. Tell him, my son, to come, that I'm waitin' for him ... I wasn't able to kill his mother. She was already dead when I found out she was no good ... But I found out about him in time ... Tell him to come. I'm waitin' for him ... Tell him to come right away ..."

He turned to his overseer, once again Colonel Horácio da Silveira commanding a fight:

"Pay the man for the favor he's goin' to do for me ... Pay him well ..."

He lay back down in the bed, his head on the hard, bare pillow, his feet still in slippers. "He died like a little bird," Felícia told the other women.

29

Beanpole's group once again lighted the roads along the cacao plantations; Captain João Magalhães planted new cacao seedlings and cleared forest; Maneca Dantas insulted Silveirinha at Horácio's sumptuous funeral; Frederico Pinto played the stock market; Julieta made love to Sérgio at the Association and dreamed of a new life; Pepe wasted away at the penitentiary; Zito Ferreira put the bite on the newly important Marinho Santos; Antônio Vítor left Raimunda in the fields for the Vamp's bed; Joaquim worked in his hiding place; Gumercindo Bessa was made manager of the new Schwartz & Silveira export company; Rita took her baby and moved to the red-light district, abandoned by Colonel Frederico Pinto; Reinaldo Bastos dreamed of a promotion at Zude Brothers and sullied Julieta's name on the streets. Cacao was affecting the destiny of each one as it underwent the greatest price rise in the history of southern Bahia. Scandals kept on coming, but nothing could stay the happiness of São Jorge dos Ilhéus, which decked itself with the lights of cabarets and laughed through the mouths of prostitutes on nights of debauchery. There was a sacred word, universally spoken with love: cacao.

Only Rosa, with her timeless beauty, wandered about the docks, sleeping on balsa rafts, indifferent to the boom, to the price of cacao, to events, and to men. She laughed with one or another, slept with those who gave her money, ate in the homes of fishermen of her acquaintance, danced in the *candomblé* sites, always at the edge of the sea, her hair redolent of salt, her lips tasting of the sea air. Rosa, whose identity was never truly discovered but nonetheless unforgettable to all who met her: Beanpole; Martins, who had stolen for her; Pepe; the students who went to the Retiro; the dockworkers and the sailors; the artist who painted her portrait; the poet Sérgio Moura, and the policeman who had roughed her up at the inspector's order. For her, and for her alone, the price of cacao at the beginning of the third year of the boom, in the city of São Jorge dos Ilhéus, did not matter. But Rosa knew every variation of the sea. That was what mattered to her.

30

The feast of St. George, at the beginning of the third harvest of the boom, was of unprecedented magnificence. The new cathedral was almost ready. Mass would be held there and the procession would originate from it. Many people came from the farms, from Itabuna, from the small towns, from Itapira. The hotels were packed. The Vamp also came, and Antônio Vítor signed a note for thirteen thousand in Carlos Zude's office. Ten was for expenses at the farm, three to spend on the Vamp. Before he left, Carlos Zude told him:

"There's a very unpleasant matter that concerns you, Mr. Antônio . . ."

Antônio Vítor thought the exporter was going to mention the Vamp. His ears burned. He was preparing his excuses to explain the affair when Carlos Zude clarified:

"It's that son of yours, Mr. Antônio. He's being sought as a communist. They say he's dangerous . . . How did he get mixed up in that? It's worse than being a thief . . ."

Antônio Vítor explained that Joaquim had always been like that, had always had a bad character. Even he didn't get along with his son. If he went to jail he'd be getting what he deserved . . . He had no call to be so stubborn. It would hurt his mother though; she loved her son . . .

Carlos Zude expressed regret at his inability to do anything for the boy. If it were anything else he could intervene, but to help a communist . . . Impossible, truly impossible.

The procession left at five o'clock, accompanied by all the important people of the city. The bishop sat on the pallium carried by the mayor, Carlos Zude, Antônio Ribeiro, and Maneca Dantas. The bells pealed in the joyous afternoon. The elegant clothes, the fine automobiles, the gold lavished on the litters bearing images of saints—everything testified to the power of cacao. Female students from the convent schools sang prayers of thanks. In his blessing the bishop expressed his gratitude to St. George for the riches he had bestowed on the city of Ilhéus and blessed the faithful. The bells pealed again. There was a dance at City Hall, a big party at the Trianon.

At Bernardino Olivença's *candomblé* site, Oxosse proclaimed misfortunes in the near future. Rosa danced in honor of the saint, as the wind shook the grove of nut palms.

As the procession made its way through the streets of Ilhéus, Julieta was giving herself to Sérgio at the Commercial Association. At twilight the procession crossed Seabra Square, site of both the Association and City Hall. From behind the curtains, their arms around each other, Julieta and Sérgio saw the crowd and the litters, advancing at a slow pace under the lights that had just come on, with prayers of thanksgiving rising to the heavens. A poem came to Sérgio's mind.

Antônio Vítor, the next morning, appeared at Carlos's office. He needed a hundred mil-réis to travel. The exporter was surprised.

"But just yesterday you took thirteen thousand, Mr. Antônio . . ."

Antônio Vítor lowered his head.

"That's true, Mr. Carlos. But what happened is that I went to the Trianon and ended up goin' out with the Ipicilone Group . . ."

Carlos Zude laughed, ordered a note for five hundred mil-réis ("Take the five hundred; you'll need it . . ."), and gave him the voucher. At the farm, Raimunda was cracking open cacao pods.

31

Sitting on Vitória Hill, across from the cemetery, on the night of St. George, the poet Sérgio Moura declaimed his poem to Joaquim. The driver was in hiding at a nearby house and Sérgio was one of the few to catch a glimpse of him. He had come that night to bring him money. Later he had spoken to him of the poem he had written that afternoon, after the procession. Joaquim asked to hear it. Below them the city glowed with a thousand electric lights. Sérgio's voice declaimed:

> *"I stand positioned on this mount*
> *Astride the city at its feet.*
> ....
> *Within the night, Ilhéus gleams,*
> *A great phosphoric buffalo*
> *That, fallen in a rutile snare,*
> *Became the treasure of the hunt.*
> ....
> *I conjure scenes of moorish lore:*
> *Within the whispers of the night*
> *To sounds of zephyrs' serenades,*
> *Ilhéus at that moment seems*
> *A great gigantic buffalo*
> *That, with the centaurs at its heels,*
> *Desirous of its diamond eyes,*
> *A creature swifter than the winds,*
> *To cower palpitating came*
> *Beneath the hill, by centaurs ringed.*
> ....
> *Within the night, Ilhéus gleams*
> *Like some great buffalo of fire."*

When Sérgio finished his poem, Joaquim stood up.

"Diamond eyes, comrade . . . That's just what it is . . . and the centaurs are tired of feeding the buffalo and are going to eat his flesh and tear out his diamond eyes . . ."

Sérgio asked:

"And can't something be done?"

"We did everything to make the colonels see. But they don't want to believe us; they say we're worse than murderers and throw us in jail."

He looked at the city below.

"But that won't make us give up the struggle. We'll go ahead until we put an end to that imperialist gang . . . It'll be tough, Mr. Sérgio, but that doesn't matter. That's why we're here . . ."

He smiled his modest smile.

"Another age is beginning, comrade. There was the age of the conquerors of the land, now it's the age of the exporters. Then our time will come . . . It's beginning . . ."

They were on the edge of the hill. They could see the city below, the "buffalo of fire" with its diamond eyes of cacao. All was silence at midnight. The two men walked together and heard together the sound borne on the wind. A sound of music and of song, an out-of-tune song. Joaquim stopped.

"What's that?"

Sérgio explained:

"It's the Ipicilone Group rounding up its members . . . Karbanks is always the one in the lead . . ."

"They're giving the buffalo something to drink, so it's easier to pluck out his eyes . . ."

The music and songs disappeared down the streets of the red-light district. The lights of the city shone in the night. The two men climbed the slope of Conquest Hill.

The Land
Changes Hands

The Bust

1

The last time that the Ipicilone Group went into the streets was January 1 of what should have been the fourth year of the boom but was only the first of the bust. In fact, at that time there was not one but three Ipicilone groups. Their points of departure were, respectively, the Trianon, the Bataclã, and the El-Dorado. But on that January 1 the three merged for a joint march through the streets of Ilhéus during the dead of night. The drunk men and women marched, with Karbanks at their head carrying the group's improvised standard, a pair of women's panties.

In the middle of the street someone suggested that Karbanks, the main figure responsible for Ilhéus's present prosperity, should be carried on their shoulders. Someone else thought that wasn't enough and said he should be carried on the women's shoulders. Thus it was. The women gathered around and, bearing the weight of Karbanks's substantial body, plunged into São Sebastião Street, where the high-priced prostitutes lived.

That was the last time the Ipicilone Group ever went out onto the streets of Ilhéus.

2

On January 2, the *Afternoon Journal* printed a cable from New York telling of a severe drop in cacao prices. From forty-five mil-réis, the peak around which it had been hovering on December 31, it had fallen to thirty. There was no major reaction, that day, among the colonels and small farmers. Still caught up in the hubbub of New Year's celebrations, most were nursing hangovers from the previous night. The following day the price quotation was twenty-nine. At that point the plantation owners became concerned; it had been a long time since cacao had been below forty-two. But someone explained that it must have something to do with the annual work suspension, that the drop in price must be because there was no cacao to be sold. Many accepted the explanation, but some asked, grumbling, why during the previous suspensions the price of cacao had risen, not fallen, with the scarcity of the product. The debate, carried out in the business district and in crowded bars, first grew heated, then became bitter and inflamed, for on January 4 both the city's newspapers published the same cable:

> New York, Jan. 3 (AP)—The price for cacao was quoted today at twenty-five mil-réis for superior grade, twenty-three for good, and twenty for standard. There were no buyers.

The *Ilhéus Daily* ran the cable in two columns on page one, under the headline HAS THE BUST COME? The *Afternoon Journal* ran an editorial in response to the cable, which it published in large type, a commentary that provided details on the harvests in the Gold Coast and Ecuador, data on prices for the last three years, the years of the boom. It concluded with some generalities that explained nothing. The commentary was neither optimistic nor pessimistic but it is symptomatic

that everyone took it as heralding the bust. Everyone understood that it
had arrived, tragically and definitively. As a curtain covers a window
previously open to the sun, a shadow fell over the face of the cacao
growers, both great and small.

In the following days the price of cacao continued to drop. If the boom
happened quickly, with cacao rising from nineteen to fifty mil-réis in two
years, the fall was even faster, a plummet from fifty to eight mil-réis
in just five months. In March, the growers could still get fifteen per
fifteen kilos for early-season cacao. Most, hoping prices would go up
again, held on. But in May, when the full harvest began, cacao was at
eleven, and the plantation owners no longer had the slightest hope that
prices would rise. In June, cacao fell to the ruinous level of eight mil-réis.
That was when the plantation owners began to realize that the boom had
been merely a ploy of the exporters. Some recalled the flyers distributed
by the communists, even remembering the rally held in Ilhéus that the
police had broken up to general applause. At a later time they would
also come to remember the idea of the cacao growers cooperative, but by
then it was too late. Because, with ever greater insistence, the exporters
were calling in the plantation owners and small farmers to settle their
accounts.

There is nothing with which to compare what happened that year in
Ilhéus, Itabuna, Belmonte, Itapira, and throughout the cacao zone. Only
Colonel Maneca Dantas's forgotten phrase, uttered to Sérgio Moura the
night of Julieta Zude's party, at the beginning of the boom, in reference
to the breakdown of the family, could do justice to the panic that gripped
the city:

"The end of the world . . ."

Only then did the colonels comprehend that they were engaged in
a struggle. A life-and-death struggle that had begun that day three
years before when, following his conversation in Bahia with Karbanks,
Carlos Zude stepped off the airplane in Ilhéus and told Martins to raise
the prices paid for cacao. A life-and-death struggle that had already
devoured Horácio; his plantations now belonged to the exporters, to the
firm of Schwartz & Silveira. The only colonel who might have been
able to resist, with his enormous capital, with his endless plantations,
his seven hundred and fifty thousand kilos that could easily be increased
to a million two hundred thousand. Only he could have led successfully
a large cooperative that could stand up to the exporters, bringing together
cacao from both the colonels and the small farmers, buying and storing
it in anticipation of the prices that must come because of the decline
in supply. He alone had not gambled in the stock market, or built
mansions, or kept mistresses, or frequented the roulette and baccarat
tables; he alone had not squandered his money. He alone. And now

he was dead. His funeral had marked the true end of the time of the colonels or, as Joaquim put it, "the end of feudalism." The exporters had understood this very well, and knew, even as they closed their eyes to the brutal methods to which Schwartz had recourse, that it was necessary to neutralize Horácio. Carlos Zude had robbed him of his political prestige. Schwartz had taken away his lands. They had taken advantage of Silveirinha, brought him over to their side. Horácio was an old man, over eighty.

He was buried in Itabuna, amidst speeches and funereal jests. Maneca Dantas tried to attack Silveirinha, who wore black and had come to receive condolences. Those present, everyone who mattered in Ilhéus and Itabuna, small farmers from Ferradas and Palestina, as well as people come from Sequeiro Grande, watched the bishop raise his hands heavenward in the prayers for the dead. No great attention had been paid to the start of Silveirinha's latest suit against Horácio. People found the young lawyer's case distasteful but paid it little heed, being avidly absorbed at the time in the Pepe Espinola scandal. At the funeral some came to realize what was happening; others understood only after the bust. As the coffin was lowered, someone provoked laughter among a small group by reminding them that Horácio must already be burning in the bonfire that for so many years the damned had been preparing to greet him with in hell. But Sérgio Moura, who had come in the special train, recalled Joaquim's words and his dramatic gesture at twilight, over three years ago at the start of the first rains. The dragon with immense claws and countless mouths that had risen to the heavens that magical afternoon, the poet now saw over the coffin in the cemetery. A dragon with a foul stomach, devourer of corpses. But no one ever fully understood the poem ("The Dragon," a little-known poem even today) that the poet Sérgio Moura wrote sometime later about the events.

Now, with cacao at eight mil-réis ("Unbelievable," said Captain João Magalhães in horror), they were talking about the colonel again. Ah, if only he were alive . . . But he had died, died in battle, his body incapable of further resistance. Maneca Dantas felt no pity for him.

"At least my friend didn't live to see this disaster . . ."

Disaster was the only word for it. "It's a disaster!" was what Colonel Frederico Pinto shouted as he settled his accounts. "What a disaster!" Antônio Vítor said dumbfounded to Raimunda, who was not surprised.

Almost all the colonels had returned to their plantations, the plantations where few had gone during the years of the boom, when the raucous cabarets beckoned with the strident voice of their orchestras, luring them with the shapely arms of women and the excitement of the gaming tables. When Ilhéus had a nightlife such as not even the state capital could boast, when cigars were lighted with hundred- and

two-hundred mil-réis bills. Where had all that gone? Where were
the cabarets, the women, the chips, the pimps, the cabaretiers, the
middlemen in the stock market game, the champagne glasses, the
jazz bands that arrived on each new incoming ship, the cocaine that
had been such a craze, the Ipicilone Group? Now desolation reigned
over São Jorge dos Ilhéus.

Almost all the colonels had returned to their plantations, their
mansions in Ilhéus closed, their cars forgotten in their garages, their
lovers abandoned. They returned, after three years of upheaval and
deep emotions, to their plantation houses and their wives, once again
promoting the raising of poultry in the front yard, cleaning the boilers
to make sweets, overseeing the planting of corn for the festival of
St. John.

But how few plantation owners saw the hominy stirring in the boilers
that St. John's Day! Sérgio Moura had a phrase to describe the colonels'
hasty flight back to their plantations. He told Julieta and Joaquim:

"It's the pilgrimage of farewell . . ."

The exporters called the colonels, along with the smaller growers, to
account. There were memoranda that quickly lost even the semblance
of conventional commercial friendliness. At first brusque, they soon
became threatening. The fearful "owners of the land" lacked the courage
to leave their plantations, as if they would be stolen as soon as they left.
Those whom Carlos Zude had called "frightened children" were now like
terrified infants clinging to their fathers' pants at the sight of the village
idiot. They clung to their plantations, to the sight of the blossoming cacao
trees, the golden fruit illuminating the shadows . . . Never had any gold
been of so little value. The memoranda arrived, the colonels opening
the envelopes in the presence of their wives with frightened eyes. The
workers were let go in droves. It was better to let them leave, despite
their debts, than to have to feed them with cacao at eight mil-réis. The
final memorandum said:

You have forty-eight hours to settle this account. If this is not
done, we shall take legal steps.

There was a time when the law belonged to the colonels. They
convicted and acquitted at will. A short time before, they had convicted
the procurer Pepe Espinola, who had shot at a colonel in self-defense.
But now they had their doubts about that same law. There was no money.
They no longer had the export companies from which to extract endless
credit. And cacao had become one of the worst crops in the country . . .
Men who had never noted the price of anything now bargained over a
few pennies in their rare purchases in the stores.

They began going in, one by one, to settle accounts with the exporters. Everything had changed in Ilhéus. It looked like a city deserted at the approach of an enemy army. The women had dispersed. Ships arrived empty and departed full. Traveling salesmen were a rare sight in the motionless streets. Shops were shut down, cabarets closed, and only the Bataclã still functioned, with a jazz band reduced to three players. Buses followed their routes almost devoid of passengers. Marinho Santos painfully watched the unhappy departures and arrivals. There were even colonels who came to him to ask to travel on credit, such was the shortage of funds. Money had disappeared. Marinho Santos witnessed the entire debacle with a certain melancholy peppered with fear. He didn't know what would happen to him. Officially he was the owner of the bus and trucking company. But in reality the exporters could discharge him at any moment and take control. Just as Joaquim had said . . . Joaquim, whom he had fired at Carlos Zude's insistence.

The small growers, first to come to the city to settle accounts, and therefore first to realize the extent of the tragedy, returned to Itabuna by second class on the train; the bus had become too expensive, an impossible luxury. Elderly farm workers, many of them incapable of working, who had previously been supported by the colonels, men over seventy, begged in the towns and cities, in the port of Ilhéus, strange beggars with the look of startled peasants, not knowing how to ask, their eyes turned aside, dragging their bodies through unfamiliar streets. New shacks appeared on the docks—hired laborers who had been let go and who hoped for help from the city in the form of one-way tickets back to their own lands.

There was no money to be borrowed anywhere. Maneca Dantas tried to sell his mansion; there were no buyers. With difficulty he managed to rent it to the elder of the Rauschnings, for a thousand mil-réis a month, a miserable income for a building that had cost him five hundred thousand.

Rui stopped running his ad in the *Ilhéus Daily*. His money barely sufficed for cocaine, now extremely rare. In bars, his hands trembling like an old man's, he repeated his favorite phrase:

"We are a generation of failures . . ."

No one was left unaffected. All those destinies had changed once again, violently. The paths of cacao were harsh that year. Before, the way had been easy, with the golden fruit hanging from trees planted in the land fertilized with blood. Everyone had been affected, severely affected.

Only Rosa, restless yet immutable, continued outside it all. Joaquim explained that she was part of the *lumpenproletariat,* but Sérgio Moura, who was a poet and transformed things and words, said that Rosa was freedom ("anarchical, Mr. Sérgio, anarchical . . .", Joaquim's voice), loose upon the docks, the only totally free being in the cacao lands. Sticking her head into the immigrants' shacks, laughing with the Syrian street peddlers ruined by lack of customers after the bust, wandering around the docks, sleeping under bridges, going wherever her feet carried her. But only she, she alone, the Rosa whose identity and whose origin were known to none.

Because all the others, men and women, colonels, hired hands on the plantations, small growers, porters on the docks, factory workers and commercial employees, shopkeepers and prostitutes—all suffered the effects of the unbelievable bust. "A disaster," they repeated to each other, but found no consolation. It was as if the virus of some strange malady had penetrated the city and spread rapidly to the neighboring areas. Even in the bars, which still had a certain clientele, expensive drinks were replaced by small cups of coffee, and even there only words of discouragement were heard, hopeless gestures. Every face was frowning and saturnine.

Thus began, in São Jorge dos Ilhéus, the time of the "beggar millionaires."

3

Elections came before the colonels could readjust their political commitments. The communists were active once again, trying to unite plantation owners and small growers behind Maneca Dantas's candidacy. But there wasn't enough time for a thoroughgoing effort, and the colonels, on the verge of losing their lands, were little concerned with politics. As for the Integralists, they withdrew Silveirinha's candidacy to support Carlos Zude, who had included two Integralist candidates for alderman on his ticket. One was Gumercindo Bessa. A similar maneuver had taken place in the other counties.

The plantation owners' electoral defeat was not limited to Ilhéus. In Itabuna they succeeded in electing only a single alderman, while the Integralists elected three and the government party won an absolute majority. In Itapira the plantation owners didn't elect even an alderman. The communists had voted for Maneca Dantas, and theirs were his own sure votes, for many who had promised their support to him and the colonels, who headed the opposition, crossed party lines for fear of the exporters.

The elections took place in an atmosphere of cold indifference quite unlike earlier times that featured rallies, gunshots, disturbances, knifings, rum distributed to voters, new shoes for workers who showed up at the polls—a sense of life that was a joy to see. The opposition had held only a single rally in Ilhéus, which took place in monotony and ended in melancholy. During his speech Rui Dantas was overcome by one of his increasingly frequent attacks of madness and began to sing an old, forgotten tango:

> "Tonight I'll drink my fill,
> I'll drain the cup till it's dry,
> And once again forget . . ."

It was the Integralists who had held marches, rallies, meetings. Carlos Zude, whom they supported, nodded in approval. He didn't like the methods of his allies of the moment, and if he used them it was because he had no alternative. But he didn't like them.

On election day a piece of news, spreading at twilight as the votes were being tallied, overshadowed the slight interest aroused by the balloting: Colonel Miguel Lima, who had lost over a million mil-réis playing the stock market, had killed himself with a bullet in the chest. Carlos Zude was elected mayor of Ilhéus by an overwhelming majority.

4

When the first large plantations went on the auction block and were sold to their creditors for a pittance, a wave of sentiment swept the city. As the bailiff called out the low offers, Colonel Janjão went around asking those present for small loans so he could buy food at the market to feed his family that week. The auctions were crowded, more with the curious than with potential buyers. The only real buyers were the exporters, who bought the plantations for scarcely more than the colonels owed them, sometimes for less. Thus it was that the land changed owners and the exporters transformed themselves into the largest producers of cacao. After the bust, when cacao returned to its normal price, varying from twenty to twenty-five mil-réis, the three largest growers in the zone were export houses: Zude Brothers & Co., the Ilhéus Cacao Export Company, and Schwartz & Silveira. Reicher and Antônio Ribeiro were also major plantation owners, though not as large as the Rauschning brothers. The plantations were spread throughout the counties: Ilhéus, Itapira, Belmonte, Rio de Contas, Itabuna, and Canavieiras. Holdings that escaped being gobbled up were divided, with the colonels invariably getting the lesser portion. The small growers disappeared altogether. From this point on, the exporters were also to become the largest cacao cultivators. Finally they had roots in the land, roots extending the length and breadth of the cacao zone. And during the bust years they were the only ones seen on the streets and highways in luxurious automobiles.

Also for their exclusive use—especially for Karbanks—were the few prostitutes remaining in Ilhéus. Almost all of them had left like migratory birds, heading for Paraíba, where cotton, known as "white gold," was creating wealth. In the streets of Ilhéus hung a melancholy air of desolation and abandonment. The overall situation seemed reflected even among the gardeners at City Hall, for the gardens—once the pride

310

of the city—lay abandoned. Even the Ilheenses' coarse jokes lost their appeal, and the most popular one at the time provoked only a sad smile. It was the one that said when two people met in the streets of Ilhéus the first one to speak would ask the other for a loan. And the other would reply, "That's why I was looking for you!" It was as if all the money from the boom had evaporated, and if someone recalled that just a few months ago the Ipicilone Group was roaming the streets of Ilhéus at night, with champagne flowing like water, it was like remembering something from far away and long ago.

But, by midyear, more than money was in short supply. In midyear began the auctioning off of fields and plantations, the foreclosures, as the land began to change hands. In Marinho Santos's trucks, returning laden with cacao from the plantations, the worn sacks no longer bore the stenciled plantation marks so often seen for the last thirty years: Auricídia, Santa Maria, Good Fortune, Dividing Line. Names the people of Ilhéus knew by heart, having seen them so often on the sacks of cacao. Now there were the marks of the Zude Export Company, or Schwartz, or the Rauschnings. Within a few months the small growers had lost their fields and the more powerful plantation owners had been reduced to small growers. Months in which one could again hear on the cacao roads a popular refrain from the days of the conquest of the land:

> It was the sorcerer's curse,
> In the name of sorcery . . .

"They're the millionaire beggars," someone had said of the colonels. The phrase caught on in Ilhéus and soon was repeated about everything. It was also repeated when Colonel Miguel Lima's funeral procession made its way through the deserted streets. His fields had gone on the block. It was necessary to borrow money to pay for the coffin. In the bus carrying those in attendance, which Marinho Santos rented on credit, there was room to spare. A poor funeral with few flowers, almost no wreaths, a handful of mourners, the weeping of the family.

The rains were violent that year. The fields, their pruning suspended at the start of the bust, burst out in shoots and useless branches that reduced their productivity. Karbanks, when he visited Colonel Miguel Lima's plantation, now the property of the Exporter, grumbled:

"The colonels didn't know how to take care of the fields . . ."

Like the other exporters, he looked at the heavily laden cacao trees, the yellow fields, the leaf-covered ground, and calculated what would have to be done to double production. The ruined small growers, returning to the place from which they had come, made excellent overseers. In their reduced fields the colonels were also returning to their frugal existence, a tinge of sadness and disappointment on the lips under their white mustaches. The field hands, let go after the bust, wandered from plantation to plantation without finding work. It was true that the communists were acting among them. Only the exporters smiled, from the porches of their recently won plantation houses, looking out over the cacao trees, their roots firmly planted in the soil. They were the new owners of the land.

5

As the group, poor stars on the cacao roads, was preparing to head out once more, to frustrate once again Florindo's hopes ("this time we'll light out . . ."), to have Capi dance, all under Beanpole's organization and well rehearsed, they were fired from their jobs. Frederico Pinto forgave their debts and sent them all away. They would have to throw their meager possessions together and leave; they could not stay within the plantation's boundaries. Only a small group, the most efficient, was kept on. It was only then that the workers became aware that the price of cacao had fallen disastrously; it was at ten mil-réis, not even enough to provide the colonels with food. It was better not even to bring in the harvest but to allow it to rot on the trees. There wasn't even enough for expenses.

They packed their rags and left. On the roads they met others who had been dismissed from other fields. On the trails new jobless laborers swelled their numbers, to whom the lands they had worked were now forbidden territory. And they began to band together, first dozens, then hundreds, and all of them hungry. Nowhere were they wanted, as they trekked from one plantation to the next, driven away by the words:

"There's no work . . ."

There were no longer any jackfruit or bananas on the trees. They came together on the main road, on the plantation roads, on the pathways. They came from everywhere, ragged, penniless, without destination. Travelers were robbed; a man from Paraíba recruited an outlaw gang from among the most courageous and departed for the backlands. Later his name appeared in the capital in newspaper articles recounting his cattle rustling exploits.

The majority banded together on the roads: men, women, and children. Among them were Beanpole, Capi, and Black Florindo; also among them were the communist agitators. They came at the start of the bust, Joaquim among them, and spread out along the roads. Strange talk began to circulate among the fired laborers. New words, perhaps the first words of hope they had heard in their entire lives. The communists imposed some order on the jobless band, brought an end to the robbing of travelers and the attacks on plantation houses, and set up collectives to distribute food. They planned to lead them to Itabuna in a huge march, a protest of unprecedented scope. The constituted authorities would then be obliged to find a solution, whatever it might be. Some were in the port of Ilhéus, but the police had forbidden the entrance of any more out-of-work laborers.

Joaquim had first come across the group camping in a cacao field. Between men and women, they numbered about forty. Night had fallen, it was raining, and the field workers were looking for trees to sleep under. All they had to eat was flour, a bit of beef jerky, and bananas picked almost green. The ripe ones were already gone. Beanpole, who through his greater experience in life had assumed natural leadership of the group, asked the militant:

"Where you come from?"

"Ilhéus . . ."

They gathered around the new arrival. The driver, born in the cacao fields, had splayed toes like any of them and seemed nothing at all like a man from the city.

"They firin' workers in Ilhéus too?"

Joaquim asked Beanpole:

"And where're you all headin'?"

"God only knows . . . We're lookin' for work . . ." It was Capi who spoke. "But don't nobody want us, say they ain't gonna be no harvest this year."

Joaquim remained with them. Little by little his influence grew. Even Beanpole came to him for consultation in times of difficulty. The third night, a light-skinned mulatto who had worked for Horácio back in the days of banditry proposed that they storm João Magalhães's house. They were near the captain's fields. Sounding out various people, he rounded up those who appeared most agreeable to the idea, among them Black Florindo. There was not enough food. They were ragged, hadn't washed for days, and seemed ready to do anything. The children looked for fruit on the trees; the women tended the fires but had almost nothing to cook.

Florindo told Beanpole the plans of the Paraiban, whose name was Romão. What irritated Beanpole most was not having been

invited to take an active role in the attack. Romão considered
him an incompetent, useless, and a coward, perhaps because of
his skinniness. He'd show him . . . He sought out Joaquim, who
was collecting everyone's leftovers to make a meal for all. His
system was producing results; the laborers, who had at first sneered
in suspicion, were coming to respect the militant. Besides, he could
do things without raising a fuss, in his own quiet way, his expression
stern, with few words and that fleeting, friendly smile. Beanpole said
in a confidential tone:

"There's gonna be a ruckus . . ."

"What?" Joaquim turned around.

"It's that Romão . . . They're a bunch of bandits . . . Us city people
don't even know what they're like . . . Nothin' but a bunch of killers . . .
All they talk about is killin' and skinnin' people . . . That's all they
know . . ."

Joaquim didn't understand anything.

"But what're you talkin' about?"

Beanpole finally blurted out.

"Don't you see that Romão guy is roundin' up people to attack
Captain João Magalhães's farm? He say they got everything
there . . ."

Joaquim went among the men, speaking with first one then the other,
and soon became apprised of the situation. At the same time, with his
usual militant's patience, he explained the difficulties of the undertaking
and the terrible results it might bring about. He managed to convince
nearly everyone, but some said that Romão was still inclined toward
the venture, along with four or five others. The group was off to itself,
talking under a jackfruit tree. Romão, an almost white mulatto some
fifty years of age, was making marks in the earth with a knife. He had a
wife and three children, youngsters who were running around the fields.
As Joaquim approached, the conversation stopped. Other workers came
up, surrounded Joaquim and the four men under the tree. Joaquim
asked:

"What's the matter, Romão?"

The mulatto pressed the knife into the ground, piercing the leaves
fallen from the cacao trees. He responded brusquely, without raising
his head:

"Ain't nobody's business . . ."

Joaquim saw that this wouldn't be easy. But he couldn't let the laborers
become outlaws; that would be the worst possible thing. They must unite,
all those thrown off the land, and together march to Itabuna where they
would demand action from the authorities. All the communists' efforts
were directed toward that end. The fruit of this practical work would be

not only the resolution of the difficult plight of the jobless laborers but
also the establishment of party bases among the peasants. These might
perhaps grow into the first cells for a great ongoing future effort. This
robbery, to be followed by others, would be a mistake, for it would
bring immediate and merciless repression by the police. The workers
would be wiped out, arrested as criminals, outlaws—a real godsend
for authorities facing an insoluble problem. Joaquim looked at Romão
digging at the ground with his knife, saw the frightened eyes of those
around him, but he had made up his mind. Sitting on the ground,
he said:

"That's where you're wrong, Romão. It's everybody's business. What
you're plannin' is bad for all of us. Not just for everybody without work
on the other roads and the trails. It's not just you they'll track down like
a wildcat in the woods. It's everybody . . . And it'll be your fault . . .
That's why it's our business . . ."

"We got nothin' to eat, we gotta steal . . . If it don't work out, that's
the way it goes . . . Can't let the women starve to death . . . Better to
be a bandit . . ."

"Not a one of us is a bandit. Not you, or me, or Florindo, or none
of us . . . We don't have anything to eat and they'll have to give us
somethin' to eat . . . We're going to unite, all of us, all the workers
out of a job, and go to Itabuna. We'll go to the city and they'll have
to give us food . . ."

"They'll shoot us . . ."

"Only if there was just three or four of us, or ten or twenty. But
there's already over three hundred people out of work and they won't
fire on so many. We're poor . . ."

"The poor ain't got no rights . . ." someone else said.

Joaquim turned to him:

"The poor don't have any rights as long as they don't unite, as long
as they don't join together to fight for their rights." He turned back to
Romão:

"But we don't get those rights through robbin' and lootin'. It's by
fightin' for them, demandin' them, showin' we're united, all of us
together . . ."

They looked at the driver. For most of them the best thing really was
to go to Itabuna. There the authorities would have to do something. This
business of wandering along the roads and raiding plantations could turn
out badly. Others, however, were unconvinced. One of them, seeing
Romão withdraw rather shaken, preparing to fight Joaquim rather than
debate with him, said:

"Look here, you ain't a worker like us . . . You come from the city,
you could even be one of them . . ."

Joaquim protested:

"I'm a worker, and the worker is the peasant's friend . . ."

But the other man's argument carried weight, and the bystanders began drawing away from Joaquim in suspicion. What saved him was the intervention of an old man who in earlier times had worked for Antônio Vítor.

"I know this young fella . . . He's the son of Antônio Vítor, the one who used to be a hired gun for the Badarós 'fore he got hisself a farm. This here fella was born in the fields, worked with a hoe . . . I even recollect him fightin' with his father to pay his help more. Antônio Vítor got as mad as a bear and hit him. Wasn't that how it was, son?"

Then Joaquim told his story:

"You see? I'll tell you so you can see what we have to do . . . My father worked the land; he was a hired gunman because in those days a farm worker had to be one. Later he planted fields and had eight men workin' with him. I worked too, and my mother and sister. But I could see the workers were bein' robbed. They earned next to nothin'. I told my father that, and he threw me out of the house. The hired hands didn't want to get mixed up in it or even talk about it. So I left, went on a ship, learned a lot of things. I learned that people like us, factory workers and farm workers, have to join together if we hope to leave this kind of life. Things are bad for you all, even worse than before. You've got no job, no food, no clothes. So the factory workers sent us, me and others, to help you, to tell you to unite so somethin' can be done . . ."

He paused. The others were listening attentively. Joaquim continued:

"When I got here, each of you was eatin' what little you had, the last of the flour. Some had more, some had less. What did I do? I brought all the food together, and now everybody is better off. Isn't that so? Am I tellin' the truth or not?"

They nodded their heads. One said:

"You're talkin' straight . . ."

Romão lifted his eyes from the knife-scarred ground:

"And what happens when the flour and dried meat gives out?"

"All of us are joinin' together . . . We're going to meet on the road to Itabuna . . . Till then we'll eat whatever we can find . . . There they'll have to give you food and do something about you . . . A piece of land for everybody . . ."

Romão hung on to his knife.

"I'm thinkin' you was speakin' straight, without tryin' to fool us. I was goin' on this job because of the wife and kids . . ." he pointed out. "They's all hungry . . . But you say that in Itabuna . . ."

Joaquim went over to him.

"You're a good man. Let's round up some food for the women to cook . . ."

They left together, gathering flour and beef jerky. Someone had held back a piece of bacon; unable to resist, he handed it over.

6

The colonels did not give up their lands without a fight. Some resisted with bullets from their plantation houses and only surrendered their plantations when the police intervened and removed them by force. One who acted in this manner was Colonel Totonho do Riacho Doce, a man past sixty, an old conqueror of the land who had tamed Itapira at the cost of blindness in one eye and the loss of two fingers of one hand. When the police—hired guns hastily put in uniform—stormed the plantation house, he was still shooting despite three bullets in his body. It was never learned why he was acquitted in the trial afterwards. To his blind eye and missing fingers was added a lame leg. He died years later, penniless and still grumbling about the exporters. Every time he saw Carlos Zude he would spit. His plantation had been bought at auction by the Zude firm for six hundred and fifty thousand mil-réis, a pittance. He owed the company six hundred and twenty. Totonho was an inveterate poker player, and when Carlos Zude bought the plantation he told his family that nobody bluffed Totonho do Riacho Doce. He'd always called a bluff, and he'd call this one too. That phrase was cited later at the trial.

Most, however, chose to fight within the law, resorting to the dodges of which they were past masters. But the exporters were on their guard and through constant monitoring of the notary offices were very knowledgeable of the complete history of the plantations. Even so, some colonels managed to salvage a part of their lands by use of legal stratagems.

Maneca Dantas was one of them. When he saw the bust arrive he understood immediately what was about to happen. Deeper in debt than most of the plantation owners, he had spent as if there were no tomorrow—half a million for the mansion alone. He had a long talk with his son Rui, just recently recovered from the attack that had overcome him during the rally. His family was already at the plantation. Maneca went to an old friend, Braz, and asked a favor; Braz agreed. It was then an easy task to convince Menezes; the aged colonel, so long a political boss, conqueror of the land, knew of every shady deal that had ever taken place in Menezes's notary office, including the dodge involving Ester's will.

"I may go under, but I'll take you with me . . ."

The fake mortgage, ceding the plantations to Braz, was signed in Menezes's office. When Carlos Zude sought out Maneca with an enormous debt of over a million to be settled, the colonel was covered. He proposed negotiations, showing the mortgage in Braz's name. Carlos Zude took the matter under advisement: Braz was little more than a small grower, harvesting his thirty thousand kilos; how could he have lent money to Maneca? But the colonel had done things right. The mortgage was for only part of his plantations. Maneca Dantas knew the best he could hope for was to save something, and even that was asking a lot. Long and difficult negotiations began between him and Zude. Rui, now in a positive phase, took the lead. Maneca proposed giving up the mansion and part of the lands, the part that he estimated to be worth six hundred thousand. But Carlos Zude rejected his evaluation, which had been made during the boom, stating flatly that he didn't want the mansion at any price. After innumerable discussions, by which time Maneca was no longer speaking to Carlos, they reached an agreement. The colonel gave up the major part of the plantation but retained approximately a fourth of the cacao he possessed. The land evaluation, done by experts, was based on prices prevailing during the bust. He sold the mansion sometime later, to the elder Rauschning brother, for one hundred twenty-five thousand. Reduced to poverty, with barely enough money to live on, even so he was one of those who came out best. If not for the dodge, he would have lost everything, even the mansion.

In the face of Maneca Dantas's stratagem the exporters redoubled their vigilance of the notary offices. They made photostats of nonencumbrance certificates for lands not yet their own. Dodges became difficult, for record keepers were frightened, and many were openly working for the exporters.

Maneca Dantas had saved something; others considered him lucky. But he was far from happy. His world had come to an end. The world he had dreamed of as a young man, when along with Horácio he had thrown himself into the conquest of Sequeiro Grande Forest. He had dreamed of his son as a brilliant lawyer, his family wealthy, respect, peace, political office. Now he was poor, living in a small house on Conquest, seeing the best of his plantation belonging to someone else, and—worst of all—his son ill, addicted, beset by sudden attacks of madness. The doctors shook their heads. "Either he gives up drugs or he'll end up in an asylum." The old colonel disliked going to the plantation. He had to cross lands that once were his, pass by the plantation house where he had lived for over thirty years, see the drying frames and kilns, the troughs and cacao groves. In the land still left to him, everything was improvised: a plantation house scarcely better than those of the workers, drying frames, kilns, troughs. At the time of division, he himself had chosen those lands. Unimproved land, nothing but cacao groves, but land belonging to Sequeiro Grande, first-class land. And he still had some young cacao trees. But he made these calculations mechanically, without ambition, without joy, without drive. What difference did good lands or bad lands make now?

At home he looked at Rui's hands, which trembled like an old man's. They were pale and drawn, and his attorney's ring hung loosely on his bony finger. Judging by his vacant stare, his son had only a short time to live. All that Maneca Dantas hoped for was to die before his son.

That way he would not have to bear seeing him dead—or worse, gone mad once and for all and taken away to an asylum. He had once seen an insane man being sent to the state capital on a ship of the Bahiana line, heading for the São João de Deus Asylum. It took six men to hold him, even though he was tied up. He was screaming obscenities, a horrible thing to witness.

Maneca Dantas looks at the fleshless, trembling hands of his son. Rui smiles gently. Maneca senses that he is under the influence of cocaine. He rises quickly because tears, which come more and more easily, well in his tired old man's eyes.

7

On the street of the lowest order of prostitutes, Rita, her unwashed son at her flaccid breast, learned the saddest song in the world, the one sung by prostitutes in the towns of the cacao zone:

> *What are you doing there, girl?*
> *I do it all, sir . . .*

The street was long, endless, the mud eternal; they had never gotten around to paving it. Even before the bust Colonel Frederico had abandoned her for a younger, more active girl. But the other woman was already there, in a nearby house, and she too sang in a hoarse voice the song that someone had made up one day as he watched those toothless, glassy-eyed women.

Why that song? Rita didn't know why it had been written or the music composed. There were songs like that on the plantations, of unknown origin. They were work songs that spoke of cacao, of drying frames and kilns. All of them were sad, but none so sad as that song of the prostitutes, known to all and sung by all, professionally by now, at the start of the evening as advertisement for their talents:

> *What are you doing there, girl?*
> *I do it all, sir . . .*

Why that song? It spoke of meaningless things: mother and love, home and despair—things no prostitute possesses. Not even despair. The street was full of them, all come from the cacao plantations. In the towns there were no expensive prostitutes, perfumed and dressed in silk, as in the cities of Ilhéus and Itabuna. Now and again one would appear, but they were incredible old women, at the end of career and life. They came from the plantations. From the hands of colonels, colonels' sons, and overseers. These men were the first; it was their right, part of the law governing life in the cacao lands. After that the women passed from hand to hand, ending up on that street, the same one in every town, the street of women, almost always known as Mud Street—when it had a name at all.

Why that song? They did not even have despair. It was a life without meaning, in which only drink brought a brief respite. The street of fallen women, abounding with fatherless children, future laborers for the fields. The colonels' children, as a rule. Now, with the bust, the number of women increased. More showed up daily, lost on the roads. There was a shortage of rooms in the houses, and of customers. The older ones looked with something akin to anger at the newer ones as they arrived. They learned the song at once, and sang it shrilly from the poorly lighted windows. There was even a girl of less than thirteen among them.

All of them would starve to death. There weren't enough men for so many women or money to pay for nights of love. On the roads, the fired farm workers attacked the women as they passed, then sent them away with nothing. Rita's father was one of those let go. All he had in the world was his daughter, the "fallen woman." Too old to wander about the road, he came to the house where Rita was living, hung his ancient whip in the living room, and took his grandson on his knee. Rita watched mutely. She asked a single question:

"Did you come to stay?"

The old man lowered his eyes in silent reply. Then he said:

"There's not any work nowhere . . ."

He seemed to be apologizing. On Rita's legs rosy wounds were beginning to open, the result of her months of prostitution. Her child futilely sought milk from her limp breasts. Rita removed her gaze from the drover's whip, worn from the work of so many years. Now she would have to support both her son and her father. Women were arriving from everywhere. The old man, sitting by the rear door, looked at the sky, the countryside, the fields beyond. At the window, Rita sings the offertory song, her work song:

> *"What are you doing there, girl?*
> *I do it all, sir . . ."*

The street was long, endless.

8

Not even Rita took any joy in the news of Colonel Frederico Pinto's misfortune. Despite having been thrown into that way of life by her father's boss in the days when the colonel was suffering the loss of Lola Espinola, in commenting on the matter with the aged drover, Rita said, pityingly:

"He's in a bad way . . . Poor man!"

Frederico Pinto's plantation had gone on the block. A strange thing happened with him: he knew he owed an absurd amount, money he could have repaid easily if the boom had continued and he had cut down a bit on his extravagances. He also knew that because of the bust his lands were barely enough to cover his debts. He didn't let it affect him. He dismissed the workers, keeping only those absolutely necessary. Dona Augusta wept, a droning kind of weeping difficult to bear. The children wouldn't be going back to school. Frederico lost his patience with his wife:

"Stop crying so much. It's more than anybody can take . . ."

She raised her obese face and kept on crying. The colonel left for the fields where the cacao pods futilely awaited harvesting by workers. In the absence of anyone to prune the fields, shoots were sprouting on the trees.

The notices arrived, one after the other. The Rauschnings, to whom Frederico had always sold his cacao, were warning that, given his indifference, they were going to take legal action to effect payment of the debt. They sent him the bill. It was enormous. He owed too much. There it was, in the itemized list: "Check to Sr. Pepe Espinola—twenty thousand." A smile flashed briefly across Frederico's face. That had perhaps been the only money well spent . . . Perhaps the memory of the procurer influenced his later decision. He never answered a single one of the Rauschnings' notices. When the judge ruled that his lands were to be sold at auction he appeared unmoved. He didn't attend the sale. He learned, also through the courts, that his plantation had been bought by the Rauschning brothers. He looked at the price. He had some two hundred thousand mil-réis left. He went down to Itabuna with his family, where at a notary office he signed a power of attorney in his wife's name and said good-bye to his children. He caught the bus, a revolver in his belt.

He entered the Rauschnings' place of business unexpectedly. Without asking permission, he went to the private office from which the two brothers ran the company. Only the younger one was present; he stood up when he saw the colonel. It was only five days since the Rauschnings had taken possession of Riacho Doce Plantation. The exporter rose, thinking that Frederico had come for his balance; the check was already made out. Or, like others, had he come to beg for a little more money? Or for an overseer's job like the small growers who had lost their lands?

He put out his hand. Frederico pretended not to notice. He offered a chair, which was refused with a gesture. The colonel asked:

"Where's your brother?"

"He's in Itapira . . ."

"Too bad, 'cause now I'll just kill you, you foreign son of a bitch . . ." And he shot, putting six bullets in Rauschning's chest.

Employees rushed to the scene, but despite his revolver being empty, they still made way for Frederico. He went to the police and turned himself in. Rauschning had died instantly.

This was yet another sensational trial. Almost everyone recalled scenes of the trial where Pepe Espinola was found guilty, at the time when the colonels were the owners of the land. Now it was Colonel Frederico Pinto in the defendant's chair, the same man who had had Pepe convicted. The trial lasted two days, with Frederico forbidding his family to spend money for a lawyer; the court had to appoint one for him. There were retorts and rejoinders, and the prosecuting attorney summed up the situation in a phrase:

"We must show, once and for all, that the colonels do not own justice, as was so often claimed in previous trials . . ."

He was the same prosecutor who had tried Pepe Espinola. It was not he who had changed but the totality of life in the cacao zone. Frederico's lawyer, clutching at straws, resorted to "temporary insanity." It was said the exporters spread money around to buy the jurors—a claim that, like so many others, was never proved. The elder Rauschning had spent copiously and hired a lawyer from the capital to assist the prosecution. He was the great sensation of the trial but his closing speech, highly literary in nature, did not meet with the anticipated success.

Colonel Frederico Pinto was tried three times. The first jury, by a vote of five to two, sentenced him to twenty-four years. The appeal led to a new trial, in which the jurors were openly favorable to the exporters. Rauschning didn't even bother to hire assistants for the prosecutor. The second jury handed down the maximum sentence, thirty years. But there was one negative vote, which left room for an appeal. The court ordered the colonel tried a third time. This last trial aroused relatively little curiosity. It lasted a single afternoon and confirmed the original sentence: twenty-four years. As Frederico left for the penitentiary, once again people gathered at dockside to see him go. The only difference between his departure and Pepe Espinola's was that the colonel wasn't tied and a son accompanied him. The curious of Ilhéus wondered how he got along with Pepe in prison. They were shocked to hear from travelers returning from Bahia that the colonel and the foreigner had become friends. And the best part of all was that they talked about only one thing: the late Lola Espinola, whom both had known and loved.

9

They begged on the highways, in the streets of small towns, in the cities. Wave after wave of ragged, hungry men filled the roads of the cacao land. The bands were enormous, coming together on the paths, then entering the towns with their hungry faces and hollow eyes. In Pirangi a group of about fifteen invaded a bakery. They ended up in jail. Among them was a woman with two children. They were arrested as thieves and sent to Ilhéus.

As long as the bust lasted, as long as the exporters had not yet become the owners of the indebted plantations, these bands of beggars grew daily. An entire family of five died of poisoning when, in the extremity of hunger, they ate a snake. The *Ilhéus Daily* published a photo and gave the story a humorous slant. The headline seemed like a joke: "Failure of a Culinary Innovation." The reporter later explained to Sérgio Moura that he had written a dramatic account that the circumstances warranted, but his editor had refused to publish it, so as "not to increase panic." The *Afternoon Journal* printed laudatory pieces about Karbanks, who had promised to find capital in the United States to open the new port of Ilhéus. The weekly founded by the Integralists, however, was now in open opposition to Carlos Zude and Karbanks, in a violent campaign against Yankee imperialism. And it reprinted wondrous accounts of Nazi Germany.

An illegal flyer put out by the communists demanded measures to resolve the plight of the jobless farm workers and exhorted them to take part in a march in Itabuna, a huge demonstration that would also have the support of factory workers. The dock workers (who were also undergoing privation), the workers at the chocolate factory, and the railroad workers went on strike. In the fields, Joaquim and other militants organized the unemployed farm workers in support of the demonstration. Even so, despite their constant political vigilance, some of the bands of jobless farm workers formed bandit gangs. But once the lands had passed into the hands of the large companies, these groups were wiped out by a spirited campaign on the part of the police, who cleared the highways not only of bandits but also of beggars and tramps.

There even arose a prophet, a bearded mulatto who roamed the roads repeating ancient prophecies that had remained in the memory of people since the time of the fighting over Sequeiro Grande, when the crazed Black Damião roamed these same cacao roads. The prophet announced the end of the world and invited the jobless masses to pray and ask God's forgiveness for their sins. At the beginning he united about himself a number of workers and drovers, but as hunger grew they preferred listening to Joaquim, who now went from group to group in an effort to unite them at the Itabuna city gates. They would all enter at once, demanding food. Despite the bandit gangs and the prophets, despite the ignorance of the peasants, most of whom were illiterate, despite the deaths from starvation, Joaquim was uniting the men; people were now coming from far away to hear him. From plantation to plantation, from one group of the jobless to the next, they spoke of him.

Romão and Beanpole, brought into the movement by Joaquim, organized collectives in the coalescing bands and directed everyone toward the highways leading to Itabuna. They began to circulate disturbing notices through the streets of the city, and the police chief requisitioned soldiers in Ilhéus to guarantee order.

10

The cacao bust found Captain João Magalhães planting new trees in the remainder of the cleared forest. Shoots of future cacao trees that would double the plantation's output and raise up the name of Badaró once again. Every day Dona Ana listened, enraptured, to the captain's news about the recently planted fields. Handpicked seedlings, the highest quality cacao trees, planted symmetrically in keeping with the latest methods. Others lost their lands through stock market speculation, because they kept lovers, became addicted to roulette, or belonged to the Ipicilone Group. João Magalhães lost his lands without any of this; he lost his lands because he had cleared the forest and planted cacao. His new cacao trees were still three years away from producing their first fruit.

When the news of the bust reached the Badaró house, João Magalhães was incredulous.

"Unbelievable!"

He repeated it so often that even Chico the parrot memorized it and added it to his ample vocabulary. "Unbelievable," but true. To the captain it was as if someone were trying to bluff him. He too was a poker player; he had started out as a player and it was as a player that he had first come to Ilhéus almost thirty-five years before. It all seemed like a bluff to him as well. But unlike Totonho do Riacho Doce (with whom he had played poker on the trip that brought him to these lands of Ilhéus), he had no wish to call the bluff.

He suspended planting and took off for Ilhéus as soon as the first letter arrived inviting him to settle accounts. In the nearly empty bus there was almost no conversation. When people did speak, it was to bemoan their fate, to complain; it left an impression on the captain. Everything indicated that the bust was not temporary, as he had first thought. In the bus he reviewed his situation. He believed he owed money to Zude, although not enough to ruin him. At the end of the first boom harvest, what with clearing of the forest and planting the new fields, he had run out of money. He had gone to Carlos Zude and the exporter had opened a line of credit for him, drawn against future crops. By his calculations he owed Carlos one crop, close to 22,500 kilos, more or less: this next crop, which was to be the fourth of the boom. But on the other hand, his new plantings were almost done; the value of his land had increased. With the boom he could pay off the debt in two or three years. Maybe sooner, if he cut back on expenses. Then would come abundance, wealth, the old power of the Badarós . . . The bust complicated matters. He wouldn't be able to pay off the debt in two or three years but would need much more time. Cacao at ten isn't the same as cacao at fifty. The main thing, though, was for Carlos Zude to be patient. He remembered the exporter's pleasant manner, his casualness when he opened the line of credit: "No limit . . ." João Magalhães, however, had only drawn the amount necessary for clearing and burning the forest, planting new seedlings, expenses connected with the older fields, and living costs. Carlos Zude would be patient; he was a good man and would understand that João Magalhães wasn't to blame. And within three years the new fields would help pay off the debt . . . In five years he'd be free, have between sixty and seventy-five thousand kilos of cacao, something like the Badarós when the zone's progress began, the old "owners of the land." And in the gloomy bus, Captain João Magalhães smiled.

The first unpleasant surprise was that Carlos Zude didn't deal with him personally. The exporter was very busy, explained the manager who had replaced Martins, a young man from Bahia; he had authorized him to settle the captain's account. The subsequent surprises were more painful. He didn't owe as little as he thought. Despite having given Carlos Zude his entire crop and despite the boom, he still owed more than one hundred and eighty thousand mil-réis. It was the interest, something he hadn't counted on—terrible, usurious interest. With cacao at ten, everything suddenly became dramatic, and the captain wrung the once fine hands that had belonged to a professional card sharp, today the callused hands of a peasant. The manager informed him that the house could not accept long-term payment. No one knew where cacao was going to end up with this price drop; maybe in a few days there'd be no buyers at any price . . . The company wanted its money.

João Magalhães listened to the commercial words, saw the still friendly professional smile of the manager. As a young man he knew how to study the faces of other poker players. Later he went into the cacao game, and lost a second time. He had lost to Horácio in the struggle over Sequeiro Grande, and now he was losing to Carlos Zude. But the first time had been a clean fight, without trickery. And in this one there was trickery of the lowest kind. But he had fought cleanly, without hiding his cards, without stacking the deck in his favor.

The manager explained the reasons and waited for João Magalhães's decision.

"I want to talk to Mr. Carlos . . ."

The manager was doubtful.

"I don't know if he can see you . . ."

"Tell him I want to settle up . . . But only with him . . ."

Carlos came unwillingly. He was, however, smiling and friendly as ever when João Magalhães entered his private office. He once again extended his hand and offered him a seat.

"How's the family, Captain?"

"Mr. Carlos, I was here with you two years ago. I needed money to plant my new field, I was clearin' forest. You opened a line of credit for me. Now I see that there was interest, high interest . . ."

"It's all standard business practice . . ."

"I know . . . I'm not arguin' . . . It may well be a clean game, I'm not arguin' that, not sayin' there was any double-dealin' . . . I just want some time to pay . . . Don't you see? I planted new fields, and in three years they'll be bearin' cacao . . . I'll pay a little each year . . . Even with cacao at ten, my twenty-two hundred kilos are worth fifteen thousand mil-réis . . . I'll pay along, workin' down the debt . . . And when cacao goes up again . . ."

"Goes up?" Carlos said. "I don't think so . . . Cacao's had its day, Captain. I'm sorry, there's nothing I can do . . . It's just life . . . You spent money planting fields. At that time cacao was high and worth a lot of money. Today cacao is worthless . . . I don't want your cacao at any price. I'm not going to buy this year . . ."

"And what's goin' to happen?" The captain's face was pale.

Carlos lifted his hands above the desk in a gesture of uncertainty.

"This isn't a straight game, Mr. Carlos. It's a crooked game. And I played fair . . ."

Carlos felt the storm about to break. But he knew how to deal with these ingenuous children who were the cacao growers.

"What was your father-in-law's name?"

"Sinhô Badaró . . ."

"He lost too, but he knew how to lose . . . What can I do?"

"That was in a straight game, with no cheatin' . . ."

"Don't get worked up, Captain. Don't get excited. Borrow some money, pay what you owe, then dedicate yourself to work. All I want is one thing: to receive what I'm owed."

The captain divined no hope in the exporter's words. There was no money to be borrowed. No one wanted a mortgage on his lands against a loan of one hundred and eighty thousand mil-réis. He said:

"If cacao isn't worth anything, then why are you buyin' up fields and plantations at the auctions? That's what I'd like to know . . ."

Carlos rose, ending the interview.

"Almost as a favor, Captain João Magalhães. I keep the lands so as not to lose everything . . . And I've helped people, lots of people . . ."

For a moment—so sincere was the expression on Carlos's face—the captain almost believed him. But he was an old poker player, used to studying his opponents' faces. Far behind Carlos Zude's amiable mask—in the mouth or the eyes or the heart, who knows?—he discovered a small detail. He rose also.

"You're lyin', Mr. Carlos. You robbed us . . ."

Sinhô Badaró was sitting in the high-back Viennese chair, in the plantation house. He had fought till the end. It had been he, João Magalhães, who wasn't even from there, who had taken his place in that game of cacao. He had lost. But at the poker table, when the game was straight and one player cheated, the others worked him over. Sinhô approves from the heights of his straight-back chair. João Magalhães extends his hand as if to shake Carlos Zude's in farewell. The slap rings out, bringing the nearby workers to a standstill. But Carlos Zude is no coward, and he grapples with the captain. Office workers come in and separate the two men. João Magalhães is thrown out of the office. But he feels satisfaction as he leaves.

At the farm he tells Dona Ana:

"They're goin' to get everything. Nothin' we can do about it . . . Cacao fields aren't worth anything . . . It's not our fault . . ."

She drew herself erect, looking into space.

"What about us?"

"Look: lots of times I wanted to leave. I was tired of this land. I stayed 'cause you didn't want to go. I did everything I could. Now I'm sayin' it: I'm leavin'. I won't stay for any amount of money, or for anybody."

She turned to look at the captain.

"I'll go with you. Wherever you want to go . . ."

He smiled, took Dona Ana by the arm and pulled her onto his lap. "I knew you would . . ."

11

Carlos Zude yanked the brush from the hands of the office boy.
"Don't bother . . . I'll do it myself . . ."

He brushed his clothes, which had gotten dirty in the fight. The
manager reappeared at the office door, after helping in the forcible
ejection of João Magalhães. Carlos said he didn't need anything else.
Occupational hazards. His face was still red. He had returned the blow,
acted like a man. That wasn't why he felt defeated, It was because Captain
João Magalhães had remained unconvinced by his words. Carlos Zude
placed great importance on his understanding of the plantation owners'
psychology. The captain hadn't been fooled. It was a defeat, and that
pained Carlos. But he turned his thoughts from the fight to Captain João
Magalhães's fields: the fields that he coveted so. They were Badaró lands,
and Carlos wanted his roots in the cacao land to lie there as well, for those
lands were symbolic; he imputed to them an almost superstitious value.
Lands fertilized with blood, conquered at the cost of bullets, corpses,
dead men along the roads. Maximiliano Campos used to speak of those
battles. The fields would go on the auction block. Carlos would buy
them. And he would build a magnificent plantation house on them, with
every modern comfort, where he could spend long solitary days of love
with Julieta . . . That would be their nest, their refuge when they chose
to flee the world of large cities. There, on the land of the Badarós, the
old owners of cacao . . .

It was too bad that João Magalhães had gotten carried away. Carlos
Zude had planned to offer him a job as administrator of his plantations.
From the porch of the new plantation house he and Julieta could
have seen Dona Ana Badaró, as courageous as a man, who knew
how to shoot, now the wife of their employee . . . But one can't
have everything . . . The captain had lost his temper. So be it . . .

333

The office boy arrived with the afternoon mail. When he passed by, Reinaldo Bastos trembled, calculating that among the letters must be the one he had written to Carlos denouncing Julieta's affair with Sérgio. He had done so for revenge, not only against the coveted and unattainable woman but also her husband, his boss. He had hoped to succeed Martins as manager. Indeed, he had taken over immediately after the other man fled. He had no doubts that the position would be made permanent. That would bring him closer to Julieta, one step on the ladder that would lead him to her bed. When Carlos sent for a new manager from Bahia and returned him to his secondary position (albeit at an increase in salary), Reinaldo felt cheated. He didn't know that Carlos had tried him in the manager's post and come to the conclusion that he wasn't up to the job. Reinaldo felt only the injustice of it all. He made no protestations but racked his brain for a way to avenge himself. He considered Julieta out of the question once and for all and he wanted revenge. The idea of the anonymous letter plagued him for days. He fought with himself. Something inside him, a certain honesty, prevented him from writing it. A scruple against which he reacted and which day by day grew weaker. One afternoon he met Julieta and Sérgio talking on the avenue, on the same bench where he had seen her one night long before, when, he thought, Julieta was inclined to take him for her lover. Then Sérgio had butted in and ruined everything. And Carlos, to top it off, had denied him his place as manager . . . He wrote the letter, on a typewriter at the Commercial Employees Association. He put it in the mail, addressed to Carlos Zude's office.

Letters from colonels asking for more time to pay their debts. Legal information about the sale of farms. Letters from firms in the south offering to serve as agents. And the anonymous letter:

Listen, Mr. Carlos Zude, you're playing the fool. Why is the husband always the last to know? While you're working, traveling, and robbing the colonels, your wife, that whore who uses your name, is making you the biggest cuckold in Ilhéus. Want to know who with? Try following her when she goes to the Commercial Association. Everybody knows she's the lover of that obscure poet Sérgio Moura. Everybody but you, Mr. Carlos Zude. If you want proof, just follow your wife. And, in case you're a tame cuckold, at least trim your horns. They're so big they're a menace to public safety.

It was signed "An unknown friend." Carlos Zude's face twisted in disgust as he read the letter. These colonels still had a few surprises up their sleeves . . . One of them had even slapped him. Who would have thought Captain João Magalhães capable of that? Now another had sent him this letter, attempting to stain Julieta's reputation. Carlos Zude didn't for a second believe the accusations in the anonymous letter. Just something the colonels did, a cheap revenge, anonymous and sordid. It was self-evident: that reference to robbing the colonels, the violent language, the dirty words. And with whom? . . . Sérgio Moura . . . Carlos knew that Julieta had cordial dealings with the poet, centering on the lending of books. Something not remotely important. His wife had never been as good and as close as during these last few years. She had forgotten all her earlier desires: outings, trips, casinos, a home in Copacabana . . . She was truly sacrificing herself . . . Now even her honor was under attack. It struck Carlos as impossible for Julieta to have a lover in Ilhéus without his being aware of it. The city was small; everyone knew everyone's else business. Now if it were Rio de Janeiro . . .

He put the letter aside and read the rest of his mail. But his thoughts were on Julieta, on the sacrifices she imposed on herself. As soon as the more pressing business matters were taken care of, they would travel. He would devote several months to his wife, exclusively. Maybe they'd go to Europe. Or the United States. To New York, while the plantation house was being built in the fields of João Magalhães, from which they would direct the destiny of the cacao lands . . .

The manager announced Antônio Vítor:

"He wants to talk to you . . ."

"Send him in . . ."

These cacao growers had their surprises. Carlos tore up the anonymous letter and threw it in the wastebasket. He opened the drawer and placed a revolver in his pocket. He had misjudged the psychology of the colonels . . . The ingenuous children were upset and capable of anything . . .

12

Beanpole was a born organizer. On the plantation he had organized the mummers group that brought light to the miserable New Year's festivities during the boom. Now Joaquim was amazed at the skinny man's ability. In great part it was to him that the militant owed the possibility of the demonstration that marched in the streets of Itabuna, asking for food and transportation. The driver was delighted with the farm workers. So much could be done with them . . . It was far different work from what he had done in the city. But it brought immediate results. He thought of making use of Beanpole, turning him into a rural agitator, a leader among the hired laborers. He worked with him every day. Beanpole had finally found something that made use of his restless personality. He had wandered through many professions and as many places, but only two things had held him: Rosa, with her shapely body, and the shepherdess group with its enthusiasm at the beginning of the year. Now Joaquim, who had suddenly appeared among them, opened new roads to him.

"You're going back to the fields . . . But this time it'll be different . . ."

He had worked with others also. But Capi spoke only of going back to Ceará. Florindo wanted to go to Ilhéus, to look for Rosa. He laughed, laughed even when feeling hunger pangs, giving the impression that all the black man knew was how to laugh. Romão was more tractable, although illiterate and understanding very little of what Joaquim said. And a few others, a group formed within the larger group, taking command, organizing collectives, directing all the unemployed workers toward the roads leading to Itabuna.

And one day more than three hundred men found themselves on the edge of the city. It was not the full complement of the jobless. Many were begging on the streets of towns and cities, others were robbing

336

travelers, some had set out on foot for the backlands. On the roads, crude crosses marked where the weakest, and the women and children, had died.

It was an impressive multitude. Emaciated and dirty, tattered, with long hair and unshaven, their enormous feet caked with mud. The news spread through the city of Itabuna. The police chief called out the troops and telephoned Ilhéus and Pirangi for help. Some Integralists showed up as volunteers to help the police. They knew there were communists among the farm workers and that was enough to assure their opposition.

Slowly, like a procession never before seen, they began to enter Itabuna. They walked silently, the women carrying the children against their breast. There was not a single weapon. At the front marched Joaquim. At the bridge separating the city, the soldiers waited. The workers carried neither banner nor flag. All they had was the hunger stamped on their malaria-yellowed faces. Families shuttered their windows, women fainted in the streets, people rushed indoors. And the demonstration ("a parade of hunger," as one communist flyer called it) penetrated the city. City Hall lay on the other side of the bridge. Trucks hurriedly left Ilhéus with reinforcements for the police. Also on his way was the special agent trained in anticommunist tactics. The soldiers were dug in at the bridge. They were under the command of a sergeant.

The mass of people stopped at the bridge. Joaquim began talking to the soldiers. Streets urchins came from nowhere and joined the mass of farm workers. The driver urged the soldiers not to fire. But the sergeant gave the order to shoot and blood from Joaquim's arm spurted in Romão's face. Then the farm worker rushed forward, toward the bridge, with the crowd following him. It stepped over his dead body, for he was quickly felled by a bullet in the chest. Wounded in the arm and faced with the impossibility of holding back the workers, Joaquim went with them. The soldiers kept firing but the multitude continued to cross the bridge. Beanpole screamed:

"We want food . . ."

And everyone began to scream, totally destroying the silence already shattered by the gunshots. The soldiers fled in panic as the unarmed workers hurled themselves upon them. They saw decision in the hungry faces of the men and women and understood that only flight could save them. They were all across the bridge by now, and Joaquim, aided by other militants and Beanpole, was trying to reorganize the clamoring mass, which was spreading out and eying the various warehouses, tempted. Some were already talking of sacking them.

How to regroup? It was Beanpole who had the idea:

"We've gotta sing . . ."
"But what?"
"A song of the fields . . ."
And they sang the song of the bloated mulatto:

> *"My color it's cacao,*
> *I'd give my love to you,*
> *But listen good, my li'l brown gal,*
> *I'm yellow, swollen now,*
> *The fever does that too."*

And the miracle of the friendly song, the song that helped them work in the fields, brought the men and women back together. They were singing it as they marched before City Hall. They were orderly. Capi quickly bound Joaquim's wounded arm. When they finished the first song they began another, the oldest of all the work songs from the cacao fields:

> *"Cacao's a good crop*
> *And I'm a good worker . . ."*

They stopped in front of City Hall. It was completely shuttered, with the employees locked inside. Joaquim shouted:
"We want to see the mayor!"
And the crowd took up the chant in a deafening din. Now pieces of song blended with the shouts for food from the throng. Finally a window opened and the mayor appeared, very pale, at the side of the parish priest. Joaquim had trained Beanpole for that moment. The gaunt man climbed onto one of the benches in the square and told why they had come. They wanted food and work. The mayor, somewhat recovered from the scare, began to reply, promising that he would send food to be distributed and provide tents to shelter them. In the cattle yards, near the city.
That was when the police from Ilhéus, led by the special agent and swelled by runaway soldiers from Itabuna, began the new round of gunfire. This time the crowd was caught unprepared and the soldiers shot from the corners of the square. It was a slaughter. One old man said later that he hadn't seen anything like it since the days of the fighting for Sequeiro Grande. At first the farm workers were terrified, seeing themselves surrounded and with no possibility of escape. But there were among them veteran hired guns, accustomed to fighting, and they were gradually able to rally. The mayor asked for calm; the priest began to pray. When the gunfire diminished, the mayor decided to move away from the window, near which a bullet had already embedded itself.

The priest, however, stood his ground and gestured toward the soldiers not to fire. Workers advanced along the walls and threw themselves, unarmed, on the soldiers in hand-to-hand combat. The multitude took heart, divided into smaller groups and attacked the four corners of the square almost simultaneously. It was as if a colossal force, restrained until that moment, suddenly made itself known. Some of the women began to sing; the firing continued.

Afterwards they carried off the bodies, both workers and soldiers. Dead, they seemed the same, all of them black and mulatto peasants, with only their clothes to distinguish them. Some thirty workers and six soldiers had died. They were buried at the same time, in a single burial witnessed by the entire city. Wooden sheds were hastily erected to house the workers. The mayor, still alarmed, ordered cattle slaughtered to feed the peasants, and the priest, who had joined them, took up a collection among the families to buy milk for the children.

Joaquim, Beanpole, and about twenty others were arrested as the movement's leaders. But that same day the general strike broke out in Ilhéus and Itabuna. The factory workers were protesting the arrests, demanding the immediate release of Joaquim and the peasants, as well as a guarantee for the farm workers of the salaries they had earned on the plantations. The situation was becoming complicated.

In the improvised sheds, the farm workers discussed the situation. Despite the dead and wounded, they were satisfied. Something concrete had been accomplished. They spoke of Joaquim with admiration. Capi, in one of the groups, had an idea:

"Why don't we get 'em out?"

Black Florindo laughed in approval. It was like a fuse. That night about fifty of them attacked the jail. The guards fled and the prisoners were freed. Joaquim laughed as he hugged Black Florindo. In the sheds they were greeted with a song that, however sad, rang like a battle anthem:

> *"Maneca died in the oven*
> *Just as sundown came . . ."*

The city of Itabuna locked its doors, the women prayed, the men said it was a sign of the times.

13

The strike spread and led to an agreement by the city governments of Ilhéus and Itabuna. They would provide transportation for the farm workers who wished to return to their places of origin, and the rest would go back to the plantations from which they had come, plantations auctioned to the exporters. Almost all of them went back to the fields, but not as they had arrived; now they took with them something to teach the others. Something that shone like a light.

One day the turn of Beanpole, Capi, and Florindo came. Capi had accepted a ticket back to Ceará. Beanpole had opted for the road back to what had been Frederico Pinto's plantation. Joaquim had given him a mission; sometime later Beanpole would travel from plantation to plantation, taking bulletins, words of revolt and hope. Neither the plantation owners' police, the watchful overseers, nor the most daring soldiers could follow his trail. He arrived at night, and every house was his own.

Black Florindo refused to return to the plantations.

"I'm goin' to Ilhéus, what I want is Rosa," he said, and laughed.

Joaquim went back also, once again sought by the police, his life untenable in Itabuna. There was a warrant for his arrest; the special agent had called him "the most dangerous of them all." He went in the back of a truck, under a canvas cover among the sacks of cacao.

14

In the immense port, deserted and dark, closed in by the dockside warehouses, opening itself to the sea of freighters, in the port of knives and sailors, cargo from Australia, cacao for Philadelphia, prostitutes and razors, mystery and bitterness—in the immense port of Ilhéus, Black Florindo searches for Rosa.

Rosa has disappeared. Where is Rosa? Who knows, maybe the trees on the hillside called to her with their hands made of branches, their hearts made of roots. Florindo climbed the hills; Rosa isn't there. Where is Rosa? Maybe in the city, in the lighted streets, the temptation for women. Maybe she's dancing in the cabaret. Her gypsy outfit looks like a typical Bahian woman's clothes. Florindo combed the streets, went into bars; Rosa isn't there.

The port dark and deserted; maybe she's gone to the sea, at the moment of sunset. To join the wind, the fishes, the waters, those drowned in the *Itacaré*. The night is windy; Black Florindo leans forward, the light from lampposts falling over him, the mystery of street corners, lengthening shadows swept into the sea. At the bridge, lights go on, illuminating strange hunchbacks: black men with sacks on their shoulders, cacao for the Swedish vessel. Black Florindo crosses the lighted areas; could Rosa be there fishing for crabs from the steps of the bridge? Maybe she's there, off to one side, with a piece of meat on a line, catching crabs for tomorrow's meal. Rosa the fisherwoman, surrounded by fish. But she's not there; who knows, she may be sitting at a table in the Flower of the Waves, Coló's bar.

A sailor greets him. He's never seen anyone that fat. A blond Swede fresh from the sea, leaning over his glass of whiskey, tying one on. It's payday and he's already had quite a few. How about a drink, Florindo? What language is that he's speaking?

Good booze, gringo booze. The glow of the glass of whiskey speaks
of sea adventures, diving for pearls, gunrunning, sailors who lost an arm
to sharks. At the bottom of the glass Florindo looks for Rosa's eyes. But
Rosa isn't there. Outside, the docks are closing down, looking like a
blind alley. At the bottom of the glass, in the glow of whiskey Florindo
finds only the lighthouse of an island, the light of the dead man, lost
lanterns, wandering boatmen, the dead man's motionless eye, watching,
watching. Go away, drowned man! It is Rosa that Florindo seeks in the
bar's ersatz whiskey. And in the eyes of the whores drinking there.
Where is Rosa? Rosa has disappeared. She was that way. Beanpole
knew that, he used to say so at night by lamplight.

The Swede laughs to himself, working up a fine binge, the payday
kind. What he needs is a good beating, but Florindo refrains. Good
booze, gringo booze. He needs a beating, but Florindo refrains. "So long,
fella." What language is he speaking? Nobody understands, and Rosa
isn't there. Outside, the docks are closing around Florindo's heart.

He must walk the entire port, from one end to the other, from the
railroad to the market, walk among the emigrants in the shallow-draft
vessels rocking in the wind. Capi has gone away, said good-bye from
the ship, gone to see his wife. In his land they have a mummers group,
and Capi is going to be Herod . . . He must walk in the darkness, between
the warehouses where the thieves hide out, walk near empty railway
cars, near Snake Island, where the cheapest whores offer themselves,
sell themselves, right there standing up, for two and a half mil-réis.
He must walk the entire length of the docks, for she is certainly not
on the hillsides or in the lighted streets. She's on the docks; neither
the trees nor the lights could hold Rosa. The docks are the home of
the homeless, doesn't everybody know that?

The ship has disappeared, leaving only fog. "Where did you go,
Rosa, with your brown body?" Black Florindo asks passersby, asks
the ships, the prostitute who calls out to him murmurously. On this
dockside night the lamppost lights, one after the other, are Rosa's eyes.
He draws close; it's not Rosa. What a sad light, devoid of people! In
the dockside night, couples seek out dark corners. From the darkness
the stars are visible, and cries of love are heard from prostitutes and
sailors. The water is black in an inkwell sea; sailors the color of coal
pass by. Rosa is dark, the color of dry cacao. Her white skirt looks like
foam, and Black Florindo looks for her in the fringe of the sea. Even
the sea foam laughs at the black man . . .

Light rains on the masts, which bend. The smoke was white; once
Rosa brought a fish in her blouse and took it out suddenly, laughing at
Beanpole's surprise. A fish inside her blouse, still alive, still flipping
its tail. "Where did you go, Rosa, with your brown body?" Could she

have gone with the fishes or the fishermen? A ship's captain had once said, in the Flower of the Waves, that there were three hundred thousand sharks inside the Ilhéus sandbar. Three hundred thousand is a lot, and they eat the arms and legs of fishermen.

And seaweed too, abounding at each bridge. Rosa used to play with seaweed, as all the winds blew through her hair. All the winds, from north and south, and the terrible northeastern wind. She would lie down on the anchored raft, her head outside and her hair trailing in the water. It seemed like a head without a body, coming out of the water; it was shuddery. Crazy Rosa, Rosa of the docks, how often you lied!

She was a woman who knew stories, and could make up others. There was never anything like her; she could have been a book, such were the stories she invented. She told one about a dead man in search of his dock. He came up to Rosa and asked if she knew where his dock was. He was a dead man with a gaping mouth, a drowning victim with a crab hanging to his chest. It was all a lie but it seemed like the truth. She also said that one day she would go away, without anyone seeing her; it seemed like a lie and she went away. "Where did you take your body, Rosa, crazy Rosa, you liar?"

It was a sea of dead islands, who had said that in the bar? Everybody was crazy, everybody said foolish things! Black Florindo, what a foolish black man! Believing everything, remembering today but forgetting later. Because Rosa disappeared and no one knows of her.

The port area is immense, a cacao warehouse. Cacao brings money, it's a good crop. It brings the money stevedores pay their prostitutes. Black Florindo asks a couple in the middle of an embrace. They stop their lovemaking to listen; they're in a hurry, and rightly so:

"I didn't see 'er . . ."

Is it that he's tired? Black Florindo doesn't get tired . . . Is it that he's tired? Or it is pain? Rosa ran away; where did she go? Black Florindo was always laughing. Rosa arrived, those nights in the fields, in Beanpole's voice, and went with them, in thought, smiling at the black man—how good it was! Black Florindo laughed all the time then; now he no longer knows how to laugh. Rosa ran away, and the docks lock themselves inside the warehouses. The thief doesn't see Rosa and pulls out a razor.

Florindo isn't looking for a fight. What he wants is to find Rosa. "Where are you, where'd you go to?" He asks for the sake of asking; Rosa is not there to answer. There's not a longer dock in the world! The sailor hasn't seen her, she's not on the ship.

Florindo bought a comb that he carries in his pocket, a pretty comb with a piece of glass shining like a diamond. It's for Rosa to comb her hair, to make her smile. "Take your comb, Rosa, come comb your hair. I'll give you a necklace, I'll buy it on installments from one of the Syrian peddlers. It's fake, I know that, everybody knows. But it's pretty like the real thing, and it's for you. I'll give you perfume, fake Houbigant. You know that Beanpole he went back to the fields, he's already forgot about you. Capi took a boat and he's gonna be Herod in a group. I'm by myself. There's the moon, Rosa, to see you by. If you don't come, Rosa, I'll drown myself."

Black Florindo has forgotten how to laugh and is going to drown himself. Rosa ran away, she's not on the docks. Black Florindo is going to drown himself.

Rosa came up to him, from behind. The black man turns; where did she come from? Crazy Rosa, so pretty to look at!

"Where'd you get to?"

"Do you want to know?"

Rosa is laughing, the black man is laughing. How good it is to laugh!

"Do you want to know? It's better not to know . . ."

What does Rosa want? Rosa's mouth, oh! Rosa's mouth, Rosa's body against his. Rosa, take your comb, forget the necklace, the perfume, the moonlight, everything but the raft.

"Were you unhappy?"

"I was gonna drown myself . . ."

Black Florindo has already drowned himself, in Rosa's body, there in the darkness of the docks. How good it is to laugh!

15

Captain João Magalhães had no desire to remain even in Ilhéus, nor did Dona Ana, who felt shame at people who looked at her now that she had lost the last of the cacao lands. The plantation had brought something at auction, more than they had expected, because Schwartz had turned up as a competitor to Carlos Zude and it became a fierce battle. That broke a kind of agreement hitherto respected by the exporters: the one who would buy the lands was the creditor of the indebted grower. Schwartz broke that law, and that was the only reason there was something left over for the captain. They could have opened a small grocery store in Pirangi; João Magalhães had received a business offer. Dona Ana was the first to turn it down. The captain also had decided to leave these lands and never return. His father-in-law had said that cacao was sticky; once it got on your feet it never let you go. But Captain João Magalhães, thirty years after he first came, had made up his mind: he will never come back.

They went to Bahia, where they bought a boardinghouse near the waterfront and provided lodging for people en route to and from Ilhéus; cacao was sticky. Bent over the pans, Dona Ana gave orders to the kitchen help, her hair white, her dark face grown old.

Cacao was sticky, it entangled your feet. In their evening talks, Sinhô Badaró had always said that. João Magalhães bought a boardinghouse and had nothing more to do with Ilhéus. He no longer owned land, nor a single cacao tree; all he had left from there was Chico the parrot, whose strident, biting voice could be heard across the boardinghouse giving order to nonexistent workers, singing work songs from the fields, calling the chickens for their feed, shouting Captain João Magalhães's old phrase:

"Dona Ana, we're going to be rich again . . ."

Then it would guffaw, bringing tears to Dona Ana's eyes, clutching at João Magalhães's heart.

Captain João Magalhães had nothing more to do with the cacao lands, where he had disembarked thirty-five years ago. Still, the first thing he looked for in the morning newspapers was the price of cacao, and if it rose he went into the kitchen, carrying the paper, with emotion in his voice:

"It's going up, Dona Ana, it's at twenty-two . . ."

She was interested too, and they would read the paper, make comments and predictions. From his cage, Chico watched, opening and closing his ironic eye.

One night, however, when things had returned to an even keel in Ilhéus, with the crisis coming to an end and the exporters producing cacao, they took a walk along the docks of Bahia. And they happened to sit on a bench near the enormous building that housed the Cacao Institute, built by the government during the boom. They looked at it with sad eyes. From Ilhéus the news had come that the bust was over and that prices were rising once more, that the plantations, now in the hands of the exporters, were doing magnificently. They looked at the Cacao Institute. Its immense shadow, cast by moonlight, fell over them.

"It grew a lot . . ." said Dona Ana Badaró.

"That's true," he answered. "It grew too big for us, old lady . . ."

It was the first time he had ever called her that. Dona Ana's hair was white now. And when they rose from the bench and walked back toward the boardinghouse they were a pair of old people without anything to do in the world. The shadow of the institute kept pace with them for part of the way.

16

One night, on his way back from a talk with Joaquim (who since the disturbances in Itabuna was again in hiding at a friend's house on Conquest Hill, from there directing the movement while awaiting its return to legality), the poet Sérgio Moura ran into Colonel Maneca Dantas. The colonel now lived in a small house near the cemetery. Sometimes he came out at night to observe the city from the heights.

He had liked Sérgio for a long time. The two talked, sitting on the cemetery walk. They spoke of life, the bust, the taking of the land by the exporters. Maneca Dantas was discouraged. He said:

"We lived our entire lives on the land, cuttin' down trees, fightin', killin' people; there was a lot of bloodshed . . ."

Sérgio listened with interest. Maneca Dantas stared at the lights of Ilhéus.

"We planted cacao, we cleared fields, never had any fun. Everything we did was for our children. And just look, Mr. Sérgio, our children turned out bad, only fit for drinkin' and whorin'." He thought of Rui: "Or worse . . . It wasn't worth workin' as hard as we did . . ."

He stopped; the poet said nothing. Maneca Dantas spoke again:

"And now they take away our lands and leave us in poverty . . . I'm old, Mr. Sérgio, tell me what good it did to work so hard, to kill, to spend fifty years buried in the woods? For what? To end up poor . . ."

Then the poet pointed to the city lights below.

"To do that, Colonel! It was worth it. You and the others made everything you see down there . . . Is that nothing?"

Maneca Dantas agreed, without enthusiasm or joy:

"Except it's not ours anymore . . ."

347

The following night, when he went to visit Joaquim again, Sérgio told the militant of his conversation with Maneca Dantas. Joaquim rose from the chair and said:

"Comrade Sérgio, their days are gone . . . Now it's the time of the exporters, of imperialism. But that day will pass too. First they're going to fight among themselves."

Sérgio passed on some news:

"Karbanks and Schwartz are already fighting. The Integralists are battling Carlos Zude . . ."

"See? The Germans on one side, the Americans on the other. Their day will end too—and ours will begin, Comrade Sérgio . . ."

They went out and walked along the edge of the cemetery. The lights of the city were below. The poet Sérgio Moura saw the dragon above Ilhéus, its outstretched claws, its hundred hungry mouths. And he thought that if the evening before he had talked to the past, now he was talking to the future. Joaquim spoke with conviction, his deep voice seeming to come from a heart filled with faith:

"First the land belonged to the plantation owners who conquered it, then it changed owners and fell into the hands of the exporters who are going to exploit it. But the day is coming, comrade, when the land will have no more owners . . ."

His voice rose toward the stars, covering the city lights:

" . . . and no more slaves . . ."

17

Carlos Zude placed so little importance on the anonymous letter ("a tame cuckold," Reinaldo Bastos told his friends) that he didn't even mention it to Julieta. Weeks went by and he had forgotten it entirely. One afternoon, however, returning from the office, he found Julieta reading. He took her in his arms and kissed her. He was a satisfied man; business was good, and Carlos Zude, whose love for his wife was undiminished, felt that the time was near when he would be able to dedicate himself to her totally, when life would repay him for all his exhausting labor. The time was right to have a child, the son that he dreamed of educating in English or American schools. Other worlds, distant and different from the world of cacao, awaited them. The immense plantations and the export house would provide everything they could ever imagine, fulfill Julieta's wildest dreams.

He took the book she was reading, leafed through it without seeing the words. He was looking at Julieta, ever younger and more beautiful. It was he who had aged. These years of struggle, of dangerous calculations, of an endless succession of emotions, had aged him, increased his gray hairs; he was no longer the graying romantic figure who had once attracted women. When his gaze returned to the book he saw Sérgio Moura's signature on the dedication page. The book was a gift from the poet. That was when Carlos Zude remembered the letter, but as something both base and comical. Just because a young man with pretensions of being a poet lent a book to a married woman the colonels immediately thought of adultery. What a backward group of people, ignorant and truly incapable of understanding the modern world. It had been a benefit to put an end to their influence over the zone. Feeling satisfied, Carlos Zude decided to tell Julieta of the incident involving the anonymous letter. She was still seated, having removed herself from

349

his arms. From the bedroom they could see the ocean through the open windows. Carlos Zude sat beside her, on the bed.

"It was the day I had that fight with Captain João Magalhães that I told you about. Remember?"

"Yes," she said.

"That same day, right afterwards the afternoon mail came. I'm certain it wasn't the captain. There wasn't time. It must have been one of the colonels, one of those who squandered their money and then didn't want to pay . . . It must've been one of them . . ."

"What?" Julieta asked, her gaze fixed on the sea.

"The anonymous letter. Saying that you were the lover of that young fellow Sérgio Moura." He laughed cheerily. "Stupid, idiotic! But I'll say one thing: I never thought the colonels would react the way they did. One killed Rauschning, others resist on their plantations, the captain attacks me, another one writes a poison pen letter . . . I thought they wouldn't react. I was wrong . . ."

That had always been a thorn in his side, his error about the colonels' attitude. He had been wrong; there was no way around it. But, in any case, the results had been the same; they were now the "owners of the land." Julieta's silence went on, and Carlos Zude smiled at his thoughts, at his now fulfilled dreams. Julieta had gone to the window, her back to him, and without facing him said:

"I'm going to tell you something, Carlos . . . It's not a lie . . ."

Carlos Zude did not immediately connect his wife's words to the letter.

"What's not a lie?"

She turned her face quickly toward him. She was like a patient whose arm is about to be amputated, in a painful but necessary operation:

"The letter . . . I *am* Sérgio's lover . . ."

He stood there stupefied, his arm suspended in the air as if all motion had suddenly ceased. It was a painful sight, and Julieta felt compassion for him.

"I'm sorry. I didn't treat you right . . . I should have told you long before this, when it all started . . . I couldn't find a way . . . Besides, in those days I didn't think the same way I do now. I'm sorry, Carlos."

He was speechless. He looked at her in disbelief. He was crushed; it was as if he had suffered successive blows to the head that left him reeling.

Julieta paced the room, with nothing further to explain to Carlos. But in the face of his silence she tried:

"Everything was wrong from the beginning. Our marriage . . ."

It was only then that Carlos interrupted:

"Is that true?"

There were no gestures, no violent reaction exploding into shouts, threats, bloodshed. He was crushed, that was all. He couldn't touch bottom; he was like a castaway. Julieta tried to encourage him:

"Try to accept it . . . You don't really need me. You have your business, your life, your world. In your way, you're a winner . . . You fought the battle and won . . ."

This gradually brought him back to reality.

"I thought that you were on my side . . . That . . ."

There was much he wanted to say, but it wasn't worth the effort. He felt like crying. His eyes dry, his throat knotted, an emptiness in his chest, he hadn't even stood up. Julieta was filled with sorrow, with infinite pity. She approached him, sat beside him on the bed, and took his hand.

"You poor dear . . . You were very good to me . . . I have no complaints against you. You're free to think whatever you want to about me . . ."

Carlos was slowly pulling himself together. Now he saw in Julieta's attitude some vague hope. It would not be easy to forgive and forget. But he loved her so much that he *would* forgive and forget. What mattered was to keep her. Only the sea broke the silence with the sound of waves falling on the beach. Carlos sought for words suddenly become difficult. What he was going to say was delicate.

"Julieta, I love you . . . You're everything to me . . . People fight for something, wear themselves down, do business, wipe out others. For something. I do it for you. I know I neglected you for a time, while I was working like a slave . . . I'm to blame too. But that fling, that folly of yours is over and done with, and we're going to forget all that, starting this very afternoon, and go away. We'll travel; we can do so now without fear. I'm only needed here from time to time. Remember when I promised you that one day we'd leave? That one day this exile in Ilhéus would end? That one day we'd be the owners of the land and then we could go? Well, we *are* the owners of the land. Let's forget everything. As if it never happened."

The feeling of pity grew inside Julieta. It was so strong that she thought of staying, giving up everything, plunging once more in the lowest and dirtiest mud. He needed her. The plantations were there, taken from the colonels and small growers. The export house was there. He needed her. But she resisted, wanting to save herself. And to do that she must stifle the pity that lay at the bottom of her heart. To save herself she would step over Carlos, even over Sérgio.

"Try to accept it, Carlos . . . It wasn't a fling or a folly. At first it was to run away from all of this"—she pointed to the house—"from your business, your dirty world . . . I myself didn't even realize what was happening. It was the 'neura,' remember? Your world. Do you think what I want is travel, clothes, dances? It's not like that . . . What I really want is to get away from this life, from this filth, this enormous filth . . ."

He was starting to understand, and a barrier began to rise between them. Julieta understood and was glad because she saw that Carlos could live without her, however he was suffering at the initial moment.

"Filth, you call it. It's the filth that supports you. It's business, and that's how business is. The smartest one wins; it's always been that way . . . You never found it dirty before you met that guy . . ."

"Don't get excited, Carlos. I don't blame you for anything. It's your life. It's just that I don't like it and don't want to live it . . ."

"You're leaving?" He was downcast once more, feeling the void around him, once again fearful.

"Yes, Carlos. But don't fool yourself. You'll only suffer for a short time. You have your business, your plantations, your new plantations, and you won't even remember me . . . It's better that way . . ."

She stopped talking, her eyes on the floor, her head down.

"I'm going away. No one will know why; there won't be any scandal. You can make up some kind of story. Later you'll ask for a legal separation, which won't hurt you in any way . . . You'll forget me, maybe even . . ."

Carlos saw it was pity and said indignantly:

"Since you're leaving there's no need to worry yourself about me. I can take care of myself." He assumed the role of head of the house. "How much do you need?"

"Nothing, Carlos. I had made up my mind a long time ago to talk with you, but I kept putting it off. It was good that you told me about that letter. I've had all my things prepared for some time now . . . All I'll take is what I brought from my mother's . . . It's enough to live on till I find a job . . ."

That was too much for Carlos Zude. Her total independence, her complete break with him, hurt him most of all. He blew up:

"A job? Maybe as a whore . . ."

"It won't be that, Carlos. Some kind of work . . ."

She felt sorry for him again. He was hurt and unhappy. She drew close and said:

"I don't want to leave as your enemy. I want you to understand . . ."

He rose from the bed, almost calm after the explosion. His voice was sad but resigned:

"I'll never understand. I love you . . ."

Julieta nodded. She began collecting her things. Carlos Zude sat down on the bed again and watched her movements. His thoughts leapt in rapid succession, with a single thing remaining at the end: he couldn't leave Ilhéus at that moment; it was still too early. She would go, fail miserably somewhere or other, and maybe return. Would he take her back? He thought about the problem:

"If you ever want to come back, you'll always have a place here . . ."

Julieta went to the Commercial Association. The windows were closed; the poet Sérgio Moura was getting ready to leave. The lights of the enormous chandelier illuminated the room where Sérgio, who was alone, was knotting his tie. Julieta came in. He kissed her.

"What are you doing in the street at this hour?"

"Sérgio, what happened to your black bird?"

"It's inside, in the veranda."

"Go get it . . ."

He brought the cage, where the bird was waking up because of the light in the room. He gave it to Julieta, who opened a window.

"Will you give me this bird as a gift?"

"It's yours," Sérgio said in surprise.

She opened the cage door by the window. The bird sprang to the open door, looked around for a moment in confusion, then flew into the immense, free night of the garden. Sérgio vaguely suspected that Julieta had been drinking. What the devil did it all mean? She turned to him, radiant.

"You know, my love, I'm free too . . ."

"Free?"

"I told Carlos everything. We're separating."

The poet was startled:

"You told him?"

She nodded. She stared at him. He was a prisoner too; his feet were also mired in the mud. But to be free she would step over even him.

"I'm leaving. I don't know where I'll go, but I'm leaving. What I'll do I don't know either, but I'm leaving." Then she ventured timidly: "Maybe someday I can work toward that world of Joaquim's . . ."

Sérgio smiled, taking refuge in literature:

"The creation escapes its creator . . ."

"I love you, you know that. I owe a lot to you. That's why I'm here: to ask you to come with me. Break the cords that bind your feet. Let's go away . . . It'll be easier and better for the two of us together . . ."

He listened to her without speaking. Literature was no help; it couldn't make the decision. Nor was irony or passion; Julieta was going to leave. And she was asking him to go with her.

"Sérgio, I came to get you. I love you very much—very, very much. But I'm leaving even without you; I want to save myself. Even if you stay here as a prisoner, I'm going . . ."

He was silent, terribly grave, his elongated profile recalling a nocturnal bird. She had never seen him like this.

"Once, Sérgio, Joaquim told me: 'There's no such thing as good or bad mud. It's all the same. It's just a question of getting out of the mud around us . . . ' It's true, Sérgio. Now I understand, and I'm leaving. I want you to go with me . . ."

Sérgio Moura stared at the night into which the bird had departed. An immense, free night. A night where a star of vivid and splendid light was being born. Julieta took Sérgio Moura's hat, which was on the table, placed it on the poet's head, gave him her arm, and said:

"Let's go, my love . . ."

18

In the port of São Jorge dos Ilhéus, devoid of ships, the aged couple begged. They were farm workers who had been fired. They were dressed in rags, their hands enormous, their feet splayed. They were singing a song from the cacao fields. Antônio Vítor dropped two hundred réis in their cup and went off down the middle of the street.

His land had been sold at auction that day, acquired by the house of Zude Brothers & Co. It hadn't even brought enough to pay what he owed. In his office Carlos Zude reminded him of his wild times with the Vamp while Antônio Vítor listened with his head bowed. At the start of the year the Vamp had run off, taking his last five hundred mil-réis with her. Back at the fields, Raimunda said nothing; going to her work every morning, she seemed as indifferent to the bust as she had been to the boom. They had never spoken about his affair with the Vamp. Raimunda had never raised the subject with him. She even seemed happy in that ruinous year; Joaquim had been exonerated and had found work in a small garage. That accounted for Raimunda's happiness, for her singing while she split the first cacao pods of that wretched harvest. Antônio Vítor had also gone back to working in the fields; he had taken on only four hired hands this year, and the house where they had lived before building the new one was deserted. Little by little Raimunda moved into the old house, taking one thing one day, something else the next. When they finally gave up the new house, Antônio Vítor never even knew how the change had taken place. He only knew that Raimunda was no longer unhappy, and that was a consolation.

One afternoon he received a summons from the judge in Ilhéus. His land was going on the block. But Carlos Zude had promised him an extension. He showed the summons to Raimunda, who was frightened.

"They're gonna take the land, Antonyo . . ."

He went to Ilhéus, attended the auction, saw Carlos Zude buy the lands for a pittance. Afterwards the exporter had spoken to him of the Vamp and the Ipicilone Group. Why that, why that mean-spirited talk about his mistakes when he had already taken all he owned? Carlos Zude ended by offering him a job as overseer on one of his plantations . . . At a salary of three hundred mil-réis. Antônio Vítor said he'd have to think it over.

The beggars' song accompanied them through the streets:

> *"Cacao's a good crop*
> *And I'm a good worker . . . "*

He didn't know why he had the urge to see his son. "Cacao is a good crop . . ." His son knew things, he had refused to stay in the fields, and in the end he'd been right . . . He stood before the door of the garage. He must look like a drunk, because an overgrown kid pulling out in a truck laughed when he saw him. Joaquim saw him from inside.

"Father!"

They went into the street and Antônio Vítor told him everything. He even told about the Vamp. Now he had no land, nothing.

"Your mother's gonna die when she finds out, Joaquim . . ."

Joaquim tried to cheer him up. He spoke of the future, but none of that held any interest for Antônio Vítor. His son told him that one day the land would belong to everyone, and the likes of Carlos Zude would be no more. But Antônio Vítor didn't believe that was possible. While his son talked, he reflected on whether or not to accept the job.

"It's three hundred mil-réis, and I'm savin' somethin' every month. Maybe someday I can buy another piece of land . . ."

He gave Joaquim his blessing at the station. The train whistled as it rounded the curve for Itabuna. He had a week to vacate the farm.

19

Raimunda received the news almost with indifference. She still went
out to the field during that week and split open cacao pods. Antônio
Vítor had decided to stay with his son-in-law until Carlos Zude
determined at which plantation he'd be working. Raimunda went
out to the fields that morning as if she would still be living there,
as if the land still belonged to them. The last day came and Antônio
Vítor called Raimunda to get things ready for the move. She
frowned.

"You plannin' to hand it over?"

He looked at his wife in surprise.

"If we don't . . ."

"If that's what you want, you can just clear out. But I ain't goin', I
ain't . . . I'm stayin' here and I ain't givin' up my land. I ain't givin' it
up . . ."

He smiled and said:

"Then we're stayin' . . ."

Around noon the employee of Zude Brothers & Co. came to take
possession of the fields; Antônio Vítor ran him off. The man went
straight to a telephone in Pirangi.

Night came and they knew the men were already on their way.
They always came at night to take over plantations whose former
owners offered resistance. They were officially called police, but in
reality they were hired guns trained as sharpshooters. Antônio Vítor
and Raimunda came out of the old adobe house, each carrying a
repeating rifle. They posted themselves forward, near the road,
behind a guava tree. They waited. It was a beautiful starry

night and the moon was shining, a good night for an ambush.
Antônio Vítor recalled other nights, from the times of the fighting
over Sequeiro Grande, when he had brought down many a man
with his sure aim. That land had cost him dearly, it had cost
him blood, and he wasn't going to hand it over. Raimunda
was right.

They did not speak. But he looked at her, and for the first time he
saw Raimunda's face without its look of anger. It was a sweet and
serene face. Antônio Vítor said:

"In Ilhéus I seen Joaquim. Gave him my blessin' . . ."

She smiled.

"You're a good person . . ."

"He's good too, I'm the one was all messed up . . ."

They fell into silence again. From far off, almost imperceptibly, they
could hear the sound of men coming their way. Antônio Vítor turned
to Raimunda.

"I was messed up . . . I even went with fancy women . . . I left you
behind like an old shoe . . ."

"You did good, you needed it. I wasn't good for nothin' anymore . . .
You did good, I ain't mad . . ."

He laughed. The steps sounded closer now. By the moonlight he could
see the armed men coming down the road. There were twelve of them,
but it made no difference. They waited for the men to come closer.
Antônio Vítor felt the desire once again to say the words he didn't
know how to say, to caress Raimunda in ways unknown to him.
He said only:

"They're a-comin' . . ."

"Now . . ."

They raised their rifles. Raimunda shot first. Antônio Vítor didn't
miss; the man fell to the road. The others ran, leaving the open road
for the woods. Approaching between trees, they located Antônio Vítor
and Raimunda behind the guava tree. They reloaded their weapons.
Raimunda moved out, raised the rifle and took aim at a man she
had spotted between the trees. She and her target shot at the same
instant. Her bullet went astray among the cacao trees; his found
its mark in Raimunda's chest. She fell facedown on the ground.
Antônio Vítor bent over her; his hand came away stained with
blood:

"Munda!"

She turned her face to him. She was smiling, she was smiling!
From the earth came a strong, good smell—good land for cacao.

He wasn't going to give up his land. No, Munda, he wouldn't give it up!

He stood up. The men were surrounding the guava tree. He supported the rifle on his shoulder, took aim, and fired his last shot. His last shot.

Periperi, Bahia, January 1944.